THE NAMESAKE

By the same author

The Dogs of Rome
The Fatal Touch

THE NAMESAKE

A Commissario Alec Blume Novel

CONOR FITZGERALD

BLOOMSBURY

NEW YORK · BERLIN · LONDON · SYDNEY

Copyright © 2012 by Conor Fitzgerald
Map by ML Design

Published by Bloomsbury USA, New York

All papers used by Bloomsbury USA are natural, recyclable products made from
wood grown in well-managed forests. The manufacturing processes conform to
the environmental regulations of the country of origin.

LIBRARY OF CONGRESS CATALOGING-IN-PUBLICATION DATA

Fitzgerald, Conor.
The namesake : a Commissario Alec Blume novel / Conor Fitzgerald.
p. cm.
ISBN 978-1-60819-845-0
1. Police—Italy—Rome—Fiction. 2. Murder—Investigation—Fiction.
3. Organized crime—Fiction. I. Title.
PR9120.9.F58N36 2012
823'.914—dc23
2012004284

First U.S. Edition 2012

1 3 5 7 9 10 8 6 4 2

Typeset by Hewer Text UK Ltd, Edinburgh
Printed in the U.S.A. by Quad/Graphics, Fairfield, Pennsylvania

For my mother, Marion Deane

FLORENCE
TUSCANY
MARCHE
Ancona
Tiber
Perugia
UMBRIA
Pescara
ABRUZZO
ROME
LAZIO
MOLISE
Foggia
CAMPANIA
PUGLIA
Bari
Avernus
Naples
Salerno
A3
BASILICATA
Positano
Taranto

Adriatic Sea

CROATIA
BOSNIA-HERZEGOVINA

N

Tyrrhenian
Sea

A1

CALABRIA

Lamezia
airport

A3

Messina

Locri
Sanctuary of Polsi

Palermo

Regio
Calabria
Aspromonte

Ionian
Sea

SICILY

MEDITERRANEAN SEA

Syracuse

| 0 | 25 | 50 | 75 | 100 miles |
| 0 | 50 | 100 | 150 | 200 kilometres |

Wednesday, 26 August

1

Milan

'BEFORE WE BEGIN,' said the magistrate, 'I want you all to know that there is no chance of a happy ending to this story.'

A policeman stepped forward. He was a young man with an accent full of the unclosed vowels of southern Italy. He said, 'Sometimes these cases work out for the best.'

'How old are you?'

'Twenty-eight, Giudice.'

'I am almost twice your age, Agente. I have had experience of cases like this before. Just one is enough to change your outlook on life and stop you from hoping.'

The other four police officers filling the small room nodded, which had the effect of isolating their outspoken colleague. The magistrate regarded them with a hint of disdain, and pressed the tips of his fingers against the polished wood of his organized desk, then shook his head in sadness at the open laptop in front of him as he set forth the essentials of the troubling case before them.

'At four o'clock yesterday, after spending two hours in the "Aqua Felix" swimming pool, Teresa Resca, fourteen years of age, was waiting for a bus that would take her back home to San Donato. A car drew up, and for some reason she climbed into it. The whole scene was captured by a CCTV camera located on the outside wall of an office block here.'

The magistrate spun his laptop around on his desk so they all could see, and hit the space bar to start the video.

'There she is, holding her pink sports bag. The camera has a narrow field of vision. She seems to be talking to someone, who moves out of frame. Now you can see the car pull up and, before you ask, yes, the camera is too high up to capture the number plate. The car is probably a grey Yaris, which might or might not be relevant at a trial held some day in the far future, but is not enough for us now. An unidentified older-looking woman goes over to the car, and you can see her talking to the driver, but we get no picture of who he or she is. She might be the same person Teresa was talking to a moment before. My instinct says it is, but let's wait for the technicians to analyse the images more carefully, see what they say. This woman starts getting in and, at the last moment, beckons to Teresa. The girl, who, her parents and friends tell me, is not rebellious or unhappy or stupid enough to do something like this, climbs willingly into the car. The car drives off. Imagine being her parents seeing this video. Imagine being her as she realizes her mistake, which happens within half a mile, because it is then that her phone goes dead and vanishes from the network. Imagine the worst, because that is what will happen.'

They watched the girl get into the car, and the car driving away. He hit replay, and they watched the scene again.

'It makes you want to reach into the screen and pull her back,' said the southern policeman who had spoken up before.

'It's like being an all-seeing but powerless god,' said the magistrate. 'We need to get through a lot of detestable business first. We need to check the father. We need to look deeper into the family and its friends. That is the most promising hypothesis of all. Why would Teresa climb into a car like that? Our first idea must be that she knew the driver. Father, all family friends, relatives, all the girl's friends, and then the mother. We rip into the lives of those who are suffering most. Let's do it immediately and quickly. We strike when the nerves are raw and the pain is greatest, and we try not to drag it out for longer than we must. Next, we look into the father's activities. He appears to be a failed journalist, but perhaps he is wealthier than he seems, and a ransom demand is in the offing, though twenty-four hours have now passed. Perhaps he owes someone something. Find out everything about his colleagues, past jobs, employment records. Go through the girl's diaries, if she had any. Her phone records have already been checked, and every contact she had needs to be questioned. Check out boyfriends, if she had any. Check out fights with teachers, with classmates and any disputes involving her or her family, no matter how trivial: a fight over an apartment-block boiler bill, an unpaid dentist bill, a broken fence.

Then, when we have done all that, we pass on to the worst scenario, worse for us because it leads to a dead-end: a random attack. Remember, though, this is a story that will not end well.'

Magistrate Francesco Fossati of the Fifth Section of the Criminal Court of Milan dismissed the police officers, and replayed the video, willing the girl not to get into the car and watching helplessly as she ignored the thought waves he was sending back in time.

2

Milan

Standing on a white pebble path at a quarter to eight in the morning towards the end of what had been another uneventful working week in an almost empty office, Matteo Arconti, now deputy head of the actuarial division of the insurance company, pulled out a pair of folding glasses to consult his new book. He pushed the glasses down his nose and raised his eyes to focus again on the tree in front of him. He had a lot of things to take in. Pale grey bark with deep fissures, a wide crown with sinuous low branches, entire leaves in alternate pinnate pairs. He was not sure about how deep a deep fissure was supposed to be, nor what 'pinnate' meant, but surely there could be no mistaking the round green fruit which, the book told him, ripens slowly over long hot summers. This was almost definitely a walnut tree, a *Juglans regia*. He had been walking past it, under it, for fifteen years and had never thought to examine it, or any of the other trees in the Indro Montanelli Gardens. He lowered his eyes to read the botanical name again: *Juglans regia*.

He skimmed through the pages to see if he could spot an illustration of the taller and thinner tree on the other side of the path, but he was already running late. He gave himself a certainty score of 85 per cent with regard to this probable walnut. In need of more data, he reached up and plucked one of the bright lime-coloured fruits. He split the outer skin of the globular casing with his thumbnail, causing it to release a scent that cut through the air like the aromatic volatiles of a synthetic detergent. He tried to prise it open to get to the walnut inside.

Unexpectedly, fluid squirted out, hitting his white shirt cuff, which poked neatly out from beneath his business suit. Damn. Watery as it ran into the webbing between his thumb and index finger, the fluid quickly became sticky. He stopped off at a drinking fountain to wash his hands, and tossed away the unsplittable case. Through the railings, he could see his dark-blue BMW 5 Series. A dirty white van drove slowly past.

He rubbed his hands under the flowing water and then stared at them in puzzlement. The juices from the smooth green fruit had tanned his skin with shades of yellow and brown. His fingers seemed nicotine stained, and the purple and black streak across his thumbnail was so similar to a bruise that he fancied he felt it throb as he looked at it. The more he washed his hands, the darker the stain became.

His wife had set him a challenge as she handed him the book: identify every tree in the park by the end of September, before the leaves fall. He liked the idea, and had even figured out how to set up a spreadsheet on his laptop to keep track. He had decided to locate the trees he identified on Google Maps, and mark the date too. Walnut tree, August 26. It would be the first thing he did when he got to the office. In these dog days of late summer, he had plenty of dead time.

'You need to change your priorities a little,' Letizia had told him that morning as he stood frowning at the unexpected gift. 'We've plenty of money. You said yourself there was no need to continue with the pretence of being a dynamic young manager. So take it easy. Spend time with your children, who love you. Sofia is fifteen already. She's going through a bad patch now, coming to terms with not being as good-looking as she once thought she was.'

'What do you mean?'

'Well, she's hardly perfect. She seems to have inherited your legs, for a start, which, well, and her chin is pointy sharp and her nose – I think that must come from your side of the family, too.'

'She's absolutely beautiful. She always has been, always will be.'

Now he glanced at his vintage Breitling watch, a gift from Letizia six years ago to celebrate his fortieth birthday. The watch lost twelve to fifteen minutes a day, but he had never had the heart to tell her and continued to wear it, surreptitiously righting it every morning against the clock on his mobile phone. One minute to eight, lied the watch. That meant it was already at least one minute past. He slipped the book into his pocket, exited the gate on the side of Via Daniele Manin. He opened the back door of his BMW and tossed his briefcase in. Shutting it, he noticed a van, the same one he had glimpsed earlier, reversing down the road at speed. Idiot driver. He was going to have to get out of the way quickly if he didn't want to get knocked down.

The van braked just in time, and its back doors burst open, to reveal a man with short straw-coloured hair, who half nodded at him, then leaped out and smiled as he landed nimbly on the road. Matteo stood absently fingering his car key, wondering if he was supposed to know the man standing next to him. Now the driver was coming around from the side, and for a split second, Matteo was worried that he had made a gesture of some sort to protest at the reckless driving. But of course, he hadn't. He was proud of his ability to resist road rage. Even so, it almost seemed as if they were coming for . . .

Someone, it must have been the driver, pulled a thin plastic cord around his neck and jerked it tight, strangling his cry. The other man, or perhaps the driver again, grabbed his hands, and twisted them behind his back with speed and violence, then jerked upwards, causing extreme pain in his shoulders, and propelling him towards the van. He went straight into the side of one of the doors, hitting it with his mouth, and felt a crack, a shooting pain, and a sudden rush of salt and slime in his mouth. He felt the van tilt down slightly as someone jumped into it. The man who had nodded in that friendly way seconds before was now grabbing a fistful of Matteo's thinning hair at the back of his neck and dragging him in. He could not breathe. The floor of the van felt strangely yielding, as if his face was metal and the floor was soft flesh. Now thousands of tiny ball bearings seemed to be rolling beneath his hands. He clutched at them desperately with his fists as if they were pearls of oxygen. A tingling sensation passed through his chest and he felt his body beginning to float upwards. Just before he lost consciousness, the cord was released from around his neck. He could hear gasping and coughing, and it took him a while before he realized he was making the sounds himself. He became aware of the man beside him and the movement of the vehicle. He was bringing his eyes into focus and getting ready to speak, when a bag was pulled over his head. Silently, the man bound his wrists with duct tape. He could hear the squeak of the sticky plastic being pulled from the roll as it was wrapped over and over his wrists and hands, stretchable at first, then tighter and tighter.

3

Milan–Sesto San Giovanni

THE JOURNEY TOOK somewhere between half an hour and an hour. Or maybe more. He had lost track of time but sensed the distance was not great. It was a short transfer from the vehicle to a damp room via a short few steps that he managed to negotiate without falling. He was thrown nose first against a crumbling wall. Still they left the bag over his head. He asked for it to be taken off, then scrunched up his face waiting for the blow that would inevitably follow. But no one answered and he realized he was alone. He could hear the muffled voices of the men speaking some Balkan or East European language. Probably Romanian, he thought. It sounded like it made sense. Romanian was full of Latin and Italian-sounding words; Albanian was unlike anything else.

Thought fragments and oddly irrelevant questions were forming a disorderly pile in the back of his mind, but they had to wait. He needed to concentrate on not dying from suffocation, on expelling the blood that kept welling up from inside his mouth and making him nauseous. To vomit would be to die. Finally, as an overwhelming question of dignity, he had to concentrate on his bowels. He began to get a rhythm going. Breathe slowly, gently, until someday someone would take this stifling hood off his head. Spit softly into the fabric to keep the blood and saliva from sliding down his throat and making him sick. Tighten the sphincter and clench the stomach muscles when the cold rush of liquid fear hit the base of his gut. The thing to remember was that they had the wrong person. As soon as they discovered their mistake, they would let him go. He had to be careful not to look at them and not to hear any names. He was able to move his fingers a little behind his back. He could use his right hand to feel the wedding ring on his left. Inside the ring were his wife's name and the date of their marriage twenty-two years ago. He closed a finger and thumb over it and started easing it off.

He was not ready to die, even though that very morning he had given a thoughtful little speech on the question of ageing and death in front of his wife and his children, sleepy-eyed and outraged at being dragged out of their summer-morning beds. They already felt underprivileged to be in Milan at the end of August when everyone else was still on holiday. The trips to France in June, the holiday camps in July, and the two weeks on the Argentario counted for nothing, evidently.

'Happy belated birthday,' Letizia had said, giving him the book on trees. He had kissed her on the cheek. She moved her lips up to meet his, but he'd gone for the cheek, because, well, the children. But now he regretted it. He should have kissed her on the lips. He felt his wedding band slip over his knuckle. Then he had kissed Sofia on the head, run his fingers through his son's hair, and said, 'Get a haircut, Lorenzo. You look like a girl.'

Lorenzo was showing signs of wanting to follow in his father's footsteps. Statistics, mathematics, probability puzzles. He and Lorenzo always had football, number tricks and puzzles to keep them in contact with each other. But his daughter Sofia had floated to a planet so far away that communications between them had become infrequent and asynchronous.

His right hand was cramping, and his wrist hurt from the effort, but he had managed to free the wedding ring from the fat of his finger. He crooked his fingertip to stop the ring from falling off immediately.

Someone entered the room. Something scraped, thin metal against cement, the hollow tube of a chair leg, followed by a fizz of static as synthetic fibres brushed plastic as the person sat down inches from him. Fingers touched his throat without violence. Then another hand, moved in under his chin, as Letizia sometimes did when she was adjusting his tie before he left in the morning. Behind his back, he straightened his finger and allowed the ring to slip into his right hand, where he nestled it protectively in the hollow made by his thumb and the edge of his palm.

The hands left his neck and the hood was lifted. Fresh cool air rushed across his face, down his mouth, up his nostrils, through his hair. It was like riding the waves in a speedboat. He looked up into the face of the man who had freed him from the constriction and darkness, unable to keep the gratitude out of his eyes. His thoughts began to clear as the oxygen returned to his brain and his eyes focused. He was in an abandoned place that smelled of urine and wet cement. He started talking.

'We don't have much money. I have a ski chalet in Aprica, just one bedroom, not worth all that much. My Generali stock options are worth 172,000 euros. I have 90,000 in the bank plus two online accounts that transfer to that account only, so I would have to be the one to do that. They have about 20,000 each in them. I lost money on the stock market. My parents rent their house and live on a state pension. Even if Letizia – that's my wife, as you probably know – even if she sells the house to get me back, which she could hardly do without the authorities finding out and freezing my assets, you're not going to get much more than a million, and . . . seeing as there are several of you . . .' He thought of the Romanian words he had heard them speak. 'Do you understand what I am saying?'

'Shut up,' said the man. 'I'm not interested. If I want you to talk, I'll tell you to talk.' The voice was plaintive and resentful, as if his captor was the one having the wrong inflicted upon him. The speaker was a *terrone*, one of those brutal southern peasants whose unwelcome presence in Milan was one of the reasons the Northern League had become so popular. He wasn't so good with the accents of the Mezzogiorno. He knew his captor was not Neapolitan. Neapolitans always sounded enthusiastic and friendly and on the verge of telling a joke. This was a more lugubrious southern accent, not Apulia. Sicily or Calabria – Calabria, probably. Where his own grandfather had come from.

'Working in insurance doesn't mean I can get my hands on money. I don't have access to funds . . . I'm only middle management. I'm not very good at my job. I can't keep up with the latest computer algorithms. I have no knowledge or privileges.'

'Is that what you do, insurance?' said the man.

The man had opened his legs a little and bent his head down, like an adult watching a child at play on the floor. Forties, tracksuit, overweight. He smelled of cigarettes, cologne, and something rubbery.

'You don't know what I do?' said Matteo, hope rushing into him like the air had a minute before.

'The Romanians said you worked in an office. They didn't go any deeper than that. No need.'

'Ah, you must have the wrong person, then,' he tried to sound

11

professional and politely apologetic, like the indemnification guys did when rejecting a claim.

The man held out Matteo's wallet, pulled out his frayed identity card. 'You are the person I want. Matteo Arconti, a Calabrian name?'

'My grandfather came from there,' said Matteo.

Like a conjurer, his captor produced the book on trees from behind his back. 'This was in your pocket. You like trees?'

'No – yes. I don't know.'

The man opened the book, looked through a few pages in the middle, and neatly pulled one out, then crumpled it up in his hand. He stepped over, and slipped the book back into Matteo's jacket pocket. As he did so, Matteo caught sight of a black pistol tucked into the man's elasticized waistband. The absence of a holster caused him despair. It meant his captor did not generally carry a weapon. So, if he had a weapon now, it had to be for a specific and immediate purpose. At the back of his mind, a version of himself was marvelling at the clarity of his thinking, promising to save the memory for later telling once this was over.

But how would it end? Matteo bent his head down, muffling his voice against his chest in the hope that a lack of clarity in the question would elicit a lack of clarity in the response. 'Are you going to kill me?'

The man pulled up his tracksuit, scratched his stomach, and picked absently at the thick black hairs around his belly button, then pulled down his tracksuit again, slipping the gun into his hand as he did so.

Matteo tucked his thumb deeper into his palm and rebalanced the ring. If he launched it behind him and his captor never noticed, it might serve as a posthumous message for the people who came looking for him when it was too late, and it would tell his wife he was thinking of her. At least he hoped she'd take it that way. But throwing away the ring was also throwing away hope.

'Why me? I have no connections to anything. I have never harmed anyone, or stolen anything.'

'We have to bow before the hand of fate.'

Matteo flipped his thumb upwards and sent his wedding ring spinning away into the darkness behind him, for anyone who was looking for him. He began speaking to hide any clinking sound of the gold hitting the floor. 'I have . . . I have done nothing all my life. And I'm not ready. I'm still learning things, you saw that. Trees.'

'I don't want to explain it. Basically, from your point of view, there's no explanation,' said the man, standing up and raising the pistol, which had a short fat barrel. He pointed it at him.

'I have a family! Two children!' Matteo's fear was tinged with outrage. 'And I am so obviously not the person you want. There must be another person with the same name! No one is making you do this, you understand that, right? Listen, like me, you probably have children, don't you?'

The man shot him in the heart, then the head.

Minchia che rumore! The noise in the concrete chamber had assaulted his ears and made him angry. He called in the two Romanians. 'Take this heap of shit down to Rome tomorrow. Do it at night. Dump it at Piazzale Clodio. There are some wide-open spaces there without buildings overlooking. Stay away from restricted traffic zones, cameras, and police, and drive so as not to be noticed. Right, who took his wallet and watch? Come on. Keep the watch, if you want to wear a dead man's watch . . . but I need the wallet.'

He held out his hand, not bothering to see which of the Romanians returned it to him. 'Keep whatever money you found, but leave everything else, especially his ID card. Leave the book in his pocket. It's a nice touch.'

4

Rome

CHIEF INSPECTOR CATERINA Mattiola walked into Commissioner Alec Blume's office and dropped an envelope on his desk.

'The results of the blood test,' she said.

'Good,' said Blume, looking up from the newspaper he was reading. 'Leave them there.' He folded over a page. As always, he was reading the local news. The watch she had given him sat beside him on the desk. He glanced up, and made a show of surprise at seeing her still there. 'I don't suppose you'd close the door when you come in here?'

Caterina went back and closed the door.

Blume waited till he heard the click, then said, 'I'm sorry I didn't make it over last night.'

'That's fine.'

Blume returned to his newspaper. 'So, you're investigating that robbery on Via Giulia,' he said as if reading out a mildly interesting headline.

'Attempted robbery,' she corrected. 'They ran off without getting anything.'

'Sure. No shots were fired. You told me the attempted robbers were probably two middle-class kids out for kicks. So, whose blood are we talking about?'

'Very funny.'

Blume pushed the paper to one side with a sigh.

'I picked up your test results on my way in this morning,' she said.

'The pointless test you forced me to do.'

'For your own good, Alec. It's not normal for a man to wake up in the morning and eat aspirin.'

'It is if you have a headache.'

'That's the not normal part,' said Caterina.

'I see you're having difficulty adjusting to my morning routines,' said Blume.

'No, I think it's working out pretty well. I am adjusting.'

'Still, I imagine it's nice to have a break from me now and again. I certainly would like to take a break from myself now and then.'

'We both need to compromise if we're going to be living together,' said Caterina.

'What about my big American breakfasts at the weekend? They seem to disturb you, too. I need to know they can continue.'

'That's a cultural thing. I can accept that. I like the pancakes too. But I don't know how you can bear to eat all that meat and eggs first thing. It'll kill you.'

'Not at all,' said Blume. 'Fat and protein are beneficial.'

'No one will convince me that those fried sausages do you any good. They put all sorts of disgusting stuff in them.'

'I know that,' said Blume. 'You know what's a big ingredient in super-market pork?'

'No,' said Caterina.

'Aspirin.' He picked up the envelope, gave it an appreciative flick with the back of his hand, and dropped it into the top drawer of his desk, which he kicked shut as he leaned back in his chair. 'Still, thanks for this.'

'You need to take the results to your doctor.'

'Sure thing. Like I said, thanks.' He returned to his newspaper.

'Now.'

'What?'

'I took the liberty of checking your schedule and making an appoint-ment for you. We have no urgent cases . . .'

'You did what? I'll make my own appointments, thank you. Also, I have one with the magistrate this morning.' He picked his watch up off the desk and reluctantly started attaching it to his wrist.

'I saw that. But it's not until eleven,' she said. 'Also, I thought he'd finished with you.'

'More or less. He probably wants to explain where the case is going. A courtesy thing. There's a certain irony in this, isn't there?'

'If there is, I don't get it,' said Caterina.

'Not with the courtesy. Magistrate Arconti is a courteous man. I meant the case itself. It involved Nimesulide, remember? Which is just the analgesic I want for my headaches, so that makes it ironic. Or is it the opposite of ironic? Apt?'

'If I knew what you were talking about I might be able to help you choose your words.'

'The case involved Nimesulide. The drug they make Aulin pills from. Chief Inspector Panebianco tells me it's the only thing that works for migraines like mine.'

'So now it's a migraine.'

'It always was a migraine,' said Blume. 'I just don't like to make a big deal of it, so I call it a simple headache.'

Caterina rolled her eyes. 'Maybe you should have taken a few handfuls of the Nimesulide when you made the raid.'

'The thought did occur to me,' said Blume. 'But stealing drugs, even if they're not illegal in themselves, and interrupting the chain of evidence in an Ndrangheta investigation . . .'

'I was kidding, you know.'

'I know. Taking you literally is my way of kidding you back. I expect Arconti just wants to sign off on the investigation. There's not much we can do from here anyhow since the person he's investigating operates in Germany, Switzerland and Milan. And Calabria of course.'

'So the case is being transferred to the DIA?'

'Probably. The DIA isn't what it used to be. Twenty years ago, with Law 41(a) and the Mafia on the run, those guys saw themselves like a cross between the Marines and the FBI, poised for victory and revenge. Now . . . Just another mistreated police force. So the investigation goes to them, or it gets kicked into the undergrowth and left to fester. I suppose the investigating magistrate's been taken off it, too. He probably wants to explain all that to me today.'

'Meanwhile, your original investigation into the "suicide" of the hospital consultant from Naples . . .'

'Stops here. For now. Foul play was not established, but at least the case opened an interesting avenue.'

'That avenue was wide open if anyone cared to look,' said Caterina. 'The consultant had never even practised. For ten years he had been

issuing prescriptions for vast quantities of Nimesulide, using hospital pro-
curement contracts to cover his tracks. It was clear he was supplying the
drug to someone who was using it to cut cocaine on an industrial scale.
All people had to do was open their eyes. His colleagues, the hospital
accountants, the Finance Police ... he was acting in broad daylight,
driving a Lamborghini on a state salary.'

'Disgusting,' said Blume. 'But, eventually overcome with remorse, the
consultant beat himself around the face, head, groin and chest before
hanging himself from his balcony in what was unquestionably suicide.'

'Are you really happy to leave it at that?'

'It's not up to me. It's Arconti's call. But it's hard to care about the
consultant or the verdict on his death. The consultant was a door into a
more interesting inquiry. Arconti had retroactive traces put on the calls
made by the consultant, which worked just fine, because it led to the
arrest of two gallant gentlemen from Calabria.'

'Your appointment with the doctor is for 9:15.' She glanced at her
watch. 'So you should get moving now. The clinic is on the way. If you
want, you can get painkillers prescribed by him. OK?'

Blume shook his head. 'You're kidding, right? You expect me to stand
up and go to the doctor, just like that?'

'Yes. You wanted something for your headaches. Go to the doctor,
talk to him. I went to the trouble of making the appointment, it's the least
you could do.'

'If I don't?'

'If you don't go, I'm going to leave this office, wait for you outside,
and then make a scene here in the station, in front of everyone. Maybe in
the corridor, you know, with voices raised and all the trappings.'

'You don't scare me. Anyhow everyone's on holiday.'

'I can embarrass you though. All it takes is for me to announce we are
half-living together.'

'Everyone knows that.'

'But it's not acknowledged,' she said. 'If I make it official, you'll have
to write up a report on conflicts of interest, and one of us will have to be
moved to a different department. Or else we'll just have to marry and
present it as a done deal.'

'So what time did you say the appointment was?' said Blume.

★

Half an hour later, Blume sat in the waiting room in the company of a desiccated old woman who avoided his eyes and fluttered her hand nervously across her throat every time he looked in her direction. He raised his arm and looked at his watch, and was about to ask her what the hell was the point of doctors setting appointment times for patients if they didn't respect . . .

The doctor appeared in person at the door of the waiting room and motioned him in. Too cheap to hire a receptionist. In the office, the doctor unfolded Blume's test results, read them, and burst out laughing.

'What's so funny?'

'What on earth do you eat?'

'Food, normal stuff.'

'I've never seen a cholesterol reading like that. Bad LDL cholesterol, I mean. I'm putting you on statins. Zocor, one a day for the rest of your life.'

'I am pretty sure you have seen a cholesterol level like that in the past,' said Blume.

'No, no. I'd have remembered a reading like this.'

'No, you wouldn't,' said Blume. 'Because I was here five years ago and we had pretty much the same conversation.'

The doctor frowned, 'I thought I knew your face.' He tapped at the computer on his desk. 'There you are. I prescribed statins for you then, too. Why did you tell me this was your first visit?'

'I didn't want to have an argument about statins again.'

'Obviously you're not taking them.'

'No,' said Blume. 'My cholesterol is inherited. Northern ancestors. Sweden, Norway, Minnesota. Places like that.'

'Why bother with the blood test then?'

'My partner insisted. Besides, I might have something else.'

'Well, you do. Poor liver function. What's your beef with statins?'

'I don't believe in taking medicine preventatively. I think it's a scam by the drug companies. Scare people to sell them stuff.'

'I remember you now,' said the doctor.

'But I do believe in prescriptions for real pain. I'd like you to write me one for Aulin, please.'

'So you have headaches?'

'Migraines, for which I need Aulin or something even stronger.'

'If I said yes, you'd need repeat prescriptions. You'd have to come back here.'

'Fine.'

'But I'm not going to prescribe it anyway.'

Blume pulled a notebook from his jacket and flicked it open. 'What about Migraless?'

'Same stuff, same answer,' said the doctor.

'Let me see . . . he also mentioned Minerol and Edemax.'

'No and no. Still versions of Nimesulide.'

'Hydrocodone?'

'Who is this maniac advising you? Take the statins, come back to me in a month, and then we can talk.'

'I'm not taking statins.'

'And I'm not prescribing Nimesulide to patients I don't know. Try over-the-counter paracetamol, less coffee and a more relaxed attitude.'

Blume slammed the door on his way out, startling the little woman in the waiting room. 'That man,' Blume told her, 'is fucking useless.'

5

Rome

BLUME DROVE FAST and aggressively through the streets to his appoint-ment in Piazzale Clodio with Magistrate Matteo Arconti. He did not have a headache yet, but he had the intimations of one. It promised to be brutal, and it would be the fault of Caterina and that idiot doctor.

When they first met, the magistrate, whose unsteady vibrato voice gave all his utterances a plaintive edge, had asked Blume about his personal life. Blume had simply and automatically lied as he did to everyone who asked questions in that area. No partner, woman, girlfriend or emotional attach-ment to anyone, he had said.

The magistrate seemed so pleased at this information that Blume sud-denly had a lurching sensation that this was the prelude to some sort of gay demand. It would fit in with the wavering voice, the ready smile. Jesus, the thought. The guy was white haired and had to be about sixty-five. Not that that was the issue. Even if he had been thirty-five or twenty-five.

'I was hoping you would say that,' said the magistrate.

'You were?'

'Yes. You see, if the criminals want to get at you, they have to get *you*, Commissioner. The same applies to me. They would need to kill me in person, since it's going to be hard to find any family. My parents are dead; I have no idea who my cousins are. My wife divorced me and moved abroad ten years ago, and even under torture, I could not say where she is. We had no children. I can be sure that no one innocent is at risk because I refuse to let go of an investigation. We might die, but no one has to die on our behalf. That is important. It gives us freedom.'

Blume, relieved to discover his magistrate had suicidal rather than homosexual inclinations, agreed, even going so far as to add: 'I don't really understand how a policeman can have a wife and family and still be effective.'

Caterina was not a wife, or even a proper partner yet. Propped up at his front door, ready to be taken round to her place, was a suitcase of belongings, mostly mementos of his parents, including their wedding rings. He had carefully buried the objects under a layer of his own clothes so that she could not see quite how sentimental he was. The suitcase had been there for five or six weeks now. Once he carried it into Caterina's apartment, the die would be cast. Apparently, her coming to his larger and nicer apartment was out of the question, because of her son, Elia, who was not to be traumatized by a change of house and school. Also, her parents lived up the road. His dead parents and lack of children gave him no counterarguments. Saying he did not like her apartment much, which was true, was not an option. She seemed to think they could rent his out, but Blume did not want strangers pawing their way around what had been his parents' home.

'I can see we will get on well,' Arconti had said after that first meeting.

And so they had, but as soon as the case began to get interesting, it had started moving away from them. Now the anti-Mafia magistrates of the DDA and the agents of the DIA were poised to take over.

It had started well enough, a trace on the doctor's phone leading to a warehouse next to an abandoned cake factory in north Rome. They set up a surveillance detail, and within a few days, two suspects had turned up in a green van. The registration traced back to a car dealer in Calabria with multiple links to the Ndrangheta. A flag went up at the DIA and DDA, and from there on it was hardly their case any more, but Arconti seemed unperturbed.

The actual raid had been carried out at dawn by an eight-man team from NOCS, the Special Forces unit of the police. They were like a rake of eager colts. Trained to stand still as they listened to their commander brief them, each one of them was visibly struggling to suppress his pent-up energy.

Blume, feeling old, had watched them through binoculars as they burst into the warehouse, pretending he didn't care that the young men in their combat uniforms and boots could all run a hundred metres in fourteen seconds or less, and eight kilometres in twenty minutes. He sometimes went on long runs that felt like they might be eight kilometres; hell, they felt like fifty.

The warehouse haul was 80 kilos of black cocaine and 10 kilos of Nimesulide in five plastic bags. Blume watched as a uniformed policeman wearing surgical gloves lifted one of the fat pill-filled sacks. Blume imagined the sack bursting and the pills bouncing and rolling everywhere as they hit the floor. One quick scoop of his hand and he'd not have another debilitating headache for ten years.

The two suspects, two brothers called Cuzzocrea, were cocooned in sleeping bags when the NOCS team broke in. The elder of the two apparently didn't even wake up, the other struggled for a moment with the zip, but lay still when a boot was placed on his throat. The police also recovered 300,000 euros in cash − a good haul.

It turned out the Cuzzocrea brothers were first cousins of Maria Itria Landolina, wife of a certain Agazio Curmaci whose name was in one of their phones, though no calls had been placed to or received from him. A trace on both phones revealed a stream of connections in Germany, but the wiretap remit issued by the Italian authorities did not extend across the border.

'I have been after Curmaci on and off for years,' explained Arconti. 'It's almost a hobby. He is based in Germany now, so there is not much chance of my getting him, but this connection via the cousins of his wife was too good to pass up.'

'Who's Curmaci?'

'Is the name completely new to you?'

'No. I looked up some records. The capo of the Dusseldorf–Duisburg *locale* is Domenico Megale, the *crimine* is his son, Tony Megale, and the *mastro di giornata* is Agazio Curmaci. The identity of the *contabile* is unknown, but may be a guy called Murdolo. Or that's how things stood two years ago, which is the best information I could find. That's pretty much it. Theoretically, those three are on the same level . . .'

'But obviously,' said Blume, 'Tony Megale, who's the boss's son and is in charge of armed operations, is going to be way stronger than the other two.'

'You'd think that, wouldn't you?' said Arconti. 'And you may even be right. But I think the most powerful one is Curmaci. There is a persistent rumour that Tony is not really the old man's son. Then there is the fact

22

that Agazio Curmaci was promoted straight up to the same level as Tony within a year of arriving in Germany. Shortly after, there was some sort of falling out between them, followed by several years that Curmaci spent in London where it seems he took a degree in history. Old Man Megale remains as ignorant as the goats he used to herd, and Tony, natural son or not, has inherited the ignorance. If I had to guess, I'd say Curmaci was the one who came up with the idea of calling the old man the Prefect. Putting his fancy education to use flattering the boss.'

'The *Prefect*?' said Blume. 'Isn't that title a bit too judicial-sounding?'

'I think it's more ecclesiastic, like Michele Greco used to be called the "Pope". When the Catholic Church is establishing itself among heathens, it sends out a mission. If the mission is successful, the mission becomes a prefecture. If the prefecture grows in size, it becomes a vicariate. If the vicariate is consolidated, it becomes a diocese. Megale, one of the first missionaries into Germany, obviously sees the Mafia conquest of the Rhine–Westphalia region as being only at the second stage.'

'Let's get back to Tony,' said Blume. 'As the *crimine*, he has the fire-power, access to killers, control over the arsenal.'

'That can be taken away from him, and you should not underestimate the importance of the *mastro di giornata*, especially when you're talking about a *locale* operating outside Italy. The *mastro di giornata* doesn't just call meetings, deal with protocol, and act as an intermediary, he is also responsible for maintaining the traditions of the Society, and that is extremely important for a *locale* based abroad. The Ndrangheta is not just a criminal organization, it's a system of belief.'

'OK, so Curmaci's important.'

'Agazio Curmaci is almost certainly a *santista*, or maybe even higher,' said Arconti. 'All the signs are there.'

'I thought a *santista* was a rank above the boss of a *locale*,' said Blume. 'It seems weird he could be both above and below the boss at the same time.'

'It's not really a rank. It's more a function. A *santista* is dedicated to interfacing with the authorities and the world of business. He will be a member of Rotary clubs, Masonic lodges, business associations, political parties, planning committees and so on. He'll exchange political favours and will appear as legitimate as possible. But, and this is where the Ndrangheta excels, a *santista* is even allowed to help the police if he sees it as being in the long-term interest of the Society. He can sacrifice his companions. If he is a *santista*, then he's sort of outside the Society and inside it too. He's allowed to make decisions that go far beyond his official title. Not only could Curmaci overrule Tony, he could even overrule Old Megale if he felt it was in the best interests of the Society.'

'But his comrades don't know he's a *santista*?'

'Not necessarily.'

'And you do?'

Arconti looked flustered. 'No, I don't. But I have a feeling.'

'A feeling that Curmaci can do what he pleases?'

'Not what he pleases. There are rules, and they are intricate. The Ndrangheta has a system that allows for controlled betrayal of parts for the sake of the general preservation of the whole. Cosa Nostra never managed it. In some ways it's hard not to admire these people.'

'Are you saying that because you're Calabrian, too, Magistrate?'

'I am proud as well as ashamed of what my people can do,' said Arconti. 'Look at Megale, the "Prefect of Westphalia", to give the murderous old goatherd his full honorific title. He controls a vast fortune that he made by buying up thousands of offices and homes in East Germany after the collapse of Communism, most of which he did from behind bars. Or take his son, Tony; or better, Agazio Curmaci. They too have untold wealth, but live like they've taken a vow of poverty. Their families live in tumbledown houses in Locri. It's not just money that drives them, Blume. Remember that.'

The magistrate paused and raised his left arm in the air as if trying to gauge the weight of something. 'Old Megale was released from prison in Germany last week. Don't you think it's odd that those two clowns with the pills, the Cuzzocrea brothers, should turn up, a few days before the release?'

'No,' said Blume. 'I don't see it as odd. I don't see the connection.'

'Maybe you're right,' said the magistrate. 'I'm just thinking out loud. Old Megale is in his eighties, and maybe he's wondering who should succeed him. Then again, maybe not. Is his adopted son the appointed heir and successor? Somewhere off to the side, above or below Tony and not so easy to place in the hierarchy, is Agazio Curmaci.'

'They sound like the sort of people who want to kill each other,' said Blume.

'Tony Megale and Agazio Curmaci have known each other since for ever, long before Curmaci went to Germany. Perhaps they are close friends. We cannot tell from the outside. And if anyone has reason to be bitter about being overlooked by Old Megale, it is Pietro, who is not only the first-born son, but, probably, Old Megale's only real child. It seems Megale decided a long time ago that Pietro was not up to the job.'

'Where's this Pietro?'

Arconti, as if he had been waiting for this question, pulled out a black-and-white photo that looked like it had been taken in the late nineteenth century. 'That's him.'

Blume looked at the photo, and handed it back. 'Is he normal? He doesn't seem to have full control over his facial muscles.'

'He's borderline retarded. He's still in Calabria. He and his wife look after Tony Megale's son, a kid named Enrico. They have no children of their own.'

'If they look after Tony's kid, then there can't be too much envy between Tony and Pietro, no? Agazio Curmaci, on the other hand, sounds like a usurper.'

'It's hard to tell. Pietro and his wife live practically next door to Curmaci's wife and children. Tony's son and Curmaci's son are the same age, go to the same school. Yet in Germany the fathers operate in two different spheres. Tony Megale's line of business is criminal, Curmaci moves in very legitimate circles. He's not going to be pleased at having his name linked, however indirectly, to those two we captured.'

'We caught them fair and square, without any tip-offs,' said Blume. 'I don't see how Tony Megale could have planned that to undermine Curmaci.'

'I agree,' said the magistrate. 'Also, it's the sort of ploy Curmaci might use against Tony, not vice versa. Curmaci is subtler. It's just that I can't be sure we really were the architects of that operation. If the doctor had not committed "suicide" and if the death had not been very suspicious, the operation would not have begun. We would not have found the connection leading to the Cuzzocrea brothers, who led us to Curmaci's wife, who led us to Curmaci. All this time I have had a sensation of being led by the nose.'

'By Curmaci towards Curmaci,' said Blume. 'It doesn't really add up.'

Arconti pushed himself away from his chaotic desk. 'You're right. I've passed everything into the expert hands of the anti-Mafia magistrates and the DIA. They're better equipped than us to deal with these things. Unless, of course, you think you would be suited to that line of work.'

'My speciality is unorganized crime,' said Blume. 'It's a bit late now to question my career choice.'

'It's never too late for that,' said Arconti. 'And you're still young.'

'Only compared to you,' said Blume.

'See, that's simply not polite. True, but not polite. I have heard people complain about your bluntness, Commissioner. But if you're interested, I know someone.'

'Interested in what?' asked Blume.

'A change of scenery. A new departure in your career,' said Arconti.

'Have you been talking about me to someone?'

'Yes, and that someone has been looking at you and your strange past. He tells me you had American parents. I was wondering about your name.'

'Did he tell you anything else?'

'Not really. Interested?'

'I don't think so,' said Blume. He had once entertained ideas of joining the DIA, but like a lot of other things in life, it had not worked out. Until a few years ago, Blume would have regarded a DIA takeover of a case as probably a good thing; now he was not so sure. Clean, focused and effective in the early 1990s, the DIA and its judicial arm, the DDA, were like erstwhile youthful idealists who had become more tired and compromised as they grew older together, both of them being absorbed into the corrupted political system they had once dared to challenge.

'All right, then. I am pleased to hear you are happy in your current position.'

'That is not what I said.'

'As for me,' Arconti continued, ignoring Blume, 'I have stayed away from the anti-Mafia magistrates, but I don't think they would have me anyway. One needs to come across as a bit more . . . a bit more . . .' He gazed wistfully out the window in search of the word he was looking for.

'Dynamic?' offered Blume.

'Yes . . . or . . .'

'Decisive?'

'Most of all, you need to be a bit uncaring, which is why I thought of you.'

'You're just sore because I called you old. I am actually a very caring person,' said Blume.

'People say you are reticent and secretive. Not very clubbable.'

'I simply believe that you should never tell a friend anything you would conceal from an enemy,' said Blume.

'That attitude is what makes you ideal for Mafia work. I've seen this happen time and again in investigations, and it has happened to me. You seek a confession from a crime boss, and next thing you know he's implicated half your colleagues, three dear friends and all your superiors. It takes a special type of person to deal with that. Someone who can survive alone. Once you have a confession, if you get one, you can't be sure who's telling the truth any more. Maybe you're being played by your informer or maybe you have been fooled for years by colleagues you thought you could trust. Capturing a boss is like holding a rabid wolf by the ears as it tries to bite your balls off. You want to release your grip, but really you'd better not.'

He squeezed his eyes shut.

'Are you feeling all right?' asked Blume after the magistrate had not spoken for a while.

'Do you ever get the feeling you are moving in slow motion?'

Blume nodded. 'In dreams all the time. Running away, legs getting heavier and heavier. Something dragging you back.' He looked at the magistrate who was sitting very still. 'But not when I'm awake.'

The magistrate lifted his left hand. 'Do you ever get the feeling one arm is really light and the other really heavy?'

'If I am wearing a watch, it makes my arm feel heavy and causes my wrist to itch,' said Blume. 'And now you've reminded me.'

'No, not heavy,' said Arconti absently. 'More like it was full of water . . .' His voice trailed off.

'My speciality is blinding headaches, not heavy limbs,' said Blume, pulling off his watch and pocketing it. He stared at Arconti, who now seemed to be stroking an imaginary beard, as if he were a doctor diagnosing his own arm trouble.

'I am stroking an imaginary beard,' replied Arconti.

27

'I see that. You can stop now,' said Blume.

'Who is your father, Commissioner?'

'My father's dead.' Arconti knew that, damn it.

'No,' said the magistrate, slowly, weighing up Blume's reply. '"My father's dead" is one of the initiation responses used by a Russian *vor*. An Ndranghetista at Curmaci's level would reply, "The sun is my father", though there are variations.'

'Is that what the beard-stroking was about? Were you testing to see if I was an Ndranghetista?'

'Of course not, Commissioner. I wanted to see if you recognized the symbolism. The imaginary beard is Garibaldi's. Garibaldi, Mazzini and La Marmora are the three secular saints of the *Santa*. Apart from all else, Commissioner, including my trust in you and your work as a policeman, racially and culturally speaking, you could never have been a *santista* in the Ndrangheta. It has to be in your blood.'

Blume shrugged. 'I just had my blood tested. It's Mafia-free.'

'Are you sure you don't want to talk to this friend of mine about a career change?'

'The DIA would never have me,' said Blume.

'It would not necessarily be the DIA. There are other groups that combat the Mafia from farther behind the scenes.'

'I would need to think about it.'

'It's a solitary life, but you would not mind, I think. Being alone frees the mind; it allows you to explore areas that others neglect, see things that others miss. Don't you agree?'

'I don't know,' said Blume. 'In my solitude, I have also seen many things that are not true.'

There was a knock at the door.

'*Avanti!*' called Blume automatically, before remembering where he was. 'Sorry, Giudice, this is your office. I had no right . . .'

An elderly man in a blue uniform backed into the office wheeling a trolley filled to overflowing with boxes and binders.

'It's no problem,' Arconti said to Blume and the man shuffled into the narrow space between them. 'We Calabrians tend to avoid the word *Avanti*. It's what drovers and goatherds shout at the beasts of the fields.' He watched the uniformed porter wipe the sweat off his brow, and carefully retreat from the trolley, lifting a clipboard off the top box. 'When addressing humans, we prefer to be more respectful. We prefer to say, simply enough, "come in." '

The porter continued his balancing act with the files, and when it became clear that nothing was going to fall off unless there was a breath of wind, he looked at the form in his hand and addressed the magistrate.

'These files are for Magistrate Matteo Arconti. I hope that is you, Dottore?'

'Yes,' said the magistrate. 'That's my name.'

Thursday, 27 August

6

Rome

CHIEF INSPECTOR PANEBIANCO delicately pinched the dead man's worn identity card between blue latex-covered fingers. 'As you can see, this guy was called Matteo Arconti. He was reported missing in Milan yesterday.'

Blume nodded. He was marshalling his thoughts and suppressing his shock. He would speak in a moment.

Panebianco allowed a few beats of silence to pass, then said: 'The victim has the same name as the magistrate you've been working with, Commissioner.'

'You think you needed to tell me that?' snapped back Blume.

Panebianco continued, unfazed. 'Same name as the magistrate but not him, right? Just to be sure.'

'What sort of dumb question . . .' He stopped himself. Panebianco was regarding him with the same detached look in his grey-blue eyes that Blume had seen him use for particularly stupid witnesses and suspects. 'Sorry, Rosario. You were right to ask. No, this is just his namesake.'

'I agree it was an odd question,' said Panebianco. 'I've worked with Arconti, and this is not him. But you know the way the dead are always a bit tricky to identify? Best to hear you confirm it, Commissioner. I wonder if he's related to the magistrate?'

'I doubt it,' said Blume.

Panebianco raised his eyebrows. 'Well, there has to be a direct connection. The body was dumped here outside the court buildings: it's hardly going to be a coincidence, is it?'

Panebianco seemed to be pushing him for a response.

Blume cleared his throat, and spoke. 'It's symbolic . . . it's . . . They are showing us what they're made of.'

'Who? The Calabrian Mafia? That's the case you were working on with the magistrate. Is this to do with the doctor and the Cuzzocrea brothers?'

'It's too early to say,' said Blume. His rage had subsided almost as suddenly as it had welled up, and was now a simmering and manageable anger, the sort that gave him energy. And deep inside, in a hardly acknowledged part of his soul, there was a feeling of reluctant admiration for the sort of person who could kill for no other reason than that the name of the victim fitted. Murder for a play on words.

'It's effective,' he told Panebianco. 'This is quite a well-structured act . . .' He looked at the splayed-out body, one arm pointing up, the other down as if to say, *Here is where I came from, there is where they went.*

As they moved around the body, a forensic technician cocooned in white watched fearfully without daring to intrude, like a possessive child who had made the mistake of lending his favourite toy to the two school bullies.

Blume tapped Panebianco on the elbow. 'Rosario, don't start from the Ndrangheta angle. If it's them, the case will be taken over by the DIA; if it's not, you're going to have to build up a different working hypothesis, so you may as well start now. Treat it as an ordinary murder.'

'You're talking as if you're bowing out.'

'I am,' said Blume. 'You deal with whoever is the magistrate in charge. Try to keep Caterina out of it, would you?'

Panebianco stood up from where he was crouched examining the black-caked exit wound in the victim's head, and waved at the forensic technician who rushed back towards the body with an air of gratitude and relief. His three colleagues followed.

Panebianco and Blume moved several yards away while the technicians continued their work with paper bags, tweezers and swabs.

'I disagree, Commissioner. This would be a good case for Caterina. Like you said, it's bound to be taken out of our hands once it's clear it is organized crime, so it would be a perfect chance for her to get some practice, and then feel the pain of losing a case.'

'I'd prefer she wasn't involved. She has a son, you know.'

Panebianco looked at him. 'She's the only one on the force with children?'

'That came out wrong.'

Panebianco did not look pleased. 'You've got no children. Why don't you handle it?'

34

'Magistrate Matteo Arconti won't be able to investigate this. It's too clearly a conflict of interest, and I think the same might apply to me. I'm going to retreat into the shadows, so to speak.'

Blume beckoned to Caterina who was still talking to the two street cleaners who had found the body. She flicked her hand at him, with exactly the same gesture she used to shoo away her son when he tried to interrupt her talking on the phone. Blume enjoyed the domestic intimacy of the gesture, but disliked the casual disregard of his authority. Even so, he let her finish her interview.

He took a walk around the area. The place was well chosen, a wide waste ground used as an overflow car park with no buildings overlooking it, and flanked by a road with fast-moving traffic and no footpath. The body had probably been lying there for hours. From what he had seen, it was unlikely that the victim had been killed where he was found. From a distance, the corpse looked like a lump of tar, a heap of clothes or a bag of rubbish.

The road, Via Falcone e Borsellino, was named after two magistrates murdered by Cosa Nostra in 1992.

He checked his phone again. If Arconti knew of the death of his name-sake, he would surely call.

Taking his time, he returned to the crime scene, now populated with more vehicles and a mortuary van. He stood at the edge and watched his colleagues go about their business. He observed Caterina whose move-ments were a little too quick. She changed direction often and twice had to retrace her steps. She spoke to colleagues, then five minutes later had to speak to them again. Lots of micromanagement errors so far, but she was maintaining authority and control, and being taken seriously – that was the main thing. He was pleased for her sake, then remembered he didn't want her on the case.

When she finally seemed to have a moment, he caught her eye and nodded at her to come over.

'The most obvious line of . . .' she began.

Blume put up a restraining hand. 'No.'

'No?'

'I think,' said Blume, 'the best way to approach this is to put a Chinese wall between us.'

She closed one eye and examined the side of his face as she often did when trying to assess whether he was being serious or not. 'A Chinese wall, no less,' she said eventually. 'A great one?'

'A Chinese wall is when you deliberately don't share knowledge or information so as not to help someone else inadvertently.'

'Sounds like an ordinary Blume wall to me,' said Caterina.

'I think you should maybe opt out of this one. You could tell the investigating magistrate your opinions are contaminated because of what I have already told you. You won't get sufficient clarity. So Panebianco's doing this until it's passed on to the DIA.'

'Or to Milan,' said Caterina. 'That's where the victim is from. He works in insurance and has no record of any sort. He never arrived at work yesterday morning, and his wife reported him missing. So maybe we should look into the wife.'

'The wife?' said Blume, intrigued. 'You mean an ordinary murder?'

'I know this is almost certainly to do with the Ndrangheta, but, like you said, I won't be influenced by you. See, your Chinese wall's working already.'

'You don't want to have anything to do with this,' said Blume. 'People who find an innocent namesake, kill him for . . . fun. Because this is a form of fun for them. Like shooting up a shop or firebombing a factory is fun for the young recruits. It is evil joy.'

'Evil or not, it does not follow that there is a particular risk for investigators. If they strike at us directly, it could spark off a war with the state, like Cosa Nostra was stupid enough to do in the 1990s. I'm in no more danger from this inquiry than any other. And you're not my protector.'

'I'm your commissioner.'

Caterina smiled and beckoned him closer, leaned into his ear, and whispered, 'Commissioner Blume?'

'What?' Blume found he was whispering, too, and grinning like a schoolboy.

'Fuck off.'

Blume stood back and scowled at her. 'There was no need for that. OK, have it your way. I don't think Curmaci or the Ndrangheta is involved in this.'

'Oh for God's sake, Alec. There is no need to exaggerate. How stupid do you think I am?'

'No, seriously,' said Blume. 'The Ndrangheta is the "quiet" Mafia.

This draws a lot of attention to them, and for what? It is not as if Arconti's investigation was going to the heart of the organization. Maybe Arconti, the magistrate, had other enemies. Maybe this other Arconti from Milan did.'

'Alec, I'm not listening to this.'

'Well, you should.'

Caterina lowered her voice. 'You spoke to me about a guy called Agazio Curmaci. Do you think . . .?'

'I hear the wife is on her way down from Milan to identify the body,' said Blume, glancing at his watch and realizing it was not there.

'Yes, she should get to the morgue in about three hours, more or less at the same time as her husband's body. But unless we bring up the Curmaci and Ndrangheta angle at once, the wife risks undergoing heavy-handed questioning from the investigating magistrate.'

'How do you know he'll do that?'

'Experience of magistrates. Unless it's a she, which would be better.'

Panebianco came over and pointed at a man strolling towards them, hands behind his back, his Venetian-blond hair visible from this distance.

'Here comes the investigating magistrate. That's Nardone.' He exchanged a look with Blume.

Caterina followed his glance. 'I don't know him. What's he like?'

Blume seesawed his hand back and forth to indicate that Nardone was less than perfect. 'There are worse. He's fifteen years younger than you.'

'No way!' said Caterina.

'Really.'

Caterina folded her arms across her breasts. 'How old do you think I am?'

'I don't know, about fifty?'

'You're not funny. Now, if I am not to think about the Ndrangheta, what line of approach should I take to the fact this body was dumped in Rome in front of the courthouse?'

'Maybe the victim came down here to Rome by himself.'

'No,' said Caterina. 'The body was moved after death, you can see that from the lividity, the way the clothes are rumpled and soiled. He's been dragged around, left lying on the ground for some time. Also, there should be more blood. If he was moved directly after death, there would be more bloodstains on his shirt and jacket. So he lay where he was shot long enough for the blood to coagulate and stop moving. Rigor mortis has completely gone, the skin has a greenish hue. The medical examiner, who seems to have a problem with women, won't say how long . . .'

'No, no. That's just Dorfmann,' said Blume. 'He doesn't hate you because you're a woman, he hates you because you're a breathing human. In his loathing of all living beings, he's a paradigm of sexual equality. He'll do a thorough report.'

'If you say so. But the time of death is at least eighteen hours earlier. And the place of death was not here. He'd have been discovered before today, and anyway there's no blood at the scene. So I'm going to assume he was killed closer to where he went missing, which probably means Milan. Which means even if this investigation is not appropriated by the DIA, it will probably be transferred there on the grounds of a "positive contrast" between the magistrates.'

'Technically, it's more likely to be a "negative contrast,"' said Blume. 'Milan won't have opened a murder inquiry, so it will be up to Nardone to declare the case as outside the scope of his competence. He will: most things in life are outside Nardone's scope of competence.'

'So you may as well let me stay on it for the day or two we have it.'

'Fine, then. But if I were you, I'd give Panebianco a coordinating role, get him to liaise with the forensic team, and help build a timeline. He has an organized mind. He's also very observant.'

'More than me, you mean?'

'Don't be so touchy.'

'Why aren't you wearing your watch?'

'I am wearing it in my pocket.'

'In your pocket?'

'It's too hot to wear a watch. It was giving me a rash.'

'So you don't like it? I can change it for something else.'

'Another watch, or an antique ring or a necklace, you mean? Don't bother. I mean, it's great and I like it very much, so there is no need to change it.'

Blume put it back on his wrist and stared at it like it was a canker. 'There.'

'Give me that watch. I'll just get the money back.'

'No. I really like this watch. And it's been fifteen years since anyone bought me a birthday present, so I'm keeping it. What's your next step here, Caterina? Concentrate on this. Never mind my beautiful watch.'

'I'm trying to collect CCTV footage from the shops and a few banks. I'm hoping they'll volunteer the videos without the magistrate having to intervene.'

'Some will, some won't,' said Blume. 'But that'll take time and as far as I can see, all the cameras are too far away from here. What else will you be doing?'

'Talking to the wife. Did you notice the victim had no wedding ring? I'll ask her about that.'

'When she gets here, yes, and beforehand?'

'Talking to the street cleaners who found the body, which I have already done.'

'Right. I suppose Panebianco can check with the victim's employers, bank, work colleagues, friends, trying to reconstruct his movements. But if we put Panebianco on that, he's not going to be able to help you here.'

Caterina stretched out her hand. 'Come on, give me back my despised gift. The watch on your wrist.'

Blume considered a little more resistance, but he relished the idea of getting rid of it. Maybe next time she would ask him what he liked rather than trying to second-guess him. He made a show of reluctance as he pulled it off. She took it and dropped it into her bag, making a point of getting the fastener to click loudly as she closed it.

'Where are you going now?' she asked.

'I need to talk to Matteo Arconti. The living one. The magistrate. And it's not going to be an easy conversation.'

7

Rome

MATTEO ARCONTI EXTRICATED himself awkwardly from his chair as Blume walked in. He stretched out a stiff arm as if he intended to ward off Blume rather than greet him.

'They have killed me.'

'Not you. Your namesake, Magistrate.'

The window beside Arconti was open, and a breeze was ruffling the stacks of papers on the desk. He wavered on his feet for a few seconds before collapsing back into his chair, all elbows, knees and anxiety.

Blume moved a heap of books and files to the floor to make room on an armchair.

'I'm sorry,' said Arconti. 'I can't say anything useful. I feel numb. Not just inside, but outside, too. It's probably a protective mechanism. I'm not sure this is real. I have even pinched myself but I can't feel it. That could mean I am in a dream, couldn't it?' There was real hope in his voice.

'This is not a dream,' said Blume.

'That's what the dream version of you would say. Prove it.'

'Our conversation is too logical.'

'I suppose,' said Arconti, unconvinced.

'Look at your left hand. Can you see it properly?' said Blume.

The magistrate stared at the back of his hand. 'I can see it fine. But I can't feel it properly.'

'I don't know anything about not feeling it, but if you can see your hands properly, it's not a dream.'

Arconti studied his hands, then Blume's face with the same quizzical expression. 'How do you know that thing about the hands?'

'An old trick my father taught me when I was little, so I could tell the difference between nightmares and real life, as if there was one.'

Arconti turned his barn-owl gaze back on Blume. 'Do you remember a while ago I was saying we were less vulnerable to attacks from the Ndrangheta?'

'I remember.'

'That's why you should have told me about your girlfriend. I thought you were unattached.'

'I'm still getting used to having someone. I sort of forgot.'

But Arconti was not listening. '. . . remember me saying that no one innocent will suffer as a result of my investigation? Do you? Do you remember that? And then they do this. They make an innocent man die as a result of me.'

Arconti pressed his chest and grimaced. 'The murder of an innocent man who was unlucky enough to have my name is more than an ironic twist of fate.' He jerked his elbow into a pile of files and sent them crashing to the floor, startling Blume who leaned forward to pick them up. 'Leave the files, Commissioner.'

Blume straightened up in his seat, put his hands on the armrests, and waited for Arconti to have his say. The magistrate was now entering into a rhetorical mode as if arguing his case in court.

'It's one thing being isolated by colleagues, derided by corrupt politicians, ignored by the public and threatened by criminals,' Arconti declaimed, his face, so white a minute ago, suddenly flushed with colour, 'it's quite another to know that your actions are the immediate cause of the death of an innocent person. Don't take this wrong, Commissioner, but if they had killed you, I could have accepted that more easily.'

'I might have found it more difficult,' said Blume.

'I can't do this. It's like investigating my own death. No one can work alone against that level of organized malice surrounded by colleagues and politicians who are complicit in it. I sometimes feel like quitting, leaving my job, leaving the country, too.'

'Could you do that?'

'Of course I could. Pursuant to Article 52 of the Code of Criminal Procedure, Abstention of a Public Minister . . .'

'Not what the law says. I meant, could you just walk away from it all?'

'Yes, I could,' said Arconti. The idea had a calming effect on him.

Speaking in a softer and more confidential tone, he added, 'And so could you, Commissioner. Maybe someday you will. Do you have somewhere to go when that day comes?'

'I couldn't quit.'

'You could. It's one of the advantages of being on this side of the law. It's the criminals who have pledged lifelong allegiance. If I sold my house in Rome, I could live out the rest of my days up north, walking in the mountains, looking after myself. I might even write a book, like that magistrate from Bari, Carofiglio. He's done well for himself. Somehow managed to eke out his magistrate's salary by writing books for a country full of people who don't read. Are you happy, Commissioner?'

'With what?'

'Life. You don't want to answer, I can see that. You probably can't. I was wrong just now about your partner. Make this woman your wife if she'll have you. Marriage is important.'

'Marriage?'

'Do you know how the Ndrangheta lets it be known you are about to be killed? They don't invite you to a wedding. So you see, a wedding is life, absence from one is death.'

'I see,' said Blume.

'You lied to me about being alone. I found out by chance about Chief Inspector Mattiola only this morning. Imagine, I thought that that was going to be the biggest shock of the day.'

'I'm not married to her. I don't even live with her.'

'That hardly matters now. Besides, I was wrong. No matter what you do, no matter where you go, no matter how alone you are, they can hurt you and they will come looking. At least you'll have someone to stand by you. You know at the start of the inquiry I called Curmaci's wife – did I mention that? The judge in charge of preliminary inquiries wouldn't grant me a wiretap, so I called her myself, recorded and transcribed the conversation. Do you want to know what I learned, but am only now realizing?'

'What?' asked Blume, more to humour Arconti than because he expected anything useful.

'I learned that not only is Curmaci invulnerable on that front, she makes him stronger. She counterattacked in a way that makes me think we're talking not just about a wife but a *sorella d'omertà*. When she replied to me, it was like she was reading from a script. Maybe she wrote it, maybe she learned it as part of the standard rebuff to magistrates who dare go after the wives.'

'Isn't that the sort of move that gets these guys really pissed off with you? Children and wives, the family is somehow sacred and off limits? Could that be why they killed your namesake?'

'You are not making me feel any better, Blume.'

'I am not blaming you, Giudice. Going after the criminal's family is perfectly justifiable.'

'They were Maria Itria's cousins that we arrested. We had justification, even according to the warped code of the Ndrangheta. Of course, she knew at once that I was interested only in her husband, but the pretext was there. Do you think I was wrong to go after her like that?'

Arconti seemed to be asking for some sort of permission, which Blume was perfectly willing to give. 'Wrong – morally speaking? No way. The criminals she helps support destroy thousands of children with drugs and guns, kill women and children with impunity. They rip apart families and communities and poison the land. They run hospitals for profit and money laundering, and leave the sick and infirm to die. Nothing is off limits in getting the bastards.'

'She could also have been acting out of love for her husband. It's hard to understand the people from my region.'

'I don't want to understand them,' said Blume. 'To understand is to forgive, and that's not my line of business. I'll understand only for investigative purposes.'

'That makes it harder to detect sincere repentance.'

'I don't get to experience much of that.'

'No, me neither,' said Arconti. He surveyed the files he had tipped onto the floor. 'Look, let me show you the transcript of the call. I gave her your contact details, too, by the way, on the off-chance she preferred policemen to magistrates.'

'What? Why the hell did you do that?'

'Good question. I had you figured for a more forgiving sort of person, Commissioner. The transcript's somewhere on the floor now. But it says nothing about her tone. She sounded sad. Aggressive in bursts, but essentially sad. She reminded me of a hostage reading out propaganda. I think there is a slight chance of her talking, if only she had a sympathetic listener.'

'Not me. You picked up all this from a phone call?'

'I'm a Calabrian like her. I have an ear for these things. It can't be nice being trapped for life in a small Calabrian village – well, it isn't nice. I should know. She's from Cosenza, you know. That's on the edge of freedom. The writ of the Ndrangheta is not total there. Almost, but not total. In my town of Gerace and the horrible new town of Gerace-by-the-Sea at the bottom of the hill, Locri as it's now called, they command everything. No one escapes.'

'You escaped.'

'You call this escaping?'

With a grunt of effort followed by what sounded like a sigh of hopelessness, Arconti bent down to retrieve a file from the floor.

'If I left the police,' said Blume, addressing Arconti's curved back, 'I would not know what to do in life. It's as simple as that. You get a chance to be good at one thing in life, and most people don't even get that. If it turns out you don't like what you're good at, that's too bad. The wrong life cannot be lived right.'

Arconti did not reply.

Pity, thought Blume, because he liked the phrase he had just made. *The wrong life cannot be lived right.* He surveyed the chaotic desk, the bowed-down figure of the white-haired magistrate. 'Did you write the transcript up yourself?' he asked. 'If you can't find it, just give me the gist.'

Arconti still did not reply. Instead, he slid silently out of his chair and fell face first into the scattered files and folders on the floor. Blume leapt up, rushed around, and flicked the magistrate over as if saving him from drowning in a pool of papers. The magistrate's face was grey, his body stiff and unresponsive.

Dead, just like that. Another dead Matteo Arconti. Two in one morning. A sudden urge to laugh welled up in him, but when it broke his lips, it was as an angry shout.

The magistrate's gaze was glassy and unseeing, but as Blume looked the right eye suddenly started blinking rapidly, and the right side of his mouth was twitching. In his left hand, he was clutching a piece of paper, which Blume yanked free, as if disarming a wounded criminal. Arconti, so silent in his collapse, was now breathing like a crashed-out drunk, full of snores, gasps, gurgles and murmurs from far down in the throat that sounded like the beginning of violent curses. Blume put his head down to Arconti's chest and listened. There was a beat there. In fact, there seemed to be several hearts beating at once.

Blume rolled Arconti sideways, stood up, went to the door, opened it, stepped out and found himself looking at a corridor full of seedy lawyers dressed for court and clients dressed, apparently, for running. He ducked back in and, finally, marvelling at the slowness of his own wits, pulled out a phone and called an ambulance.

Then he sat down in the middle of the papers, and did his best to comfort Arconti, whose right eye had stopped moving but whose lip continued to twitch.

'I don't know if you can hear me, Magistrate – Matteo? I think you've had a stroke or a seizure. The ambulance is coming. You'll be OK.' He tried to think of some other comforting thing to say, pulling the piece of paper he had taken from Arconti's hand out of his pocket in the hope it might inspire him. He saw it was the transcript Arconti had been reaching for. 'See, you found the transcript,' said Blume. 'I'll read it.'

Blume started rifling through the files on the floor, picking them up, stacking them on the desk.

In the corner of the room sat Arconti's fat leather briefcase. Blume went over, glanced inside and saw papers from other cases. He dumped them on the desk. Working quickly, he started leafing through the files scattered on the desk and then those on the floor. He spent almost ten minutes going through them, trying to pick up something he could use, even if only as a benchmark to test the integrity of whatever magistrate would now take over. But it was too much. He could never pick out the essential documents in time. Already he heard the commotion and buzz working its way up the corridor. He grabbed handfuls of files at random, choosing the most densely typed ones he could find, and stuffed them into the briefcase. The piece of paper he had taken from the magistrate's frozen hand he dropped into his inside pocket. Then he stood up, took a deep breath, and calmly opened the door, signalling to the ambulance crew and guards who were coming down the corridor. While the three of them piled into the small office, the fourth remained behind to repulse the horde of curious onlookers and concerned colleagues that had suddenly materialized.

Blume stepped over and looked down at the magistrate whose working eye seemed to have gained some focus. 'Don't worry, Dottore. Our case continues until you tell me otherwise.'

Arconti did not reply.

8

Rome

B ACK AT THE Collegio Romano station, the only other person from the *squadra mobile* to be found was the unloved Agente Rospo. When Blume passed him, he was speaking with quiet truculence, his lips almost touching the mouthpiece of the phone, and did not even look up.

Blume shut himself into his office, and slid closed a thin bolt that he had installed himself. He felt at peace here. The room was not pleasant or comfortable, but it had accrued institutional dignity over the years. It seemed as if some long-term policy was in place to renovate it at forty-year intervals. The process must have begun in the 1890s with the installation of the mahogany desk, an impossibly heavy object with dull brass handles on the drawers, topped by an expanse of bulging but still intact green leather. Forty years later, the Fascist authorities had added the heavy grey filing cabinets and a modernist interpretation of a chandelier of gunmetal and glass with sockets for three low-watt bulbs, whose light never reached the ground nor even managed to make the metal shine. The ripped club chair in the corner next to the door was from the same period. The rest of the room, including the ugly orange-and-brown painting in a steel frame on the wall, belonged to the 1970s. Forty years on, and they had supplied him with a multifunction fax-printer-scanner-photocopier and a laptop, and curly energy-saving bulbs for the chandelier.

The window looked into a shadowy void between buildings and never received direct sunlight. The soot on the window filtered out most of the light, and the dark walls of the office absorbed what was left. If he read, it was always in the yellow pool of the light of his desk lamp. While it might invite depression and introspection, the room did not admit panic. It was a good place to plan in.

His mother would not have approved of him being here. She had never dispensed nearly as much advice as his father, but he remembered her warning him about not seeking out too much solitude. It had been a day of a bad school report or something, and she had come into his room where he sat mute, alone, angry at finding himself in a strange country, fed up with having to study his school companions from a distance to see what made them tick rather than just joining in with them and making friends. First, she apologized and promised he would find his way in Rome, Italy and then the world soon enough, and then she comforted him with thoughts of going home to Seattle someday.

'But loneliness is never a real friend, Alec. Beware of when it creeps up on you disguised as solitude, peace, independence or self-sufficiency. Do not invite it into your life because it will never leave. It will even pretend to be its exact opposite, a companion.'

Even then, she was probably too late with her advice. Besides, sometimes, such as now, solitude was a tactical necessity. He wanted no one, not even his own fully conscious self, to watch as he set about composing a forgery to entrap Agazio Curmaci.

Chief Inspector Panebianco had described the murder of Matteo Arconti as a 'cowardly' act. But he was wrong. Cowardice was failing to respond with conviction and power to a challenge, a description that did not fit Agazio Curmaci or whoever was behind this.

Mafia bosses were either traumatized killers or, worse, killers who were not in the slightest bit traumatized by the things they had been made to do when young. The upshot was they were always stronger than politicians and public servants, the police included. The fight against the Mafia, Blume liked to say, would never be won until the politicians did for themselves what they ordered others to do. According to Caterina, his was an argument for a police state. Fine, then. Why would a police state be worse than this Mafia one?

Agazio Curmaci was certainly senior enough to order a killing without compromising his own safety, but he could just as easily have carried it out in person. A man such as that would not take great pains to cover his tracks. With any luck, forensics would be able to get traces of his DNA from the victim, and then place him at the scene of the killing, if they ever worked out where that was.

The challenge, then, was to force the bastard out of his hiding place in

47

Germany and draw him back into the open, back to Italy. As Blume sat in his quiet office reading the transcript of the phone call Magistrate Arconti had made to Curmaci's wife, he saw with perfect clarity how this might be done.

According to the date stamp, the call had taken place several weeks ago. Blume read the one-sided conversation, a monologue effectively, several times and, as Arconti had already observed, the woman's words offered absolutely nothing that could be used against her husband. On the contrary, they had been spoken with the opposite intention. It was a typical Mafia call containing the characteristic mixture of veiled threat and whining accusations of victimization. It was practically a template declaration, and there was no doubt but that she had read it out. Evidently, she had been prepared as soon as her cousins were arrested. Arconti's side of the conversation was missing, but Blume doubted it would have made any difference to what this woman, this *sorella d'omertà*, said.

Dottore, I appeal to you as the mother of two children. I lay out my truth before your ideals of justice, and I beg you to resist the temptation of making such hurtful, dangerous and damaging charges against my husband, who is guilty of nothing other than being a noble father and a shining example to his children and the hardworking people of this modest town. Unable to make a living in a land too long forgotten and despised by the state, he was compelled to travel abroad, but would sooner cut his own throat than his ties with his beloved homeland. Even in my pain at his absence, I am comforted by the love and respect of the entire town for my husband, for they know him for what he is. Every man must respond to his own conscience and God, but the man you have described, the evildoer to whom you have outrageously attached my husband's name, is unrecognizable. I pray that God will forgive you for this injury of our name when the time comes, and may the time come slowly.

I am speaking to you as a woman of peace.

It was effectively a declaration of affiliation to the Honoured Society of the Ndrangheta (*I am comforted by the love and respect of the entire town for my husband, for they know him for what he is*) and a threat on Arconti's life with the references to God's forgiveness, cut throat, and injuries. Finally, it was a way of letting Arconti know he was not going to get anything from a wiretap except elaborate declarations of innocence.

48

Blume phoned the Palaces of Justice, found the assistant who worked with Arconti, and asked if anything had been heard from the hospital. His concern was real, but he also knew it was too early for news and that the person he called would be more interested in hearing what Blume had to say. After confirming that there was no news, the assistant said, 'You were in the office when it happened, I hear.'

'Yes, yes, I was. He just keeled over. Poor man. But people can come through a stroke.'

'His files are all over his floor. What happened, did he knock them off his desk as he fell?'

'Yes,' said Blume. 'He was going to show me something when it happened.'

'It is such a pity. Any idea what he wanted to show you?'

'It was a confession of some sort. No, that's not quite the word he used: an admission.'

'By who?'

'I never found out,' said Blume. 'He collapsed before he could show me. I hope you've got those files in a safe place now.'

'Safe?' the *sostituto* sounded uncertain. 'We have to sort through them. There's a lot there, and some notes from another case have got mixed up. This was the investigation into the hospital consultant who committed suicide?'

'Originally, yes,' said Blume.

'You're saying there was a confession involved?'

'I'm not saying that. Did I say confession? Arconti said something about an admission. A telephone call he transcribed. I don't know any more than that. It'll be in there somewhere among the mess of papers.'

The *sostituto*, whose voice was at once young and tired, said, 'I hope so.'

'By the way, in all the confusion, I left my notebook in there. Do you think I could pop round and collect it? It's got some witness statements from a different case in it.'

'Do you want me to see if I can find it?'

'No, it's all right. I'll come round. It's no trouble.'

He hung up before he could receive any more offers of help. The next call he made was to a reporter from *Il Messaggero*, a young woman – no more than a girl, really – who covered some of the *cronaca nera*, the local crime and bad-news section. He told her about Arconti's collapse and the scattered files that were found in his office, omitting to mention he was there at the time. The reporter was not all that impressed until he mentioned that no one else knew about the mysterious mess in the office, which suggested that someone might have been looking for something. Her voice suddenly became chirpier and harder, her questions more direct, her gratitude for the call more effusive.

Blume sat down at his computer and began rewriting the words that he wanted Curmaci's wife to have said. He was halfway through his first draft when his phone went. It was a reporter from the Rome section of *La Repubblica*. Blume hated the paper and disliked the reporter, so had some fun in being tight-lipped and uncommunicative, ending the call with an angry outburst about the police having no duty whatsoever to answer questions just because a reporter spoke about the 'public interest'. He felt confident his comment would intensify suspicion that some sort of attempt was being made to suppress a leaked document. It would take them no more than a day to find the document and a night to construct their own journalistic fantasies around it. He was on his final rewrite of the bogus confession when a reporter from *Il Corriere della Sera* phoned him.

'What's this I hear, Alec?'

Blume gritted his teeth. He had met this man once in the flesh. It did not put them on first-name terms. 'That depends on who you've been listening to.'

'About a magistrate being hospitalized, his office ransacked.'

'I have heard no such thing,' said Blume.

'A Mafia case, apparently. Ndrangheta to be precise.'

'Nothing you can publish. No story there.'

'Missing papers?'

'No, nothing,' said Blume. He hung up as satisfied as he knew the reporter was not. If past form was anything to go by, the reporter would get in contact with someone in the police who would get in contact with Agente Rospo who, not being very much in demand, had plenty of opportunity to act alone.

Blume took some scissors, cut the heading of the original transcript with Arconti's handwriting on it, and glued it on top of his new version of the transcript. He deleted the file from the computer using the antivirus program, which promised to overwrite it seven times, folded the original into his pocket, and made three copies on his dinky new multi-function scanner.

He took one of the copies and placed it in the middle of his desk and gazed critically at the new version of the transcript, and compared it with the old.

He had left the opening lines intact. *Dottore, I appeal to you as the mother of two children. I lay out my truth before your ideals of justice, and I beg you to resist the temptation of making such hurtful, dangerous and damaging charges against my husband . . .*

But where she had spoken of her husband being forced out of his native land, Blume made a few adjustments so that it now read: *. . . guilty of nothing other than being a noble father and a shining example to his children who has been placed in an impossible position by the arrogance and power of the judiciary of two countries.* That's how Mafia informers usually justified themselves. He decided to keep the part about Curmaci preferring to cut his own throat, but now it read:

He would sooner cut his own throat than his ties with his beloved homeland, but nor would he ever betray the love of his wife and children whose very lives are now in danger as a result of the intolerable pressures you have brought to bear on him. My pain at his absence is intensified by the suspicion and evil mistrust of the entire town. Every man must respond to his own conscience for the sins and crimes he has committed, but the man you have described is no infame. He is an honourable man whose conscience is good and strong and whose love for his family too great. I pray that someday the people of this town will be free enough to forgive us for what they, in their ignorance, now regard as a betrayal. Allow his sincere repentance, I beg you, to save the life of two innocent children and a woman of peace . . .

and so on.

An affiliated woman who had made a statement like that would not last through the week. He was pleased with his work. The more he read it, the better he liked it. He had turned a statement of defiance into a confession tinged with cowardice. The accusations against the town, the claim that they had no choice, the same dishonest tone, the same refusal to take responsibility for their misdeeds all struck a convincing note. It was still wheedling, still obscurantist, still bitter but, plausibly, the words of an *infame*, by far the worst insult in the rich Mafia vocabulary of hate and fear. The punishments for an *infame* were brutal. If Curmaci had any feelings for his wife or his reputation as a husband with honour, he'd have to intervene now.

Blume hid the confession in the middle of some of his papers. If the copy he was about to plant in Arconti's office was not found, then there was a good chance this one would be.

Rospo accepted bribes from the newspapers, lawyers, unknown superiors and even rival magistrates. He was the source of half the leaks from the office and was dumb enough to think no one knew. One of the newspapers would have called him already and even for a modest sum he would hunt through Blume's files like a truffle dog till he found whatever they had asked him to find, caring nothing for plausibility or truth.

Blume's next stop was the courthouse, where he had no problem gaining readmittance to Arconti's room, though accompanied by the *sostituto*, a young man with a wispy beard and round glasses, who looked like some early-twentieth-century radical. Gramsci, maybe.

The papers had been picked up off the floor, but were piled haphazardly on the desk. Blume said, 'I can hardly search through the papers of an investigating magistrate.' With a slight push, he sent a few files sliding over the desk. A few of them flopped onto the floor.

'Oops.' He slipped in the false confession as the *sostituto* was looking at the floor and swept the fanned-out papers back into an unsteady pile.

'Look, it's pointless. If you come across my notebook when sorting through the files, let me know, please,' said Blume.

The *sostituto* nodded, uninterested and, it also seemed, unsuspicious.

Friday, 28 August

9

Milan–Sesto San Giovanni

WHEN HE HAD been a young man, he made the mistake of storing 40 million lire in an abandoned house on the outskirts of the town. Foolish youth that he was, he had secreted the cash in a cavity between one of the outside walls and the rotten floor, thinking the plastic wrapping he had put around the bundles of notes would protect them from decay.

He was sixteen and had just been inducted as a *picciotto* and was only then beginning his apprenticeship to become a *sgarrista*. For a year he had studied the initiation ceremony, overlearning it till it was like the alphabet or the times table.

– *What seek you, young man?*
– *Blood and honour.*
– *Have you blood, young man?*
– *I have blood and I have blood to give.*
– *Who was the man that told you of the existence of this organization?*
– *My father, Domenico Megale.*
– *May the bread become lead in your mouth and the wine you drink turn to blood if ever you betray us . . .*

Once sworn in, he was convinced they would ask him to kill so that his accession from *picciotto* to *sgarrista* might be accelerated, as befitted his pedigree. His family had form, history and honour. But they seemed to have no such exalted plans for him. In what was to be the first in a life of insults received, he was entrusted with the mean task of collecting 'rent' from shopkeepers. Worse still, they had assigned him to the oldest and weakest, to the most supine, intimidated and accommodating tradesmen,

men completely without hope, honour, or courage. He could not understand this failure to put him to the test. Heaping on the indignities, they
did not bother to ask him for the *pizzo* he was collecting from the businesses, yet prohibited him from spending or investing it. And so it was
that he stored it in a damp alcove where it sat for three years. He could
not bring himself to look at the growing pile of bundles, symbol of his
shame, money taken from beings that were less than human. He pushed
them deep into the cavity in the wall, and never noticed the mould that
bloomed on the banknotes. When he at last pulled out the hidden packets,
three-quarters of the banknotes inside had turned into a greasy black
sludge. Those that remained were disintegrating.

He prepared himself for death, and reported his incompetence and loss
to the *contabile* of his *locale*. But his story of the rotten money was greeted
with laughter.

'Burn what's left, Tony. And find a better hiding place.'

'I shall repay my debt.'

'You made an honest mistake, did you not? 40 million lire. That is not
even the salary of a hospital administrator. Let's write it off as capital
invested in experience.'

But he did not like the easy laughter that had greeted him, nor the way
in which his expectation of death and willingness to accept it had been
treated so lightly. For months, rumours about the circumstances of his
birth, about his blood, had been circulating. Not only had his natural
ascent been blocked, but there was, he could feel it, a collective snig-
gering behind his back when his name was mentioned.

But he always knew there was one way he could silence all the laughing
and sweep away the scorn. When he decided the time had come, he acted
without asking his father or his stupid but faithful elder brother Pietro for
their opinion or blessing. For who could bless a son who kills his mother?
A man who commits an unforgivable sin and shows no fear of certain
eternal punishment is a man with no fear. Not only was he prepared for
hell fire, he expected it immediately, since his foster father would surely
put him to death for what he had done. Instead, they both left the village
and transferred to Germany while the story of the boy who murdered his
natural mother was quietly absorbed and mythologized by the town.

It had been harder than he imagined to plunge the knife into the old
woman. She was sleeping when he came in, and her face was upturned,

displaying so many of the fine lineaments of his own: the sharp chin, the tiny ears like two commas, the way the eyebrows swept upwards. When he saw all this, he hesitated, and as he hesitated, she awoke, and spoke his name in a way that filled him with rage, and allowed him to strike. Once she screamed it was easier, and, as when he was killing a suckling pig, the pity and revulsion merged into pleasure and fascination.

The sports bag he was now holding in his hand contained 5,000 euros. The bag and the money in it were to attract the attention of the Romanians, and excite their greedy minds.

He did not despise the two Romanians. He even felt some liking for them. They had carried out his instructions to the letter. It was hard to find reliable people nowadays. If they had not been Romanian, and if the situation had been a little different, he might have eventually put their names forward as potential *contrasti onorati*, faithful men worthy of being baptized into the organization.

He stood in the shadow of a tall tree that grew straight out of the cement paving. He was standing on what used to be the storage yard of the Falck steelworks, and yet here was a tree as tall as the factory walls fifty yards behind him. He remembered news reports about the works closing in the 1980s. It did not seem possible that the tree could have grown so tall since then.

His car was parked behind a pile of twisted rebar and rubble, out of sight. When the Romanians arrived, all they would see was him and the bag. Two of them in a vehicle, just one of him, on foot, in a wide-open space, ready to part with money and perhaps ready to commission a new job. They would wonder whether he was really alone. Well, he was.

The traffic on the highway made a steady hushing sound like the sea, and, in the tree, two birds of some sort seemed to be squabbling over a single purple berry, pecking at each other, fluttering, hopping on and off the same branch, ignoring the hundreds of other branches and thousands of other berries. The only other sound was the creaking of the steel girders and corrugated roof on the part of the factory that had yet to be torn down.

He heard the diesel engine before he saw the vehicle. Probably the same vehicle they had used to transport the body. Always a van with the fucking Romanians. You never saw a Russian in a van, never saw a Romanian in anything else. It stopped fifty yards away and flashed its headlights. He raised his hand in greeting, bent down, and picked up the bag, held it aloft, then put it down again. Did they think this was a kidnap exchange of some sort? He waved them over. The van drew closer, slowly, suspiciously. He signalled impatience, but saw no increase in speed. Dirty suspicious animals, the Romanians. Gypsy in all of them.

Finally, it stopped and out got Teo. Behind the wheel sat the other Romanian. Teo was upon him, his face all bristles and smiles, his thin cheekbones twitching, his eyes moving side to side.

Tony pointed to the bag on the ground. 'There you are. You get to keep the bag, too. Pity. It's Adidas, same as this tracksuit. I bought them as a matching set.'

'Great,' said Teo, making no move to retrieve it.

'You want me to bend down and open it, show you the money?'

'No, no,' began Teo, but Tony bent down, unzipped the bag completely, and opened it so Teo could see inside. He could feel the Romanian's eyes being drawn towards the grip of the pistol protruding from the waistband of his tracksuit bottoms.

'You came armed,' said Teo.

'I live in a dangerous world.' Tony picked up a broken piece of rubble from the ground and tossed it in his right hand, then from hand to hand as he straightened up. 'This,' he showed the lump of concrete to Teo, 'is all that remains of Italian industry.'

Teo glanced quickly at the rock in Tony's fist, but his gaze was drawn inexorably to the cash-filled bag. He lifted it up, and casually ran his hand inside it.

Tony slipped the piece of concrete into the kangaroo pocket on the front of his tracksuit top, adjusted his crotch, pulled out the lump of rubble again, and rubbed it with his thumb. 'You're not going to count the money?'

'No. You need us again, you know where to come. Always glad to help.'

He turned around.

'Hey, Teo!'

The Romanian spun around, his dark eyes widening in alarm.

'Zip up the bag or you'll lose the money. Two days' work and nothing to show for it. What would your wife say to that? She'd be suspicious, wouldn't she?'

Teo smiled, then nodded, and zipped up the bag. Tony watched him, giving him a friendly wave as he opened the door of the van and got in beside the driver. He allowed them to say a few words, waited till he saw the driver begin to turn the steering wheel, then called out again:

'Hey, Teo!'

The driver stopped his action. Tony dropped his hand into the kangaroo pocket of his tracksuit, pulled out a black object the size of a computer mouse, and tossed it casually from hand to hand as he approached the van. He got to the window, which was a little higher than he had anticipated.

'There is one thing you could do for me next week, but . . .'

Teo rolled down the window.

'I didn't hear that. You said something about next week?'

'Yeah, I was saying there is something you could do. It's a little harder than this job.'

'What?' asked Teo.

Tony stretched his arm out and dropped the black object at Teo's feet.

'What's that?' asked Teo.

'A Mecar something or other. I forget the make.' He fell to the ground and rolled to the rear wheel of the van, hoping the young Slovakian dealer who had explained this trick to him was right about the 'relatively contained' explosive force.

Teo and the driver managed to get a lot of words out between them before an enormous thud caused the entire vehicle to jump from the ground. The sound banged against the wall of the factory and bounced back. The Slovak had told him the fragmentation grenade would not make much noise, but he'd been wrong.

Megale stood up, a little unsteady. His ears felt as if they were full of water, and he realized he couldn't hear the traffic on the highway any more. He surveyed the front of the vehicle. The blast had lifted the windscreen out, frame and all, peeled back part of the roof, and knocked out Teo's door, which was hanging on the buckled remains of a hinge. Teo lay on his seat, his head back. Something blunt and harmless looking, like a piece of soft plastic, was sticking out of the front of his throat. The driver had found time to turn around, because his head was draped over the back of the seat. The blast had blown the shirt right off his back and embedded thousands of red and black fragments across his body, almost as if the cuts had already turned to scabs. The cab was filled with countless droplets of blood, something sticky and black, and a frothy white substance. Many of the banknotes looked unharmed, but he would not be touching them.

The thing was, the Romanians were alive. Both of them. The Slovak had told him they would never survive. He said it would blow their fucking heads off in an enclosed space like that, and yet here was Teo, not well, but definitely alive, his eyes not only open, but also slowly turning towards Tony as he stood there by the door. The driver, half kneeling in his seat, seemed to be whispering, like he was making a confession. Again, not dead. Megale wrinkled his nose against a stink of sewage and burnt oil that seemed to be coming from the driver.

Teo seemed to be smiling, but his eyes were becoming glassy. Tony pulled out his pistol, and put it into Teo's eye, and pulled the trigger. He had to clamber halfway into the van to lift up Teo's head to shoot him through the second eye. Then he went around to the other side, and pulled the driver off the seat. The man fell back, dead now, his intestines visible, slick and shining. So that's where the stink was from. Tony shot out his eyes and, for added meaningless symbolism, shot him in the mouth, too. Now they would waste time wondering who this slob had been talking to.

He went back to his car and drove up to the van. All told, it had been a bit disappointing. He had seen car crashes that produced worse damage than that. The entire back section was intact. He lifted the jerrycan out of the boot of his car, and doused the two bodies, then sprinkled the petrol around the cab, and soaked the seats. He loved the aromatics of petrol. He'd always loved it. Shoe polish, too. He had once set fire to a bowling alley, pouring the petrol down the lanes and setting them alight, watching the river of fire.

He retreated, pulled out a cigarette, lit it and took a few drags before flicking it into the van. It bounced off the seat, dropped into a shining pool of petrol on the floor, and fizzled out. He moved his car out of the way, then returned and, walking backwards away from the van, poured the remaining petrol on the ground. Then he lit it with his lighter. The flame was slower and feebler than he thought it would be, and there was no explosion as the fire in the cab took hold. As the flames caught, the van rocked, as if being buffeted by wind.

Here I am, he thought to himself, twenty years on, burning money again.

10

Rome

THE YOUNG POLICEMAN pointed to the screen with a triumphant air not yet diminished by the grinding repetition of tasks that his career had in store for him. 'There!' he said. 'That vehicle there.'

Blume leaned forward, allowing the side of his face to brush against Caterina's hair. Businesslike, she moved away from him and pointed to a blurred blob on the screen.

'Not very clear, is it?' said Blume.

'No. It's an old traffic camera,' said Caterina. 'Over here, we have RAI offices, which are definitely going to have a surveillance camera, but we've got nothing from them yet. And there is the court of the Giudice di Pace, where most of this footage comes from. Show him, Claudio.'

The young policeman smiled at Caterina. He was probably good-looking, if you were into white smiles and muscles obviously toned through excessive workouts in a gym. As he brought up images on the screen, he strained Blume's forbearance further by explaining what Blume already knew.

'This is a bar, which closes at 12:30, and this is a restaurant that closes half an hour later. The cooks and the owner usually leave at around 2:30 in the morning. They all cross the open piazza to where their cars are parked. Inspector Panebianco interviewed them all and none of them reports seeing anything, so we know it was after 2:30 . . .'

'Look, just show me what you got,' said Blume.

Claudio pressed a button on his fancy control panel, and another grainy image in washed-out colour appeared on-screen. Blume recognized the crime scene. In the background, practically the only vehicle in sight, was a van, stopped by the kerb.

'Three-twenty in the morning, we can see the van at the crime scene. This is taken from the offices of the Giudice di Pace. It is too far for us to make out any detail, even with enhancement techniques, also because it is dark. The camera takes frames every thirty seconds. The vehicle is stopped here, see? Afterwards we can just make out the body on the ground, but we miss the moment they put it there.'

'But maybe we'll see that from one of the other cameras we have not examined yet. It could be useful for prosecution purposes,' said Caterina.

'Uh-huh,' said Blume, not all that impressed so far.

'If we go back ten minutes,' said Claudio, 'we catch the same vehicle passing a camera on the banks of the Tiber and . . .' he pressed a button, 'there it is going past the crime scene, this time without stopping. If we go forward, there it is again, heading away from the scene. So the vehicle, which I think is a Ford Transit, drives by what will be the crime scene, like it was checking, goes down the banks of the Tiber, takes a right, goes down 200 yards where we capture it here, goes back to the crime scene, stops there, then back to the banks of the Tiber for the second time, where the cameras pick it up again.'

He sat back, ran his thumb down his sternum in satisfaction, and beamed at Caterina, who beamed back at him. Agente Carini looked quite dashing in the short-sleeved summer uniform he was wearing, and his hazel eyes were shining and full of enthusiasm for his job and the success they were having. He drew a breath to continue his explanation but was interrupted by Blume.

'I'm taking it you got the number plate.'

Agente Carini's face fell as he realized he was not going to get a chance to explain his brilliance.

'Sorry if I spoil your fun and save my time,' said Blume. 'You've reported the registration number to Milan, I presume?'

The young policeman pouted, 'Of course we did. Forty minutes ago. Not just Milan, a general request to all patrols.' He folded his arms and tried to ignore Blume's stare.

'Was the van headed out of north Rome on the A1 back towards Milan?'

Agente Carini nodded reluctantly.

'OK,' said Blume. 'So the vehicle will have arrived in Milan early this morning – but you still don't have images for it leaving the highway?'

'Not yet, we have to guess its probable arrival time. Obviously we're going to see if it gets picked up on the security and speed cameras, in service stations . . .'

Blume held up a hand and cut him off in mid-flow. 'From about half an hour ago there has been an APB out on it. Who's the van registered to? Is it stolen?'

'It's not reported stolen. It's in the name of some shopkeeper in Latina,' said Agente Carini. 'It looks like he figured he'd save on the vehicle transfer tax. So the van's still in his name. He's just now gone into the police to make a sworn statement to the effect that he sold it eight years ago. We're waiting for news, but he's probably got nothing to do with it.'

'People should pay the damned tax to transfer ownership. They don't realize they can be liable, especially if there is an uninsured accident,' said Blume.

'It is a bit steep, that tax,' said Caterina. 'My car's in my aunt's name.'

'I don't think the commissioner meant people like you, Caterina,' said Agente Carini.

This was too much.

'*Caterina?*'

'I meant to say Inspector Mattiola. Sorry, sir.'

Blume looked at Caterina, and shook his head disbelievingly. 'Inspector, why are you still here? Shouldn't you get back downtown?'

'If we get images of the van on the highway going back to Milan, that will be useful,' she said.

'Leave that job to the Boy Wonder here. Anyhow, I don't understand you. Useful for what?'

'Useful as evidence,' said Caterina in her iciest tone.

Blume poked the young policeman. 'Hey, Calogero . . .'

'Claudio. My name's Claudio.'

'You look like a Calogero to me. Go get me coffee.'

The policeman stood up without looking at Blume, then made a point of going over to a female colleague at the next desk and whispering something and nodding at Blume and Caterina. Eventually he slouched off.

'How dare you humiliate me . . .' hissed Caterina, then stopped as she realized a dozen young cops at the data centre were straining to listen in.

'No, you listen to me, Caterina. You got the number plate, now move on. Evidence for what – the pretrial conference? For the trial, which may never be held? How is it the recipe for hare stew goes? First, catch your hare. This stuff can wait. For God's sake, Caterina, you're the one who wanted this. You have twenty-four hours to find out what the victim and the suspects were doing in the twenty-four hours before the murder. Or have you forgotten?'

The young policeman came back, and sat down close to Caterina and glared at Blume. 'The coffee machine's broken,' he said.

11

Rome

BLUME HAD A shower, lay down, closed his eyes and breathed in the familiar air of the bedroom. It had been his for more than twenty years, but he still thought of it as his parents' and of the bed he slept in as theirs.

He was just beginning to drift off for a deliciously early night, when his mobile phone rang. He placed it under the pillow. The muted trill and faint buzzing from beneath his head was quite soothing. If it was urgent, they would phone again.

They phoned again.

'What?'

'Commissioner Blume,' said a voice he had not heard before: a voice that harboured no doubt it had the right number and was speaking to the right person. 'My name is Captain Massimiliano Massimiliani. I would like to see you as soon as possible, if I may.'

'Who did you say you were?' asked Blume.

'Massimiliano Massimiliani. Primo Capitano. Carabinieri. I am seconded to the DCSA. Where are you at this precise moment?'

'I am in the San Giovanni district.'

'Where in the San Giovanni district?'

'Via Orvieto,' said Blume.

'Do you mean to tell me you are at home?'

Blume groaned in exasperation as the intercom by his front door rasped. Now what?

'Commissioner Blume?'

'Just a minute, Captain.' He took the phone from his ear, ignoring whatever the captain was saying, went into his living room, and picked up the intercom, held it to one ear, put the phone back to the other. 'I'm still here, Captain. Someone's at the door . . . Wait a second . . . Yes?'

'It's me. At your door, downstairs. I'll hang up,' said Massimiliani.

The mobile phone relayed the words a full second later than the intercom, giving Blume the unpleasant feeling of the captain's voice going in one ear, passing through his brain and out the other.

Blume put his phone away, grabbed a polo shirt and pulled it on. The intercom rasped again. He had forgotten to press the button to open downstairs. He did so now and went back into his room to fetch some trousers.

The captain rapped rhythmically at the door like an old friend in a good mood as Blume was doing up his flies. He had not found any socks. He answered the door to a well-turned-out man in his early thirties, dressed in expensive casual clothes. Early thirties, already a 'primo capitano', a Carabiniere grade that had no direct equivalent in the police, but could be said to be ever so slightly higher than the rank of commissioner.

'How did you know I was at home?' demanded Blume, standing aside to allow his visitor in.

The captain held one arm down by his side; in the other he had a thin leather portfolio with which he rhythmically swatted the side of his thigh. He entered the room with two long strides, and tossed the portfolio carelessly on the coffee table. The captain was not gym-toned like the idiot cop Caterina had seemed to like so much, but there was not an extra pinch of fat on him. Blume recognized the look. It was the easy confidence of someone with long military training, of one who has seen action. The easy gait, the ready smile came naturally to a man who saw no one in his sights who could possibly threaten him. The only sign of tension and, possibly, a lack of control were in the hands, which the captain could not keep still.

'I needed to find you as quickly as possible,' said the captain, as if this were a sufficient answer. 'Also, I told you, I work for the DCSA. Electronic surveillance and tracking mobile phones is what we do.'

'For drug smugglers and criminals. Not for police commissioners,' said Blume.

'Were you going somewhere?' the captain pointed to an outsized, shiny hard-shell suitcase next to the door.

'That's been there for weeks,' said Blume. 'Why did you pretend not to know where I was?'

'You're the one who seemed reluctant to mention that you were at home. It seemed impolite to insist. May I sit here?'

'It's a bit . . .'

The captain sat down on Blume's sofa, which received him in a soft sinking embrace so that his knees were soon on a level with his eyes. He struggled back up and eyed it then Blume with suspicion.

'I was going to suggest the armchair,' said Blume. 'That's basically just a pile of cushions. The springs went and then the webbing.'

The captain sat in the armchair and beat out a tattoo on the cracked leather armrests. For himself, Blume chose a cheap IKEA chair that Caterina had made him buy for her apartment and rejected as soon as he had finished assembling it.

'You should dispose of that sofa,' said the captain.

'I know,' said Blume. 'It's been here for years. I'll get around to it someday.'

The captain interlaced and cracked his fingers. 'I need your help for Monday morning, think you can do that?'

'Sure thing,' said Blume. 'You need to move a piano, paint a room, have someone killed?'

'Ah, sarcasm. Here's my ID card if you need to check my credentials.'

He neatly flicked a plasticized card into Blume's lap, then clicked his fingers impatiently as Blume examined it. The badge showing the inter-force symbol of the DCSA: three swords, the flaming grenade representing the Carabinieri, a walled crown representing the police, the yellow flame of the Finance Police, and the motto: *Trigemina vis cor unum.*

'Three forces and one heart,' translated Blume. 'Beautiful concept.'

'Let's get down to business, Commissioner. On September 2nd, the Ndrangheta are holding their annual general meeting in Polsi after the Feast of the Madonna. This year, same as last, we're fitting the place out with hidden cameras and mikes, keeping an eye on who turns up. We'll be logging number plates, taking photographs. They know we'll be there, but, as always, they don't care, and no matter how many devices we plant, they don't have any problems making sure we pick up nothing that is vital. The bosses from all over the world turn up, or give powers of proxy to their seconds-in-command. This year, for the fun of it, we're hosting a delegation from the German Federal Police, the BKA. The delegation arrived a few hours ago, and we meet tomorrow morning, then again on Monday and during the week. There are some tensions between the BKA and the Italian authorities, but more co-operation than you might think. The Germans have occasional moments of humility when it comes to organized crime, or, at least, they are willing to acknowledge our greater experience. Now that they have moved beyond the "mafia-doesn't-exist-in-Germany" stage, they are interested in learning. A visit to Polsi is part of that. Your friend Agazio Curmaci could well turn up, too.'

'My friend?'

'You know what I mean. You come recommended, Blume. Magistrate Arconti speaks highly of you. In fact he says hello.'

'He said hello? Not *hyyuhhaggh*?'

Massimiliani shrank back as if unnerved by Blume's zombie imitation. 'If you're referring to the fact he was taken ill today, he's already far better. He was sitting up in bed when I saw him. It's true, he can't speak properly, though I don't think that's an excuse for you to mock . . .'

'You've seen him today?'

'Yes. He recommended you a while back, of course. Today I went to visit him as a friend.'

'Oh,' said Blume, taken aback. 'And what did he recommend me for?'

'As someone who we might turn to for an extra hand. Specifically, someone who had a perfect command of English, a smattering of German, professional integrity, intelligence, experience, willingness to travel, no family commitments.'

'A hand in what? I'm busy right now.'

'It looks to me like you were taking an early night.'

'I am on standby. Is Arconti really sitting up?'

'He had a stroke, they administered the drugs. It remains to be seen what damage there is and how long it will take him to heal. But he's already regained movement. Look, Blume, I'm not a doctor.'

'Now that we're on the subject, who are you exactly? Who do you work for? Apart from the DCSA?'

'In order of importance and pride, I would say I am first and foremost a Carabiniere. I also work for AISI, and I have been seconded to the DCSA.'

'AISI. You didn't mention that before. SISDE, huh?'

'AISI, not SISDE. SISDE's the old name. It hasn't been used for a while.'

'That's because you fuckers had such a reputation for subversion and corruption you had to change your name like a criminal on the run. More of a conspiracy of crypto-fascists, thieves, Freemasons and Vatican financiers than a secret service.'

'I was a kid back then, but most of your criticism is justified. Even so, there was always a public-service ethos. Good people. Same as in any institution in this country. Layers of deadwood and corruption, but a core of good people in the middle, fighting against the odds. There is no conflict between homeland security and my duties as a Carabiniere. They are complementary. You know what the motto of the AISI is? It's *Scientia rerum Reipublicae salus*, which means . . .'

'The salvation of the Republic comes from knowing all about other people's shit,' said Blume.

'That's a very free translation.'

'Tell me some of the Republic-saving intelligence you know.'

'I know your colleagues are spending all night following up an investigation that has already ended. And you, sensing this to be the case, have wisely decided to take an early night.'

'Explain.'

'A few hours ago the police in Sesto San Giovanni got a call reporting an explosion and fire in one of those giant disused industrial areas. They found a van with two charred corpses. The bodies have not been identified, yet. But the van is the one your colleagues have just put out an APB on. The investigating magistrate in Milan has decided not to inform the investigating magistrate in Rome until tomorrow or even Monday.'

Blume retrieved his home phone from among the cushions of his collapsing sofa.

'What are you doing?'

'They're my colleagues. I'm going to tell them. So they, too, can get an early night.'

'I'd prefer you didn't.'

'They'll know soon enough; why not immediately, give them a proper weekend?'

'Because I would be breaking my word to my friend in Milan, if Rome were to learn about this before he was ready.'

'So you shouldn't have given him your word.'

'I told you this because I thought I could trust your discretion.'

'You're one of these people who can't keep a confidence. Immediately you hear one, you rush off to tell someone else, me in this case, and then you get all moral and uppity if it looks like I want to do the same thing. A secret service man who can't keep a secret,' said Blume.

'I can keep secrets, Blume. For instance, I am not going to tell anyone that you falsified a confession by the wife of a powerful member of the Ndrangheta.'

Blume started to put the phone back on the sofa. But before it touched the cushion, it started ringing.

12

Rome

BLUME ANSWERED THE phone, taking his time. He knew without looking it was Caterina, the only person who ever called him on his landline.

'Hi.'

'I'm back in the office,' said Caterina. 'I took your advice and got to work on other things.'

'Maybe you should call it a night,' said Blume, staring at Massimiliani who raised his hands in a gesture of mild exasperation, but whose face did not betray much.

'Are you calling it a night?' she asked.

'Yes, you should go home, Caterina.'

'You know Elia's on holiday at the sea with my parents?'

'Even if you don't need to get back to him, it's good to get some sleep,' said Blume. 'You can get back to the investigation in the morning.'

'I see,' she said coldly. 'I was phoning for another reason.'

'What?'

'That book Arconti's wife gave him for his birthday. It had a page missing.'

Blume was surprised. He had been expecting some personal stuff from her. This was more welcome.

'The wife bought the book at Feltrinelli at Piazza del Duomo a few days ago,' continued Caterina. 'I called her to check. It was brand-new, yet damaged when we found it. The pages skipped from 156 to 159. One sheet – pages 157 and 158 – had been torn out. You could see the ragged edges where it was ripped. I had one of the uniformed guys, Bonanni, pop round to the Feltrinelli store on Largo Argentina and get a copy while I was examining the CCTV, and it was here on my desk when I got back.

The torn page corresponds to a description and drawings of oak trees: the *Quercus petrea* and the *Quercus robur*, the Sessile oak and the Pedunculate oak. I looked them up in combination with various search terms, including *Ndrangheta*, and this brought me to a series of webpages on the "Tree of Wisdom", which is also called the "Mother Tree", the tree of the Ndrangheta. Depending on the webpage, sometimes it seems as if the tree is mythological, sometimes as if it is an actual oak that has been growing for hundreds of years near the sanctuary of the Madonna di Polsi, above the "Infernal Valley". The trunk is five metres in circumference.'

'That's very interesting.'

'You don't have to be sarcastic.'

'I wasn't being sarcastic. That's interesting: the Tree of Wisdom.'

'I think the missing page is a buried reference. Ripped out by the killer in a symbolic gesture. The Ndrangheta sees itself as a tree. The main trunk, the *capo bastone*, is the boss, the leaves are the latest recruits, the least important, the branches are their commanders, and so on. The roots feed on the blood of traitors and the soil of the land. I'm still reading up on it. If you want, we . . .'

The captain slapped out a fast rhythm on his knee, and stood up briskly and started touring the room.

'Another time, Caterina. I need to go.'

'Wait. He did have a wedding ring. His wife told me. For some reason he threw his ring away or they stole it from him.'

'Probably the latter,' said Blume.

'No, I don't think that fits the . . .'

'Later. Tell me later.' He hung up. Massimiliani was now strolling around the room, picking out books at random, looking at them, putting them back.

'A lot of art books. History, too.'

'My parents'.'

'They were art historians. I read your file. But three of the books I just looked at were published after their death, so you must have bought them.'

'It's a hobby.'

'No novels.'

'Stories are a waste of time unless they're true,' said Blume.

'Or unless they serve a purpose. We all tell stories to ourselves that we know aren't true. The Ndrangheta, for example, has a lot of stories that are useful. That Tree of Wisdom you were just talking about with . . .?'

'They make stories up as it serves their purpose,' said Blume, ignoring Massimiliani's cue.

'That's just what you did with that confession, isn't it?'

Blume tried to keep his gaze steady, but he felt disoriented. He had reckoned it might take two or three days for his falsified transcript to leak through the system. Instead, it had been a few hours. Even by the lousy standards of secrecy in the force and among the magistrates, that was far too fast.

'Look, Blume, I admire your enterprise here. It tilted the scales in your favour. But let's not waste time in denials. If there had been a confession from Curmaci's wife, I'd have heard about it from Arconti. He mentioned that he had called her, fishing for information, but there was no talk of a confession. It had to be you. I think it was a good idea, and I like the way you both buried it in your office and in the Palaces of Justice. You made us look for it so that when we found it the thrill of discovery would make us reluctant to consider that we were led to it. I think you might be a natural.'

'You keep saying "we". Who else was with you?'

'Your direct superior, the Vice-questore. Well, he accompanied one of my men. So he sort of knows, but he is not aware it was a forged document. Let's hope he never finds out.'

'Great. So my office was searched. Was Arconti relaying everything back to you? I trusted him.'

'And you were right to, and you should continue. Casual chats. Of course, he's not in a fit state to talk at length, but if we were to phone him now and ask whether he had received a confessional phone call from Curmaci's wife, what would he say?'

Blume stayed silent.

'We soon found out you were planting the story in the press, too, along with hints of a break-in and a cover-up. If we try to deny or kill the story, it will only gain more credibility. So it's out there, now, with a life of its own doing whatever you wanted it to do. So, tell me, what did you want it to do?'

'Disorient Curmaci, maybe force him back into Italy to defend his family before he's ready. Get him in trouble with his associates. Just get back at him some way. Drag him into the open, discomfit the bastard.'

'I like that. We can let it run its course,' said Massimiliani. 'Curmaci was probably planning to attend the Polsi summit anyhow. But for all your cleverness, Blume, you made a mistake that, to my mind at least, makes it incontrovertibly a forged confession.'

The nagging doubt Blume had had from the start in the back of his mind seemed to step forward and take an ironic bow. 'I got the tone wrong,' he said.

'I was really hoping you'd recognize your own mistake – another good sign. You kept to the same tone of the original denial. But that was a prepared statement full of insinuation and warning. If she really had been confessing and seeking help, the tone would have been less coherent.'

'Ah, well,' said Blume. 'She's still in the shit, though, isn't she, once this gets known?'

'Probably,' agreed Massimiliani. 'Her name's Maria Itria.'

'I know.'

'She's got two children.'

'So had the unfortunate insurance salesman, Arconti.'

'He was an actuary.'

'Whatever.'

'You seem convinced it was Curmaci. Any particular reason?'

'Well, Magistrate Arconti is the main reason. He told me a bit about Curmaci, and this seems like the sort of thing he might do. But I am not assuming it is Curmaci.'

'So why did you go to all that trouble of falsifying his wife's statement?'

'If it wasn't Curmaci, it was one of them. Getting Curmaci will do fine, since they're all the same.'

'Interesting attitude. You don't care whether this really was Curmaci or not?'

'Like I said, it may as well have been him,' said Blume. 'Curmaci or someone else in the organization. All the same. Only the name changes.'

'Now I'm on your side in this, Commissioner, be assured of that, but can't you see a slight similarity between your approach and Curmaci's carelessness about killing an innocent man just because his name happened to match the magistrate's?'

'No, I see no similarity at all,' said Blume. 'But I did notice you attributed the killing to Curmaci.'

'Suppose the murder was not even related to the Ndrangheta?'

'It is,' said Blume. 'It's too symbolic. It fits with how Curmaci operates.

74

Killing a namesake, putting the body next to Via Falcone e Borsellino in remembrance of martyred magistrates, the torn page.'

'What torn page?'

Blume hesitated, then told Massimiliani about Caterina's discovery.

'You think that was some sort of calling card left by Curmaci?'

'I looked up the name Curmaci a while ago. It means "tree trunk", so the symbolic gesture fits. Then there were the victim's dirty stained fingers.'

'What does that signify?'

'I haven't the slightest idea,' said Blume. 'But it's bound to have some sort of symbolic meaning.'

'Maybe you're right. But it is not nearly enough for an international arrest warrant.'

'Nothing ever is,' said Blume. 'Which is why forcing him down to Calabria gives us a chance to pick him up.'

'Us?'

'You. Someone.'

'Curmaci would be worth getting. The Ndrangheta reproduces like a cell. First, they make a copy of the rules for building another cell; then, they send someone like Curmaci with the rules abroad. Once the rules are laid down, other members of the original cell start moving abroad, too. You could compare Curmaci to a string of DNA.'

'A string of RNA would make a more accurate metaphor,' said Blume. 'And Arconti compared him to a Catholic missionary. Anyhow, priest or protein, it still seems to me getting rid of him would be a good thing. When I say get rid of . . .'

'No need to reassure me, Commissioner. I know you're not in favour of assassinations, even of the worst. That emerges from your files. But wouldn't you say Curmaci is too important to be carrying out assassinations in person?'

'Like I said, do we care if it was him? He killed in the past, at least that's what Arconti told me.'

'Oh, he did that,' said Massimiliani. 'Definitely. He was an executioner for Old Megale in the 1990s. Then he stopped. It would be unusual for him to start again now.'

Blume shrugged. 'So he ordered it.'

'Possibly. Every Ndranghetista who goes abroad, Curmaci included, has to leave family members at home. That way they can operate more freely in the new territory. Their family members gain respect and wealth, but basically, they are hostages. The local Calabrian Ndrangheta can get to them at any time.'

'That sounds like a weakness waiting to be exploited,' said Blume.

'Which is what you are trying to do with your forged confession.' Massimiliani walked over and tapped Blume lightly on the shoulder. 'I like that attitude, too. You have convinced me we can work together, now can I convince you?'

'That depends. What would I be doing?'

'I can't say yet.' Massimiliani pointed at the portfolio he had tossed on the table. 'Read what's in there. It will take you about an hour to read, two hours to learn.'

'What is it?'

'An old DIA report on the Camorra in Naples and environs. It gives descriptions of their activities, the names of the main families. It's pretty basic stuff. Actually, I pulled most of it off the internet.'

'I thought we were talking about the Ndrangheta. What's the Neapolitan Camorra got to do with anything?'

'Ah, what indeed? If only we knew.'

'I'm sure you do know.'

'As a matter of fact, I don't. I am not going to talk about it until I know you're on board. The situation is still developing. I can arrange for the Questore to give you time off, or, if we go down the official route, I can get the Prosecutor General to sign off on your temporary transfer of juris-diction. If I were you, I'd take the time off. You get paid, and that can be topped up with some travel expenses.'

'Where would I be travelling to, Naples, Calabria?'

'I can't say until we're agreed. I can say, however, this could open a whole new career for you.' Massimiliani strode over to the door and looked again at the suitcase. 'Looks to me like you are already packed and ready to go.'

Massimiliani opened the door. 'Monday morning, nine o'clock, Polo Tuscolano Operations Centre. Go in the north gate. Use my name. If you're there at seven, you're there. If not, no problem. You decide.'

Saturday, 29 August

13

Milan

IT WAS AFTER watching the girl waiting for the number 45 bus climb into the car for the fiftieth time that Magistrate Francesco Fossati suddenly realized why he had been doing this. With a knot in his stomach in case he was too late, he called up the police at the Monforte-Vittoria station immediately and ordered them to sequester all the video recordings from the office building for the previous weeks, only to be told, with a certain tone of disdain, that this had already been done. An hour later, he and an inspector were sitting in his office watching grainy images of the girl as she left the sports centre every other weekday at the same time.

Teresa Resca had been going to the swimming baths on Via Piranesi on Mondays, Wednesdays, and Fridays ever since she finished school in June. She took the 45 bus from her house in San Donato at around two and took it back again at around four. It was almost a door-to-door service, but, to be safe, her father sometimes liked to meet her as she got off and walked back to the house through a narrow, isolated orchard path leading to the apartment block. She always phoned as the bus was drawing close to home. If he could not make it, then she took the long way round, increasing her walk by five minutes. When she failed to call or show up, they called the police immediately.

The father said he knew who it was, what they were doing, why they had done it, and as the investigation moved forwards, it looked like he was right. Giovanni Resca published essays, wrote a blog, gave talks and even put on earnest theatre performances, all for the sake of alerting the Milanese to the fact that the Ndrangheta was very much among them. He had received so many threats from the very start that over a period of five years of campaigning journalism, he had made the fatal mistake of becoming almost blasé. He thought they might kill him, because this is what they had threatened, but they had never threatened his wife or their one child. Then the threats stopped, along with Giovanni Resca's embryonic career in journalism. Branded an agitator, his shows of political satire drew shrinking audiences to ever-smaller venues and newspapers stopped publishing his articles. The upside was that the threats dried up along with his work.

The magistrate had been true to his word and conducted a ruthless and invasive but quick and efficient line of inquiry that day by day rapidly extinguished theories of kidnapping for ransom, incest, fraud, substance abuse and voluntary flight and elopement until they were left with two options: what the father had been saying all along, which many of the police thought improbable and a symptom of his deluded tendency to see the Ndrangheta everywhere, or a random snatch of a young girl by sex traffickers or a killer. None of the endings was going to be good, and yet the parents still seemed so hopeful it was almost irresponsible of them. Despair was better than hope, he knew; but his job was to bring home a body.

'Watch the woman,' the magistrate told the inspector. 'You never see her properly because the camera's too high and far away, but from the dyed-yellowish shade of the hair, the shape of the body and the way she moves, I could tell it was the same person. The technicians agree with me.'

The woman had turned up four times in a row and stood waiting at the bus stop with Teresa. They could be seen chatting a little. She was always there at the same time as Teresa. Possibly they chatted in the bus together. Together, they watched new video footage from the San Donato metro station, the terminus of the number 45 bus. Teresa got off several stops before the end of the line, but the woman, along with other passengers on their way to the metro station, stayed on to the end.

The police had put in the hours and expertise to filter down the video to one telling moment. Helped by the absence of commuters and traffic in August, they had captured a video feed of the woman getting off the bus at the metro station, then, instead of taking the metro or another bus, she got into a car, which resembled the one Teresa was to climb into a few days later. The car could be clearly seen turning and heading back in the direction the woman had just come from. Again, the number plate proved elusive.

'She did not need to make that bus journey,' said the magistrate. 'She got on that bus specially to be with Teresa.'

The inspector nodded in agreement. 'We're checking other cameras for that car. Eventually we'll find it.'

'What were Resca's articles about?'

'Money laundering, construction companies and the financial crisis.'

'And he loses his child for that?'

'Giovanni Resca wanted his voice to be heard. He wanted people to read his articles and hear his truth. Now, with politics on vacation, every national newspaper and even the foreign press are following this story, and linking it to Resca's articles, talking about his shows and his leftist politics. He got the fame he wanted and lost his child.'

'We can't find any connection to the woman. No one has any idea of who she might be,' said the inspector.

'That's because she is no one. Let's say you want to abduct an innocent but not stupid girl in broad daylight, how do you do it? First, you send a woman. This woman casually stands at the bus stop and strikes up conversation, almost certainly about how slow the bus is in coming. They get on, Teresa gets off, and the woman stays on board. A few stops later, the woman gets off and is picked up by her accomplices. Next time Teresa's at the bus stop, there's the woman again: more friendly conversation. Now Teresa knows the woman gets off at a later stop. One more meeting, more friendly conversation, by now they may be on first-name terms. Then, in for the kill. The woman is there chatting away, a car pulls up, and, why, a stroke of luck, it's a friend who has spotted her there at the bus stop, offers her a lift home. The woman accepts and is halfway into the car when – where are her manners? – she extends the offer of a lift to Teresa. The driver, a friendly type, could even be another woman, has no problems with this: they're going past Teresa's house anyhow, as Teresa knows. In she gets. Fourteen years old, never harmed anyone, still full of trust and hope.'

14

Resca, G. (2009, July 30). How the Ndrangheta saved the banks: an analysis by Giovanni Resca, *Il Manifesto*, pp. A1, A6

OSINT stands for Open Source Intelligence. It refers to the sort of information you can pick up in the public domain just from reading government papers, chamber of commerce records, company balance sheets, newspaper articles, planning permission applications, land rezoning agreements and local news. It is what we journalists used to do all the time, but now we prefer to be spoon-fed, and like fat, coddled toddlers, we accept digestible pap from the corporations and government. But who makes the pap? Someone has to produce it, and make it easily digestible and even tasty for a gullible public. The pap-makers may deserve censure for what they do, but they are today's true journalists. Often venal, calculating and dishonest, always inventive, they are the great storytellers of our time. First, they plant their memes, their exposés, distractions, half-truths or downright lies, then they build a narrative around them. They are the world's secret artists.

The trick in OSINT is self-reference. You create a news story that is completely or partially made up, then you circulate it quietly until it is picked up by someone else. You bide your time until it goes viral or simply becomes part of the background noise. The important thing is it must no longer have a single identifiable source. You let the Chinese-whisper effect distort some of the details of the story, then you pick it up again and bring it to prominence attributing it to others. That's how most of the Iraq WMD stories were created. This is the storytelling skill. But, and this is the mistake that many of us on the Left often make, not all OSINT is false. On the contrary, most of it is true, for otherwise it would not work. The trick is to weave separate threads into a convincing fable. As in advertising and publishing, two other meretricious pursuits, the hardest part of OSINT is making sure that it's your *story and not someone else's that gets out there.*

Borrowing from the OSINT experts, then, I should like to propose my own version of recent economic developments. Using open sources, I have looked at the events since the collapse of Lehman Brothers and drawn some inevitable conclusions. Unlike many of my colleagues, particularly those who work for Berlusconi, I want to make full disclosure at the outset, and say that the reason I am telling this story, which is a true one, is that I want the Ndrangheta to become known. I want to publicize the name. I want the organization to become as notorious and ill-famed as Cosa Nostra. I want to put them in the limelight so that that part of the state they do not yet control might wake up and do battle.

As the readers of this newspaper know, capitalism needs a lot of propping up. It always has. Most of the direct support is through military spending, but capitalism can also rely on the public to provide collateral when things get tough. When billions are being made (but not distributed), the public is told capitalism works; when billions are being lost, the public is told it needs to pay up to rescue capitalism, because only capitalism works.

Sometimes plutocrats dispense with the effort of intellectual justification. They simply back capital accumulation with military force and the constant threat of violence, and kill those who resist. This is how it works in Russia, Albania, Bulgaria, Romania and most of Italy. We call it the Mafia, but we could just as easily call it deregulation. The only difference is the veneer of legitimacy.

But it is an important difference. For capitalism to appear legitimate, people must keep believing that it works. So when it stopped working, when people realized the banks didn't trust one another enough to lend, capitalism faced an existential threat. The whole money supply — the whole concept of money itself was on the brink of becoming a story in which no one believed.

In the USA, the Treasury Department introduced quantitative easing. Likewise, in the UK — basically, they printed money, and put off the day of reckoning. In Italy, Berlusconi said the banks were fine, and threw parties in his Sardinian villa. But for a few nights, before the institutions could react, before the trillions were pledged by western governments, there was a risk that ATM machines would stop paying out. Banks needed cash, and they needed it quickly.

Now what sort of organization has a whole load of cash, serious cash, billions upon billions in banknotes — enough to make a difference for a few vital days? The answer comes spontaneously: organized criminals. Specifically, the Russians and the Ndrangheta. There were others, too, but these two had more cash than anyone *else. The Ndrangheta needs to burn through its money. Cosa Nostra, an older organization, has interests, contacts, influence, clout and a certain establishment respectability by now, because it has so many non-cash assets. The Ndrangheta is flush with cash. In fact, it has too much, and needs to convert it into capital investments.*

The symmetry was perfect. The Ndrangheta has too much liquidity, because it has accumulated cash too fast since the late 1980s. The banks had too little liquidity, and the governments had too little time.

Using open-source intelligence, which means intelligence available to anyone who cares to investigate for himself or herself, I have been able to establish, beyond all reasonable doubt, that the three major British banks and at least two large American banks received enormous deposits in cash during the crucial hours and days of the banking crisis. In exchange, and again, I have listed sources at the end of this article, it was agreed that neither the tax authorities nor anyone else would look too closely at where this money came from. It was the biggest money-laundering operation in history, and it was sanctioned by members of government and the upper echelons of law enforcement. It was a quantum leap for the Ndrangheta. It gave them proper financial power.

Capitalism was saved by blood and drug money to live another day, but we shall pay the consequences of handing enormous financial power to a Mafia organization so disciplined that even its name is unknown to many people in its own country of origin.

But check the facts, look at the evidence. The Ndrangheta is already in control, a virus that has taken over the body politic. As long as we are a useful and unwitting host, we will suffer only slight discomfort, but when this virus is ready to infect stronger hosts, it will kill us and move on.

Magistrate Francesco Fossati powered down his laptop, slid it into his desk drawer, and glanced at his watch. He needed to hurry now if he was to make it home in time for supper with his family.

15

Locri, Calabria

'SALVATORE, HOW MANY times do I need to tell you this? Put the white cap on your head when you are in here.'

'But I'm completely bald, Capo.'

'That is why I am not making you wear a hairnet, too. Put on the cap and carry that bag of sugar over here while you're at it. Mind your step, the tiles are treacherous with lemon juice.'

Salvatore, seventy-two years of age, arms as thin as tendrils, his face as dark as a rusty nail, lifted the thirty-pound bag of refined sugar as if it had been filled with feathers, and set it down on the zinc counter beside his boss, Basile. As well as lifting heavy weights for Basile, it was his job to keep the conversation serious and on-topic while Basile feigned disinterest. So, putting the sugar down, he returned to the conversation he had started ten minutes before. 'It is unthinkable that a *sorella d'omertà* would spontaneously report to a magistrate like that. Especially her. She has been treated with nothing but the greatest respect, even though she comes from outside.'

'The things we have lived to see, Salvatore. Personally, I'm not inclined to believe it for one moment.' Basile swiped his hands together, in what looked like a gesture of finality, a closing of the argument for good, but also happened to be the most efficient way of getting the sugar and starch off his hands. Salvatore waited to see which it was.

Basile turned his back on Salvatore as he washed his hands under the tap. 'Who is the source of this accusation against Maria Itria?' he asked.

'One of our people in the Palace of Justice in Rome. It's part of the swirl of rumours around the dramatic warning issued to the magistrate.'

'And we really have no idea who decided to drop a corpse outside the Palace of Justice in Rome?'

'Not yet. Everyone seems to think Agazio ordered it; no one is sure.'

'And this magistrate to whom the message was directed, he has a confession from Maria Itria?'

'So it is rumoured.'

'Rumoured?'

'Reported. Yes, he does.'

Basile pulled sheets of green paper from the wall dispenser, dried his hands, crumpled up the paper and dropped it into the rubbish bin below. 'None of this makes much sense. Least of all the intimidation of the magistrate. Excuse the noise, Salvatore. I want to beat these egg whites.' He threw the switch on a white appliance and dialled up the speed. 'Come closer to me so you don't need to shout.'

Salvatore came closer, but remained silent, as he knew he was supposed to, watching the white foam rise in the copper bowl.

'One of the churning blades in the Vita 30 60 ice-cream maker needs replacing. Apparently it needs to be shipped from China,' said Basile. 'So now the Chinese are in the ice-cream business. Nicaso repaired his own machines, re-pumped the refrigerants, and calibrated the compressor so you could hardly hear it even when it was cooling a full batch. He was the real artisan, not me.'

Salvatore knew Basile was thinking and wanted the conversation to drift towards neutral topics until he had made his decision. 'Some people find it strange that you should want to ply a trade at all.'

'What, am I supposed to spend my days playing *briscola* and inspecting my lands? Did you try the last orange sorbet I made?'

'You know I cannot taste sweet things, Capo.'

'I think it was even better than the *turruni gelatu* I made last winter. I added three grapefruits and reduced the sugar by about one-fifth. It was a bitter sorbet, which I thought you might like because there is no sweetness in you, my old friend. And you say you didn't even try it?'

'You never told me you had changed the recipe.'

'Pity. It's the first real experiment I have made since taking this place over. When Nicaso was in charge, he was always experimenting. Licorice in the coffee granita, kiwi and figs together. I never had the courage or the imagination. And I am too old.'

'Nicaso was always breaking with tradition. That is one of the reasons he lost his *gelateria*.'

86

Basile's laugh was joyless and asthmatic. 'That is not the reason he lost his *gelateria*.' He pointed to a heavy steel cabinet with fat glass jars filled with red and green liquid. 'My strawberry and mint is commercial concentrate, sent down from Naples. Nicaso never did that.'

Basile pulled open the door of a refrigerator as large as the backdoor of a truck, and nodded to Salvatore to lift out a deep lozenge of stainless steel brimming with bright green ice cream, which started steaming as it entered the warmer air of the kitchen. Salvatore's hand stuck briefly to the icy zinc, and he felt momentary pain.

'Leave it to soften, Salvatore.'

Salvatore discreetly blew on his cold hands, and adjusted his white hat.

'Would Agazio goad the authorities into inquiring into the activities of the Society in Rome?' asked Basile. 'Killing in Milan, which itself requires permission, and disposing of the body in Rome and mocking a magistrate as he did so? I am supposed to think that Agazio, who has always been subtle, disrespected the families in Rome and Milan?'

'Perhaps he obtained permission from one or two of the families.'

'And we heard nothing about it? That would be the worst option from our point of view. We can talk at the Feast of the Madonna next week, but I hope that that is as unlikely as it seems. For Curmaci, the assassination of the magistrate's namesake is doubly destructive. It angers other *'ndrine* and will make the authorities determined to get him. It is better to assume this is the act of a hotheaded and rash person. To my mind, that would exclude Agazio.'

'You realize I have great respect for Curmaci,' said Salvatore.

'Of course you do.'

'I also have great respect for Maria Itria.'

'Naturally. She is a good woman.'

'The magistrates and police grow more despicable by the day. I believe it is quite possible they used Curmaci's wife to generate suspicion and dissent. Indeed, we do not even know whether Maria Itria received a phone call from the magistrate or made one of her own volition.'

'Or whether the call took place at all,' added Basile.

'Indeed. But would you not say that Curmaci, who is above all a man of principle, might have allowed himself to be swayed by his rage at this dishonouring of his wife and delivered an unambiguous message to the magistrate? The fact that he did not kill the magistrate himself and cause an overreaction by the authorities in Rome stands to his credit and would be typical of the man's admirable combination of severity and subtlety.'

'You make a plausible argument, Salvatore. Even so, where self-interest blinds many, it enlightens some, and I have always considered Agazio an enlightened man . . .'

'Another thing we must bear in mind, Capo, is the unfortunate trend towards independence in Lombardy and Germany. That has already led to the need for punishment expeditions to the north and forceful realignments. We are constantly working to maintain the faith and loyalty of the *locali* in Milan and Germany.'

'That is a generational problem that affects the younger men in the *'ndrine* of Lombardy. These youths speak with Milanese accents and deal with northern separatists who despise the south. But Agazio Curmaci is in some ways the opposite. He reinforces the rituals and maintains the tradition. He is not interested in independence. He was born in Gerace.'

'Typical of the rebels is their willingness to use persons external to the Society. It seems East Europeans were used in this case,' said Salvatore.

'Why did I not know that?'

'We have only just found out.'

Basile slowly removed his apron. Although it was splashed and stained, he folded it up as neatly as if freshly washed and ironed. 'Salvatore, it pains me to say this, but could your suspicions of Curmaci be connected to your kinship with Tony Megale? Your father and Domenico Megale's father were cousins and blood brothers.'

'They were, and my sister married Domenico's martyred brother.'

'What happened to him was tragic. Some things are not healed by time.'

Salvatore bowed his head in memory of a brother-in-law killed thirty years earlier. Then, his posture still prayerful, he said, 'It makes no sense for Tony Megale to have done this.'

'Who was the fool who says otherwise?' said Basile.

'Not a fool, Capo. I can see his name in your thoughts.'

'So now you read my thoughts and call me a fool?' said Basile with a smile.

'I would ask again,' said Salvatore, 'what interest could Tony have in doing something such as this?'

'To make good men like you have evil thoughts about the Curmacis,' said Basile. 'If he and Agazio have had another falling out, as they did in the early years, Tony might have tried to frame Agazio.'

'I think we must appeal to Domenico,' said Salvatore.

'Sadly, Domenico cannot make it to Polsi this year. They say he grew old in prison, though I believe he is no older than me. If Agazio and Tony have become enemies, it may well be a battle for succession. I would not wish to put Domenico in a difficult position. He has always expressed full faith in both Tony and Agazio, and, apart from that misunderstanding many years ago when they were immature, they have since expressed full faith in each other. Curmaci's son Ruggiero has been partly brought up by Tony's sister-in-law. Domenico cannot be seen to choose the wrong side, and it is inhuman to ask him to. It may be a decision we have to take for him. For now, his very silence is a message.'

'We do nothing?'

Basile tested the thawing of the ice cream by pressing a small indent with his thumb. 'Quarrels would not last long if the fault were on one side only. It might be both are to blame, it is more likely neither is.'

'May I speak frankly?'

Basile sighed. 'I would prefer to have this argument done with.'

'So would I. But we will achieve greater peace and harmony by promoting the cause of Tony Megale. I say that not because we are related, but because his father . . .'

'Not his natural father,' interrupted Basile.

'Even so. The Megales are more established. The Curmacis are new. Agazio's father was the first. They have no roots.'

'The Megales have few people left here. Perhaps they are on the wane.'

'They have a man, Pietro.'

'Pietro is limited.'

'But he is a man. Curmaci left only his woman and her children.'

'I say we do nothing for now.'

Salvatore nodded. It was time to play his trump card. He pulled out a phone, and placed it on the counter, amid the droplets now falling from the sides of the ice-cream container. 'As you know, the Finance Police have tapped Agazio's home number. This conversation took place last night. I had it sent to me as a matter of urgency. A captain of the Finance Police is about to get a new car, thanks to this act of cooperation.'

He pressed a button, and a woman's voice could be heard. 'That's Maria Itria. The man she is speaking to is Agazio.'

'I recognize their voices, Salvatore. They are talking about his arrival . . . what's incriminating about that?'

'Wait . . . coming up now.'

Maria Itria: '*What do you want for your dinner on your first night home with your family? Something special? A* spezzatino d'agghjiru. *I know just the person who can get me the ingredients.*'

Agazio: '*Too fancy. And you always overspice it. A good plate of* Maccarruni cu'zugu ra Crapa e ru Porcu. *That's what I prefer.*'

Maria Itria: 'Maccarruni cu'zugu ra Crapa e ru Porcu?'

Agazio: '*Si. Boni! Also, it's legal. Imagine if some policeman were listening to us now. If they had nothing better to do than to listen to us, then maybe they'd try to arrest you for killing and cooking a dormouse for your returning husband. Better cook me some pork and pasta!*'

Basile raised his hands. 'I don't see what's so damning about that.'

'Capo, that was code.'

'It may have been a joke code, Salvatore. They know the Finance Police are listening. Agazio even teases them.'

'It was emergency code, Capo, and you know it. He sent her a warning.'

'My ice cream is melting, Salvatore.'

'He was telling her to flee.'

'He was telling her eating dormice is illegal.'

'He was trying to cover up the shocked pause she made when he asked for *Maccarruni cu'zugu ra Crapa e ru Porcu*. He knows about the confession and he's trying to save her.'

'Bring the tray of ice cream out into the cooler in the bar, Salvatore.'

Salvatore did as he was told, removing his white hat and flinging it onto the counter as he left the kitchen. He dripped the tray into the slot, and picked up a star-shaped sign on the end of a short spike, and sunk it into the green mass, muttering to himself, 'Sickly . . . sits in the stomach like a brick, tastes of . . .'

'Did you just stick the mint sign into my pistachio ice cream?' said Basile, his voice coming from directly behind Salvatore's head.

Salvatore kept his head bent down and his voice casual. 'Silly mistake, Capo. I must be preoccupied with other things.' He stuck in the right sign, and turned to face his boss.

'I want the children to taste my latest ice cream,' said Basile. 'Have a group of them brought here after football practice tomorrow morning. Remove their phones, and we shall keep them out of circulation for a few hours. Agazio's son Ruggiero and Tony's son Enrico must be among them. They are best friends anyhow, aren't they?'

'Yes, they are.'

'Good. They can stay here all afternoon.'

'You know Enrico's aunt will panic immediately if Enrico misses his lunch. You know what Rosa is like.'

'I know about Zia Rosa. She has overfed and coddled that child. It is hard to imagine he is really Tony Megale's son. Old Megale could at least disown him as not his flesh and blood, but Tony must claim him as his own. That child needs some toughening up. Ruggiero, on the other hand, is like a reincarnation of his father. I see something in him.'

'I agree that Enrico is hardly a worthy successor, but he's young yet.'

'Not so young he can't start acting like a man. Perhaps it is time to give him some lessons in courage.'

'As I say, Zia Rosa will certainly panic when Enrico vanishes for a few hours. That could be misconstrued.'

'I told you, I know. We shall consider how the families react and draw conclusions later,' said Basile. 'If Maria Itria, who keeps her neighbours at a distance, were to start phoning and visiting them inquiring in worried tones about Ruggiero, that, too, might signal a bad conscience. Do not forewarn the Megales or any other family, Salvatore. Make sure the sons of several families are here tomorrow. We must be seen to be just.'

16

Milan

'I'LL HAVE THE sea bass,' said Magistrate Bazza. 'And you?'
Magistrate Fossati shook his head. 'I can never get used to the idea of fish in Milan . . .' He looked at the menu without enthusiasm. 'I'll have the mix of cold cuts,' he told the waiter. 'Just water to drink.'

The waiter collected the menus and left.

'You should try the fish.'

'You know I'm from Livorno, Ezio. When I visit my parents' graves, I eat fresh local fish. My mother used to make a fantastic *cacciucco*. Actually, I don't usually eat at lunchtime. I'd have preferred to meet for dinner in the usual place.'

'I wanted to meet as soon as possible,' said Magistrate Bazza. 'Have you got the file on the missing girl?'

'Teresa Resca. Yes.' Fossati glanced around the room, then handed the file to his friend.

Bazza ate breadsticks as he glanced through the pages, then handed them back.

'No,' he said. 'I can't help.'

'No?'

'Definitely not organized crime. But that I can't help is in itself an important pointer. For one, the modus operandi is needlessly complicated. From what I can see here there was a long stakeout in broad daylight, they depended on public transport and relied on a certain amount of luck. But I had my mind made up before I even looked at your file. This is not a Mafia abduction.'

'Are you supposed to make up your mind like that before you even see the file?' said Fossati.

'There's not much in that file that isn't already in the public domain. Nothing to make me change my mind. This has nothing to do with the Ndrangheta or any other Mafia.'

'Don't the bastards you deal with ever reserve unpleasant surprises for you? Don't they ever act out of character? I mean if you really knew everything about how they operate . . .'

'You know how it works, Francesco. Intelligence gets you only so far. We know a hell of a lot but can't act upon it. The Northern League and Berlusconi have cut our funding. Did you know that my colleagues in Calabria have to wash their own cars? And they can get fined for insubordination if they don't. Then that creep Maroni with his pervert's moustache and red glasses comes on TV and says his Ministry has done more to combat . . .'

'Aw, don't start that conversation again, Ezio,' said Fossati. 'I'm here about the girl.'

'It's not organized crime. That's not where you should be looking. I would have heard a whisper. I spent the morning with a team of excellent Carabinieri analysing intercepted communications over the past six months, focusing on any reference to the girl and her father. The father got mentioned twice. It's not enough. He hasn't written any exposés in months anyhow. It makes no sense for them to decide to silence him when he is already silent.'

The waiter arrived with Fossati's platter of cold salamis and hams. Fossati lifted a length of speck. 'Help yourself,' he told Bazza.

'No. I'll wait for my fish. So tell me about the rumour mill on your side of the building.'

'Everyone's interested in the murder of that insurance broker. The poor bastard with the same name as Magistrate Arconti.'

'Interested, as in displeased the case went down to Rome and got bounced up to us in the anti-Mafia wing without anyone else getting a look-in?'

'No. Just interested. Or not interested, as the case may be. There isn't even enough belief or passion for magistrates to feel strongly about jurisdiction rights nowadays.'

'They're right to feel disheartened,' said Bazza. 'Almost everyone you and I investigated in the '90s is in political office now. All we did was raise the cost of bribes. I don't understand how you managed to stay on there.'

'An ordinary magistrate manages to solve a lot of cases, put away people who have done real harm. I don't know how *you* bear it in the anti-Mafia. Huge rolling investigations that never come to an end, the constant reminders of the extent of the infiltration of organized crime, the cowardice of politicians.'

'When we manage to break a case, we order arrests in the hundreds. That's always gratifying. We shut down entire systems, even if only temporarily. Ah, here's my sea bass.'

Bazza smiled happily as he slipped off the shining skin, peeled away a layer of brown flesh and unpacked the fluffy white meat beneath, sucking his fingers as he did so. He fell silent until he was halfway through it, then said, 'You had a strange run-in with that magistrate in Rome once, didn't you?'

'Arconti? Yes,' said Fossati. 'It was some time ago. I think it's safe to say he won the bout.'

'But you became friends afterwards?'

'Friends . . . no. We wear different political colours. *Magistratura Democratica* versus *Magistratura Indipendente* and all that, though of course those allegiances were more important then than now. Arconti's a Catholic conservative, but one of the better ones. At the time, I thought he was a pawn of the Christian Democrats, but I was wrong there. He's not beholden to anyone, though I resented the way he assumed I was acting out of left-wing prejudice.'

'He was right about you. At the time, you were highly politicized.'

'And so were you.'

'Those were the days,' said Bazza. 'Remind me how Arconti outsmarted you.'

'I was investigating illegal party political funding, and Arconti's name came up,' said Fossati. 'It looked to me like he had deliberately mishandled an inquiry into donations, and then intervened to persuade the preliminary judge to throw out the case for lack of evidence. Everything magistrates in Rome did back then was suspect.'

'Such was the mood of the day. Turns out, we were no better here in Milan.'

'I would contest that. But I was wrong about Arconti. I assumed he was obeying a political master, and I ordered a wiretap on him. It was easy to do that in the '90s, remember? I had a go-to guy in the Finance

Police, and he set it up, then reported back to me. By then, I was already beginning to guess that Arconti was clean. Remarkably clean, as a matter of fact. But being clean didn't stop him from being a sly southerner. Somehow, he found out what I was doing. He took elements from several investigations and combined them in a way that dumped a lot of suspicion on the guy from the Finance Police I was using. He then applied for a wiretap on the policeman. So every time my man reported back to me on what he had heard Arconti say, Arconti was sitting there in Rome listening in. And the clever thing was, if he had tried to wiretap me directly, I would have probably found out. We were listening into one another for four months, and then one day he called me up himself, invited me down to Rome, and we spoke. He said he could see I was doing my best in difficult circumstances, and hoped I could see the same was true for him. The Finance policeman, by the way, got caught accepting bribes two years later.'

'Arconti is in hospital. He was taken ill after the murder of his namesake.'

'I am sorry to hear that,' said Fossati.

'This is confidential, Francesco, but we like a guy named Agazio Curmaci for the crime. He's Ndrangheta.'

'If it's confidential, why are you telling me?'

'Because we've been friends for twenty-five years, and I trust you and I thought you might like to know.'

'Don't exaggerate, it's been only twenty-three years.'

'Just after *Mani Pulite* ran completely out of steam and I jumped ship to the DDA, Curmaci was a young *camorrista*, freshly inducted into the "Honoured Society", he killed five people.'

'At one go?'

Bazza neatly peeled the skeleton from his fish and put it on the side of his plate. 'All at one go. It was the detail of the killings that got my attention. He shot four, stabbed one to death. The one he stabbed was nineteen years old. Here's the thing though, he had been told to kill one person only, a guy called Cava . . . Gra . . . I forget the name. Instead, he killed the guy's parents, sister and brother. That was the one he stabbed. The only person he did not kill was the target. Transversal revenge, as they say.'

'What happened to the target?'

'He was so enraged and terrified, he tried to turn to the authorities for help, but his evidence was not seen as reliable, and he lost his right to protection. So that was the end of him. Vanished without trace. Shortly afterwards, Curmaci went to Germany. Within one year he was reporting directly to Domenico Megale, also known as Megale Senior, *Megale u Vecchiu*, or the Prefect of Westphalia.'

'Prefect of Westphalia. The arrogance of these people.'

'It didn't stop him from ending up in jail. He got put away by the BKA, one of their first successful operations against an Italian boss, thanks to an investigation into a tax scam involving VAT, but I don't think prison made much difference to him. He's out now, by the way. Just got released two days ago. His son, a killer called Tony, held a homecoming party. I don't know if Curmaci was there or not.'

'You've been looking into the Megales and Curmaci for a while, then. This is not something you picked up just the other day,' said Fossati.

'You're right. And one of the people who has been helping me is Magistrate Arconti. That's why I was interested in your opinion of him.'

'Favourable, I suppose. I have finished my salami, Ezio, so can you say why you want me to know all this?'

'I told you, because you know Arconti.'

'That's all?'

'Actually, there is something else. Arconti became involved in this case when he was called in to investigate the suspicious suicide of a doctor who was prescribing one of the admixtures they use to cut cocaine. He and a Roman commissioner, Alec Blume, quickly moved from that to an operation that led to the arrest of two low-ranking members of the Ndrangheta. Arconti should have passed the case on to the anti-Mafia before he got that far, but he didn't.'

'Understandable.'

'I disagree, but never mind. He and this commissioner arrested two brothers who were cousins of Curmaci's wife. Arconti then started looking into Curmaci, which even you will admit is beyond his scope of competence. But I know the reason he did this. Arconti is from Gerace in Calabria, the same town as Curmaci, though a generation separates them. It's personal for him. In the meantime we have another case, or perhaps a development of this one.'

'Those bodies discovered in the Falck steelworks in Sesto San Giovanni?

I got the impression it was low-level stuff, Albanians murdering each other or something,' said Fossati.

'Romanians. Thanks to some decent and rapid work by the commissioner and an inspector, a woman, Mattiola, a direct link has been made between the bodies found there and the Arconti murder. For the time being, we have decided not to let the investigators in Rome know about this.'

'That's a shame for the police. They do their job well, and their reward is to be excluded.'

'I will put them back in the picture when the time comes. The point is, we might be seeing the start of an upset in the balance of power.'

'You know I am in the middle of this kidnapping of a girl, which you yourself just told me is unconnected with the Ndrangheta?'

'I know. I'll let you go now. But just one more thing.'

'You said "just one more thing" five minutes ago, Ezio. I'm going now. You get the bill, I'll get it next time.' Fossati stood up.

'Wait. Domenico Megale – the boss in Germany?'

'What about him?'

'He has two main points of reference. One is Agazio Curmaci, who is the *Mastro di giornata* of the German *locale*. The other is his son, Antonio, who's always been known as Tony. Tony is the *crimine*. Tony was once married, but his wife died, leaving him a son, who's in Calabria. His wife's surname was Mancuso.'

Fossati sat down again. 'For God's sake, Ezio, you could have told me this at the beginning.'

'No, first I needed to tell you the girl's kidnapping is not Mafia related.'

'And now you're telling me the opposite. Giovanni Resca, her father, wrote article after article detailing the investments made by the Mancusos in Milan. His article specifically names that family, time and time again. They made threats against him.'

'So are you going to investigate the Mancuso family?'

'I already am, to the best of my ability with the resources I have.'

'I told you, it's not Mafia related. It's not them.'

'How can you know?'

'Like I said, the modus operandi isn't right, but mainly because we've been monitoring the Mancusos closely for some time now. We recently picked up a lot of chat between one of them and someone in Germany.

97

We can't identify who, but it could be Curmaci and it could be Tony Megale or even Old Megale. But my point is, there is no indication that they are really concerned by Giovanni Resca and his anti-Mafia blogs and articles. I'm telling you this because I think you'll be wasting your time if you pursue that path while looking for the girl.'

'Duly noted. It's not the only line of inquiry I am following.'

'My advice is don't concentrate on the Mancusos, OK? It's not them.'

'I'll take that into account,' said Fossati.

'But you're still going to look into them?'

'Of course I am. How can I not?'

'I knew you wouldn't drop that line of inquiry just on my say-so. That's another reason I wanted to talk to you. Seeing as you, despite my advice to the contrary, will be looking into the Mancusos and their properties, will you let me know if you find anything interesting?'

'Anything in particular?'

'Anything at all. Specifically, anything that might be connected to Curmaci, East European criminals, or the murder of the insurance actuary Matteo Arconti.'

'So while I hunt for a stolen child, I carry out a covert check for you guys in the anti-Mafia?'

'Only if you are going to waste your time looking where you won't find the poor child. Don't get me wrong, Francesco, I would prefer you to find the missing girl, and I wish you would take my advice and follow any other leads.'

'I will follow other leads, and I see why you think this was not organized crime. But I need to follow this one, too.'

'Let's hope you find her, even if . . .' Bazza looked down at the discarded skin and bones of his fish.

'I know,' said Fossati. 'Too much time has already passed.'

Sunday, 30 August

17

Locri

'PEPÈ, LUCA, GIOVANNI, Enrico, Ruggiero, Rocco. All of you, get over here.'

Pepè rolled his freshly lit cigarette between his fingers, then let it drop lightly to the ground. Luca, Giovanni and Rocco stopped aiming karate kicks at each other, Enrico received a pass from Ruggiero and flicked the ball up and into his hands. They all started walking towards their football coach.

Enrico cast Ruggiero a questioning glance. Ruggiero ignored him. He felt the others picking up on Enrico's uncertainty and storing it away for future use. Almost certainly none of them knew what the coach wanted, but they knew it was important to look as if they did. Pepè was even nodding, as if he had been expecting this.

'What is it, coach?' said Enrico.

'A little discussion of tactics, down at Mr Basile's place,' said the coach. 'Now.'

'Not on the pitch?' asked Enrico, his voice a squeak of protest and surprise.

Luca spat on the ground, just behind Enrico's heel. 'You heard him, Enrico.'

'Are you coming, coach?' asked Enrico.

'Maybe later.' Their coach pulled a clear plastic bag from inside his Adidas tracksuit, and held it open in front of Enrico.

'What's that for?' asked the boy.

'It's for putting things into, Enrico. Let's start with your mobile.'

Enrico turned around and looked at his friends uncomprehendingly. Pepè already had his iPhone out, and was the first to drop it into the bag. Luca, Giovanni and Rocco followed. Ruggiero delayed a little, carefully pulling out his phone, giving Enrico all the time he needed to see what he was supposed to do, then dropped it into the bag. He nodded at Enrico, trying to communicate to him the need for silence and obedience.

His hints weren't enough.

'My aunt wants me to call her. She said I have to call if I'm not going straight home after practice.' He slid open his phone. 'I'll call her now, tell her we're going to the bar. She won't mind.'

Ruggiero stepped forward and plucked the phone from Enrico's hand, and tossed it towards the coach who opened the mouth of the plastic bag wide to catch it on the fly. The coach turned quickly on his heel and walked away from them, saying, 'I'll see you kids later.'

Pepè was already on his motor scooter, gunning the throttle, checking his lean face and the fit of his sunglasses in the rear-view mirror. Luca clambered on behind him, but Pepè hit him hard in the throat with the heel of his hand, knocking him sprawling to the ground. Luca stood up, dusted himself down and laughed, like it had been a rehearsed stunt. Rocco, who had the other scooter, nodded to Giovanni, who climbed aboard, and they were off, leaving a swirl of dust and a scent of fuel behind.

Pepè said something, his words drowned out by the rip and roaring of the scooter motor as he revved it. Then he let go of the throttle and spoke into the sudden silence, 'Enrico, get on.'

Enrico looked in panic at Luca, who turned away in disgust, then to Ruggiero, who shrugged. Finally he found his voice. 'Thanks, Pepè, I can walk. It's only ten minutes.'

Pepè turned off the motor, dismounted and moved towards Enrico, who retreated behind Ruggiero.

'You don't want to ride from me?'

'I can walk.'

'Yeah.' Pepè looked down the hill and over the half-built run-down houses. 'You'll be there in ten minutes, right? No detours.'

'No detours,' promised Enrico.

Pepè ignored him. 'Ruggiero, you'll see to it, won't you?'

Ruggiero said, 'I'll bring him straight there. Along with myself.'

'You need a scooter to get around on. What are you waiting for?'

'My mother thinks it should be my father who gets it for me.'

Pepè nodded. 'That's good. When is he getting back?'

'I don't know these things, and I don't ask.'

Pepè stared at Ruggiero, before giving him the slightest of nods, imperceptible to the others. Then he jerked his head and Luca, nervously laughing and fingering his throat, climbed aboard again, and they left.

Ruggiero took Enrico by the elbow and propelled him forwards. 'Come on.'

They set off down the hill together. Almost every house they passed had added a second floor years ago, but none of them had ever completed the work. The most advanced were those that had managed to put up pillars and a roof, but no walls, giving the buildings the look of having been gutted by bombing. Some homeowners had ambitiously begun work on a third level. Twisted steel rebars protruded from every roof. Everything was still in the early stages of construction and in the final stages of decay. Enrico hesitated for a moment as they passed the intersection leading to his house where he lived with Aunt Rosa and Uncle Pietro, but Ruggiero gave him a push. 'We were told to go directly. They took our phones. We're not to talk to anyone. That has to be clear even to you.'

'What have we done?'

'I don't know, Enrico. Probably nothing. Maybe it's someone else who's done something, or just a test of obedience. Or maybe it's some sort of preparation for the festivities on September 2nd or tactics, like Coach said. We'll find out.'

'I'm worried something's going to happen. Why did they take our phones?'

'To make us disappear for a while.'

'My aunt will be worried sick if I don't contact her,' said Enrico. 'Sunday lunch. You know what she's like.'

Ruggiero nodded. Zia Rosa, as he also called her, though she was not his aunt, lived her life in a state of fretfulness and, according to Enrico, slept no more than three hours a night, though how sleepy Enrico would know that was a mystery. Perhaps Enrico's uncle, the strong-smelling and slow-witted Pietro, had told him, but if so, that would mean he would have had to speak, which is not something Ruggiero had often heard him do.

They entered the silent piazza and headed towards the bar. Two empty chairs and a tin table sat next to the door, which was covered in a heavy bead curtain. A faded chart showing ghostly Motta ice creams and smudged prices still quoted in lire was nailed to the wall.

'It's already closed for the afternoon,' said Enrico in relief. 'The scooters aren't here. They must have gone home.'

Maybe Enrico was right. Mr Basile's bar and *gelateria* kept irregular opening hours. On any given afternoon it could be closed while its owner sunned himself on the white sand. Closed meant unoccupied by Basile or Salvatore. They never locked the bar, because no one for any reason would ever think of taking anything from it, not even a glass of water, without permission. Basile loved the sun. It had burned him deep brown, caused melanomas to prosper on his back, and wrinkled the skin of his face, but still he went, the only sunbather on the horseshoe-shaped beach, sitting in front of the half-built villas, rusting metal cages, breeze blocks and paralysed cement mixers, soaking it all up.

He never swam in the bright blue waters of the sea in front of him, just lay there all afternoon, smiling up at the sky, his wife dead these ten years, his three sons lost in 1991, the year the war between the Cataldo and Cordì families finally ended.

Ruggiero realized Mr Basile would have told the others not to park their scooters in front of the bar, which explained the empty piazza. Just as he was about to point this out to Enrico, the bead curtain parted and Basile's faithful ancient retainer, Salvatore, thin and sprightly, waved the two boys inside.

Walk in if invited, even if you know. His father had told him that that was the sign of true courage. He would have felt better if his father were here now. But all their fathers were abroad, in Milan, Turin, Spain, Slovenia and Germany. He was not alone in being alone.

With Enrico right behind him, Ruggiero brushed the beads aside with the back of his hand, and stepped inside the dark bar.

18

Locri

THEY HAD BEEN inside the bar for an hour and a half now, and no one had said anything to them. The only absolute if unspoken condition was that they remained there until told they could go. Ruggiero watched as Enrico made his way through the pistachio ice cream, then quietly offered him his, saying, 'I haven't touched it.'

Enrico waited impatiently until Ruggiero had put the ice cream in front of him, then set to it like he was being chased. Ruggiero thought no one had noticed, but then Salvatore, who served at the bar without anyone ever thinking of him as a barman, came over.

'You don't like Mr Basile's ice cream?'

Enrico raised his eyes for a moment, smiled sleepily at them both, then returned to spooning the sweet green cream from the wafer cup into his mouth.

'I'm just not hungry,' said Ruggiero.

'It was a generous gesture. What sort of ingrate would turn down a gift from Mr Basile?'

'I'm not hungry,' repeated Ruggiero, knowing, without being able to do much about it, that he was speaking in a tone of detached contempt for Salvatore, and that this would do him no favours. He could have said more. The ice cream was bright green and over-sugared. Its sweetness made him gag. The bits of nut that Basile left in to give it a natural taste were surrounded by crystals of frost, and chewing through them felt like a chore. Ruggiero could remember when the *gelateria* was run by Pino Nicaso, a man who knew his trade and then was pointlessly put out of business by Salvatore and Basile, bringing to an end the only happy place in town.

Salvatore left them alone and did not, as Ruggiero had feared, return to force-feed him one of Basile's special treats.

The other kids had started playing table football. Abandoning Ruggiero in the corner, Enrico went up to join in, but was made to watch instead, and then pushed roughly aside by Luca who blamed Enrico's flab for getting in the way and allowing Giovanni to score.

Pepè had chosen to play the poker machine, and remained impassive as the machine dealt him hand after hand in defiance of all rules of fairness and statistical probability. He had a thunderbolt design shaved into the back of his crew cut. He kept his face turned towards the screen and away from his companions, but Ruggiero knew the screen also had a mirror effect, and he was watching them as they stole surreptitious glances at his back.

Ruggiero, as sometimes happened, seemed to have become invisible in his corner. He was hungry, but for real food. A Sunday meal prepared by his mother, not the vile ice cream or, worse still, one of the stale bar sandwiches wrapped in plastic. He was bored, too. Bored with the table football and the tough-guy curses of his companions, bored with defending Enrico from attack, bored with the ugly furniture and the sly bald Salvatore, said to have used a meat cleaver to cut the arms, legs and cock off a policeman in the 1960s. The policeman, the story went, survived and lived the rest of his days in bed, though without female company. Maybe none of it was true.

Once again, as so often happened, the joshing and casual teasing of Enrico's lack of skill had hardened and grown colder. Enrico, sweating with effort, still lost nine–one to Luca and was told to fuck off and stop wasting everyone's time.

He came back over to Ruggiero and sat down heavily beside him like a wet seal. His arrival put Ruggiero back inside the exclusion zone in which Enrico lived. When Enrico was near him, Ruggiero could clearly see the hostility and contempt of those who looked in their direction. All he had to do was step outside the zone, away from Enrico, and the hostile looks became almost invisible again. Yet Enrico's father Tony was both feared and respected: more the former than the latter. His uncle Pietro was at least feared. It was the contrast with them that did Enrico no favours. As to his own family, Ruggiero knew that no one quite trusted his father, his mother or him. They were regarded as excessively reserved and insufficiently local. Most of the time he was quite comfortable with it; now he felt under pressure, and he knew, even if Enrico was too dim to recognize it, that some sort of test was being done on them, not on the other kids.

The front door of the bar, closed to the public, was opened to admit a small man with dirty skin and a white beard, whom Ruggiero recognized as a friend or relation of some sort of Salvatore. He was dressed in the dark-green working clothes of the forestry protection corps, the one state uniform that it was no dishonour to wear. Ruggiero was not entirely sure of the status of the scruffy visitor, but he knew it was surprisingly high. His name was Tommasino and his job was to clear the woods of undergrowth and cull foxes. Occasionally he lit summer fires that raged for days and were reported on the national news. The burned-out land was perfect for construction developments, and the firefighting equipment and firefighters themselves were all part of a supply racket run by the *locale* of the town, whose boss was Basile.

'What are all these kids doing in the bar, Salvatore? I come in here after a day's toil expecting a quiet grappa, and I find myself in a schoolroom, or is it a Cubs' meeting?' He grinned, showing yellow teeth. One of his incisors was snapped in half. 'Get them out of here.'

'You heard him,' said Salvatore. 'Time to go home.'

Obediently they moved away from the table. Pepè made one more play on the poker machine, then casually walked towards the door. Enrico took larger and faster spoonfuls of ice cream.

'Wait!'

Tommasino lifted a stinking jute bag off the floor and handed it to Pepè. Pepè glanced into the bag, and smiled, then pulled out their six phones and dropped them on the counter.

'I happened to meet your coach,' said Tommasino. 'He said he was sorry he couldn't make it and asked me to give you these, and I was happy to do a favour. Go on, take them, turn them on. You'll need to phone your mothers and apologize.'

Salvatore motioned Pepè over to him, and whispered a few words.

The forester looked across at Enrico, who was just now finishing his ice cream. 'You're Pietro's nephew.'

'I am Tony Megale's son,' said Enrico, an unexpected upsurge of pride and defiance in his voice.

'That goes without saying. I happen to know Pietro, not Tony. How about a beer?'

Enrico looked around for help, but Ruggiero, fed up with it all, cast his eyes down and looked away. He just wanted to go home. He stretched out his hand to pick up his phone, but Pepè snatched it up first.

'Give me that,' said Ruggiero, more bored than intimidated by Pepè's antics.

Pepè tossed it to Salvatore behind the bar. 'Ask him for it.'

Salvatore stepped back and allowed the phone to hit the floor in front of him. He stood there immobile, his bald head balanced like a skull on the top of his thin body. Pepè whitened and apologized, then came around the bar to retrieve the phone from the floor and put it on the counter beside Enrico's. Then he and the other three left in silence.

Salvatore fixed Ruggiero with a stare that lasted only a few seconds, then turned his back. Ruggiero left his phone where it was.

A minute later, the silence of the piazza was ripped apart by the noise of souped-up scooters.

'What about it, Enrico, will you buy me a beer?' asked the forester, when the noise had died away.

'I don't think I have the money,' said Enrico. 'I would if I had it. Maybe I could borrow some from Ruggiero?'

'*Figluolo mio.* I am joking. I am the one who buys the beers in here, isn't that right, Salvatore?'

Salvatore draped a damp bar cloth over his shoulder and said nothing.

'I don't want a beer,' said Enrico, making to stand up then deciding to sit down again.

Ruggiero puffed out his cheeks in exasperation, and went over to sit next to Enrico, who was going to need help.

'Thanks,' whispered Enrico.

Ruggiero shrugged. The forester came over and sat down beside them, bringing with him a smell of wood chippings, urine, sweat and tobacco.

'Then you're having a grappa.'

'I don't drink,' said Enrico. ·

'Maybe if you learned to drink, you wouldn't eat so much, Enrico. Salvatore, no more of Basile's ice cream for the boy.'

Salvatore, who was bent down and talking through the serving hatch to someone in the kitchen, presumably Basile, raised a hand either in acknowledgment or to tell Tommasino to be quiet. Either way, the forester lowered his voice and spoke in a furious whisper to Enrico. 'You don't refuse a drink from me when I generously offer you one.'

'Sorry,' said Enrico.

Tommasino called out, 'Salvatore, let's put some water in Enrico's grappa. Make it half water half spirit, like Enrico himself.'

Salvatore nodded. Out of a satchel, Tommasino produced some dark bread and a shiny yellow cheese studded with hot chili peppers. He started paring his cheese with a wooden-handled curved knife. Salvatore arrived with a bottle of grappa and a jug of water.

Tommasino poured Enrico a glass and sat watching as he drank it, then poured him another, then another, ignoring Enrico's burbling protests and clicking his knife open and shut.

'What about you, young Curmaci? Want a drink?'

Ruggiero refused with a barely perceptible lift of the chin and a slow closing of his eyelids. No one should expect him to have to speak to the stinking, unlettered forester. He chose a point behind Tommasino's head and focused on it, allowing the forester's murderous gaze to hit the wall behind him. If they were alone, he might have returned the gaze, see what came of it. He felt calm enough.

After half an hour, Salvatore came over and said, 'Enrico, you can go home now. Pick up your phone on the counter.'

'What about Ruggiero?'

'You can tell your aunt he was delayed here.'

Enrico tried to bring his eyes into focus. 'My aunt will tell his mother. So wouldn't it make more sense . . .' – but he lost track of his line of argument.

'Tell his mother, too,' said Salvatore, 'if you think that will help.'

Enrico reached over and grabbed the bottle and poured himself another grappa. 'I'm not leaving without Ruggiero!' He downed the glass in a single gulp and spent the next few minutes coughing and wiping the tears from his eyes.

Another half hour passed and now the bottle on the table was empty and the glass in front of Enrico had tumbled over. Enrico's face was flushed, his eyes shone bright and his head was lolling from side to side. Cheese rinds lay curled on the table.

'Salvatore?' asked Tommasino.

From behind the bar, Salvatore nodded.

He brought over their phones and placed them on the table, giving Ruggiero a wink as he did so. Ruggiero remained impassive, and waited until Salvatore had withdrawn before picking up his phone, and standing up.

Enrico had begun moaning and muttering something incomprehensible.

The forester cackled as if at some private joke, then left the table and went up to the bar counter. 'Young Megale has drunk too much,' he said to Salvatore.

'That's fine. His good friend Ruggiero is here to look after him. The Curmacis are renowned for their loyalty. The Curmacis and Megales are old friends, working together in faraway hostile lands.'

'Let's hope the alliance lasts. It seems to me Enrico is as much a liability as a friend. Here, young Curmaci, what do you want us to do with Enrico?'

'He's my responsibility,' said Ruggiero. I'll look after him and take him home.'

Monday, 31 August

19

Rome

'INTERESTING TIMES, BLUME,' said Massimiliani, ushering him through the visitors' area without a pass. He lowered his voice as they walked quickly down a corridor towards a tinted window that turned the outside world dark orange.

'I have a good friend in the German Federal Police. You'll be meeting him later. This morning, he started talking about Curmaci, and so I pushed him a little and he said he had heard Curmaci was cooperating with the Italian authorities. I said I would have to look Curmaci up, find out who he was, but my BKA friend did not believe me. He seemed quite agitated at the idea that Curmaci might be talking to some Italian magistrate. Isn't that good? Your lie has gone international over a single weekend.'

'Why would they be agitated if Curmaci were cooperating with us?'

'Good question. It makes me wonder if Curmaci might be cooperating with them. I doubt it, but even if he is not actively cooperating with the BKA, he could be partly under their protection thanks to his high-level contacts. We almost never get high-level informers from the Ndrangheta. Ten a penny in the Mafia these days, but not the Calabrians. It would be very frustrating if the Germans got there first. I just think they are worried that if Curmaci were talking to us, we'd find out about things happening in Germany of which they are unaware.'

'And we don't really want him talking to the BKA in case he tells them about things in Italy we know nothing about.'

'Fear of losing face is the greatest impediment to international cooperation, but we actually get on reasonably well with the BKA. Better than you might expect. I'm going to take you down to meet him in a minute.'

He led Blume into an empty conference room with large screens.

'This is where we show off what the DCSA does. Like the war rooms in the movies? Except when the globe lights up with red lines, they are mobile phone connections we are tracking rather than nuclear missiles. Let me check the BKA guy's in my office. I'll send someone down to collect you.'

Blume sat in the room alone, and looked around for something interesting to do. On the podium, he found a laser pointer, and spent some time causing the green dot to play over the DCSA emblem.

The conference room door opened and a small man in a wide brown tie and thick glasses looked around in confusion at not finding anyone within his immediate field of vision. Blume danced the laser beam at him, and the man held up his arms over his face. Blume half expected him to shout, 'Don't shoot,' but all he said was, 'I was told to fetch you.'

As he followed the man down a long, featureless corridor flanked by closed doors, his phone came to life and started pulling in missed call messages. Caterina had phoned twice.

He stopped and called her back, allowing the man in the brown tie to reach the end of the corridor before realizing Blume was no longer at his heels. He came beetling back wagging an angry finger, but Caterina had already answered.

'Where have you been?' she demanded.

Blume glanced at his wrist where his watch used to be, and said, 'It's still Monday morning. I've been in bed.'

'I mean yesterday and the day before.'

'That was a Sunday. It was my day off. Saturday ... stuff to do. Paperwork, mostly.'

'You're not allowed to do paperwork at home. Anyhow, I don't believe that's what you were doing.'

'I don't have time for a to-and-fro between us. If you want –'

'They've taken the case out of our hands. They found the van in Sesto San Giovanni and,' she paused for effect, 'it was burned out and two bodies were found inside. I had to find this out for myself. Only now has the Milan magistrate admitted it to me.'

'When did they say the van was found?'

'Friday. They've been sitting on the information, making a fool of us. Not of you, though, you backed out of this from the start, didn't you?'

'I was giving you breathing space.'

'Don't worry about that. I get all the air I need in the large empty spaces you like to leave between us.'

'I was talking at a professional level. You don't want me there all the time.'

'But you knew from the start my investigation was a dead-end.'

Blume started to make a protesting noise, then decided not to bother.

'You knew and you said nothing,' she insisted.

'No. Not at all,' he said. Accurate or not in her reckoning, it was not right for her to accuse him like this. He turned his back on the man in the brown tie, who was literally hopping with impatience, like a fat chaffinch.

'Liar,' said Caterina, and hung up.

He swung round savagely at the bouncing functionary. 'Next time you wag that finger you'll be wagging it up . . .' But he stopped. The man in front of him, who barely reached his chest, seemed on the verge of tears.

'I have a very tight schedule,' he squeezed his legs together and twisted his body as if he was holding his bladder. 'Can you please hurry?'

Blume took pity, and they proceeded at a smart pace down hallways and up stairs, and then the small man popped open a door and led him into a dark, narrow room, the size of a large utility cupboard. A small hopper window near the ceiling slanted inward, allowing in dark air that reminded Blume of the smell of Line A of the Metro. The gunmetal desk spanned the narrow space between the walls, leaving the tiniest gap for the man to squeeze through, which he set about doing at once, as if anticipating that this would take some time, as indeed it did. Blume reflected that it would have been quicker to clamber over the desktop, which had nothing on it.

The man finally reached his seat behind the desk and sat down. He then looked up with a slight frown of annoyance as if he had been sitting there busily working away and Blume was an unexpected and unwelcome visitor. The pleading demeanour evident in the corridor was quite gone now, and he nodded curtly at the third object in the room, a seat, identical to his own, on Blume's side. He pulled open a drawer, extracted a thin phone and placed it on the table.

'This is your new phone,' he said. 'I need to see the one you have now.'

Blume was interested in seeing where this was leading. He took his clunky old Nokia out of his pocket and set it on the desk between them next to the sleek new Samsung.

'I see,' said the man, looking at the Nokia with disfavour. 'This new one is a Samsung Smartphone – I have forgotten which model, but it will tell you its name when you turn it on. For now it has but one phone number in it, listed under "Mamma". That's us. If we call, please answer. We have a trace on this phone, of course, so we'll know where you are . . . umm . . .' He drummed his fingers on the empty desk trying to think of other features.

'Anyhow, you can keep it afterwards. Like a perk. That's something. Touch screen, Android operating system, built-in GPS navigator, MP3 player, Bluetooth, internet enabled, and it will connect to all four providers, TIM, Vodafone, Tre and Wind. I don't know how they did that. Don't use it for personal calls for the next few days. Nothing sinister, just our standard practice.' He pointed to Blume's old Nokia. 'I am going to take that, OK?'

'No,' said Blume. 'Not OK.'

'Is it police issue or personal?'

'Both,' said Blume. 'Police issue, but it's the one I use for everything, You're not having it. It's not legal for you to have it.'

The man nodded in complete understanding, but stretched out his hand anyway. Blume grabbed his phone back. The man withdrew his hand as if bitten by a snake. The Smartphone sat on the table between them.

'If you take the Samsung, I'll have accomplished 50 per cent of my task. Will you at least take it?'

Blume took it and slipped it into his pocket. 'Thanks for the gift. You realize I have no idea who you are or what this is about?'

The man relaxed. 'That explains it. You haven't been briefed yet. Let me check.'

He pulled out a phone, identical to the one he had just handed to Blume, and pressed its screen. 'Yes, me . . . He came here first . . . Right. He still has his old phone by the way. Oh yes, I suppose that makes more sense . . .'

He dropped the phone back into his pocket and extended his hand. 'Well, it's been a pleasure.'

As Blume took his hand, the door behind them opened and Captain Massimiliano Massimiliani entered.

'Sorry about that, Alec. You were taken to the wrong room. Or the right room in the wrong order. We're just down the corridor here, will you come through?'

Pausing before a door, Massimiliani put his hand on Blume's shoulder. 'Just before we go in there, two things. First, the German agent is the liaison officer of the BKA to the anti-Mafia and he really is a friend of mine. He's completely trustworthy.'

'Completely?'

'Oh, yes. I don't tell him much, of course, but if I did, I am pretty certain he would treat the information responsibly. Now, as much as I have great faith in my friend, I would ask you not to fall for his absent-minded stoner act. He often claims he does not understand, but it's all an act. Mind what you say.'

Massimiliani opened the door and ushered him in. The man inside stood up and introduced himself rapidly, almost before Blume had taken stock of him.

'Kommissar Blume, I am Kriminaloberrat Winfried Weissmann,' he spoke English. 'Please call me Winfried.'

'Winfried?' Blume had a distant memory of his father mentioning a great-grandmother who had the same name. Or was that Winifred? The man in front of him must once have had a full shock of Afro-style hair in his youth. What was left was still frizzy and wild, but it was also snow white and had receded so far from his forehead that it now sat like a pile of freshly shorn wool on the back of his head. Although at least sixty years old, he wore a denim jacket and a red-and-green checked shirt, but, whether in deference to his official function or in recognition of his age, he also wore a shiny pale-blue loosely knotted tie. Winklepicker boots with silver buckles peeped out from below his drainpipe trousers. Blume was not surprised to see an ankh-shaped earring hanging from his fleshy earlobe. Behind him, Captain Massimiliani was nodding in approval as Blume took all this in his stride.

'*Lei è il capomissione? Sind Sie Oberbefehl . . .*' said Blume, holding out his hand and smiling pleasantly.

'Ah! You speak some German!' The BKA man suddenly seized Blume's hand in his own, clasped the other hand over it, and pressed it rather emotionally, as if they were childhood friends now reaching a parting of the ways. 'But we can speak English. *Oberbefehl* is a bit of an exaggeration.

117

I am the chief of this mission. I don't think Massimiliano has explained everything to you?'

'No.'

'It's very simple and – hah! – it is very embarrassing, yeah?'

'If you say so,' said Blume, taking a step back.

'I am embarrassed!' shouted Weissmann, then lowered his voice, glaring suspiciously at the closed door. 'We have an agent by the name of Konrad Hoffmann, who has been working in the BKA for fifteen years and has a perfect record. I do not know him personally, although I have met him. For the past five years, this officer has been specializing in inquiries into the management of industrial waste and organized crime. Most of his inquiries have focused on the export and disposal of heavy metals produced by German firms. So far, his investigations have focused on the Camorra and the illegal dumping of toxic waste in the region of Campania. The Camorra is not the only Mafia involved in this sector, but Hoffmann's inquiries have been focused on that particular organization rather than any other.'

He paused and regarded Blume with an appraising look, as if seeing him for the first time. Blume nodded gravely, which seemed to satisfy him, and he continued. 'Nine months ago, Konrad Hoffmann made an application for vacation leave, which is his right. In fact, he has not even claimed for as long as he might, and it is absolutely normal for him to ask for time off in the summer, just as it is also perfectly normal for him to take a camper van and drive south into Italy along with thousands of other Germans. So none of this was noticed.'

'No one noticed a German with a camper van driving to Italy in August?' said Blume. 'I understand why this might not make the news.'

The BKA chief found this extremely funny and filled up the room with throaty laughter.

'That was very humorous. So many Germans with camper vans and motor homes . . .' He lowered his voice, 'Not as bad as the Dutch, though. You can't move on Italian roads for the Dutch and their yellow number plates and little camper vans! Yeah, so, Konrad Hoffmann. He left on Thursday, spent Friday night in Tyrol, Saturday in Mantua, and last night in the "Tiber Village". He is on his way from there to us now. You understand this?'

'I'm following what you are saying,' said Blume, 'if that's what you mean.'

'You are following me. That is good. I cannot ask for more. Now, as you know the boss of the Dusseldorf colony of the Ndrangheta, Domenico Megale . . . wait, wait . . . I have to say this right.' He cleared his throat. 'The Italians call him . . .. *Megale u Vecchiu*. That means "Old Megale". Did I pronounce it right?'

'Sounds fine to me,' said Blume.

'Did I pronounce it right?' insisted Weissmann, a note of aggression creeping into his voice.

'It's Calabrian. In Italian it would be *il vecchio*, in Rome we'd say *er vecchio*.'

The mistrustful glint returned to Weissmann's eyes. Massimiliani darted an anxious glance at Blume, as if to appeal for his greater understanding, but did not intervene.

'We will call him by his proper name, Domenico Megale,' decided Weissmann.

'Great idea,' said Blume.

'So, this Domenico Megale was released from prison after a series of trials and sentences. He is too old to face trial again, but we think he will probably not be boss for long. Maybe already he is not.'

'I would not presume that,' said Blume. 'Italy is a country for old men. Death rather than age, sickness or incarceration stops a boss from being boss, or a prime minister from being prime minister.'

'Excellent point! Italy is controlled by evil old men: I must remember your observation. We have been watching Megale's house since his release. It is located between Duisburg and Dusseldorf, in a village called Grossenbaum. We have been noting down the number plates of vehicles, taking photographs of visitors. And one of those visitors was Konrad Hoffmann, who is now in Italy on business we know nothing about. That is the problem.'

'He is freelancing?'

'We don't know. This is what is such an embarrassment. We are very surprised at this. We wanted to see who would turn up at Megale's house to welcome him back, but we did not expect one of our own agents to go there. He arrived wearing a false moustache and unnecessary glasses. It was the worst effort at disguise anyone on the surveillance team had ever seen, and this is one of the reasons they took a particularly close look at him and circulated the image immediately. I would like to

119

put the photo of Hoffmann in disguise on the BKA intranet so everyone can be amused, except it is a serious matter,' said Weissmann, then suddenly guffawed. 'Hoffmann is a person who likes to work on his own as much as possible, and he has done well like this. The logical thing to think was that he was investigating some Eco-Mafia connection between the Ndrangheta and the Camorra. So we sent round an agent last week to his office to have a chat, but discovered he was on leave. We started looking for him, casually, with no big hurry, then it was discovered he had crossed into Italy.'

'Well, have you asked him?'

'We contacted him by phone yesterday and asked him if he was enjoying his holiday and where he was. He told us the truth. Perhaps he knew if we were calling we already knew, and were tracking his phone. He's a BKA agent, after all, and a very good one, but only behind the desk. In the field he is a disaster, as we can see from his attempt at disguise and his failure to notice a stakeout by his own colleagues. I do not think he has many friends in his department. But his record is impressive, as are his qualifications. Yeah, so . . .' Weissmann fingered his earring.

'Did you ask him where he was going?' prompted Blume.

'Ah sure, that is what I had forgotten! We asked him where he was going next, and he said he was on holiday and could not be sure. So we, very politely because he is a colleague who has contributed much, insisted that he must tell us. He said then he was going to Campania, which, of course, is an area he knows something about. But,' Weissmann paused for dramatic effect, 'what is the connection with Domenico Megale and Calabria? We are still looking through his files, but we see no evidence of a connection between the Camorra and the Ndrangheta in this area.'

'Your files can't be much good. The Camorra and Ndrangheta cooperate all the time.'

'If there is a connection and it involves German firms, which is very plausible, our man has not been sharing information with his superiors or colleagues. It would be useful to know what he is up to. This is where you come in, Commissioner.'

Massimiliani clapped his hands in a businesslike fashion to indicate that they had said enough. He nodded at Weissmann, said 'thank you' in English as if they were at a conference, then switched straight into Italian.

'Winfried likes me to speak Italian now and then so he can practise,' he said to Blume. He raised his voice, '*Tutt'a posto se faccio così*, Winfried?'

The BKA commander gave the sort of cheery wave like Blume and Massimiliani were two friends visible from a distance but out of earshot.

'I don't think he does understand much,' said Blume, watching the German's face for signs of comprehension.

'You'd be surprised, he's a wily old bastard. He phoned Hoffmann himself this morning, and told him that the Italians needed a favour, and that he and Hoffmann just happened to be in the right place at the right time to do it. He told Hoffmann to come here, saying we Italians, disorganized as always, suddenly need to send an undercover agent down to Campania. Konrad was asked to provide the cover, and of course he could not say no, holiday or no holiday. I don't imagine he really believes we need him, a German, to infiltrate an Italian into Italy, but Weissmann put him on the spot.'

'One of those tricky lies that you can't challenge without revealing that you, too, are lying,' said Blume.

'Right. So everyone is pretending that we need to attach an undercover police officer to him for purposes that we would prefer not to talk about. The pretend undercover agent is you, of course.'

'What's my cover story?' asked Blume.

'You are going to tell him you are investigating toxic dumping, but obviously you can't say much. That's why the material I gave you on Friday night should be enough for you to bluff with. You know a bit about the subject now. You tell him that your mission is secret, and that your bosses thought it would be good to have you join him and pretend to be one of two German tourists travelling into Campania, the Amalfi coast.'

'He won't believe that if he's smart.'

'He wore a false moustache and missed a stakeout by his own colleague so he could visit a Mafia boss just out of jail. It is possible he is not smart at all.'

'They've had three days already to find out what this Hoffmann is up to. He doesn't sound as if he's going to fall for my undercover stuff. If he starts asking me about the Camorra, that file you gave me the other night was pretty thin even for bluffing purposes.'

'I realize that. If at any point you feel that he should simply be stopped, let us know. Bear in mind also that we or his bosses in the BKA might come to the same decision and intervene. But in the meantime, why not see what we can find out? I see this as a perfect opportunity for you to get a feel for what working undercover might be like.'

Blume looked doubtful.

'The best way to see what Hoffmann is up to is to let him start doing it without letting on. Covertly track where he goes, who he meets. Not assign someone to him.'

'That's exactly what the BKA wanted, but we really can't let that happen. We can't have a German agent apparently freelancing in a delicate area, just ahead of the Ndrangheta summit, too. Our first idea was just to stop him. Assigning someone to him was a compromise, and we only agreed to that once we were as sure as we could be this was not some sort of set-up.'

'Good job you trust them, I'd hate to see what distrust looks like.'

'Use that phone to report to us and keep it on you at all times so we can see where you are.'

Blume turned to the BKA chief and said in English, 'Your rogue agent will cancel whatever plans he had as soon as I turn up.'

'*Ich bitte Sie, das ist doch offenkundig!*' Weissmann muttered something else that Blume failed to catch, then laughed, stood up and, for some reason, gave Massimiliani a blow on the back, presumably intended as a friendly gesture. 'Sorry, I must speak English.'

Massimiliani had claimed he liked the German commander, but Blume caught a flash of outrage on his face at being thumped so heartily on the back.

'I just said it was obvious he would have changed his plans,' explained Weissmann, 'if his plans are something he means to keep secret, which they may not be. It is also possible that he has something so urgent that he means to do it anyhow, or it is possible that by putting you in his company we are preventing him from doing something. We will continue to examine his files and movements until we find out something.'

'Why not just follow him discreetly?' asked Blume. He could see Massimiliani was annoyed he was repeating the question to Weissmann. 'I mean before now,' he specified.

'That is what we have been doing since Friday evening,' said Weissmann. 'But we have been monitoring him only at a distance, using his phone and credit card, without the direct involvement of any Italian police. He has been in the Tyrol, like many Germans, but now he is heading south.'

'You called him,' said Blume. 'So now he knows his movements are being observed. Frankly, this does not seem to have been particularly brilliant.'

Weissmann grinned and gave him a thumbs-up. He had a fat silver ring on the base of his thumb and a tiny cobweb tattoo on his palm. 'It was so dumb, yeah, so dumb.'

But it was not so dumb. To follow a rogue agent in Italy, the BKA either had to launch a large and expensive surveillance operation using their own people, and risk getting caught and losing trust with the Italians, or they had to rely on a team of Italian police doing the surveillance for them on one of their own men, which he could see was not an attractive prospect either. Add to that the fact that Blume and this Hoffmann character seemed to be tilting more or less in the same direction against the same *locale* in Germany, and were both prepared to use unorthodox and secretive ways to do it, and they seemed made for one another. Blume also realized, with a flush of shame, that he and the German must also appear as two fools on an errand. Hoffmann's disguise had been penetrated at once, Blume's forging of Maria Itria's transcript was discovered within hours.

Weissmann gave him a friendly nod and, for good measure, another thumbs-up.

'Babysit him and talk to him,' continued Massimiliani in Italian. 'Try to find out whatever you can while we and the BKA try to find out about this new connection between Domenico Megale and the Camorra.'

Weissmann came up and extended his hand, but vertically, like he wanted either to high-five or do one of those hand-grab, shoulder-bump, buddy-buddy moves that young people seemed to favour.

Blume chose to ignore it. Weissmann dropped his hand by his side, smiled understandingly, then aimed a left-handed punch at Blume's bicep.

'I appreciate this, Commissioner. You will do good work.'

Blume left the room, rubbing his arm.

20

Rome

A DIP IN THE terrain outside the perimeter fence of the DCSA compound gave the illusion that the area towards which they were headed was contiguous with the car park surrounding the IKEA emporium about half a kilometre away.

They left the air-conditioned building, and Blume thought the heat outside was not as bad as he had feared, but a few paces and the soaking sensation on his back reminded him that Roman heat was cumulative as well as humid. The no-man's land that separated them from IKEA was filled with yellowing fennel, run to seed, which clogged the air with a scent of hay and aniseed that threatened to make him sneeze. As he kept up with Massimiliani, who walked at a quick pace, he caught flickering glimpses through the railings of broken ancient Roman brickwork and low mounds, beneath which lay tombs emptied of their treasures.

'You were meant to hand in your phone, Blume.'

'What's this thing about my phone?'

'It's standard undercover procedure. You get a phone full of innocuous-looking numbers, nothing that connects back, nothing that can compromise.'

'I see,' said Blume. 'Except I'm not going properly undercover, am I?'

Massimiliani hesitated.

'Am I?' said Blume.

'No,' said Massimiliani finally. 'We considered it. We even set in process a procedure to get you some different ID . . . but you've never been trained. A three-day course will do at a pinch . . . Just try to sell Hoffmann the idea you are working undercover and have more to hide than him.'

'I'll try.'

'Great! There it is: that camper van parked under the pink mimosa.'

'There is no such thing as a pink mimosa,' said Blume. 'That's a Persian silk tree.'

'Really?'

'That's its proper name,' said Blume. He pointed to the vehicle underneath the tree. 'Look at the state of that piece of junk. Thirty years old if it's a day. It's hard to tell how much of that brown and orange is design from the '70s or whenever, and how much is rust. I'd be surprised to see it move.'

'It's a Fiat Hymer,' said Massimiliani.

'Where's the car we're using?' said Blume. 'You guys have a load of great cars confiscated in asset seizures. If I could choose . . .'

'I'm sorry, I thought you understood. You're going with him in the van. It helps to hide your identity and his. A camper van is just the sort of thing a pair of German tourists would use. Two men in a saloon car: police; two men in an camper van . . .'

'Queer,' said Blume.

Massimiliani nodded sympathetically. 'I can see how you might think that,' he said. 'But think of it as an advantage in undercover terms. I don't expect you to sleep in there with him. I've made some bookings in a nice place, a hotel in Positano,' said Massimiliani. 'Separate rooms,' he added.

'Jesus,' said Blume. 'Also, is it normal for people with camper vans to use hotels?'

'Probably not, but I figured you might not want to go along with what Hoffmann professes was his original plan, which was a campsite in Salerno.'

'I've never been inside a camper van,' said Blume. 'You?'

'Dear God, no,' said Massimiliani.

Despite its age, the motor home had evidently been well looked after. 'No one in the cockpit or whatever the front bit is called,' said Blume. 'But the engine's running. What's that about?'

'He must be in the back,' said Massimiliani. 'I suppose the engine is for the air-conditioning.' He knocked on the side of the van, and the door swung open.

The man who stepped out was painfully thin, remarkably tall and, worst of all, bare-chested, apparently feeling unselfconscious about his cream-white skin and the wispy strawberry-coloured hairs that branched out beneath his nipples. His hair was fiery red, and his arms, neck, throat and face were covered in long brown freckles. He was barefoot, and as he touched the hot ground, he winced, showing teeth that seemed glassy and translucent, and were surrounded by an excess of gum.

'You are the man whom I must accompany?' asked the German in English.

'That's me. Commissioner Blume, Alec Blume.' He reluctantly held out his hand, expecting the German's hand to be sweaty, but it was perfectly dry and the handshake seemed normal enough: as robust and unenthusiastic as his own.

'Konrad Hoffmann. We can go now. I have been waiting too long already.'

The German's English pronunciation was almost perfect, slightly American even.

Blume turned to Massimiliani and, speaking Italian, said, 'I get into this freakmobile from the '70s and we drive down to Positano. That's it?'

Instead of answering him, Massimiliani turned to the German who, thankfully, had retired to fetch a white T-shirt and was pulling it over his head. He stood there watching them for a while, then climbed into the cab, pointedly slammed shut the door, and sat in the driver's seat gunning the motor.

'Oh,' said Massimiliani. 'Almost forgot . . .' He pulled an envelope from his inside pocket and handed it to Blume. 'Cash. That's to pay the hotel and expenses. You can sign for it when you get back.'

'I didn't bring an overnight bag,' said Blume.

'Did I not mention you would need one?'

'You didn't even mention the journey.'

'Sorry. We only decided on our tactics definitely this morning, while you were in the conference room.'

'But the idea was there since Friday?' said Blume.

'Yes,' said Massimiliani. 'I am so used to working on a need-to-know basis . . .'

'That you can't even tell someone to bring a change of clothes?'

'That's one of the reasons I gave you that money.'

'Underpants money. Great.'

The camper van gave a blast of its horn.

'See?' said Massimiliani. 'Leave a German in the sun for a bit and he turns into an Italian. I bet he never hit his horn outside a police headquarters in Dusseldorf. He's not going out of that gate without my clearance or without you. By the way, I've had your car sent back to your station at Collegio Romano.'

'How thoughtful of you,' said Blume. 'At least promise me that if you find out anything useful about this guy and why he went to visit Megale, you'll let me know.'

'We'll keep you informed, you keep us informed. Enjoy your trip.'

Blume climbed into the camper van beside the German who had had the decency also to put on a pair of white trainers. As soon as he was in, the security gate started to roll slowly open.

'This is a farce,' said Konrad, revving the engine in a threatening manner, but then driving out of the gate with exceeding care.

'I agree,' said Blume.

'I want you to know that this camper van was built in 1989, the year the Berlin Wall fell. I bought it second-hand in 1990.'

'World Cup year. You guys won. Unless you're East German. Did you buy it to come down here to see the matches?'

'That was one reason.'

Blume reflected for a moment. 'Why do you think I care when this camper was made?'

'You said it was from the 1970s.'

'You mean when I was talking to Captain Massimiliani. True, I did say that. It was for rhetorical effect. I also remember saying it in Italian. So this is your way of telling me you understand Italian and I had better watch my mouth?'

Hoffmann turned to look at him. The bright sun through the dirty windscreen illuminated the tips of his pale eyelashes in a way that made Blume think of insect wings.

'My spoken Italian is good even though it is not a useful language to speak. My comprehension is perfect. For your sake I have decided we can use English.' Hoffmann signalled right. The camper wobbled and squeaked as he moved into the next lane.

'For my sake?'

'You are American-born, I am informed.'

'Who told you this?'

'His name is Weissmann.'

'Yes, I met him.'

'He is not my commander. He is from *Abteilung IK*. International Coordination. That is not my department, so he is not my boss.'

'Is he your superior officer?'

'Yes.'

'Well, then,' said Blume. Hoffmann started to reply, but Blume interrupted: 'No, don't take this exit.'

'I was told I could continue with my trip as planned, now you are telling me I cannot?'

'I want you to stop by my house first. It won't take too long,' said Blume. 'It's nearby. I have a suitcase packed and waiting by the door. It'll take me three minutes once we're there.'

'*Unter der Bedingung dass, ich bereit zu warten bin.*'

'Of course you'll wait for me, Hoffmann. I trust you.'

'You understand German?'

'I worked in a BMW factory in Munich in my youth. Every summer, almost all summer, for five years. It got me through college. I don't speak it well, but that's fine. It is not a useful language.'

21

Rome

BLUME GRABBED AN empty backpack, then opened his wardrobe only to find almost no clothes there. He was three or four washing loads behind. The only viable clothes, along with his favourite possessions, were locked in the cream-coloured hard-shelled suitcase which dated from the days before someone had thought to attach wheels to luggage. It was even older than Hoffmann's camper van. He grabbed some socks and underwear and stuffed them into the backpack, then, willing blood and power into his biceps, finally lifted the suitcase and carried it out of the apartment. He had imagined this action several times in his mind, thinking that once the suitcase passed the threshold he would have made an irrevocable decision to move out of his apartment and in with Caterina. He was relieved to discover that it was not so.

He dragged the suitcase across the courtyard and out the front gate, making sure his arm and not his back was taking the enormous strain. As he made his way down the street towards the camper van, his phone started ringing, and he cursed volubly, to hide his relief at having an excuse to drop the weight and answer. But when he saw Caterina's name on the display, his relief turned to anxiety. He hit the hang-up key with his thumb and carried the suitcase the rest of the way. Hoffmann left the cab, opened the side door, and stood inside waiting to receive the suitcase.

'Thanks,' said Blume. He counted a one-two in his head and one-two out loud as he swung it up, anticipating the pleasure of the sudden release of the weight. Hoffmann caught it with excessive nonchalance and staggered backwards, looking gratifyingly shocked at the weight of the thing.

'How long do you think we are going to be travelling for?' asked Hoffmann.

'I packed it for a different reason,' said Blume. He did not feel like adding any more but if he was supposed to find out as much as he could about Hoffmann, he needed to make an effort to seem friendly. 'It's been there for some time. I'm supposed to be moving in with my girlfriend.'

'Girlfriend. Ah. That's good. Have you been with her for long?'

'A while,' said Blume. 'She's a colleague.'

'Super. So you see each other all the time.' Konrad stepped out and closed the camper door, then locked it.

'Yes. Being always in contact with her is . . .' His phone rang again.

'You can answer that,' said Hoffmann. Blume glanced at it, saw Caterina's name, and cut it off. 'It's stopped. Look, can I just check something in my case before we go?'

'Inside the camper?' Hoffmann's blue eyes widened in exaggerated surprise.

Reluctantly, he unlocked the door and Blume stepped inside. He noted two matching soft leather suitcases nestling against each other in the back, and beside them, his own oversized and antiquated cream one. The interior was furnished with plastic wood and the metal edges with fake wood-grain siding, which suddenly disinterred a buried memory of a Buick station wagon someone's mother used to drive. He remembered sitting in the back, his bare legs stuck to the vinyl bench seats, as the car, an enormous thing, glided down the freeway like a fat boat on a muddy river. In Europe, you could always feel the rumble of the wheels. You were always aware of the surface of the road.

Stuck to the fake wood-board above the curtain that separated the living area from the front cab was a photo of a young woman. To judge from the pale-blue tint that had washed away most of the bright colours, it was at least fifteen years old. The girl was blonde, smiling, and possibly pretty, but the flat colour and absence of shadow made it hard to form a clear idea of what she was like. She was standing in front of a camper van, which, Blume guessed, was the one he was standing in.

He felt Hoffmann's eyes on his back and realized he had been under observation. What with the careful positioning of the photo in the dead centre of the small living space, above a stiff divider curtain that reminded him of a tabernacle. Blume stretched out his hand as if to touch it.

'Don't touch that!'

He turned around, making a show of being surprised to find Hoffmann there. 'Touch what? Oh, you mean the photo. Who is she?'

'An old friend.'

'You mean a young friend,' said Blume. 'But I guess you were just as young when this was taken.'

Hoffmann tapped a clear plastic watch on his wrist. 'Thanks to you we will be driving in the hottest hours of the day.'

'It's only two and a half hours to Naples, maybe a bit more in this thing. And from Naples to Positano another hour.'

Blume sat down in the passenger seat beside Hoffmann and, in a second effort to come across as friendly and helpful, began to explain the best way to get from Via Orvieto to the A1. 'Basically, back the way we've just come. Straight on till Cinecittà, then we need to go . . .'

Hoffmann pulled out a SatNav from the glove compartment beside him and stuck it to a suction mount on the windscreen.

Blume folded his arms and lapsed into offended silence.

As they left the city limits Hoffmann accelerated and the camper van responded with a soft lurching movement as if its suspension was made from marshmallows. It was showing an alarming tendency to yaw as well as pitch and roll as Konrad, like any northern European driver dealing with Italians, found his efforts to set an example of careful driving being undermined by his own paroxysms of rage, resulting in much braking and accelerating.

'Take it easy, Hoffmann.'

'My name is Konrad.'

'Konrad, OK.'

'What about you?'

'You can call me Alec, if you feel you have to.'

'OK, Alec. Why have you been assigned to ruin my holiday?'

Blume considered his response.

'I am here because I've been told to keep an eye on you, and find out what you're up to. So maybe if you just tell me, I can get out, get a taxi back, and return in triumph with a complete report.'

Konrad pointed at a fast-moving swarm of vehicles ahead. 'In Germany, we would never have vehicles come on the road before vehicles go off.'

'I have no idea what you are talking about,' said Blume.

'This is what I mean.' Konrad pointed out the window. 'Those cars are coming on to the road from the right and must come into the flow of the traffic. That is the entrance, no? And here, fifty metres farther on, we have the exit. So all the cars that want to go off must cross at high speed in front of all the cars that are coming on. This is very bad engineering.'

'Our apologies,' said Blume.

Ten minutes later, Konrad pointed to the side of the road. 'Do you notice that?'

Blume checked. The road signs seemed normal, the hilly land behind the guardrail was so dry it looked like a collection of sand dunes. One sign told him the next Agip service area was fifteen kilometres. No cars were coming on or going off the highway in an unGerman manner. 'Notice what?'

'Evidently you don't.'

'Is this some sort of German version of I-spy?'

'*Ich seh' etwas, was du nicht siehst.* Yes.'

'Konrad, I have a headache and a loaded gun. Please tell me what you are talking about.'

'I am talking about the rubbish. It is constant in Italy. There has been an unbroken line of rubbish along the road from your house to here. I was just wondering if after some time you stop noticing.'

'Sometimes I notice,' said Blume.

'Italy is like Africa in this respect. Have you ever been to Africa?'

'Does Morocco count?' said Blume.

'Technically yes, but not Arab Africa. Below. I was in Conakry for a week. They have the same problem as you. Plastic refuse everywhere. It's a sign of a failed state.'

'It gets tidier as you move north in Italy,' said Blume. 'By the time you get to Germany, everything is perfect.'

'Have you read Jeremy Bentham?'

'Can't say I have,' said Blume.

'He founded utilitarianism – but he copied Kant, of course. As a utilitarian, I say there is an argument to be made for inflicting the death penalty on someone who throws rubbish on the street or defaces a public building.'

Blume was trying to read his companion's face. Right now, Konrad's mouth was showing an excess of gum, which possibly meant he was smiling.

But as Blume began forming a complicit grin, Konrad closed his mouth into a tight line and straightened his face. 'It is a serious point. Take a landscape that has been ruined as completely as this. We can calculate it on the felific index. First, you must add up all the distress of the hundreds of thousands of people who pass through it, the sense of disgust and depression, as well as the anger, frustration and what I must imagine is self-hatred and justifiable sense of inferiority among many Italians. If you total the negative emotions, and keep in mind that these are feelings people experience over and over, every day, as they drive or walk by all these ruined sites, then you can say that the sum of human harm done must exceed the harm done by a single murder, or even multiple murders.'

'Throwing an ice-cream wrapper equals mass murder . . . You're not Catholic, are you?'

'I am atheist,' said Konrad.

For the next forty minutes they continued in silence. The road was clear and they were making good progress.

Eventually Konrad said, 'Do you like music?'

'That definitely depends,' said Blume warily. He had heard German death metal, Bavarian brass bands and the alienated electronic squawks of experimental stuff from Berlin. He looked at the flaking silver buttons on the car stereo.

Konrad followed his glance. 'I was not saying I would play music, I just wanted to know if you liked it.'

'Yes, I do,' said Blume.

'I like *lieder* by Schumann, Schubert, Wolf and Mahler. I know the entire *Winterreise*. Do you know it?' Konrad unexpectedly took an exit from the autostrada.

'No. Where are we going? We should have stayed on the autostrada.'

'Schubert's most famous song cycle? I learned it many years ago, and I can play the piano accompaniment, too. They say I have a very fine singing voice.'

'Do they? Why are we taking this exit?'

'It is my holiday, no?' Konrad rolled to a stop at the toll gate, and slotted a credit card into the machine. The machine sucked it in, thought about it a bit, then spat it out and flashed a message.

Konrad tried again, without any better luck.

'Use mine,' said Blume. 'I've got *fastpay* on it.'

'That is very kind.'

The machine deducted another 14 euros from Blume's disastrous bank account and the barrier lifted. As Konrad handed back the card, Blume's phone, his 'proper' one as he now thought of it, started ringing.

'Caterina! I was just about to call you.'

'Are you avoiding me?'

'No. I've been busy. I couldn't take calls. Has anyone been on to you about me?'

'Nobody has contacted me.'

'Someone from the DCSA or the Questura should. Basically, to explain that I'm going away for a few days –'

'Where?'

'At the moment, we're just entering Campania. But I'm not sure if I am supposed to tell you even that. I'm sure I can talk about it later.'

'You said "we". Who else is there?'

'Another policeman. A sort of policeman. Really, I'm not going to say more.'

'How many days?'

'I don't know. Two, three. Caterina, stop asking questions.'

'Fine. But you . . .' Her voice became a metallic stutter as they passed an area of poor reception, but Blume did not ask her to repeat whatever she had said. It sounded like a reprimand of some sort, or maybe it was the robotic quality of her voice.

'This is not a good line,' he said.

'I can hear you perfectly well. Why aren't you calling me?'

'Stuff, you know. Unexpectedly busy, I'm calling you now.'

'No, *I* called *you*.'

'Yeah, well we're both holding a phone and talking, so my basic point still stands.'

'If holding the phone is tiring you . . .'

'No, no. Of course not.'

His new phone vibrated and chimed cutely in his pocket. Having two phones was going to be as stressful as having a watch. The display showed a message: 'Text from Mamma.'

He jabbed at the icon, but the touch screen had evidently been designed for some future elfin race with tapered fingers and a steady aim. Even giving it his full attention, he could not manage to tap the animated envelope on whatever magic spot might reveal the text they had sent him. He pulled out a pen and struck at it in vain. He slapped the phone several times against the top of the dashboard, which drew a disapproving scowl from Konrad who was now hurtling down a secondary road at full speed like he knew where he was going and someone's life depended on it.

'Alec?' said Caterina.

'Yes,' said Blume, throwing his new phone on the floor in front of him. 'I'm still here.'

'I have to go up to Milan in a few days. Magistrate Bazza, the one who took over the case then decided not to tell me anything? I don't much like the sound of this magistrate.'

'No?' said Blume. 'Why not?'

'I just said: he held back information from me when I was investigating.'

'That's normal enough, Caterina.'

'I know, but a good magistrate holds back for strategic reasons. The point is to trip up the suspects, not the investigators.'

'Maybe you're being too sensitive.'

'Too emotional and female, you mean?'

'That's not what I meant at all, but now that you mention it . . .'

'A good magistrate's interest in a case is always based on a desire to know what might be useful. That's what Arconti was like, wasn't it?'

'I guess,' said Blume.

'From what I've seen, this Milan magistrate is interested in this case because he likes to know things that others don't.'

Blume was about to advise her to be careful dealing with the magistrate in Milan, if only for the sake of her career prospects, but Konrad decided to roll down his window and fill the cab with thunderous warm wind, and then started singing.

'*Soll denn kein Angedenken*
Ich nehmen mit von hier?'

'Just keep doing what you're doing!' Blume roared into the mouthpiece and pressed his phone harder against his ear.

'It's noisy where I am!' he explained, motioning at Konrad to roll up the window and shut up. Konrad ignored him. Blume cupped both hands over the earpiece.

'Alec, you would tell me, wouldn't you, if your journey was connected to the Arconti case?'

'No.'

'No you wouldn't tell me, or . . .'

> *'Wenn meine Schmerzen schweigen,*
> *Wer sagt mir dann von ihr?'*

Blume put the phone down. 'For Christ's sake, Konrad!' He brought it back to his ear. 'Listen, let's not mix things up, Caterina. I'll call you back soon.' He hung up abruptly.

Konrad stopped singing. Blume couldn't decide whether he had been serious or was engaging in some sort of exercise in humour that only Germans appreciated. Konrad's tenor voice had, in fact, been quite good.

The real problem was Konrad's driving. He was bouncing in his seat and swinging the steering wheel left and right like a five-year-old pretending to steer as he swerved around the potholes and sought to avoid the bumps in the road. The sunlight was lighting up his fiery hair and streaming directly into his face so that there was no way he could possibly see where he was going.

'That was not the right exit for Positano, or Naples, or even Salerno,' shouted Blume above the rushing air.

'I am perfectly aware of where I am going,' said Konrad, his tone now scornful. He swerved around one pothole but hit a second, larger one, almost bouncing Blume into his lap.

Blume steadied himself. 'Oh yeah, and where might that be?'

'To the gates of hell,' shouted Konrad, facetious as ever.

22

Near Pozzuoli, Naples

'We could get a bite to eat at that *osteria*,' suggested Blume.
Konrad continued driving.

'I'm hungry,' said Blume. 'It's past two. We're going to miss lunch if we don't stop. If I skip a meal, first I get a blinding headache, then I start killing Germans. Seriously, I need to eat. It's a blood-sugar thing.'

'You are a diabetic,' said Konrad. It did not sound like a question; it sounded more like a reprimand. 'That *osteria* is abandoned. You can see it has not been painted or restored in fifty years. I did a course in urban tracking in 2002. We were taught to see things at a glance. The trick is to see the whole thing and the details, and keep moving, while you consider the implications of what you have captured in the first glance.'

The camper van dipped and its suspension groaned as Konrad drove them through a series of potholes and over a lattice of tree roots that had burst out of the tarmac.

'So you'll have noticed the five cars and the van parked outside it?' said Blume, when the rocking had stopped.

'Yes, of course I saw them.'

'So, Konrad, it is not abandoned. It is still serving lunch.'

Konrad slowed down. 'My point is that eating at this time of the day is bad for clear thinking.'

'OK. Forget it. You're obviously in a hurry to get to . . . where is it you want to get to?'

'Lake Avernus,' said Konrad. 'But now I am looking for a place to turn, so that we can go back.'

'To the abandoned *osteria*?'

'I now recognize that it is not abandoned. I was not focused at the time. Now it is all clear in my mind's eye.'

The *osteria* served food directly to the table without any menu. Two bottles of water, a jug of wine and a basket of bread sat between them. Walking quickly by, the waiter placed two dishes of *caprese* in front of them. Konrad tried to say something in Italian to the waiter, who listened patiently, an expression of pity verging on concern in his eyes. When Konrad had finished his incomprehensible sentence, the waiter gave him an encouraging smile and moved away to deal with normal people.

Blume quartered his mozzarella, speared a tomato slice and, with the help of a piece of bread, pushed the mozzarella on to his fork. It was sweet and creamy.

'My speaking skills are rusty,' said Konrad.

'Corroded, I'd say,' said Blume. 'I didn't understand a word.'

'*Non è che io non sappia parlare italiano, sai?*' said Konrad.

'Now I understand you fine,' said Blume. 'How come you didn't speak like that to the waiter?'

'I was speaking Campanian dialect.'

This time, there seemed to be no humorous undertow in Konrad's demeanour. 'Are you serious?'

'Of course. Perhaps the waiter isn't from these parts.'

'Apart from the fact you were entirely incomprehensible . . .' Blume replayed Konrad's phrases in his mind and began to laugh. 'Dialect . . . with that accent. You should be on *Zelig*.'

'What is this *Zelig*?'

'A TV show for stand-ups.' Blume tried to suppress his laughter. The trick was not to think of . . . No, it was no good.

Three minutes later, drying his eyes with the back of his hand, Blume said, 'No foreigner can ever speak dialect. You might pick up some of the accent if you stayed here long enough, but you can't speak dialect.' He looked at Konrad's plate. 'You haven't touched your *caprese*. Why are you not eating that mozzarella *di bufala*? That is local produce, and this is the best area in the country for mozzarella.'

'I am not sure I like it. I would have preferred to choose from the menu.'

Blume stripped a crust off a piece of bread and crunched it between his teeth. 'No menu here.' He pressed the flat of his knife on the mozzarella, bleeding milk across his plate.

The waiter came back, stared wordlessly at Konrad, then removed his mozzarella and tomato. The next course was homemade pasta and San Marzano tomato sauce with plenty of basil.

Once again, Konrad sat immobile, ignoring his food.

'No wonder you're thin,' said Blume. 'What's wrong that you're not eating your pasta?'

'I must not be hungry.'

'Then leave the fucking bread alone.'

Konrad took his hand out of the bread basket and tucked it guiltily under the table.

'That's better,' said Blume. 'Now eat up. And let's get some business out of the way.'

'What business?'

'Your colleagues saw you in the company of an Ndrangheta boss. Domenico Megale, to be precise.'

Konrad looked so utterly shocked that Blume burst out laughing. 'I can't quite work out when you're trying to be funny, but there's no mistaking when you're shocked. It seems you wore a disguise so bad they want to use it as a sort of reverse example.'

'As soon as Weissmann called me, I realized there was a good chance they had seen me.'

'Why the look of shock, then?'

'I am only very surprised they should have told you this. After all, who are you?'

'Don't try to turn the questioning around.'

'Are you particularly expert?'

'No,' said Blume.

'Then you must have a direct interest in this. What is the link between you and Megale?'

'The questions are still flowing in the wrong direction, Konrad. I have already levelled with you. Time to reciprocate. Give me something I can put in a report.'

'I am observant,' said Konrad. 'I saw immediately that you have no ring on your finger, but you have a girlfriend.'

'She is above all a colleague,' said Blume.

'Tell me about your relationship with this woman.'

'Fuck off.'

Konrad blinked a few times as if he was trying to compute something. His long nose, pointed chin and sad mouth gave him the appearance of a mistreated horse. Eventually, the cogs of his logic stopped whirring and he delivered his finding. 'If there is a woman in your life, then you must be happy,' he told Blume. 'But you are running away from her.'

The suddenly personal turn in the conversation disconcerted Blume. The least he could do was regain his function as the person asking the questions. 'Do you have a girl?'

It was unlikely, surely, but women were strange. Sometimes they became overwhelmed with such intense feelings of pity for spectacularly ugly men that they ended up marrying them.

'Not any more,' said Konrad. 'Not for a long time.'

'That can be good. It gives you time to concentrate on your work,' said Blume. He did not believe this for a moment. All the extra hours made available by not being in a relationship were filled obsessing on what was so wrong with you that women could not bear to be near you. Then as soon as you found someone, you began to long for the solitude you thought you hated.

Blume steered the conversation back towards pertinent issues. 'Have you found some connection between the Camorra and the Ndrangheta? Is that what this is about? They both specialize in poisoning the earth, which is your area of expertise, right?'

'It is one of my areas of expertise,' said Konrad. 'I have been engaged in a long investigation into toxic dumping, and that involved the Camorra, of course. The investigation is now over, prosecutions have been made. I am an acknowledged authority by now. There is talk of me writing the preface to Saviano's next book. As an expert in Italian crime, I obviously know a good deal about the Ndrangheta, but I have no evidence of a direct connection between the organizations.'

'What about the visit to Megale's house?'

'Did they see me leaving or entering?'

Blume racked his brain. He couldn't remember what he had been told. 'Both, I imagine.'

'But you don't know. I will admit that I have been privately studying the Ndrangheta a little, and maybe talking with an exponent of that organization.'

'Well, that's a start,' said Blume.

'I am very surprised at what I have found.'

'And what is that?'

'It is a very effective and quiet organization and extremely efficient. I thought Italians could never be that organized.'

'That's because you've been dealing with the Camorra. They are chaotic,' said Blume. 'With 100,000 men they can't control Naples, but with around 30,000 the Ndrangheta controls Europe, Australia and fifteen African states as well as Central and South America, and has a turnover about the same as the GDP of Slovakia, or Slovenia . . . or Serbia. I can never remember which.'

'The obvious conclusion is that Italians are organized only in crime,' said Konrad. 'I think that is undeniable.'

'That sort of facile conclusion is why you Germans are so useless as investigators,' said Blume. 'The Ndrangheta has taken over East Germany better than the Soviets ever did. They own all the seafront houses in the Baltic, they control half the municipalities in the Ruhr valley and all the drug money in all your cities except for Berlin where they allow the Moroccans to sell hashish, on a franchise basis. They import metals for your industries, take out the waste, and clean the money. They mediate between the Russians and your industries, and they help capitalize your banks. They know how to wait, to accept sacrifice, to tough it out, to hide wealth, to remain mute, help each other, bide their time. They can do that better than any German criminals, and they can do it better than your politicians and businessmen. They own you.'

'You sound almost proud of what they do.'

'Italians are better at self-sacrifice, discipline and savings than anyone else in Europe and, above all, they – we – are extremely organized. The problem is that we divide into units that are too small. We organize into families instead of neighbourhoods, neighbourhoods instead of towns, towns instead of provinces, provinces instead of regions, and regions instead of a country. The same goes for our industries. They're always too small. We have the same problem in the police. Basically, we should have just one force. But we are an organized people. Just look at an Italian travelling. Neat, clean, everything planned, budgeted. The northern Europeans are chaotic, dirty, dishevelled, lost, drunk, loutish . . . As for your police and their efforts to stop drug smuggling, words fail me. Eat your lunch, what's the matter with you: are you some sort of fucking anorexic?'

141

'Dioxins,' said Konrad.

'What?'

'This food. It is probably all poisoned. We are in Campania. I know about this region. People burn rubbish in the streets and fill the air with dioxins from burning plastics. The Camorra has filled the land with heavy metals and maybe even nuclear materials. You keep telling me the food was produced locally. But I don't want to eat produce grown from the toxic soils of Campania. These are filthy people, *ein Dreckvolk*, and I do not want their food.'

'You ate the bread.'

A gratifying look of panic crossed across Konrad's face.

The waiter, who had taken back Konrad's untouched plates one after the other, now came over to find out what was going on.

'*Non si sente bene*,' Blume explained. '*No, figurati, il cibo era ottimo. Poi, è un tedesco, quindi non capisce un cazzo né della buona cucina, né delle buone maniere.*'

Konrad had pulled out a notebook and was writing something down. In the middle of all Konrad's extravagantly curly hair was a great bald patch where the freckles looked like liver spots. From above, Konrad looked like an old man, and this pleased Blume immensely.

Konrad paused in his writing for a moment to look up and smile at Blume, saying, quite mildly, 'You forget I understand when you speak Italian and insult me to the waiter.'

'I didn't forget. I just wanted to make sure the waiter understood. What are you writing?'

'Some of what you said is interesting. I am making a note. One of the reasons I am good at my job is I am willing to learn.' Konrad put away his pen and notebook.

'Konrad, just tell me why you visited that Ndrangheta boss. Personally, I don't give a damn. In fact, if it leads to your imprisonment or death, that's fine by me. It's between you and your superiors. I just need something to take back so it looks like I did some work here. You get that, don't you?'

'You are so full of suspicions but do you . . . do you know anything about me, Commissioner?'

'I am rapidly forming some ideas.'

'Years ago I was on my way to becoming a professor or an archaeologist,' said Konrad, 'but I switched universities and became a federal policeman instead.' He downed a glass of wine, then cleared his throat. 'My Latin and

Greek are excellent,' he continued. 'My Latin professor once asked me to explain my method for learning vocabulary so fast, so that he might teach it to his other students.' He paused and peered at Blume, then shook his head sadly. 'I don't think you have the right sort of mind for my technique. You lack patience and humility, as well as a classical background, of course.'

'You're making me feel really small.'

'But I think even you may know that Ndrangheta is a Greek word, it comes from *andrangathos*, which means "courageous man".'

'Are you absolutely sure about that?' said Blume. 'You're convinced you are not talking bullshit?'

'Of course I am sure. Calabria was part of Magna Graecia and ancient Greek words are still spoken there.'

'So you're telling me Ndrangheta is an ancient name?' asked Blume.

'Yes. I am assuming you have not studied these things. Obviously, you have no knowledge of ancient Greek.'

'Italian kids still do Greek and Latin, at least if they go to a *Liceo Classico*, which I did. There's nothing ancient Greek about those Calabrian thugs. Don't believe anything they say. Even their name is a lie. The organization you have placed back in the mists of time basically came into being in 1975. So, once again, you have understood nothing.'

'I hate to correct you . . .'

'Then don't. It's all made up. There's no ancient custom. When I was a student, the name was hardly even used. It doesn't date back much further than the War – you know, the one you guys started and lost.'

'Italy lost first,' said Konrad.

'Italy was misrepresented by its leaders, and changed sides. And I was speaking as an American there.'

'I have studied the rites of the Ndrangheta. Some of them are based on ancient custom.'

'It's all bullshit,' said Blume. 'All those rites are taken from the Freemasons, another bunch of bullshit artists. This Ndrangheta mythology was basically invented yesterday. Like I said, until the 1980s they were just called the Calabrian Mafia. For a while it was called the Maffia, with two "f"s; before that, people just called them the Camorra, or bandits.'

'So they do go back in time.'

'Sure they go back in time,' said Blume. 'Everything and everyone goes back in time. We all come from somewhere.'

23

Locri

ROBERTINO AWOKE AS his mother was making lunch, and, noting she was not within touching distance, began to make his displeasure known through a mixture of griping and straining efforts to escape from the trap of his baby bouncer.

His mother seemed to be more stressed than usual by his antics, and sensing this, the child raised the stakes, adding cries to his grunting efforts to break free.

'Please, not now. Ruggiero!' she called. 'Come in here! Pick up your brother. Keep him quiet for ten minutes, would you?'

Despite arching his back and going red from the strain of trying to break out of his bouncer, it turned out the last thing in the world Robertino wanted was to be removed from it, at least not by his brother. Griping became screaming.

'Shut that child up!' shouted his mother. 'Get him out of here.'

'But he's hungry,' protested Ruggiero.

'What the hell do you think I am doing, standing at this stove for the fun of it?'

Ruggiero eventually found a game that Robertino liked, which consisted of singing pee-poh-pah-dah on a sliding scale and touching him on the forehead, nose, chin and tummy, over and over and over again. By the time lunch was ready, the infant had dissolved into peals of laughter, which quickly became infectious and lifted the mood.

As she finished spoon-feeding Robertino a pap made out of meat stock and semolina, his mother said, 'Your father will be here in a few days. He can't say when. He'll sort things out, if anything needs sorting out, of course.'

'I know.'

'Because something is going on. Yesterday Zia Rosa was in a panic about Enrico not coming home. I tried not to let her infect me with her fear, but I was worried, too.'

When Ruggiero had arrived home the evening before, this mother had been studiously casual about his temporary disappearance. He had been at once hurt by her indifference and proud of her strength.

'It was bad for Enrico. Not me.'

'Was it?' His mother was fond enough of Enrico, though she tended to use him as a yardstick with which to measure the superiority of her own son.

'Who else was there?' asked his mother.

'Pepè, Luca, Giovanni and Rocco.'

'What did they tell you?'

'Nothing, Mamma. It was all about football.'

'You say they treated you well and Enrico poorly? Who is "they"?'

'The others. My friends,' said Ruggiero.

'Friends,' she said contemptuously. 'The only friend you should trust is an ex-enemy, because then you have the measure of him. What was said?'

'Nothing was said.'

'Did you feel isolated?'

'A little. But that's just part of being a Curmaci, isn't it?'

His mother spooned up semolina from Robertino's chin and deftly dropped it into his mouth. Robertino made slow fish-like movements with his mouth, still tasting the semolina broth, interested in, but wary of, the flavour. 'One day, you're at the market buying some fresh spinach, and you see someone you sort of know, and you suddenly realize he is standing on his own in the middle of the crowd. The flow of people past him divides too early to avoid him, as if he were a large obstacle rather than a single person.'

'Who are we talking about, Mamma?'

'Someone you never knew. But it could be anyone. Then as you watch him, you realize no one has mentioned his name in weeks. Then, one day he's gone, and you are not surprised. Either his body is found in Filadelfia with no face left on it after a shotgun blast, or he disappears from the face of the earth. You wonder why he didn't see it coming, but the answer is that he did. But he could not think what to do, and could not imagine leaving.'

'Papà is not like that.'

'Of course not. He's far stronger.'

'I don't think I'd be like that either,' said Ruggiero. 'I'd fight rather than wait like a lamb for the slaughter.'

'If you couldn't fight, what then?'

'Would I run?'

'Yes.'

'I don't know.'

'My last phone call with your father was . . . strange.'

Ruggiero shifted uncomfortably in his seat. He wanted to hear, but she was drawing him into the intimate sphere of husband and wife, a place he had not been before. It sounded like she was looking for advice, and he was not sure he could give it.

'We have a sort of code . . .' She took his arm and stroked it. With a smile to lessen the significance of his action, he drew his arm away.

'Sorry. You're getting too old for my caresses,' she said.

'It's just that . . . Tell me about your code.'

'There isn't much to it. Papà said all we needed were a few key words and a tone. The words themselves don't matter. For instance, if he mentioned the toy box in Robertino's room, it indicated urgency.'

The box had used to be his, and before that his father's. It was bright red with sharp edges, and it snapped shut like a shark over bait whenever you leaned into it to pull out a toy.

'Did he mention the box?'

'Yes. And he warned me both about the authorities and about our neighbours. But then he reminded me he was on his way down in a few days. He said that plainly. Then we spoke of meals in a way that made it sound like code, but it wasn't. In the end the messages were so mixed I couldn't understand what he was telling me.'

'Anyone listening in will have picked up that he was coding messages, even if they didn't understand the meaning,' said Ruggiero.

'Listen to you, the expert,' said his mother with affection, instinctively reaching out to caress his arm again, then stopping herself. 'He often has fun like that, teasing any judicial police that might be listening in, but in this case he wanted anyone, not just the police, to be suspicious and confused.'

'So his message was that he can't pass on messages.'

'Which means he's worried about more than just the police, and he wants us to be, too. And then yesterday, you . . .'

'That was nothing, Mamma. But he'll be here soon. All we have to do is wait.'

Ruggiero trusted his father, and believed in his strength, but sometimes had to concentrate a little before he could call up a clear picture of his face. When his father did come home from Germany, he was always an unhealthy white colour. His clothes smelled foreign, and he sometimes seemed to have a slight difficulty with speaking Italian, exaggerating the dialect when talking to Ruggiero, but soon running out of things to say. Then he would start talking about the funny things the Germans said and believed, and he would praise their cars and roads. His father and mother would retire into their bedroom, speak in private tones, then the volume would drop still further, and yet he could still hear them hushing each other and stifling sounds that were already muted.

He knew now what they were up to. Luca once claimed to have watched his parents through the keyhole, but then altered his story when Pepè accused him of perversion.

Even without Luca's graphic eyewitness accounts, by now they all knew what their returning fathers did with their mothers – hence the arrival of Roberto, or Robertino as he immediately became known and would probably remain for the rest of his life. All the kids had a father who worked abroad, except Pepè whose father ran the garage. Enrico, of course, lived with his aunt and uncle. His mother had died from breast cancer several years after Enrico was born, and his father showed no interest in finding a replacement either in Germany or Calabria. Enrico claimed he remembered his mother's face, but she was dead before he was four, which made his claim as unreliable as most of what he said.

The one thing Ruggiero knew for certain was that no matter what happened, his father would do the right thing, and that anything his father told him to do he would do. The Curmacis might not be the most loved family, but Basile, too, was unloved, had few surviving blood relatives, yet his writ extended as far as Filadelfia. People might whisper about the Curmacis, but no one would ever dare say out loud that Agazio Curmaci was an *infame*, which made the atmosphere of intimidation in the bar yesterday hard to accept.

He went up to his bedroom. His father would soon return to the village and on September 2nd they would attend the procession of the Madonna di Polsi and enjoy a fine picnic afterwards, where he would be encouraged by his father to drink wine and warned by his mother not to. Together he and his father would display quiet confidence.

Downstairs, his mother was moving back and forth as if cleaning the house. Ruggiero lay on his bed, closed his eyes and inhaled its familiar smell, the smell that had accompanied him through his childhood. He wished his father were here already, guarding the doors, fighting for his family.

24

Lake Avernus, Pozzuoli–Naples

KONRAD WAS TALKING again.

'It is logical for people with serious communication problems, or who are autistic or aggressive or sociopathic or suffer from Asperger's syndrome, to choose to leave their home environment and live in a foreign land. I think this might explain some of the characteristics of the American people. Maladapted Europeans and captive Africans.'

'Indeed?' said Blume. Most of his energy was going into keeping the camper van on the road.

'Yes, because people with serious problems in their relationships, if they are intelligent, travel away from their home and stay away. When they are abroad, they always have a pretext for acting alienated and their incapacity to relate to normal society becomes part of their foreignness. People will often justify their strange and sometimes unpleasant behaviour on the grounds of cultural differences and homesickness,' said Konrad. 'America was built by people like these. Also, if I might add, they were not very efficient people. These "pioneers" had an entire continent at their disposal as well as slave labour, yet their empire has lasted less time than the Macedonian kingdom. And as for comparing it with the Roman or Greek empires . . .'

'You're just in a bad mood because you haven't eaten,' said Blume.

'I am not in a bad mood. But you are not a relaxing driver.'

'You shouldn't have drunk so much wine on an empty stomach, then you could be at the wheel.'

'You are right. You will take me to Lake Avernus before we go on to Positano.'

'Was that a question or an order?' said Blume.

Konrad bent his head down so he could look out the window at the scenery around him. From the doleful head-shaking that followed, Blume knew what turn the conversation was about to take.

After several minutes Konrad said, 'This country is filthy. So far every verge has been filled with rubbish and every road is full of potholes. Everything is falling down.'

Blume nodded, pleased at having guessed right. 'I thought you might be about to say that, because you've already said that.'

'But it is a disgrace,' said Konrad. 'Is this not a sign of inferiority? Be honest.' But instead of giving Blume a chance to be honest, he added, 'I do not think Italians will ever defeat organized crime. I think your theory about small units is quite plausible, but I don't think it fully explains the Italian tendency to illegal behaviour. Of course, I do not think the Italians are racially inclined to violence and theft . . . and bad driving. I am hardly,' he laughed at the absurdity of the idea, 'a racist.'

'The thought never even crossed my mind,' said Blume.

'. . . I think perhaps they have a virus.'

'If you're talking about the Mafia, remember that viruses spread, and Germany has been infected for some time.'

'You must understand that I am not using a metaphor. I am referring to a real virus, a biological virus. Are you all right, Commissioner? You seem to be sucking.'

'Sucking?'

'*Mist.* That is not the right word. You have tremors in your face and you are pressing your eyes closed.'

'I suffer from headaches,' said Blume.

'You should try transcranial magnetic stimulation,' said Konrad. 'It also gets rid of depression and reveals your hidden artistic abilities. Unfortunately, the effects are not permanent.'

'I'll tell my terrific doctor. What's this virus you're talking about?'

'It is called *Toxoplasma gondii*. It is a virus like the one that causes malaria, and it is common throughout the world, but I believe it is particularly common in Italy. This virus enters the bloodstream, then invades the brains of its victims, in this case Italians, and causes neurosis. This is not to say all Italians have *Toxoplasma gondii*, but perhaps more have it here than in other countries. It causes poor driving and an inclination to risk taking and rule breaking.'

'Where does your mysterious virus come from, Konrad?'

'Ultimately, all viruses come from outer space.'

'Same quadrant as you?' asked Blume.

'This virus,' continued Konrad, 'resides in cats and rats and other mammals. A rat with the virus altering its brain might be unnaturally attracted to cats – this is the risk taking at work, you understand. So the rat goes to the cat and says chase me . . .'

'So it's a talking rat?'

'Obviously the rat does not speak,' said Konrad. 'You are not taking this seriously. You are a superficial man.'

'I am sorry,' said Blume. 'The rat, without speaking, informs the cat – in writing perhaps? – that it wants to be chased.'

'It makes this clear by virtue of the fact it approaches the cat. An animal that deliberately approaches its predator and seeks death is an unnatural thing.'

'So the cat kills the rat,' said Blume.

'Absolutely!' said Konrad, pleased that Blume had followed him this far in his reasoning. 'The rat gets caught and dies, but the virus goes into the cat and from there it gets passed to humans. But it is also passed from the eating of raw meat. I am thinking of the raw pig that makes prosciutto, the raw beef in *bresaola* and Florentine steaks, raw milk used for cheeses, salami and lamb, but also contact with the soil.'

'This is science fact?'

'Unfortunately, Italy does not regularly screen its pregnant women for the virus, but all the contributing factors and symptoms are plain to see, so it is a reasonable scientific hypothesis.'

'So maybe we should be concentrating on rounding up the cats, and after a few generations our women will stop giving birth to baby Mafiosi.'

'You know I can tell when you are mocking me,' said Konrad.

Ten minutes later they arrived at the lake.

'I forget,' said Blume. 'Why are we here?'

'You said you studied Latin in school,' said Konrad. 'You must have read Virgil?'

'We had to.'

'Ah.' Konrad fell silent and consulted the SatNav and then surveyed the landscape, a frown on his face.

Blume cut the engine and climbed out of the camper van. It was good to stretch his legs. The two of them were the only people in sight. They walked down to the low wall bordering the lake. Blume jumped up onto the ledge and walked along it, looking down at Konrad's bald patch. 'This is Lake Avernus. I can see you're disappointed. Is it the smell? That's sulphur. It's supposed to be good for you.'

Konrad followed Blume along the wall, then called out after him. 'It's not the smell. It's the cement buildings all around. Also I thought Lake Avernus would be bigger.'

'It's just a large pool on the top of an exploded volcanic crater,' said Blume.

Reluctantly, Konrad caught up with Blume. 'But for such an important place . . .'

'What's important about it?' asked Blume, leaping off the wall. The walk was doing him good.

'In mythology, this is the Gate to Hades, the entrance to the Underworld. I thought you said you had to read Virgil in school.'

'Doesn't mean I have to believe him. Mythology again. You're really into this stuff,' said Blume. 'Konrad, it's just a lake. Virgil made all that shit up to please the new emperor. He probably didn't even bother coming here to look at it.'

'But there are real ruins of the Cumae sibyl over there. Those are real.'

'Real in that there are Roman ruins there, yes. We don't have time for a visit.'

'Shh! I need to control something,' said Konrad.

'Check something, you mean, unless you're talking about a Teutonic urge to take over a country, in which case . . .'

'Please. You must be silent.'

Konrad appeared to be scanning the sky and listening hard, like a gunner waiting for an air attack. Eventually, he began to smile. 'There. What do you hear?'

By way of reply, Blume popped another aspirin.

'Can't you hear the silence?' said Konrad, his eyes still skyward.

'I can hear a television,' said Blume. 'A motorbike, a girl having an argument, someone hammering metal on the other side of the lake, a dog barking, now I hear a car . . . and a passenger jet coming into Capodichino airport. Tell me when to stop.'

'No, no, I meant the silence. Listen to the silence!'

'Behind all the noise, there's always silence,' said Blume.

'I meant the absence of birds. Virgil wrote that no birds fly over this lake, because it is the entrance to the Underworld. And look, just as Virgil said, there are no birds! Avernus, you see, comes from the Greek *a-orni-thos*, which means without birds.'

'Do ducks count?' said Blume, pointing to a bunch of reeds from which a loud quacking sound like laughter was emerging.

Konrad folded his arms and stared disapprovingly at the reeds, before striding off like a damaged wind-up toy back to the camper van, and remained there making his own contribution to the silence.

Blume, fed up with driving, decided Konrad was sober enough to get back in the driver's seat. This seemed to cheer the BKA man up some-what. He disappeared into the back of the camper and emerged with a packet of wholemeal biscuits and black *Vollkornbrot*, a piece of which he offered to Blume. Blume declined the bread and pointed instead to Konrad's SatNav. 'Use your navigator to get us out of here and plot a route to the hotel. Put in Campi Flegrei to Positano, see if it forces us to pass through the middle of Naples, which it probably will.'

Konrad was pleased to do this, and they were soon on their way again, bouncing down a crumbling lane, branches scraping the sides of the van. By Blume's reckoning the pointless expedition to Lake Avernus, a place far below Konrad's classicist expectations, had cost them no more than an hour and a half.

After ten minutes of driving, Blume stopped believing the SatNav and told Konrad to take a left, then another. The SatNav announced that it was recalculating, and then instructed them to go right where no right was to be seen. Blume realized they must have missed a turn, and were now heading inland, away from the Naples Tangenziale.

Konrad, who had maintained a beautiful silence all this time, now stopped dead in the middle of a crossroads and read out the road signs: 'Quarto, Manano. We are in Campi Flegrei now, I think . . . where is Pozzuoli? It must be behind us.' He pulled the camper to the side of the road.

'That's your stupid navigator for you.'

'I have very good orienteering skills, but I need to be outside the vehicle,' said Konrad.

'No, you stay there. I'll do this,' said Blume. He got out of the camper van and stood on the bonnet to see over the hedges. He caught a glimpse of the sea, which was enough. If they headed that way, they couldn't go wrong.

Konrad got out too.

'No, you get back in. I don't want advice from you or your navigator.'

Konrad stayed where he was. 'I got out because I think your reckless driving damaged the engine,' he said. 'I think it is beginning to overheat.'

Blume had noticed the burning smell, too, but had put it out of his mind. He sniffed at the bonnet. Nothing.

'I think it's coming from somewhere over there,' he said. 'Someone is burning stubble in a field.'

Konrad tilted his head back and sniffed. 'It is melting plastic,' he announced. 'Naples is famous for this sort of behaviour. But perhaps it is a house?'

'It's not.'

'You will run that risk?'

'More of a risk for whoever's in the house than for me.'

'That's your attitude?'

'Jesus. Look, I'll show you it's not a house. Come on.'

The pair of them walked in the direction of the smoke, now getting thicker and yellower and sweeter. It reawakened Blume's headache.

'There,' said Blume, pointing. 'Someone is burning plastic in a field.'

'Like that, in broad daylight. In front of neighbours,' marvelled Konrad. 'In Germany . . .'

'This isn't Germany,' said Blume.

'No. In Germany we have a society and the law is the same for every-one. *Gesellschaft* is the word. Here it is all *Gemeinschaft*. The law is not equal and justice is achieved through private channels.'

They had reached the edge of the field, on the far side of which a pile of plastic sacks was smouldering. There were houses about, but no one in sight. Blume waved his hand at the dreary dump and said, 'Satisfied?'

'If we were in Germany and I was showing you my country, and we discovered something like this, I would intervene as a policeman.'

Blume clambered over some woody briars and stood at the edge of the field, watching the white and yellow plumes of poison floating straight up, until a breeze from the sea caused them to swirl and drift towards him. He covered his mouth and nose with his arm and walked forwards. There was no one about, and there was no way of knowing to whom the field belonged. The wind changed direction again and blew the air clean, allowing him to breathe and see better. He could probably stamp on the smouldering heap and put it out.

He turned back and looked at Konrad, who had moved closer to the camper van. Another stream of air from the sea lifted up a new type of blacker and harsher smoke, smelling of diesel fumes, which clung to the ground, turning over and over on itself. Fuck this, he thought to himself, and turned back.

A sudden dull thump made him look around as, fanned by a crosswind, the rubbish heap burst into orange flame. The heavy oily smoke merged with the faster-moving yellow clouds to create an opaque fog that billowed outwards and upwards, far higher and faster than the quantity of material seemed to justify. There was no question now of approaching to investigate. If the blaze became any more intense, maybe one of the neighbours, or the arsonist himself, would call the fire brigade and ask them to save his house. If they turned up too late, he would appear on national television to denounce the government authorities for his misfortunes.

The subsiding black soil in the middle of the flame seemed to writhe and emit a hissing and screeching sound. As Blume stood fascinated, something scampered across the top of his shoe, and a moment later another object, soft but with compact mass and moving at speed, knocked against his ankle.

Blume felt his flesh tighten against his bones. Fleeing rats, many of them, were rushing towards him, escaping the fire and smoke. The writhing mass on the ground was almost upon him, as he broke into a run.

He was far too late to escape the living tide. Hundreds of rats overtook him, fanning out in front of him as if he were the pursuer and they the pursued. As he drew near the camper, gathering pace all the time, he saw Konrad leap in and slam the driver's door behind him and vanish.

Faster rats from behind mounted the backs of the slower ones in front, sometimes leapfrogging them, sometimes tumbling in the process, causing a pile-up, into which other rats would run until three or four of them stacked on top of each other, momentarily as high as his kneecaps.

Konrad was invisible, still deaf to his appeals, so Blume adjusted his flight and headed for the side of the camper van, which he hit at full speed. The door was unlocked, but he had to stop and pull it outwards. He jumped in and kicked it closed, but had the feeling that something else had leapt in with him. He surveyed the floor, the walls, and thought he saw a movement near Konrad's suitcases. Well, one or two rodents wasn't a problem. He shoved his head through the curtain separating him from the cab, where Konrad lay across the two seats, as white as if he were dead. When Blume appeared, Konrad let out a low moan of abject terror, before making a slight recovery, edging himself out of his prostrate position into one that was merely slumped.

'Keys,' demanded Blume, climbing with difficulty through the gap and into the front.

Konrad started fumbling around in his pockets. The soft thuds against the side of the camper and the dancing and trembling sensation from the ground beneath were like heavy rain. Blume manoeuvred himself into the driver's seat. Konrad was now waving the keys in front of him, but Blume was staring transfixed out the window. The rats had gone already, and the sea wind had snatched the toxic smoke and whipped it away into the clouds to poison the raindrops.

Blume, still pumping adrenalin and overcome with a desire to laugh and whoop, found it difficult to keep his hands steady as he inserted the key in the ignition, and started the engine. He turned the steering wheel slowly, to give any lurking rodents a chance to escape. He did not want to spare them, but he did not quite relish the idea of driving over their hunched grey backs like they were furry cobblestones. As he reversed he felt a suspicious bump under a wheel, then another.

'Jesus Christ,' said Blume. 'That is something else.'

Konrad was sitting up almost straight now, and was in the process of composing himself when, out of nowhere, a rat skidded across the bonnet so fast it seemed to Blume that the animal had cleared the front of the van with a single leap. Konrad screamed. Instinctively, Blume slammed on the brakes, sending himself and Konrad lurching forward against the window. The vehicle shuddered to a halt, the engine cut out, and they sat in the unexpected silence, looking at each other.

156

Konrad had frozen up so much that when he spoke it was almost without his lips moving. 'Please, take me away from this place.'

Blume pulled the key from the ignition and swung the key ring on his finger, looking thoughtful.

'What are you doing?'

'Waiting for you to tell me what you're doing in Italy, Konrad.'

25

Milan

THE INSPECTOR TURNED on the light, which shed a blue-tinged glow and bathed the young policeman beside him in a deathly pallor. The room contained a plastic bucket-seat chair with rusting legs, and the floor was made of unlevelled cement.

The building they stood in had belonged to the Mancuso clan, one of the principal Ndrangheta 'ndrine in Milan. The seizure of the property by the police was supposed to have a symbolic effect, which it did – but not the intended one. Private investors turned out to be too afraid to use the building and the City failed to do anything with it. The final message was that the Ndrangheta was stronger than the state.

'Give the walls a kick, see if they sound hollow.'

The young policeman was more conscientious than that, and methodically worked his way across the narrow space tapping the wall every inch from bottom to top and back again. His older colleague, shamed, did the same. After ten minutes, they were pretty sure nothing was hidden behind the walls.

'There's some staining here,' said the young policeman.

'That's just damp.'

'Maybe, but then it has to be recent because there is no mould and I can't smell much damp in here. Some, but not a lot. Also, there's a patch on the floor. It's like they hosed down the place not too long ago, which would be strange. Who'd want to clean up in here?'

The inspector hunkered down and touched the floor with the back of his hand. 'It seems fairly dry.' A dull sheen near the corner of the room caught his eye, then disappeared. He went over to investigate and found himself marvelling at the fact they had not seen it immediately.

'Look here,' he said.

'What? I can't see anything.'

'It's a gold ring. It looks like a wedding ring.'

Magistrate Francesco Fossati held the clear plastic bag up to the light and examined the ring.

He handed it to a white-suited technician. 'Can you use luminol spray in here, and examine those stains?'

'This place is overrun with rats and stray animals who have been shitting all over the place,' said the technician. 'The whole place will light up blue. The important thing is to get a fleck of blood from the wall or floor, if that's what you're looking for.'

'You're the experts,' said the magistrate. 'Get scraping, or whatever you need to do.'

The technician handed the magistrate back the evidence bag. 'There's something written on the inside of the ring. A name . . . date. See?'

Fossati pulled out his reading glasses and perched them on the end of his nose. 'Letizia,' he read. 'And then there is a date. "23 July 1985."'

'Some wife is going to be pissed off with her husband for losing that,' said the inspector.

But Fossati knew what they had found. 'Was it covered in dirt?' he asked the young policeman, who immediately reddened.

'I don't think so, but I didn't touch it.' Then he brightened up. 'But they took photos. You can ask the technical team . . .'

'Asking you was supposed to be a shortcut. Did it look like it had been there for long?'

The policeman decided to risk an opinion. 'No. It looked newly lost.'

'Yes,' said Fossati, mainly to himself. 'From a few days ago.'

Fossati had listened to his old friend Bazza and had not been concentrating on the Ndrangheta as likely perpetrators of the kidnapping. But Mafia-owned or not, this was an abandoned building that lay close to the place where the girl was last seen. And now he had a piece of vital evidence for Bazza, who would be grateful but would forever remain convinced that Fossati had ignored his advice and focused on a Mafia connection.

Fossati realized he had probably found the place where Arconti had been murdered. Letizia was the name of the wife of the murder victim. It was a good find, but he felt no triumph. Teresa was still missing, Arconti was still dead.

The technician appeared at the doorway. 'Someone or something was shot in there.'

Fossati nodded. 'Yes, that makes sense.'

The technician looked at him in surprise. 'There is even a small pock-mark on the wall. We can look at the RNA ratios to see how old the bloodstains are. We need arc lights and more manpower in there.'

Fossati called in the inspector and the policeman.

'Well done on finding the ring, but you two seem not to have noticed a wall covered in blood.'

The young policeman looked mortified, but the inspector stood his ground and returned the magistrate's gaze. 'That's because you told us to look for something else: the body of a girl, a hiding place.'

'So it's my fault?' said Fossati. 'Maybe you're right. You found some-thing I wasn't looking for, but I know someone who was.'

26

On the Road to Naples–Amalfi

'I AM INVESTIGATING A possible new connection between the Camorra and the Ndrangheta for the dumping of toxic waste,' said Konrad, glancing nervously out the window as if the rats might still be following them.

'In your own time?'

'I am dedicated, and I work best alone.'

The Camorra, the 'system' as they called it locally, was seeking to expand its drug operations into Lazio and was organizing a deal with the Ndrangheta for better wholesale prices and services in kind, namely the illegal dumping of toxic waste into the aquifers of Naples. Crime bosses drank only mineral water these days, observed Konrad.

His story was perfectly plausible. In fact, it was probably true that the Camorra and Ndrangheta were colluding, but Blume didn't believe for a moment that it had anything to do with Konrad's trip. No, the man, who now sat hunched and defensive in the passenger seat, was still not telling the truth. Blume could understand the anxiety of Konrad's superiors. For all his academic precision and pretention, there was something reckless and irrational driving him, as if once untethered from a lifetime of desk-based investigation, he no longer cared for consequences.

Blume figured the best tactic was to nod and look as if he accepted the explanation. He knew from experience that suspects who had unconvincing alibis that they thought no intelligent person could accept were often more annoyed than relieved if their unlikely stories seemed to be taken at face value. Disappointed by the stupidity of their questioners, and unable to overcome the human need to be understood, they often started hinting at the truth. That was not how it always worked of course, but Blume figured Konrad would not be able to bear it for long, and he was right.

'I am glad you told me that,' he told Konrad. 'Now I have something to put in my report. I guess you were worried about your investigation being leaked?'

'No. I mean, yes. That's it.'

'Great. I don't see why you couldn't have told us that earlier. And told your bosses. I'm guessing you're working on a hunch, and you don't want to make a big deal of it until you're ready.'

Konrad was growing increasingly uncomfortable with every rationalization Blume gave to his story, and merely nodded unhappily.

Blume drove on for another ten minutes, whistling as if a great load had been taken off his mind.

Suddenly, Konrad could bear it no more. 'I know who you are,' he said.

'Well, we were introduced.'

'Not like that. Your name appears as a lead investigator appointed by the prosecuting magistrate Matteo Arconti into a case that involved a relation of a person called Agazio Curmaci, who is Megale's right-hand man. I know about the murder of a man to intimidate Arconti. I don't believe you were appointed by chance to stay by me. I think you are also conducting an investigation into Megale or his son or Curmaci.'

'What an inventive mind you have,' said Blume. 'When you say "you also", do you mean you are doing the same thing?'

'I do not understand.'

'Or do you mean "I, among other things, am also conducting an investigation"?'

'Are you attacking my grammar?' asked Konrad.

'Never mind,' said Blume. He took the Tangenziale, and they were soon cruising along in a long loop around Naples on their way to the Amalfi coast.

'Are you intending to go down to Calabria?'

Konrad shrugged his thin shoulders.

'Are you working for Megale?'

'I am offended by your suggestion.'

'You visited him.'

Konrad shrugged again.

162

'Follow my reasoning, here, Konrad. Megale is not a BKA asset, not your asset, not your paymaster, and yet this visit. There are only two explanations left.'

Konrad perked up, as if he, too, was interested in hearing his own reasons.

'You went to him for help or information,' said Blume, 'or both.'

'I needed to find out some things, and I need to find out one or two things here, then I will go home. It is a personal matter that has nothing to do with anyone else.'

'How did you get Megale to talk to you? Bosses are not naturally helpful to federal agents.'

'I am very good at database mining,' said Konrad. 'If I get the numbers, I can see patterns. I have built up a good picture of the shell companies and money-laundering methods that Megale and his men use. I explained to him some of what I knew about how his German *locale* was operating, and he was interested in me and listened.'

'So he thinks you're suppressing information that could be used against him? Are you?'

'I will be reporting everything I know when I get back,' said Konrad. 'I am proud to say criminal bosses have no reason to trust me.'

'But first, you got him to tell you something in exchange for your silence? Or temporary silence as you say it will be.'

'I am not answering that,' said Konrad. 'I just showed him I know about his shell companies, though I don't know as much as I pretended, and I proved I knew some details about his money laundering.'

'What details?'

'Money laundering comes in three stages.'

'Placement, layering and investment,' said Blume.

'Exactly. When it comes to investments, Megale seems to work more with Agazio Curmaci than with his own son, or with the *contabile* who's supposed to be in charge of finances,' said Konrad.

He paused to measure Blume's reaction. Blume kept his eyes on the road ahead.

'Curmaci comes between the layering and investment phases,' continued Konrad. 'He's the last connection back to the Ndrangheta. Everything downstream of him is clean. He's like a filter.'

'I see,' said Blume.

'And that is why his violent and rash reactions to his wife's cousins being arrested are completely out of character. I am wondering if your Investigating Magistrate Arconti managed to provoke him in some way.'

'Not enough to justify what happened,' said Blume. 'I find it odd to be talking about Curmaci all of a sudden with you.'

'The criminal world gets small at the top of the pyramid,' said Konrad. 'Curmaci rather than Megale junior seems to be second to Megale senior. Would you say that's right?'

Despite himself, Blume was impressed. Without any change in his characteristic mixture of self-aggrandizement and moodiness, Konrad had reversed the direction of the questioning.

'Am I right in thinking,' said Blume, 'that one of the reasons you agreed to travel with me was you were hoping *I* might give *you* more information on Curmaci?'

Konrad shook his head. 'No, I don't need any more information. I had no choice about accepting you. I would prefer to be left alone for this.'

Blume guided the camper van halfway into the emergency lane to avoid being sideswiped by the vehicles passing them. Eventually he said, 'The main reason I am here is I am interested in joining the DCSA or maybe getting a recommendation that would allow me to apply to the DIA. I wanted to get away from my colleagues and my desk. But I have nothing special to give you on Curmaci.'

'I thought you said you had a girlfriend who worked with you?'

'Yes . . . what of it?'

'Why would you want to leave her behind and spend your time travelling on missions?'

'That's got nothing to do with anything,' said Blume.

'It seems to me you are running away.' Konrad might have said more, but an unmistakable thump followed by a scuttling noise from behind caused him to freeze and whiten.

'Yeah,' said Blume casually. 'There is a rat in there. Maybe two. They must have got in with me.'

Konrad made a choking sound and he grabbed at the door handle, as if intending to hurl himself out of the vehicle and into the path of the cars speeding past them.

'Please, stop. We must get out.'

'I can't stop in the middle of this highway, Konrad. And the emergency lane has just disappeared. I saw a sign back there for a service station. We'll pull in there.'

Konrad unbuckled his seatbelt and twisted around in his seat to watch the back. 'How far?'

'A few kilometres. We'll be there in a minute or two. You really don't like rats, do you?'

Konrad had a wild look in his eyes and his teeth were clenched. He was attempting to stand, back to the windscreen, and his whole body was twisted into a hideous shape, his limbs jutting out like bent straws.

'I think it's fair to call this rat thing a phobia,' said Blume, 'but no problem, we're there already.' He headed towards the ramp leading into the service station. 'I don't like them either, but I keep my fear in check. But I suppose you're terrified a rat will bite you and you'll get that virus that turns you into an Italian. Go on, hop out, go into the Autogrill, and get yourself coffee and a sandwich or something. I'll deal with the rat in the kitchen. Tell you what, get me one of those frozen coffee things. You know them? You pull out a tab, shake the container and the coffee goes really cold? Don't make the mistake of getting the red container, which turns the coffee hot. And get me some sweets. A pack of fruit Mentos would be nice. Are you listening?'

Konrad had the door open before Blume had even stopped the camper van.

27

Rome

CATERINA KNEW THAT this fair-haired magistrate with his chin-strap beard was bullying her because he in his turn had been humiliated. Appointed to conduct an investigation into a potentially important case, he, like her, had spent his weekend gathering evidence and background information. In fact, he had been playing catch-up with her, since she was further ahead with her inquiries. Then the whole thing was taken from him and transferred to the Milan section of the anti-Mafia magistrates before he had had the chance to issue his first executive order.

'The police in Milan have just confirmed that the burned-out van in Sesto San Giovanni was the same one you were attempting to trace from Rome to Milan. Presumably the two burned bodies they found are the people you were looking for.'

Caterina and her colleagues had spent almost three full days on the reconstruction of the movements of the van, tracking it at the north Rome Tollgate, picking it up again using the traffic speed cameras near Florence, getting decent-quality images of the occupants when they stopped at a service area after Bologna. Their best stroke of fortune had been when the driver paid for fuel by credit card. They were able to get an identification of the driver, a certain Teodor Popescu. The card and the van were registered to an office-cleaning company set up by a building renovations group associated with a real-estate management firm specializing in decommissioned and disused buildings whose holdings included warehouses in Sesto San Giovanni where, as it turned out, the driver and occupant of the van were both killed. Dutifully and promptly, Caterina and her team had handed all the information to this young magistrate, practically in a gift box with a bow on it. The magistrate had somehow botched his effort to steal all the credit for it as he passed it on to Milan, since the head of the investigation there had asked not for the opinion of the magistrate, but had asked for her by name.

Caterina merely nodded as he told her that she should have spent more time investigating the scene of the crime. He conceded it was hardly her fault. Her commander had vanished and left her, a woman with a child and insufficient experience, to run a full investigation.

'Thank you, Caterina,' he said as she was leaving. 'Are you sure you have held nothing back from me?'

'Nothing. But call me Inspector Mattiola, Signor Giudice, not Caterina.'

She left the door open on her way out, hoping it annoyed the magistrate as much as it annoyed Blume, which, she admitted, was hardly possible.

Unlike Blume, Caterina was a glutton for the summer heat, even in the city. She loved the way it bounced off the pavement back at her face in the early afternoon, then radiated from the buildings in the evening. When the sun heated her hair, it felt like a soft electric current was running through every strand. In the heat everyone walked more slowly and deliberately. She loved the way Roman drivers eschewed air-conditioning, preferring to leave the window open and droop an arm against the side of their car, raising their hand sometimes to direct a refreshing airflow up their arm, sometimes to greet people, more often to insult other drivers with languid gestures. The gleam of the light off the windscreens and metal of the incessant traffic lifted her spirits. The blaring horns, which were full of violence and irritability in the winter, seemed now to be celebratory and bear no ill will. Happy motorbikes and scooters roared through gaps in the traffic and across dangerous intersections, the riders sounding their horns in delight at the way the rushing warm air kept them dry and alert. She passed an old man sitting on a broken bench milking the sun, oblivious to the traffic. She remembered her grandfather sitting on a park bench like that, his face pointed up, as blissful as a lizard.

And yet she wished Blume were here to spoil it all for her. He'd have a jacket on and be sweating underneath it. He'd clump around in his heavy shoes, which he wore off duty and on, contemptuous of men wearing 'Jesus sandals' as he called them, appalled at the ugliness of people's feet. When it became too much even for him to wear heavy clothes, he'd appear wearing the T-shirt he had had on in bed, shiny running shoes and shorts, and pretend day after day that he was going to the park for a run until eventually he did go running, if only to save face (but not his knees, as he would make perfectly plain for the next few weeks). If he were here now, instead of avoiding her and sneaking off on a mission, he'd be complaining of the dust and the grime, and would be seething in rage at the people walking too slow, the drivers driving too fast, the stench of the unemptied skips, the starling droppings and the sticky residue of the lime trees on the bonnet of his car. But he was always funny, intentionally or not, when raging against the heat and his adopted city.

Caterina entered the Gelateria dei Gracchi, to which Blume had introduced her. He said their ice cream was better even than Toni's on Colli Portuensi, and he was possibly right, but still she preferred Toni's. He had brought her here on one of those rare days they had been able to spend in each other's company.

She now ordered herself a rich yellow, cream and walnut cone, and ate it, reflecting on how well she had handled that little shit of a magistrate. The sun had disinfected him out of her mind. Blume absorbed all his rage deep into his body and let it seep out slowly through sarcasm and head-aches and intestinal problems he never mentioned and would be mortified to think she knew anything about.

Caterina was considering whether or not to eat the cone. It seemed ridiculous to worry about the few calories left in her hand after she had said yes to the whipped cream on top five minutes earlier. Her minor quandary was resolved by the trilling of an incoming call. She dropped the cone into the overflowing rubbish bin outside the *gelateria*, and kissed her fingers clean, before fishing the mobile phone from her bag. She glanced at it and saw an unknown number of a few digits. An institution of some sort, she guessed.

'Inspector Mattiola?' A woman's voice.

'Yes.'

'I am Doctor Silvia La Verde, Consultant Neurologist at the Gemelli Hospital. I am phoning on behalf of Magistrate Matteo Arconti, who is unable to make the call.'

'He's awake?'

'Absolutely, and he's sitting here right beside me. He has some diffi-culty in holding a phone and pressing buttons . . .'

Like Blume, then, thought Caterina.

'. . . but I am confident we can deal with that over the next weeks and months. He has no problems, or only very minor problems relating to muscle control, in speaking. I'm going to put the phone to his ear now.'

Caterina waited a moment.

'Eeeola?' said the voice, which sounded like it was coming from the other side of the tomb.

'Eeola?' she said.

'Attrina Eeeola?'

'Caterina Mattiola, yes, sir, that's me. How can I help?'

Silence. Then some voices in the background, someone exclaiming something.

'Chief Inspector Mattiola,' said the same voice, almost perfectly normal now, apart from a slight slurring. 'Magistrate Matteo Arconti here. Sorry about that. It turns out I can speak perfectly fine if the phone is at my right ear, but I become almost aphasic if it's at my left. Half my brain seems to be numb. Dr La Verde here is very interested in this. I think she's writing a book about people like me.'

Caterina allowed her silence to convey that she had no idea what he was talking about.

'I was wondering, could you find time to pay me a visit. Just you, mind. I have a few things I'd like to ask you.'

'Can't you ask me about them now?' said Caterina. She had just used up her last stores of tolerance for pompous magistrates.

'I have a consultant neurologist acting as a phone holder. I really think you should come here, Inspector.'

They always did that, conversationally demoted you by one rank when they sensed a lack of deference.

Perhaps sensing an imminent refusal, Arconti added, 'If you really want to know, I don't so much want to ask you questions as to tell you a few things. They concern Commissioner Alec Blume, and a little trouble he has made for himself.'

He could have said that to begin with.

'I'm on my way,' she said.

28

Castellammare di Stabia, Naples

B<small>LUME WAITED TILL</small> Konrad had gone in, then, instead of parking in front, backed up and drove the camper van around to the rear and squeezed behind a semitrailer. Moving quickly, he left the cab and opened the door to the living quarters, and stomped in, lashing out with his feet at anything he thought he saw moving. He flicked on the light, but it only cast a buttery glow on a section of the ceiling, and illuminated nothing. He saw he could let in more light by opening the curtain that closed off the driver's cab.

The rat, the size of a small cat, was attached to the curtain, perfectly motionless, its pink feet digging into the fabric. It had positioned itself right behind the passenger seat, inches from where Konrad's head had been. Its nose was pointing up towards the ceiling, its tail swinging almost imperceptibly to and fro to offset the gentle sway of the curtain.

Hickory, dickory dock, sang Blume to himself, his eyes seeking a weapon as the animal continued to gaze upwards, pretending not to have seen him as he pretended not to have seen it.

Blume moved deeper into the camper, quietly unlocked a cupboard, and pulled out the first thing his hand touched, which turned out to be a can of insecticide. Fine. He'd use it as a baton. As he transferred it to his right hand, the rat did a 180-degree rotation, turning his nose from twelve to six. Blume, momentarily experiencing some of the horror he had seen written on Konrad's features, launched the canister. With a casually insulting backward flip, the rat executed a somersault in the air and landed on its feet on the floor, walking rather than running out the door just as Blume's useless aerosol hit the curtain. Blume stepped to the door, just in time to see the rat slip under the rear wheel of the camper van, very much with the air of one prepared to bide his time until the human persecutor had left.

He pulled the door to. Without the breeze, the room immediately became airless and hot. He made a very rapid survey of the camper, pausing again to look at the faded picture of the girl. Then he went over to Konrad's two leather suitcases and lifted the larger onto the misery-inducing Formica table bolted to the floor. It was closed with a small combination padlock of the sort that could be sprung with the help of a mini-screwdriver and the sudden application of force. But he had no such screwdriver to hand. Patiently, he pulled gently on the latch, seeing which of the dials felt tightest. He zeroed it, tested again, found the third dial was now tightest, and worked at that. It took him less than two minutes to get the combination.

Sweating profusely now as the sun outside turned the camper into a Dutch oven, Blume opened the suitcase. As expected, Konrad's clothes were neatly folded and separated by type. Blume stood back and looked carefully at the contents, studying patterns, memorizing the order. Then he started taking out the clothes item by item and running his hand over each.

He had to open the door for air. He glanced down at the wheel, seeing nothing. 'Hey, rat?' he called. 'Want to climb in here, make a nest in Hoffmann's underpants?'

Comforted by the breeze, he returned to his task of feeling his way through the contents, stroking the silky lining of the suitcase with the back of his hand. He double-checked to see if he had missed anything in the front pocket, then set about putting everything back. The second suitcase had the same combination as the first.

The contents here proved more interesting. He immediately found a notebook, with an expensive vellum cover. Inside were neat handwritten notes, all in German. It would take him too long to work out the meanings. He could make out some words, *Ehrenabzeichen*, *Geschäftsfreund*, *Kontaktperson*, *Rache*. Hoffmann also had some headed paper with the lettering BKA and the black eagle symbol, but the sheets were blank. Below some neatly folded shirts, he found a sheaf of papers held together by spiral binding. There had to be eighty sheets at least and, Blume noted, many of them were in Italian. He glanced quickly through, and saw they referred to the Ndrangheta. He caught some names of major families and that of a heroic magistrate Nicola Gratteri, who was one of the leading experts on the organization. Blume hesitated, then decided to transfer the entire document into his own suitcase. It meant Konrad would find out about this in an hour or two when he went to unpack his bags, but that was fine.

He was looking for a weapon. If Konrad had one, it had to be in here, because he was not carrying one on his person. Blume had carefully and surreptitiously checked from the first moment they had met, and had finally been able to rule out the last possibility of a concealed weapon when Konrad had lifted his feet off the floor in fear of rats, revealing that he wore brown-and-white striped socks, but no ankle holster.

He lifted out three books. One was a guidebook to 'Kalabrien und Basilikata', one of the more useless guidebooks crammed with glossy photos of places that, presumably, you would be seeing for yourself. He held the book by its spine and made a fan of the pages and shook, but nothing fell out. There was a novel, *Selbs Betrug*, again with nothing hidden inside. More interesting, but ultimately unrevealing, was a book called *Mafialand Deutschland* by Jürgen Roth. Konrad also had a neat little halogen penlight that Blume wasted a few seconds playing with. He reached the bottom of the suitcase without finding anything else of interest. He swiped his hand through the inside pocket, finding nothing more than what seemed to be the torn and crumpled remains of some old-fashioned postcards. One showed the 'doors of Malta', another was an image of an English seaside town called Brixham. Judging from the faded turquoise colour of the sea and the single brown car parked in the port, the photo dated from the 1970s. There was a ripped postcard of a caravan site in County Cork in Ireland framed by bright red fuchsia, and a close-up of the Glockenspiel at Marienplatz in Munich and another of the nearby Frauenkirche. There was nothing written on any of them. The postcards were so old that the paper formed tiny fibrous pills as he rubbed his thumb along the edges. They did not fit in with the neatly stacked clothes, the high technology, the cleanliness and order of the bags. He had an idea, which immediately crystallized into a conviction, that the camper van in which he now stood had been to those places in the distant past. These were fragments of Konrad's memory, pieces he wanted to keep for personal reasons. Something here explained his presence in Italy.

He pulled out the last postcard, which turned out to be ripped

172

vertically in half. He felt around for the other half, but the pocket had given up the last of its treasures. The postcard, more of a holy keepsake, was of the type religious people bought in churches. It showed a vaulted ceiling, a side chapel, a Madonna with a massive crown on her head and the beginnings of a second crown, presumably on the head of the Christ child in her arms. The vertical tear obliterated the rest. But Blume recognized it at once. It was an image of the Madonna of Polsi, also known as the Madonna of the Mountains, the goddess of the Ndrangheta. This was the very Madonna that the bosses lifted on their shoulders and paraded through the steep streets of the village clinging to the sides of Aspromonte. He turned the card over and saw it was signed in a careful childish hand with rounded large characters: Domenico Megale.

Old Megale wrote like a five-year-old. If that was his signature. Blume looked closely at it, bringing it over to the door to get more light. The glistening of the ink, its fresh darkness on the old paper convinced him that Domenico Megale, or someone purporting to be him, had signed the back of this torn Madonna recently. Either Konrad was such a fan of the Mafia boss that he carried around his autograph, or this had some specific purpose. It had to be Konrad's passport to somewhere, he reasoned. It certified that Konrad was to be allowed to enter somewhere, or was a man to trust. Someone else held the other half of the image, so they could check this was authentic.

And yet, even as he looked at the signature and the torn image, Blume could not believe that Konrad was really an envoy from Domenico Megale. He could not say why he was so certain except that Konrad had little of the perpetrator and much of the victim about him.

He closed the van door again and started putting everything back into the suitcase, including the torn Madonna. When the lanky German came knocking on the hotel door a few hours from now, angrily demanding an explanation for his missing notes, Blume would ask him about it.

Someone hammered on the door he had just closed. Blume snapped shut the case, put it back on the floor, opened the door.

Konrad stood holding two plastic bags. 'I thought you'd be out front.'

'No parking space. I tried to use the shade of the trucks to keep the camper van cool.'

Konrad peered in. 'Are they still there?'

'No,' said Blume. 'There was just the one. It might be near your feet.'

Konrad gave a satisfying leap, like a colt learning to show-jump. Then he got in the driver's side, slamming the door behind him. 'Close the door, please.'

'Did you get that coffee?' said Blume from behind him. 'Wait, I'm coming around.'

Blume sat down in the passenger seat and Konrad gingerly handed him the bag. Blume peered inside and pulled out a packet of fruit pastilles and popped one in his mouth. 'You remembered, well done. I love these sweets. But where's the coffee?'

'When I asked for what you said, no one understood me,' said Konrad.

'It's sold with the sweets, in a blue container . . . never mind.' He popped another in his mouth, adding synthetic strawberry to the chewy lemon he was already enjoying. 'What?' he said to Konrad's outraged and incredulous expression. 'I like sweets. I never grew out of it. It's my only vice. You want one?' he pulled back the wrapper and held the tube towards Konrad, who recoiled.

'Did you wash your hands?'

'You mean the rat? I was kicking at the rat, not tickling its stomach.'

'European rats carry a flea which carries a bacterium called Bartonella. It causes serious coronary damage.'

Blume popped a green sweet into his mouth, then mimicked a man having a heart attack, clutching at his left bicep, then throat.

'You're not funny, Commissioner.'

29

Rome

Arconti was sitting up waiting for her and managed to lift his arm as she entered the room. A box of Kleenex sat by his side.

'I have a private room, which is good,' he said, plucking one out and dabbing the side of his mouth. 'Excuse me if I drool a little.'

Caterina, who did not know the magistrate, was unsure what sort of tone to use. Sensing this, Arconti said, 'I am going to use *tu* and call you Caterina. I want you to do the same. Call me Matteo.'

'Signor Giudice, you are asking too much. I can't possibly use *tu* . . .' she trailed off as the magistrate fixed her with a haughty and unblinking stare.

'I am not that old, despite present appearances,' said Arconti, his lip curved into a sneering expression of command.

Caterina bristled. 'I am not using the familiar form with a magistrate I don't know. You had something to tell me, now tell me.'

The magistrate continued to regard her balefully, but his voice sounded incongruously cheerful. 'That's fine by me. Sorry if I embarrassed you. May I call you Caterina?'

'Yes,' she conceded.

'OK, Caterina, now will you please look at this side of my face, the side that doesn't look like it's had the mother of all Botox injections? I'm sure the frozen half is fascinatingly creepy, but I have feelings, too.'

She looked at Arconti's face full on, and saw half his mouth smiling. His right eye was moving up and down and there was a humorous glint in it.

'They are hopeful that other side will start thawing out within a few days,' he said.

'I'm sorry,' said Caterina. 'I was staring, wasn't I?' She glanced surreptitiously at the left eye which glared murderously back at her, while Arconti laughed good-naturedly.

'Never mind. And as for the honorifics due to a magistrate, you can forget that. I'm quitting. I know it was probably cholesterol or cigarettes or something, but I blame my work for this. That and my parents of course, they gave me the genes.'

'I'm sorry to hear that,' said Caterina. She hooked some strands of hair over her ear and turned her head so as to look only at the magistrate's good side.

'You're lovely,' he said. 'And now you're blushingly lovely. I found in the past few days it's become easier for me to speak my mind. I find you lovely, and the fact that that big brooding bastard of a commissioner didn't see fit even to mention you in all those hours we were together is . . .'

'Hurtful,' said Caterina.

'Yes. Blume isn't always upfront, is he?'

'Not always,' she agreed.

'I think he probably communicates more with you than with me, which is as it should be and as I hope it will be,' said Arconti. 'Do you know where he is now?'

Caterina hesitated.

'I'm not fishing for information. I know where he is,' said Arconti. 'I'm just wondering if you do.'

'Yes, I do. I think so. Tell me anyhow.'

'He's been recruited by Captain Massimiliani from the DCSA to accompany a German who may or may not have something to do with the Ndrangheta and may or may not be acting as a go-between for the Ndrangheta and the Camorra. He left you here investigating the murder of Matteo Arconti, which, I have to say, still makes a certain impression on me when I say the name. You were briefly under the direction of a magistrate from my office, right?'

'Magistrate Nardone.'

'Can't quite bring him to mind,' said Arconti.

'Natty little beard, young . . .'

'Nope. Can't picture him, but it's all irrelevant now because the case has floated up to Milan and into the all-devouring embrace of the anti-Mafia magistrates.'

'You are very well informed, Giudice.'

'Call me Matteo, and, really, use the familiar form,' he attempted a smile, and Caterina's eye was drawn back to the sneer stamped on the left side of his face. 'I'm informed because I've been talking to this Massimiliani I mentioned. He wanted to know a few things about Blume.'

'When was this?' asked Caterina. 'I was given to understand that you were in a coma. In fact I was surprised when the doctor called.'

'Yes, it was Massimiliani's idea to say I was totally incapacitated. It was such an opportunity for a plausible lie he simply could not let it pass, even if it served no purpose whatsoever. Not that I'm up and dancing yet, but no coma. Is Blume a principled man?'

Caterina fell silent.

'If it helps,' said Arconti with another lopsided grin, 'I think he is but . . .'

'But?' asked Caterina. 'What has he done? Or what are you going to ask him to do?'

'I am not going to ask him to do anything, Caterina. But he took a doubtful initiative. I think his motives were pure – well, not pure but justifiable – and I think he was looking out for me . . .'

'Don't make excuses for him,' she said.

'You're right. Still, I get the feeling that Blume has embraced a philosophy he doesn't believe in, and it's led him in the wrong direction. I'd be interested to know whether you are accompanying him on it . . . You haven't a clue what I am talking about, have you?'

'No.'

'That means he's on his own.'

'You are still talking in riddles, Giudice.'

'When Massimiliani found out I was not a vegetable, he came in to ask me about a confession apparently made by Curmaci's wife, Maria Itria. When I said I had spoken to the woman but never received any confession, quite the contrary really, he showed me a transcript, adding that copies of the same had been leaked to the press, and one in particular could be tracked back to a policeman in your office who is known to do anything for a bit of cash and is therefore usually kept away from sensitive information . . .'

'Rospo,' said Caterina.

'So the confession was fed to him, or left where he would find it.

Massimiliani anticipated this by conducting his own search, and meanwhile Blume takes a leave of absence . . .'

'I understand,' said Caterina. 'Blume falsified a confession by a Mafia wife.'

'Exactly. You're very quick on the uptake. Massimiliani was full of admiration for this technique, and I think he might really want to recruit Blume whose name, I admit, I am responsible for putting forward. Me, I have my doubts that Blume's action was such a good idea. He put the woman's life in direct and immediate danger, and perhaps the lives of her two children.'

'Blume is a stupid, arrogant bastard,' said Caterina. 'He can deal with this himself.' A thought struck her. 'I hope you're not implying I had anything to do with it?'

'No. I am not accusing you of complicity. I meant what I said: I am not going to be a magistrate after I get out of here. I just want to make things as right as possible on my last case. Has the arrogant bastard been phoning you?'

'He has been avoiding me more than anything. He's been avoiding me for a year now, come to think of it. We were supposed to . . . sorry, you don't need personal details.'

'I would like to help.' The magistrate closed his right eye sympathetically, while his left eye continued to glare at her.

'Commissioner Blume is a coward,' said Caterina.

'That's very harsh, Inspector.'

'He has it in his power to do good for himself and others; he refuses to do it through fear, and calls it principle.'

'He did it to draw Curmaci out. I think he did it for me.' Arconti dabbed the side of his mouth again and asked Caterina to help him drink a glass of water. It was an awkward moment, and she kept apologizing as the water ran in rivulets down the lifeless left corner of his mouth. All the while, his left side regarded her with loathing for her clumsiness. Eventually, the magistrate had swallowed half a glass and dribbled the other half.

'That's fine. I'm used to it already, though the therapist tells me I must never get used to anything. Apparently I must fight like hell to get back to how I was just the other day, which is rather depressing.' He dabbed his mouth and laid his head back, addressing his thoughts to the ceiling.

'Blume is treating Curmaci as if he were a common criminal, which is a mistake. It is far easier to isolate a common criminal than one who operates in an organization. When dealing with the Mafia, it is almost impossible for us to restrict the consequences of an operation. I am not sure Curmaci is the sort of prey you'd want to catch. I withheld some information about Curmaci from Blume because . . .'

'Because you're a magistrate and that's what you guys do,' said Caterina. 'You withhold stuff.'

For a moment both sides of Arconti's face regarded her with the same expression, but then he relaxed. 'It's the system, not the people. Magistrate means master. We do the thinking, you do the doing. That's why you are called agents. It's not how things work in reality, but it's what the law says.'

'Yeah, well . . . Plenty of magistrates need to be taught stuff by us agents.'

'True. Look, Blume is making a mistake. I want you to tell him that. For his sake. This is organized crime, not ordinary crime. People like Curmaci aren't in it for the money. It's the power, the prestige, the fear they can instill in others, the power to corrupt, the revenge against the classes that kept them down, the ability to design the political landscape. The Ndrangheta is like an order of murderous monks, and Curmaci is one of the high priests.'

30

Positano

THE CLEAN WHITE hotel in Positano was set into cliffs overlooking the sea. It was still Campania; the stinking chaos of Naples was only up the road, but they had entered another world.

The girl at the reception desk gave them a bright smile as they entered. When they had filled out the visitor cards, the girl glanced out of the door and saw the camper van.

'Is that vehicle yours?' Her smile seemed a little more forced.

Blume jerked a thumb at Konrad, who was looking around the hotel lobby with an appreciative air. 'Not mine. His.'

The girl nodded as if in understanding. She looked at the ragged back-pack drooped off Blume's shoulder.

'Is that your luggage?'

'I have a suitcase in the camper, too heavy to bother moving.' He patted his backpack appreciatively. 'Got all I need in here.'

The girl was now avoiding his eyes.

From the front, the hotel seemed like a single-storey house, but the entrance and lobby areas turned out to be the top floor of a building of three levels that developed in a step pattern downwards towards the sea. From a window on the left, they could see the roof tiles of the next two levels down, the lower of which jutted out into what seemed to be empty space. It was as if the entrance lobby where they now stood was the only part of the building sunk into safe ground. Konrad was unabashedly delighted with the place, at one point even nudging Blume and pointing at the vertiginous prospect, as if Blume, who felt a little giddy, could miss it.

Blume was sure the buildings below were actually nestled safely into the rock and resting, at least in part, on solid earth, but he still walked down the hallway with the same cautious tread he used when shuffling up the aisle of an aeroplane in flight, thinking of what would happen if his foot went through the floor. Konrad's room was in the lowest of the three buildings to the far left, Blume's in the building above to the right.

Blume was reassured to find the back wall of his bedroom was thick and uneven and it followed the contours of the rock face. It was cold and slightly damp to the touch. He had a shower to wash off the memory of rats. Then he opened his backpack and took out fresh clothes rescued from the suitcase. Fresh, but wrinkled, so he decided to put them on, lie on the bed, force them into some shape against his body.

The wide rectangular window, which swivelled open on a central hinge so that it could complete a 180-degree turn until the outside panes faced in and the inside panes out, framed nothing but sea. He had to stand right next to it and peer downwards to see the cliff into which the building was embedded. He caught a glimpse of a tiny garden set on a narrow ledge fifteen feet below, large enough for maybe one child to play in, a child with very laid-back parents. A ball dropped from his window would bounce once, bang in the centre of the garden, then fly over the cliff edge and down into the sea for ever.

The air that came in was salty but not clammy. The temperature was perfect. A three-masted tall ship lolled halfway to the horizon, headed out west. He opened his mouth wide and with three deep breaths cleared his mind and gratefully exhaled the threatened headache that had been lying in wait all day.

He expected Konrad any moment now, demanding his notes back, accusing him of bad faith. He flicked through the binder he had taken from Konrad's suitcase, shaking his head at the sheer number of pages in German. Blume's German was just good enough to see that the texts dealt with the ceremonies, history and beliefs of the Ndrangheta. One or two articles were in English and the rest in Italian. The leaves were filled with marginalia in blue and red. Konrad Hoffmann was a conscientious and fastidious scholar. No surprise there.

Blume took out the small curved black notebook he carried around in his back trouser pocket, which he used only when he had forgotten or deliberately set aside his larger one. His intention was to note down any points of particular interest among Konrad's papers that caught his eye, but he gave up after ten minutes to focus instead on the image of the torn

Madonna signed on the back by Domenico Megale. Konrad's putative passport to somewhere, a membership card for something. What was the etiquette about ripping a Madonna in half? The Ndrangheta initiation ceremony involved the burning of images of the Archangel St Michael. For all he knew the tearing up of a Madonna was fine. But Konrad should not have it in his possession. Far from a voucher or token of safe conduct, the half Madonna was a death sentence that the foolish German was going to deliver with his own hand.

He picked up the reassuringly heavy handset of the bedside phone and called reception. Yes, the girl told him, they did have a fax and of course she would be happy to send something.

Blume took his Samsung and, after moving icons back and forth like he was trying to solve a tile-puzzle from his childhood, finally found the number pad, pressed '1', held it, and waited.

Massimiliani answered on the third ring.

'Nice of you to call in. Do you know how many times I have tried to contact you?'

'No, but I'm sure this clever phone can tell me,' said Blume.

'It looks like you're near Positano.'

'Very clever phone. Actually, we're there, in the hotel. We took a bit of a detour to Lake Avernus, which was the mad German's idea. No reason that I can see, except he says he studied Latin once. Do you have a fax number up there?' asked Blume.

'A fax . . . I suppose we must still have one. Hold on.'

Blume heard the plop of a hand being placed over the mouthpiece, as if Massimiliani felt it was important not to let himself be heard calling out to someone in the room about whether they had a fax.

Finally, Massimiliani was back with a number, which Blume noted down. Very much to Massimiliani's surprise and annoyance, he hung up as soon as he had finished writing.

The girl behind the desk smiled at Blume as he walked over, but the smile faded as Blume slapped the 83-page document on the desk in front of her and said, 'You told me you had a fax.'

He wrote the DCSA number on the back of the first page. 'These need to go out immediately.'

The girl picked up the file and seemed to weigh it in her hand. Then, with what sounded like relief, she said, 'I can't fax this: it's in spiral binding.'

'That's all right,' said Blume. 'You fire up the fax machine or what-ever you have to do, and I'll rip the pages out and hand them to you one by one.'

'That'll take hours. Look, when I said we had a fax . . .'

'And that you'd be happy to oblige,' added Blume.

'Yes, I did say that but . . .' The girl picked up the phone and pressed a number. 'Dad? I need you up here.'

When the hotel owner arrived at reception, he immediately dismissed his daughter with a curt nod of the head. He then turned to Blume with an expression of loathing, which Blume couldn't justify unless the girl had telepathically communicated his unreasonable fax demands. He began to explain about the fax again when the manager interrupted him.

'I'm afraid we're going to have to ask you to leave. Both of you.'

Blume turned around, looking for Konrad, but he was alone in the lobby. Through the window of the hotel he could just see a small part of the rear section of the ridiculous old camper van.

'Your skinny boyfriend isn't here. You know how I know that?' said the manager. 'I know that because he is at this moment lying naked on a ledge beneath our private garden. There have been complaints. Three children and a very respectable woman have seen him so far. Lucky for him my daughter has been spared the obscenity.'

'My boyfriend?'

'Partner, whatever you people call yourselves these days. I should have guessed, two men in a camper. There's a campsite in Salerno, an hour from here, I'm sure you can park for the night there.'

'Look, he's German,' said Blume in his best soothing voice.

'Not only that,' continued the manager, his voice trembling now, 'he took two of our white towels and a bathrobe with him, when it is expressly written in large red letters on the door that they are not to be removed from the rooms.'

'He's still down there?' asked Blume. 'On the ledge?'

'Yes, he is. Unless he's taken off his bathrobe and dived into the water again. There's a sign that says no swimming, dangerous currents, but if he can ignore our polite request about the towels, I suppose he's not going to pay any attention to public notices. He'll probably dash himself to pieces against the rocks. I'm calling the police.'

Blume pulled out his police badge, placed it on the counter between them, and tapped it with his forefinger, where 'Commissario' was written. 'Before you do that,' he said, 'consider that this strange German and I have separate rooms.'

The manager looked at the badge, then picked it up and examined it closely. He looked back at Blume and, for the first time, noticed the fat document on the counter.

'What is that?'

Blume made a show of checking that they were alone in the lobby, then opened the file, pointing at the German text. 'These are files belonging to the German. He doesn't know I have them.'

'So you two are not . . .?'

'I'm investigating him.'

'Really? Sex crimes?'

Blume shook his head with great sadness and ambiguity.

'It's part of an operation. See the number on the back of the first page here? It's an 06 number to a fax in Rome. It would be good if we could get this to them before the German finds out. The pages will have to be detached leaf by leaf before it can be faxed.'

'That means he'll find out,' said the manager.

'Can't be helped,' said Blume. 'But once it's been transmitted to Rome, there's not much he can do about it. Of course, he mustn't be allowed to see that you have this.'

'No, I suppose that makes sense,' said the manager.

'Now, as I was about to explain to your beautiful daughter,' Blume pulled out two fifties from his wallet and put them down on the counter, 'I realize it will take time and effort, and then there's the question of the phone bill.'

'Oh, that,' said the manager, waving a dismissive hand. 'We pay a flat rate every two months. We could fax all night without paying a cent more.'

Blume slid the two fifties across the counter. 'But it's such a terrible waste of your time. And I am asking for discretion, too.' He pulled out another two fifties. 'That one's for the towels and bathrobe, and to buy some drinks, dinner and ice cream for the lady and the children the German has offended.'

The manager eyed the money and said, 'Luckily the fax is in the back room, so no one will see. My daughter could do it, if that's OK, or is it too confidential?'

'Absolutely fine. I was counting on it, because that way you can give her the two fifties as extra pocket money. The others, of course, are for your guests. I'm paying damages here, and you're being very helpful.'

The manager hesitated, then, with a look of agony crossing his face, pushed the notes back towards Blume.

'I am willing to help, but I cannot accept payment for my duties as an honest citizen.'

'If I have to pick that money off the counter, I'll charge you with bribery of a public official,' said Blume.

The manager paled, and his hand froze over the bills, unsure whether to push them away, claw them back, or just let go.

'I'm kidding,' said Blume with a laugh.

The manager laughed, too.

'But I insist,' added Blume, pushing the notes at him and turning on his heel.

He guessed there was nothing of any use in the series of files being faxed to Rome. They could check if they wanted. The important thing was to seem to be doing something. He returned to his room to wait for Konrad. He opened the window and lay down on his bed, kicking off his shoes and then using his big toes to peel off one sock, then the other, and thought again about the torn Madonna.

His phone vibrated, but did not ring. He must have activated silent mode setting by mistake when he tried to answer it the first time. That would explain all the missed calls.

'What are you sending us, Blume?' asked Massimiliani, when he finally relented and answered.

'Proof that Konrad Hoffmann is interested in the Ndrangheta,' said Blume.

'Well, that was pretty well established once his colleagues spotted him leaving the home of an Ndrangheta boss, don't you think?'

'Fine, then,' said Blume. 'Proof he's no expert on the Society, despite having met the boss of an important *locale* in Germany. He's learning the rudiments of Ndrangheta history and ceremonies. I don't consider myself a real expert, but I do know that it is a cardinal sin for any member to carry about information on the mysteries and secrets of the Society, so take this as proof he has not been inducted into it. Or maybe he's doing a double bluff, but I just don't see it. Konrad is not operating on behalf of the Ndrangheta. I am sure of it.'

185

'How did you manage to get these files from him?'

'I took them. He doesn't know yet, but he will.'

'I suppose that's good work, then. Anything else?'

Blume thought about the torn image of the Madonna, and couldn't bring himself to tell Massimiliani about it until he himself had a clearer idea. He'd talk to Konrad and see what he could find out. He realized he wanted to give Konrad a chance to explain before reporting to Massimiliani.

'No, nothing else at this point,' he said.

'Keep up the good work,' said Massimiliani. 'I think we may be about to learn something this end about Hoffmann and his motivations. I'll let you know as soon as I hear.'

Blume dropped the phone by his side, put his hands behind his head and closed his eyes, trying to work out Massimiliani's tone. The waves broke against sharp rocks at a regular rhythm forty metres below. Far away, seagulls were kicking up a terrible fuss.

A cooling air swirled around his feet, and he flexed his toes, pulled his trousers up to free his ankles, pulled his polo up, and lay there with his stomach bare. Lovely. It would be nice to have Caterina here now, but it was nice, too, maybe nicer, to be all alone on a large smooth white bed. He could stretch out in an X-shape and catch more of the air coming in, along with the distant noise of people shouting, motorbikes, or maybe outboard motors. The seagulls had stopped their clamour, a plane was passing high overhead, and some insects were clicking and chattering near the window. He flipped the pillow over to the cool side, pressed it against the back of his neck.

Damned phone. It was still under his hand, he picked it up – no, it was the one beside the bed. He rolled over, realizing the air had darkened considerably and grown cooler and wetter. 'Pronto?'

'Room 17.'

'Huh?'

'I'll meet you there,' said the manager, his voiced hushed with boyish excitement. 'You'll see. I've sent my daughter down to you. She'll be there any moment.'

Someone knocked gently on the door, and Blume jumped out of bed and opened the door.

'My father said to give you this.' She handed him a neat stack of A4 paper. 'And to go down to Room 17 immediately. Down those steps.'

The manager was waiting in the corridor below. 'The German is not back yet but it's getting dark. He'll be here any moment,' he said. He stopped outside Room 17 and opened the door. Beaming from ear to ear at his own cleverness, he then placed the spiral-bound notes in Blume's hands. 'I managed to get them all back into the spine. My fax machine is also a photocopier, so I thought I could copy them for you as I sent them, see? Then you can put this back in his room and the German will be none the wiser.'

Not bad, thought Blume, though he did not like the idea of the hotel manager being in too much on this, and definitely did not want him to watch as he opened Konrad's suitcase and slipped the document back in. He nodded, took the file and closed the door in the eager manager's face.

The manager knocked immediately.

'No,' said Blume. 'You can't come in here.'

The manager's voice, hoarse with panic and excitement, came from behind the door. 'The German's walking up the steps. I just caught a glimpse of him. He'll come in the door at the end of the corridor. It'll take him only seconds . . . He's going to catch us . . . Wait.'

Blume heard the manager move away from the door and his footfalls pounding down the corridor. He took his time even so, placing the document carefully in the position he remembered finding it. If Konrad walked in, well, it would be embarrassing, that was all. He closed the suitcase, walked quickly to the door, surveyed the room once more.

He slipped out of the room as the manager came running up the hall, breathless.

'I pulled hard at the door so he couldn't open it from the outside. Really hard like it was locked, not like someone was pulling it. He'll have gone up the cliff path to get in, and then he'll come down the stairs . . . that's him. Quick, we can get out here.'

He ran down the corridor again. Blume followed reluctantly, and they exited the door the manager had been blocking. They ascended the steps back up to the parking area, past the camper van, and back into the hotel. The daughter and her father exchanging theatrical glances, Blume went back down to his room, dissatisfied.

Konrad had been willing to leave the documents unattended for hours. It wasn't unreasonable to conclude that he didn't care too much if they were discovered, which meant they had no real importance. Or, at the risk of being too Freudian, it meant Konrad unconsciously wanted them discovered. Maybe he wanted someone to stop him. But from doing what?

31

Positano

A FEW MINUTES later, Konrad, his raw neck and head sticking out of the white cotton bathrobe, knocked on the door to announce, much to Blume's surprise, that he had made reservations for dinner. He said he would take a quick shower and meet him in the lobby in fifteen minutes.

'Where are we going?'

'A place called I Partenopei,' said Konrad, making a good job of the pronunciation. 'Recommended by the hotel manager who looks at me funny.' Konrad lowered his voice, '*Schwul*, definitely. Despite the daughter.'

Blume went up to the lobby to wait where the manager, full of solicitation and goodwill, immediately informed him he had ordered them a cab, even though it was only ten minutes on foot.

'Far too dangerous that road in the dark,' the manager said.

The taxi turned out to have a fixed rate. Fifteen euros there and back. 'Call here when you want him to come down and pick you up.'

'That's not a taxi,' said Blume.

'Not exactly,' agreed the manager. 'It's a sort of courtesy car for some of the hotels on this side of the headland.'

'A courtesy car is free.'

'I'll pay, of course,' said the manager quickly. 'It's not as if you haven't already been generous.'

'I'll get the German to pay. He can pay for dinner, too.'

Konrad arrived wearing a wide-collar paisley-design shirt, a crumpled linen jacket and drainpipe black jeans. Adidas running shoes and a powerful stench of Denim aftershave or something else that belonged to the 1970s completed his get-up. His hair, still wet, was sleeked back into a ducktail.

The restaurant was perched on a rocky outcrop overlooking the harbour. Looking down, Blume could see their table reflected in the dark water and the waiter coming towards them like a black shadow moving just beneath the surface. Running the length of the wall was a fish tank with crabs and lobsters, the pincers disabled by plastic cuffs, and red reef mullets, ready to be netted and fried without needing to be gutted.

They ate well, but mostly in silence. Konrad, who said swimming had made him hungry, announced that from the point of view of toxins, he had more confidence in the produce of the sea than the land. He had swordfish steaks. Blume, being adventurous, went for aubergine with chocolate and peppered mussels, and they both chose *acqua pazza* as their first course.

The restaurant was full for a Monday night. Blume glanced at the swarthy bulky men sucking at their fingers and reaching across each other as they stretched to help themselves from central platters of fish. At another table a woman bedecked in gold jewels and wearing a white tracksuit was explaining to the waiter that the roly-poly kid in the blue football strip of Napoli sulking beside her had coeliac disease and would die if any pasta passed his mouth, but he could, and did, eat meat and fried potatoes, though he might possibly be allergic to fish. Five youths at another table, all in tracksuits, drank limoncello and kept a careful eye on Konrad and Blume.

'I'm glad to see you do eat,' said Blume. 'You even seem to be enjoying yourself.'

'There is something liberating about this place.'

'This restaurant, the Amalfi coast, or southern Italy?'

'All together. I am not a romantic anarchist. I am, after all, a policeman. But there is great freedom in the absence of rules. And I feel like we have travelled a great distance, even though it was only a few hours from Rome this morning. That seems so long ago.'

'The south is separate from the north,' said Blume. 'The broken roads and railways turn journeys down here into tiring odysseys. Even when southerners speak standard Italian, they use a different grammar. Everything is said in the remote tense. That has to mean something.'

'It means they still use the Latin past tense,' said Konrad. 'It is very fascinating to me.'

'If it were up to me,' said Blume, 'I'd give this region back to the

Spanish, the north back to the French and the Austrians, and Sicily back to the Arabs.'

'And so, logically, you would give Rome and central Italy back to the Pope.'

'Oh, no,' said Blume. 'I couldn't do that.'

'Why not?'

'Because he's German.'

Konrad, recovering his confidence in the purity of the produce, ordered *sospiri di limoni* for dessert. Blume asked for coffee.

'I am paying for this of course,' said Konrad. 'You are my guest.' He called over the waiter and got the bill, scribbled on a piece of graph paper.

Blume shrugged. 'It's the other way around if anything, but you can still pay.'

Without quite knowing why he was doing it, especially after he had made such an effort to cover his tracks, Blume now found himself saying, 'Konrad, listen to me: if you're thinking of going down to Calabria, don't. They don't want visitors. That would definitely include a federal policeman from Germany.'

'Why do you say I am going to Calabria?'

'Because you are.'

'Just because I met Domenico Megale . . .'

'I saw that torn Madonna with Megale's signature. Take that look off your face, you left your bags unattended in the camper van, and then your room. Some part of you wants to be stopped. A well-hidden sane part.'

Konrad's eyes were shining. Perhaps it was the drink. 'I have a private matter to attend to. It is not police work. I would be grateful to be left alone,' he said.

'Is that icon of the Madonna some sort of code? What's the idea, someone down there has the other half of the torn Madonna, you fit the two halves together, they see Megale's signature, they know you are good and true?'

Konrad stared into the middle distance avoiding Blume's sympathetic gaze and struggling to compose his features into an expression of indifference.

'Are you planning to kill someone, Konrad? Or are you trying to get yourself killed? Or both? All I can say is you are making a bad choice, and I am giving you a chance not to make it . . .'

Blume stopped, as the waiter returned.

'If I make a bad choice, there is another universe in which I make a good choice,' said Konrad. 'I believe in multiverse theory.'

'That's handy. Meanwhile, back in this universe, the waiter's just asked us if you would prefer to pay in cash.'

'What?'

'Cash. The credit card machine is mysteriously "broken".'

'I don't have enough cash.'

'Fuck it,' said Blume. He pulled out two fifties from the envelope Massimiliani had given him and paid for the meal.

32

Positano

BLUME WAS LYING in bed, his stomach heavy with fish, searching for the willpower to read through Konrad's notes when his Samsung vibrated.

'Massimiliani, I suppose?'

'Of course it's me. I hope you're not using the phone to call other people.'

'No. What do you want?'

'You can forget about Hoffmann.'

Blume sat up straight, causing some of the papers to slip off his bed. 'No! I was just getting somewhere with him. He has a torn Madonna. I think it's a pass of some sort.'

'Sorry, I'm not following. Are you talking about some immediate threat?'

'No,' said Blume. 'I was . . . never mind.'

'Good. We'll pick you up in the morning, both of you. Hoffmann's superiors have finally worked out the reason for his trip.'

'Well?'

'They won't tell us yet. They say they need to check up on one or two final details. Personally, I think they are embarrassed at having overlooked something obvious, or maybe they have discovered Hoffmann was working for one internal department, which neglected to tell the other. It's their problem, not ours.'

'Just like that? We no longer care about Konrad?'

'We never did care about him. We cared about what he might do, but it seems he's not going to do anything that bothers us. He's not armed, is he?'

'No.'

'See? It's not a serious matter, at least that's what they say.'

'You suddenly trust the Germans?'

'I always trusted my friend and associate Weissmann.'

'But you don't know what it is they have found out?'

'I am afraid not. I expect them to tell us tomorrow. It's rather late in the day now. They want to talk to Hoffmann himself beforehand. In fact, they are probably talking to him now.'

'OK,' said Blume slowly, concentrating on keeping the anger out of the two syllables. It was clear the Hoffmann threat, and hence Blume's contribution, had never been taken very seriously. He knew all along the mission was not crucial, but this was humiliating.

'What was that you said about a Madonna?'

'I'll tell you that later, sometime tomorrow. After you've heard from the Germans.'

'Tell me now, Blume.'

'It's late. It's a complicated thing and you just told me it doesn't matter anyhow,' said Blume, hanging up on Massimiliani for the second time that evening.

Blume picked up the bedside phone and dialled Room 17, and was quite surprised when the inside line did what it was supposed to do and put him in contact with Konrad, who sounded as if he had been asleep.

'Curmaci,' said Blume. 'Agazio Curmaci. I don't quite know why, but that's who you are interested in. So am I. That's why they threw us together. If he's your enemy, maybe I can help. If he's your friend, then . . . I don't know. You don't want him as a friend.'

Konrad said nothing.

'Do you know what sort of man he is?' said Blume.

'Yes,' said Konrad quietly, his voice muted with sleep. 'I know what sort of a man he is. I think I was just dreaming about him now. Go to sleep and we can talk in the morning.'

But Blume no longer felt as tired as before. He retrieved the fallen papers from around his bed and started looking through them. Konrad had copied out songs, dialect words, stories, history and even recipes connected with the Society. Occasionally, a word was underlined here, an exclamation mark added there. Finally, Blume found a page with underlining and translations of dialect words on which Konrad had committed himself to a comment, although it turned out to be no more than a hastily scrawled '*sehr interessant*'.

It was a description, no doubt out of date, of the protocol for making contact with an *'ndrina* that did not know you. Was that Konrad's plan?

Q. Are you a wolf, a bee or a goat dropping?
A. I am a wolf who will devour you, a bee who will sting you, and a goat dropping that follows you.
Q. Do you walk, sir, above the road or below it?
A. I walk both above and below the road, for I am an artful scoundrel.

'Oh, no you're not, Konrad,' muttered Blume. He flicked through till his eyes landed on more marking by Konrad, this time at the top of the story of Osso, Carcagnosso and Matrosso. Blume knew the legend. It was just the sort of thing an impressionable German like Konrad . . .

His phone, his real one, not the one supplied by Massimiliani, was ringing. Wearily, he got off the bed, half hoping it would stop before he got there, knowing full well who it would be. He hesitated; the caller, Caterina of course, was insistent; she was in a fury with him by the time he answered.

'Apart from everything else,' said Caterina, following up her long opening sentence in which she had called him a coward, a sneak, an *infame*, a liar, childish, stubborn and uncaring, 'you are a fool.'

Now would be a good time to put down the phone, thought Blume, but then Caterina mentioned she had been to see Magistrate Arconti.

'He's talking, and he's talking about you. He's also talking about a mysterious confession made by Curmaci's wife.'

'Ah,' said Blume.

'Captain Massimiliano Massimiliani appreciated the subterfuge. Is that what you want, to earn the approval of people like him?'

'What's wrong with him? You haven't even met him.'

'Massimiliani's father was involved in the Borghese coup attempt.'

'That was his father,' said Blume with an authority he did not own, since Caterina's revelation was news to him.

'But you didn't know that, did you? You were so anxious to get away and play boy soldiers that you did not even question him, look him up or check him out like I did. Since when do you trust some creep from SISDE or AIMI or whatever they call themselves these days?'

'He's probably listening, you know.'

'Yeah, I can smell him from here,' said Caterina. 'Did he give you a Masonic handshake, Alec? What lodge will you be joining, P3, P4, the Circle of the Illuminated Thieves?'

'Now you're exaggerating. Maybe Italy needs people like him now,' said Blume.

'No, it doesn't, but people like him need errant fools like you to follow their directions. Gallivanting about as if anyone would ever take you seriously. A middle-aged homicide cop pretending to be fifteen years younger and playing at secret agent.'

'You can't talk to me like that.'

'Shut up, Alec. I mean . . . shut up. Christ. Put this right or forget about me ever speaking to you again.'

'Put what right?'

'You've put that woman's life in danger, just to place yourself at the centre of an affair that does not properly concern you. Tell Massimiliani to deal with it differently and you come home. But first, make sure that woman and the people around there don't get hurt.'

'So you think she deserves help, sheltering her criminal husband, nurturing criminal children, hanging out with other criminal women, the *sorelle d'omertà* as they call themselves, perpetuating the Society, obstructing inquiries, intimidating the few good citizens left? Whatever bad comes to her, she had coming.'

'Including death? You'd be all right with that?'

'If she dies, it won't be by my hand, but by the hand of someone she knows, someone who will have more innocent blood than hers on his conscience. Someone whose murdering of innocent people she accepted, hid and respected.'

'Alec,' said Caterina, disorienting him by suddenly softening her tone, 'you don't have to talk tough like that to me. I know you.'

'Then you should know these are my opinions.'

'No, they are not. And even if they are, I happen to know your opinions don't always match your feelings.'

'I hate it when you try and persuade yourself that I am what you would like me to be. Next time I fail to live up to your expectations, don't come looking for me.'

In the old days when he was receiving the silent treatment from a girl on the phone, he used to be able to hear the pops, gurgles and whooshing sound of the telegraph wires punctuated by the sighs and breaths and involuntary voiced murmurs that allowed him to judge the mood and seriousness of his soon-to-be-ex-girlfriend on the end of the line. But digital technology, the source of much evil in the world, he felt, had killed that, too. A high-pitched whine just within his audible range suggested the connection was still live, but the silence from the other side was total. He could not analyse her silences or anticipate her responses. Or maybe it was just Caterina and digital phones had nothing to do with it.

'How's your head?' she asked eventually.

'My head?'

'Yes, Alec, your head. The large hairy thing full of evil thoughts that sticks out of your collar. The part of you that aches and talks about itself all the time.'

'Fine. Mostly. I was on my way to a headache twice today, but it passed both times.'

'When will you be home?'

'I don't know and I can't say. Maybe as soon as tomorrow.'

'I hope so.'

After he had hung up and stuffed his phone under the pillow, Blume found he was unable to banish his thoughts, concentrate or properly distract his mind. In the end he read the story of Osso, Matrosso and Carcagnosso, until he felt his eyes close.

33

The Three Knights

© *Domenech K. & Nisticò G., 2007. Die Heldenunternehmungen der drei Ritter. Vorwort In Lange Kunst Vol I (3): 3–15. Frankfurt. Germany. Fachverlag Klett-Vauk.*

In that place where now stands the Mosque of Al-Asqa in the sacred city of Jerusalem, a band of warriors, founded by twenty-five good men who took up arms only with reluctance, established their seat of command. The band was known as the Poor Fellow-Soldiers of Christ and of the Temple of Solomon. We remember them today as the Knights Templar.

They wore snow-white mantles displaying a scarlet cross, symbol of our Saviour Jesus Christ, symbol also of their faith and their fair-dealing in business and of their readiness to afford protection, even at the cost of blood, for those who had the humility and wisdom to seek their help. Even when their help was not sought directly, the knights sacrificed their own comfort to protect the pilgrims travelling to the Holy Land across desert kingdoms under the cruel and heathen rule of Islam.

The first Grand Master of the Order was Hugh De Paysn, cousin and vassal of the Count of Champagne; the second-in-command was Goffredo di Saint Omer. The committee in charge was made up of nine Knights, all of whom had taken a vow of poverty. They defended the Latin states of Edessa, Antioch, Tripoli and the Kingdom of Jerusalem, conquered by the valour of Franks and Normans. The Knights Templar were officially recognized as an Order of the Church by Pope Innocent II in 1139. This Pope, from the Papareschi family in Rome, grew up in Trastevere where he founded a church now called Santa Maria, a place that has remained holy through the ages.

The Knights Templar continued for about 150 more years until, on Friday 13

October, 1307 Clement V ordered the dissolution of the Order and the arrest of the members. Dozens of Knights Templar were burned at the stake in Paris.

The surviving knights dispersed and fled to all corners of the world. Three blessed brother Knights fated to live an accursed life, Osso, Matrosso and Carcagnosso, travelled together, and on the road they met a tall man with a diamond where his left eyeball should have been. The man, an ageless descendant of Balqis, Queen of Sheba, gave them spools of magical thread. Anyone who touched the threads and looked upon another man would see into the blackness of his heart, and anyone who touched the threads and looked up to the sky would see all the evil deeds mankind had yet to commit. For, as the Jews believe and as it is written in the Targum Sheni to the Book of Esther, the fabrics of the land of Balqis were spun from the fibres of plants that date from the Creation and were watered by a river that ran from the Garden of Eden.

The brother Knights brought the threads to an old spinster who wove them into five fine cloaks. The Knights then put the spinster to the sword so that she might never tell of their secret. Each of the brothers took one cloak for himself. Osso, the eldest brother, gave the fourth to the poet Dante to accompany him safely into exile from treacherous Florence, as well as on his long voyage into hell, purgatory and heaven. Who wore the fifth cloak remains unknown to this day.

Osso, Matrosso and Carcagnosso, deeply touched by the glimpses of future evil deeds, fashioned a fine ship with three masts of living trees and five sails and travelled across the world seeking to warn peoples of coming calamities. They travelled to the noble races of the Americas, the Aztecs, Mayas and Incas, and forewarned them of the terrible fates that would befall them when the next white men arrived in tall ships.

The people listened to the Knights, and their warning was passed from generation to generation. But those peoples who forgot their traditions, also forgot the story of the Knights, so that when the time of the catastrophe came, they were unprepared.

The Knights then performed many acts of courage, and their fame spread far and wide. They travelled to Tibet, Samarkand and prospered for some time in the city states of the Hanseatic League.

Finally, wearied of travel, Osso, Matrosso and Carcagnosso sought peace and tranquillity in the Holy Kingdom of Spain. But their renown travelled faster than they, and ere they had set foot in Spain, they had already become hateful to the vengeful nobles of the Kingdom. Unjustly accused of ignoble deeds against a maiden of Spanish royal blood, the three Knights were forced to flee the

Kingdom. They settled on the island of Favignana, north-west of Sicily, oppo-site the ancient city of Trapani.

There, the three brother Knights decided to go their separate ways. Osso, who dedicated his life to the Lord Jesus Christ, chose to travel the narrow body of water to Sicily and settle there. Carcagnosso, beloved of Saint Peter, travelled the length and breadth of Italy and, finding that Naples was the most beautiful of all the cities he had seen in his long travels, chose it for his home. Matrosso, who turned all his prayers to the Archangel Michael, crossed the Straits of Messina to the region of Calabria, and there he made his home among the proud descendants of the Normans.

Each Knight brought with him a code of honour. As they took up their new and final abodes, they enshrined these codes of honour among their followers, who formed societies of honour. Osso's Honoured Society became known as the Mafia, which means virtue; Carcagnosso formed the Most Excellent Reformed Society, the Camorra; Matrosso formed the Society of Valorous Men, the Ndrangheta.

Some say the cloaks were unravelled and the magic threads distributed to the most faithful, others that they are still worn by a secret elect who may be seen by those who have eyes to look . . .

34

Locri

THE STORY OF Osso, Matrosso and Carcagnosso, his father had told him, was like the story of Jesus Christ. It was absolutely true, and where it evidently was not true, it contained symbolic truth. Symbols were to be accepted in absolute solemnity. Names were sacred, oaths even more so.

His father told him variations of the Osso, Matrosso and Carcagnosso story, some of which he already knew, others he had not heard. Each variation, his father explained, was a possibility, and each was spoken with reverence. Sometimes there were deeper truths, sometimes there were pieces of history left out or suppressed. Osso, Matrosso and Carcagnosso, if not Templars, if not the three founders of the three honoured Societies, may well have been Norman brother knights. Calabrians were often Greek, his father explained, and some of them, the weakest, were of Byzantine stock. Others, whose hard blue eyes could be seen among the leaders of so many of the top families, were the direct descendants of the Norman conquerors.

'In the year 999, a handful of men from the north, the Normans, came down and seized control of Apulia, Calabria and Sicily,' his father explained one night during a brief visit. 'They expelled the Lombards, the Byzantines and the Arabs, and commanded with an iron fist. But they did not disdain the people of Apulia, Basilicata, Campania, Sicily and Calabria, a people whose exceptional beauty was the result of mixing the blood of the red Germanic Lombards with the dark-skinned Arabs and Africans, and the pampered Greeks, Albanians, Illyrians and descendants of the ancient Romans. The Normans and then their descendants melted into the local people, but without losing any of their fierceness. They set out to conquer the Holy Land, while their cousins on the Atlantic coast of France, lacking land and with warrior fathers who did not want to pass on any of their wealth even to their own sons, conquered the British Isles. Ours is warrior blood. That, son, is why your eyes are blue and why I named you Ruggiero and your baby brother Roberto. In history, the Norman Robert was earlier, but Roger was greater. You are named after the Norman Knight who created the Kingdom of the South. Learn about him.'

Ruggiero had done as his father asked, reading books he barely understood, then reading them again. He even read three in English. And when his father returned six months later, he was dying to show off his newly acquired knowledge, but his father asked him nothing. A full year later, he appeared one night at the doorway of Ruggiero's bedroom and returned to the subject.

'Your mother tells me you have been reading those books about the Normans. What have you learned?'

Ruggiero started listing the dates and places of the battles through southern Italy, the leading knights, the Norman families, and their long war with the Byzantines, the Pope and the Lombards. His father listened, nodded, asked him some dates, corrected a few things, and gave him no praise.

The following night, he asked him what else he had learned, and Ruggiero spoke of the conquest of the Holy Land, the Italians and Normans in Antioch and Jerusalem, all the way up to the final defeat of the last of the Norman kings in Benevento.

On the third and final night before he left for Germany, his father again asked him what he had learned, but Ruggiero had come to the death of Conradin and the books his father had given him went no further.

'So, what did you learn?'

'I don't know.'

'Think.'

'I learned what sort of people they were.'

'And what was that?' asked his father.

'They were men of faith, who believed in Jesus Christ and the Holy Apostolic Church, but they still went to war against the Pope.'

'Excellent. Even as they held him captive, they begged his forgiveness. What else?'

'Brother fought brother, cousin fought cousin. And they had a grand council. When they had a common enemy, like the emperor of Constantinople, they came together. But they also fought each other, and sometimes even in the middle of a joint operation one family would try to gain the lands of another.'

'Yet each battle was eventually resolved by the other families if ever a dispute threatened to undermine their right to rule southern Italy,' said his father.

Six months later his father, speaking to him after dinner while his mother was upstairs with the newborn Robertino, said, 'I will not sit by your bedside and tell you stories any more. You are too old for that.'

Ruggiero nodded, sad and pleased.

'But a little modern history won't hurt. I'm talking about the 1960s, a long time before you were born, but a period which to many people still seems like yesterday. It was a period of change and internal war. Since then, we have become ever stronger, which is only natural. Do you know why?'

Ruggiero rightly considered this a rhetorical question and said nothing.

'Threats and restrictions are what make us strong. Threats above all, provided they are external and not internal. Outside enemies make us strong. Restrictions and obedience also make us strong. Someday, it may be good to find yourself facing a powerful enemy, especially one who thinks he knows your weaknesses. And you will have a weakness. We all do.'

'So how do you stop them from exploiting it?'

'You change it at the last moment. The regular drunkard who turns up for a fight with his mind alert, focused and sober, the coward who puts his life on the line, the miser who throws away all his wealth to confound his enemy, the joker who turns deadly serious − these are the people who suddenly emerge victorious. But first you need to see where your weakness is. For this you need an enemy, because your enemy will always be nearer the truth in their opinion of you than you are yourself.'

'What's your weakness, Papà?'

'Find out your own first before you ask me, and find it from someone who hates you.'

'Is that how you found out yours?'

'I had many weaknesses, but I have worked for years in a foreign and hostile land in the company of someone who hates me more with each passing day, and that has kept me alive, alert and strong.'

'Are you talking about Enrico's dad? I thought our families were close.'

'We are. But let me tell you a story about Tony. In some ways, it is a story that redounds to his honour. I want you to know it so that you understand something of the character of the man. I also want you to imagine how it would feel to be the enemy of a man such as this. Are you following me?'

'Yes.'

'In 1963, a faction of the Society was still aligned with the Communist Party. This was because the party was not in government and was regarded as being a sort of anti-state. All the Society's income came from providing business protection and seizing hostages, or kidnap victims as the press always called them, from the wealthy north for distribution to the people of our land. So the *melandrini*, the Ndrangheta gangs, were doing in deed what the Communists only promised. That year, a feud broke out between the Mazzaferro and Neri families over the control of the bergamot orange plantations of Reggio Calabria. The Mazzaferro represented an old version of the Society based on ideas of socialism and land reform. Not collectivization or real socialism, since there always have to be landlords and tenants, but they wanted more social justice. The Neri represented a new right-wing version of the Society. In those days, they were very interested in what was going on in Greece where the colonels had taken power. The Neri got mixed up with monarchists and fascists and princes of the Church, as well as magistrates, Christian Democrats, and even elements of the armed forces and police. It was a strange time of strange ideologies, none of which survived for long.

'The feud between these two families would not usually involve people from our side of the country. But one family from our area, the Megales, with great strategic acumen, decided to offer assistance to the Neris. They sent an expeditionary force up the mountain to help them. So it was that one night in May 1964, a group led by Domenico Megale – you know of him now as *Megale u Vecchiu* because he is old, but then he was still in his prime, and everyone called him Mimmo instead of Domenico. They say he brought with him his son, then twelve years of age, to show the people of the town that even if his son was slow in his speech and thought, he was fast and merciless in his action. I'm not sure if that's true.'

'You mean Zio Pietro?' Ruggiero tried to picture Enrico's truculent and silent uncle as a boy, but couldn't.

'Yes, Zio Pietro. Now, where was I?'

'Domenico Megale was leading an expeditionary group,' said Ruggiero.

'Right. Domenico Megale and his group breached the defences of the Mazzaferro fort, which was nothing more than a drystone house on the slopes of Aspromonte, and destroyed its inhabitants, wiping out an entire branch of the Mazzaferro. That night of slaughter ended the feud, and relegated that branch of the Mazzaferro family, or what was left of it, to obscurity.'

'But the Mazzaferro are still in charge in Gioioso Ionico.'

'Different clan, same surname. Don't interrupt,' said his father. 'When Megale and the Neri squad left, there were twelve males and eight females left dead, their ages ranging from seven to seventy-seven. Four more were seriously injured, three of them maimed for life, and if you look you may well see one of them, disfigured of body, who remains among us yet, pardoned and reinstated by Basile himself.'

'Was Basile involved in any of this?'

'Basile was the deal-maker and peacekeeper. He did not take sides, which is his speciality. He never takes sides until the dust settles, and is always ready to mediate. Basile's only interest is this area, and now he has this *gelateria* . . . You interrupted me again.'

'Sorry.'

'That's OK. It means you're listening. Some of the very oldest were left alive, to bury their dead and bear witness. A beautiful young mother, whose husband was away at the time, was also allowed to live. But perhaps it was better she had died, for her child of one year, her only son, disappeared during that night of slaughter. After the feud was declared officially closed, the woman's husband, who lived in northern exile, like so many of us, was allowed to return. He was supposed to comfort his wife and give her new sons to help her overcome her grief, but this never happened. The body of the child was never returned. It was given to understand that a *picciotto* who had snatched the abandoned child from his cradle as the mother cowered in the next room lost his life soon after the end of the feud.

'Some said that it had not been a lowly *picciotto* but the chief *sgarrista* himself, Domenico Megale, who was in that room. And some also said that he had held the infant in his hands, ready to dash its head against the wall, but overcome by sudden compassion, had spared the child's life. But Domenico Megale never spoke of it, and no one dared to ask him, and the memory of the bloody night began to fade.

'The young mother never had another child, and for years she never mentioned what happened that night. In 1982, when I was a young man hardly older than you, the mother had a vision. Her child, now a young man of nineteen years, she claimed had appeared to her in a dream, accompanied by the Blessed Gioacchino da Fiore dressed in rags.

'Most people felt great sympathy for the woman, who was now leaving child-bearing age behind her. People said her dream had been sent as a message of farewell to her youth and fertility. As it was evidently her grief that was speaking to her, she was treated with the utmost kindness by the town. But their patience was soon exhausted as she continued in her delusions. As the years passed, she continued to report that her son, now aged twenty, now twenty-one, and now twenty-five, was visiting her while she slept, sometimes accompanied by the Madonna, sometimes by Padre Pio but more often by the Blessed Gioacchino da Fiore. She began to make pilgrimages to the town of San Giovanni in Fiore to visit the Abbey of Florens, and when her story became known, the monks there did what they could to console her and pray for her, even holding a special mass one night in November.

'Then, in 1989, she did the unthinkable and went to the Carabinieri and denounced Megale for the events of a quarter of a century earlier. She did so at five o'clock in the evening, walking straight up to the barracks under the eyes of the whole town.'

Ruggiero blinked his eyes in acknowledgment of the sense of shock that must have been felt.

'Now it turns out,' continued his father, 'that for all the rumours, no one had ever really asked her about what happened that night in 1964. Sometimes people prefer not to remember. And yet, this forgetting was also the right thing to do. The slaughter that night was a terrible act, but it had its historical causes and necessities. It was also the beginning of a restructuring and a reexamination of conscience that has served everyone well since.

'The people of the town were sickened by this woman's blatant act of treachery, but they were also dismayed in their hearts because over the years her talk of seeing her son in the company of saints had assured people that the child was at peace with God, and was accompanying his mother through the rest of her life, ageing with her, until she, too, would be at peace. But when the benighted old woman went to the Carabinieri, she told them her son had been seized but not killed by Domenico Megale. She said that when Domenico burst into her bedroom, she was suckling the child. He was so struck by the sanctity and tenderness of the image that he found himself rooted to the spot, or so she claimed. She approached him and offered the child in exchange for her own life and a pledge to remain silent for ever. She then commended her infant into the hands of Domenico and said he was now the father. She told the Carabinieri that Domenico Megale had taken her child and left. Upon leaving, he had warned her never to come looking for the child, but now she was breaking that pledge.

'The woman's husband went to Megale and begged forgiveness. The people in the village were instructed to shun the deluded woman, but she seemed not to notice. A local magistrate opened an investigation, letting it be known that he did so with reluctance. He sent two young Carabinieri to ask Megale about the night in question. Megale told them he had no memory of the night, lost in the mists of time. The case was archived.

'Then in 1990, the woman invited in television reporters. You probably know the show, *Chi l'ha visto*, which is dedicated to tracking down missing persons.'

'It's still on,' said Ruggiero.

'Back then it was a new show, presented by an interfering albino bitch called Donatella Raffai. They sent down a team of reporters who interviewed the mother. Now she aggravated the situation by speaking far too freely about the night of the massacre, naming names and describing the abduction of her son, and saying how she was warned never to look for him. The national newspapers took up the story, and reporters swarmed the streets until our dignified reticence, as well as some low-key resistance that took the form of attacks on their vehicles and equipment, persuaded the vultures to fly back to Rome and Milan. The husband, now in his late sixties, asked permission of Don Matteo to divorce; it was not given, which was unlucky for him.

'The woman, prodded and urged by the vile reporters who were too abject to visit us, went up to Rome. There, in the studio, she allowed them to show the face of the man she claimed was her son, a man whom they had covertly filmed as he went about his business in the village, and a man whose face was familiar to everyone. That man was called Tony, the younger of Megale's sons.'

'Enrico's father,' said Ruggiero.

'When he saw his Tony on television like that, Megale, who around this time people started calling *u Vecchiu* because by then he had lost his wife to cancer – same as would happen later to his daughter-in-law – and looked far older than he really was, sued the television station for defamation, and the case dragged on for five years before ending in a settlement in his favour. Around this time, too, Communism collapsed in Europe and Megale foresaw the great fortune to be made from buying property and businesses in East Germany, and moved with his younger son, Tony, to Dusseldorf, where there was already a small Calabrian presence. He left Pietro here. As for the case against RAI Television, the judges declared that Tony had become an object of hatred for a woman devastated by loss and childlessness. She stood on the steps of the court with a placard on which she had written 'No Hatred Just a Mother's Love'. And the newspapers ran with that line, of course. God, they loved it. After the scandal had died down, Tony married a girl, Angela Mancuso, who came from an important family settled in Milan. Six months after, baby Enrico arrived, but Tony was already in Germany with his old man. He came down for the christening, though. His next visit was for Angela's last day on this earth and the funeral two days later. Cancer like wildfire through her body. I remember seeing her, thin, yellow, suddenly old. When she died, Zio Pietro and Zia Rosa decided they would take care of the baby.

'A few months later, the ignorant old woman, uncaring about Tony's bereavement, crawled out into the open again to say Enrico was her grandson. Encouraged no doubt by a reporter, because she could not even read and knew nothing about these things, she demanded a DNA test, which Domenico, Tony, Pietro and Zia Rosa all turned down with contempt.

'By now, the old woman's husband was having difficulty living in the town. His failure to exercise his authority over the woman was punished, so they say, by seven *zaccagnate* on his chest and shoulders, his age being taken into consideration, followed by expulsion. He stayed in the village with his wife, a humiliated being despised by all. Can you remember what happened in the end?'

Ruggiero remembered it as if it was yesterday. 'The woman and her husband were both stabbed to death on the same night. Him on the way back from the bar, her in her bed. It was in September, not long after the Feast of the Madonna di Polsi. School had just reopened.'

'Almost correct. The old man was shot at close range with a low-velocity bullet. Just one small entry wound at the back, no sign of violence from the front. But the woman was stabbed repeatedly in the belly and groin as she lay in her bed. The killer opened her up and tore her very insides out. It was a cruel thing. There was a big funeral and, even though they had no family, everyone turned up, including Tony Megale. He had recently returned from Germany. He had come home several days before the killing took place to celebrate the Madonna di Polsi – and visit Enrico, of course. He spent a day in custody being questioned. On the same day he was released, he asked me if I would join them in Germany, and I did.'

'Did he ever tell you anything about his mother?'

'So now you think that that woman was his mother?'

'Wasn't she? Isn't that what you just told me?'

'Draw your own conclusions quietly, decide on your own course of action quietly, act quietly.'

'So you never asked Tony?'

'You are still asking too directly. I have never even spoken of the story to anyone until this moment. In Germany, *u Vecchiu* treated me well, but I soon saw it would be necessary for me to pursue a different path from Tony, and that is what I have done. Our paths often cross, but I thought we had succeeded in dividing our responsibilities with respect and without rancour. I may have been wrong.'

'Have you and Enrico's dad fallen out?'

'Too many direct questions. If you ask direct questions, you'll be disappointed by the evasive and uncertain answers. Sometimes there are no answers, and in the meantime, people will stop talking to you. Learn to infer.'

'*Megale u Vecchiu* is now truly old,' said Ruggiero.

'That's more like it. Now that he is a free but ailing man, Tony's time may have come. At the Polsi summit, Tony may announce his intention to take over the German colony from his father. Pietro will never raise any objection, because he fears Tony. Tony seems to think this is a good thing, but having members of your own family fear you is an evil.'

'If Tony Megale really is part of the family.'

'I am letting that pass once more, but never say it again. Many people think they know the truth about who Tony is, but they would be advised to keep their counsel. I think Enrico has also heard the story. But if he has not confided in you, then you must not know. Consider the story, weigh it in your mind, draw your own conclusions, and keep them in your heart – and speak to no one, not even me, about it ever again. Carrying secret knowledge in your heart, and never speaking, is a heavy burden, and it is time you started to feel the weight and learn how to deal with it.'

'But . . .'

'Shh.' His father put a finger to his lip. 'Imagine Old Megale fearing all of a sudden that Tony is not the right person. Maybe he thinks he should have tried harder with Pietro.'

'That might be good for Enrico,' said Ruggiero.

'Enrico is young, and is reputed to be weak.'

Ruggiero instinctively began to defend his friend, then fell silent. His father was right: Enrico was weak.

'If Megale, who is expected to retire, chooses to stay in charge until his death, or just stay on until he reaches a final decision, Tony might object. There may be a period of instability, a search for successors. That is pre-cisely what the Society does not want. Anyone who is the source of insta-bility or who attracts the attention of the authorities or acts unpredictably is a threat.'

'But Enrico?'

'Enrico is your friend, but he is also Tony's son. You are Enrico's friend, but you are also the son of a man whom Tony might feel has risen too high and moved beyond his control.'

'Zia Rosa would not let anyone do anything to harm me.'

'She is a good woman. Her husband is a decent and simple man whom I trust. Tony is my honoured companion abroad. Individually, every Megale is a close friend. Collectively . . . I want you to be prepared when the time comes. Promise me that?'

'I promise,' said Ruggiero.

Tuesday, September 1

35

Locri

ENRICO MEGALE, IN the guise of a fat infant, was standing in a garden of roses, slicing at the branches of a short tree, which bled as it was cut. Thirteen men lay at its feet, thirteen was the number of branches . . . Someone was shaking him, and his dream slipped under his pillow. He tried to grab it with his hands, but the person shook him harder, and then unexpectedly kissed him.

'Ruggiero?' said his mother's voice.

He knew immediately from the tremor in her voice that fear had taken hold of her.

'We're going to make a surprise visit to my sister in Catanzaro,' she said. 'And then maybe we'll travel up north to do some shopping. Rome. We could go to Florence.'

The clock beside his bed told him it was 3:30. Wearily, knowing that whatever his mother had planned was not going to work, he climbed out of bed and sat staring at his feet.

'Get dressed as quick as you can, and come downstairs, quietly,' said his mother.

She was his mother, so he did as he was told. Reaching around in the dark, he grabbed the same clothes he had been wearing the day before. They felt a bit sticky and cold going on. He had changed his underpants and socks, which were the important things. He turned on the light and blinked at the brightness. His father might have called and told them to flee. His father was courageous but also practical and despised acts of bravado. 'You are worth more than the fool brandishing a knife in public, showing off on his motorbike. Let him end up with his own knife in his throat, his skull fractured by a car. You have a duty to preserve yourself.'

The upshot of that reasoning was that, like Enrico, he was not allowed a scooter. His father's philosophy and Zia Rosa's womanish fears had the same result. But Ruggiero had a knife, which he did not brandish in public. It lay snug beneath his mattress at night.

Sitting on shelves were books and some soft toys that he thought he was saving for Robertino, but, he now saw, were already too old and faded for a new child. On his wall was the amaranth-coloured flag of Reggio Calabria, the only Calabrian football team ever to reach Serie A. In an approximation of the same red colour on a piece of paper he had written 'Amaranto si nasce'. But in these parts, people were not really 'born amaranth'. The team belonged to the other side of Aspromonte, where other families and other interests held sway.

A click and the light went off. He had not heard her come in.

'Keep the lights off, love,' said his mother who stood there with an empty suitcase in hand. 'Are you ready?'

Ruggiero pulled on his shoes and watched as his mother, moving swiftly and quietly, added some of his clothes and a pile of battered story-books that she used to read to him until Robertino was born.

He carried it downstairs for her, and was surprised to find Robertino sitting there in his baby bouncer, in gurgling serenity.

'Robertino's always awake and quiet at this time,' said his mother, picking up on his surprise. She went over to the high chest of drawers in the corner of the room, and ran her hand over it like she did when looking for dust, only this time she did not examine her hand.

'Did I ever tell you my parents gave me this? My father got it from his grandfather who got it from his father. It was made in the 1500s for the monks of the Abbey of San Giovanni in Fiore. It must be worth thousands. Go upstairs to your room, check to see if your bed is made.'

'It is made.'

'Well, go up again. Straighten the cover. Just make sure it's perfect.'

'Should I close the shutters on my bedroom window?'

'No, keep your shutters open. Don't close any shutters. I am going to put Robertino in the back of the car. You check your room, then come down. Pull the front door closed behind you.'

Ruggiero did as he was told. When he came down, the other two were already in the car. He shut the front door softly behind him. He climbed into the Fiat Panda next to his mother. The car was filled to brimming with jumper suits, little white T-shirts, baby bottles, toys, suitcases, plastic bags and bottles of water.

Behind him, the baby was asleep in a stroller bed that his mother had secured with a crisscrossing of all three seatbelts in the back. She turned around, gave him a smile of reassurance, then slid the key into the ignition and turned the key.

Nothing happened.

It was as if there had never been a connection between the ignition and the engine. She turned it again, but the only sound was the soft breaths of Robertino in the back, the squeak of the suspension as she leaned forward and made a third vain attempt.

Ruggiero plucked the house key out of his mother's bag, which lay open on the seat between them, without her seeming to notice. He climbed out of the car and walked back towards the front door. His mother remained in the dark car, embracing the steering wheel.

36

Locri

RUGGIERO EVENTUALLY COAXED his mother out of the car, back into the house. Robertino had dozed off in the back seat, then woken up when moved, and was now in no mood for further transfers. He needed feeding, comforting, changing, cuddling, petting, lulling and laying down again.

As his mother carried out these rites, Ruggiero could see she was beginning to shake off the shock that had momentarily disabled her when the car would not start. In calming the baby, she had calmed herself. Even so, he felt the grip of her fear when, as he was passing, she suddenly grabbed him and held on to him, her hand hard like a claw, and said, 'Get all our stuff out of the car and back into the house.'

Detaching himself, Ruggiero said, 'So Papà's in trouble and we must flee?'

She shook her head. 'Something's wrong. He called earlier, while you were asleep. He said he could not make the flight to Lamezia Terme, and might even miss the Polsi celebrations.'

'He will never abandon us,' said Ruggiero with total conviction.

'Of course not,' she said, her voice laced with doubt. 'Will you please get the stuff out of the car back into the house? I'm going to lie down with Roberto now,' and so saying she lifted the sleeping bundle, whose small fists were clenched in a communist salute, and took him upstairs.

Ruggiero went out the front door, leaving it slightly ajar. Closed or open made no difference. If they killed his father, they might come looking for his family, but then again they might not. If they failed to find his father, however, they would inflict pain on his family to punish him or draw him into the open. Who would the executioners be? Who would know in advance? Basile, obviously, since not a leaf stirred in the town without his say-so. Pepè and his family were likely to know, and any one of them, Pepè included, would be capable of pulling the trigger, plunging the knife, tightening the wire, igniting the blaze. Or, as his father had intimated, Enrico's family, the Megales? Not Enrico, because he was weak. Never Zia Rosa. That left Pietro. Yes, Pietro could do it, but he would not be capable of working alone. Pietro needed to be told what to do.

Had his mother done something she should not have? She was acting fearful and seemed unable to find or bring comfort. She would never have gone to the police or anything like that, and her opportunities for an illicit affair were nil. Another possibility was that they were at the start of a new, wide-ranging feud. If it was a feud, the Curmacis would emerge as the winning faction: he could feel it. Soon he would command full respect from all of them. Magnanimous, he would extend protection to Enrico, set out rules for how young heirs to the Society should behave among themselves. Some of the old rules needed to be reinstated. The old stories needed to be heard again.

If his mother wanted to flee, then it was his filial duty to help. But to help her to the best of his ability implied seconding her intentions, not following misguided orders. So he walked by the car, ignoring his mother's instructions to empty it. He had a better idea to try out first.

He left the overgrown front garden, which protected them from prying eyes, turned on to the unpaved and unlit side street, his thoughts as dark and deep as the night air. If there was a feud in the offing they needed allies, but Ruggiero had not registered any improvement in attitudes towards him. The afternoon in the bar without telephones had indicated the exact opposite. He had convinced himself that Enrico was the target, and the main point had been to teach Enrico not to be so soft and complacent. Before a large-scale feud, some people would change cafés, others would suddenly prefer one side of the street to the other, one petrol station to another, many would vanish. If there was a feud, some people would sit three-quarters turned from him, others would come up and warmly greet him in the street, make loud jokes and recommendations for all to hear, and move on. But no one had approached, no one had visited, and no one was offering friendship.

He arrived at Enrico's rusty gate. He lifted the deadbolt and began edging the gate inwards, pausing after every creak and crunch. Enrico, Zia Rosa and Zio Pietro had a dog, a vicious, sheep-mauling, sly mongrel that had arrived when he and Enrico were still toddlers. The dog, never allowed in the house, spent most of its day running after traffic, yet had never been hit by a car. Its unnatural luck had been noted, especially since it was assumed that some people in the neighbourhood must have deliberately tried to crush the beast below their wheels and put an end to its reign of terror over small children and other dogs. The animal had every reason to like him more than Enrico who had never treated it with any kindness, but it was still capable of emerging from the prickly mesh of bush where it lived, and growling and baring its teeth, just to say it knew he could not have a legitimate reason for being here at this time of night. But no white fangs and shiny eyes appeared in the darkness. The beast was probably off killing chickens somewhere.

The car he was aiming for was parked directly in front of the kitchen window. It was an old, uninsured Fiat Ritmo, treated almost as badly by Zio Pietro as the dog. They used the old car to drive across fields and drag pieces of farm equipment around. When they wanted to arrive in style at church or in town, they drove the Range Rover with tinted windows and polished hubcaps that they kept locked in a cowshed.

The door on the driver's side did not even close properly, let alone lock, but on opening it creaked almost as much as the gate. The kitchen window in front of him remained dark as did the window above that, where Zia Rosa and Zio Pietro slept in separate beds. Enrico's room was on the other side of the house, overlooking a disused vineyard, defined by a line of crumbling cement posts linked by sagging wires.

Ruggiero climbed into the front seat, holding hard on to the door to stop it both from creaking open and from banging closed. He figured he could afford to slam it once he had the car out of the gate. Sometimes Zio Pietro left a few keys in the glove compartment, any one of which, with a bit of twisting and turning, could be used to turn on the ignition and engine: and there they were. Good. He would start the engine on the road outside, halfway between their gate and his own – or maybe he'd push the car down the last few yards of road as far as his own house, just to be on the safe side. The Ritmo had a shuddering motor that sounded like a two-stroke, and was audible from a distance. The important thing now was to freewheel quietly out of the gate on to the road. He eased the driver's door inward towards himself with exaggerated care, and so when it struck the object that had invisibly interposed itself the impact, though soft, ran through him like an electric shock. The car door was being impeded by something heavy, dark and alive. Inches from his wrist a white smile of sharp teeth appeared at the same time as the dog growled.

Ruggiero felt his fear melt into rage, which ran down his arm as sweat, and he knew the dog would smell it and react.

'Shh. It's me. Shh. There's a good boy, you lousy stinking filthy animal, get away from here.' He put out his hand, and the dog growled again and bared its teeth. 'Me,' repeated Ruggiero. The dog growled again, and Ruggiero pushed his upturned wrist into the mouth so that one bite could split his veins. 'Me. It's me, the only human who ever loved you, you fucking evil beast.'

The dog pushed its head forward so that when it closed its mouth on Ruggiero's hand it merely massaged it with its blunter back teeth. Ruggiero ran his hand against the side of the hot mouth and then slapped the animal on the side of the neck. 'Stop it, good boy, now move.'

The dog backed away, vanishing almost at once, and Ruggiero released the handbrake and pressed down on the clutch. The car began to roll very slowly backwards, the driver's door swung out and he pulled it in again. As he did so, he caught a glimpse of movement at the bedroom window. For a moment, he thought it was a reflection of the dog moving, but the image was pale, and the dog was dark. Besides the image had appeared on the second floor, at a height where the dog could not be. As the car gathered some speed and rolled away towards the gate, he imagined a face staring out at him from behind the glass, but he had to turn his head back to guide the car, which was moving faster than he had expected. It took all his force to avoid sideswiping the hanging gate. He spun the steering wheel to direct the car into the road, and the gravel below crackled and snarled beneath the bald tyres. Suddenly the steering column lock engaged, and the car, now losing speed, made a slow but inexorable turn towards the low wall. He braced for impact, but before he hit the wall, the back wheels dipped into a dry ditch, and Ruggiero was thrown backwards and then forwards, hitting the horn with his chest. The horn sounded for no more than half a second, but it was the loudest noise he had ever heard.

He kicked at the stupid door till it opened. He was not going to be able to push the car out of the ditch, and revving the engine to get it out would simply draw a large audience. By now he was not even sure he knew how to break the lock without breaking the whole thing and whether he should have attempted this to begin with.

It would be more manly to await his fate at home and defend his mother and brother there. Passing by the gate he looked up to Enrico's house, and this time what seemed like an afterimage of Zia Rosa was watching him from behind the window. He almost lifted his hand to wave. If she had seen him, the next time he sat at the kitchen table eating one of her meals, she'd give him a significant look and say nothing, then, as he was leaving, she would ask him if he had anything he wanted to tell her. That had been her method when she had discovered his unconfessed misdemeanours in the past: a broken window here, a missing jar of Nutella there, or that dangerous excursion into the collapsing outhouses at the end of the garden when he had gone rat hunting. He never had anything to tell her, but appreciated the gesture and her discretion.

By the time he reached his house, he was beginning to rethink the experience. It could never have been her. It was too dark and too far for him to have seen her face at the window as he was passing on the road. His imagination was playing tricks on him, because it was 4:15 in the morning, and his brain had decided to go back to dreaming without telling him. And now, finally doing as his mother had asked him, he lifted two suitcases from their car and took them back into the house, expecting her to be there waiting fearfully and angry at his delay, but there was no sign of her. He put them down quietly in the hall so as not to waken her, and went back outside to collect the other things from the car.

It was on his fourth trip in that he heard his mother's voice, speaking softly as if from far away. He moved quickly and quietly to the kitchen door, then walked in suddenly, catching her unawares. She swung her body sideways away from him, and clasped the phone closer to her ear. She seemed to express a few words of gratitude and clicked the phone shut and slipped it with mock casualness into a kitchen drawer. It was 4:35 in the morning and she was making or receiving secret calls. He felt he had a right to know.

'Who was that?' demanded Ruggiero.

'None of your business.'

'Of course it's my business.' He went over to the kitchen drawer. His mother shrank away for a moment as he approached her, which gave him a hard, righteous feeling of gratification for a second or two, before it was submerged by a sudden wave of panic, followed by sadness as he realized that she had just ceased to be the all-knowing source of total love on whom he could always depend. She should not be shrinking from him, she should be reaching out to him, pulling him into her embrace, and telling him everything would be fine. But as he looked at her, he realized that was what she was hoping for from him, which angered him all over again.

He opened the drawer, pulled out the phone. 'I've never seen this before,' he said.

'No?' She was still trying to sound casual.

'Who did you call, Papà?'

'Nothing to do with you.'

'It's everything to do with me.'

'You are not the only child in this house.' She sat down at the table, brushed the back of her hand over its grainy surface, then rubbed it against her own cheek. 'You didn't wipe the table like I asked you, Ruggiero. You never do as I ask.'

'Who?' Ruggiero demanded again. 'Was it a local call?'

'No. Not local. Is that Robertino crying?'

'No, not yet. But if you don't answer, then I'm going to bed,' said Ruggiero and went upstairs.

His mother was still downstairs. Maybe she was making more phone calls, appealing for help, for he knew that was what she had been doing. He was ashamed of her, but he wanted her to succeed, too. He wished his father were there to tell him what to do next.

Over five days in March, in the middle of which they celebrated his fifteenth birthday, his father had begun by telling him things he already knew, calmly and so slowly that he began to feel impatient. He was a *giovane d'onore*, the son of a man of honour. Ruggiero almost rolled his eyes at this. He knew whose son he was. He had an idea of where he fitted into the hierarchy, but he lacked the absolute precision of others like Pepè and even Enrico. They knew who should respect them more, who less, and who they need not even consider as entitled to an opinion, which included more than half the class and all the teachers, except for the coach. But in six visits over two years, his father had slowly started unpacking small and mostly unwelcome surprises, things Ruggiero thought he knew, but hadn't. First, a *giovane d'onore* did not automatically become inducted into the honoured Society at the age of sixteen.

'I know that,' said Ruggiero, aggressive because he had failed to hide his surprise. 'Everyone knows that.'

'We may postpone the date, because study is also important.'

'I'll be the only one.'

'Once in, you'll move up quickly. There is no rush. I want to make sure that you are suited to it.'

This made Ruggiero angry, but his father had been unmoved. 'First I shall test your mettle. When we are certain about what you can do, then we can let others conduct the initiation rites. Think of it like knowing the answers to an exam beforehand.'

'How will you test my mettle?'

'Good question. I hope the occasion does not present itself too soon. But it will eventually.'

Another day, his father told him, 'Don't always look for explanations. Sometimes there aren't any.'

'Explanations of what?'

'Anything. A disappearance, an accident, an earthquake, a sudden violent death, the tragic killing of an innocent man. Don't look for explanations.'

On his second to last day before leaving, his father had told him that the important thing was to persuade people. 'When you are persuading people, you must not distinguish between friends and enemies. Everyone must be persuaded. You yourself must be persuaded.'

'What if it's not true?'

'Your belief makes it true. If you believe something to be true, then it becomes true.'

He didn't really get that bit. Nor did he quite understand his father's claim, on the morning before he left for Germany, that things that were equal could also be different.

'Like what?'

'If I gave you two fifties,' and here he handed him two 50-euro notes, 'is that the same as my giving you five twenties?' and here he handed him five 20s. 'Or ten tens?' This time he handed him nothing.

'Sure. Five times twenty is the same as two times fifty.'

'Well, you're wrong. They are different acts.'

'OK,' said Ruggiero, resolving to think about it later.

'That money is for buying treats, not for clothes, shoes or any necessities,' his father had said. 'If you need new clothes, your mother will pay.'

'Thanks.'

'I want you to spend three-quarters of what I gave you on buying things for your friends. If I'm not back by June, your mother will give you another €200. Three-quarters of the total on your friends, right?'

'OK.'

'And take good note of who always lets you buy and who never lets you buy for them. Beware of both extremes. The ones in the middle, who let you buy sometimes and then treat you sometimes, are more trustworthy.'

'Right.'

'But don't rely on just that. There is never just one trick, never just one answer.'

'Supposing something bad happens?' He had not meant to sound so childish and helpless. The words just tumbled out.

'If something happens, your mother will let me know, and I'll get here.'

Or had he imagined that response?

He unbuttoned his shirt, and stood there bare-chested, thinking of the car in the ditch, the opened gate. He often practised trying to overcome the feeling of vulnerability that being bare-chested gave him. Logically, it made no sense, since a knife or bullet wound inflicted through a shirt was exactly the same as one inflicted on bare skin, and yet he could not help feeling that it would be worse.

His mother had stopped moving around downstairs. In the next room, Roberto sighed in his sleep. The effect was always comical when he did that, the sigh sounding so world-weary.

A foot scraped on the gravel outside the house. It was an unmistakable sound, the same that his own feet made day after day. Ruggiero froze. Downstairs he heard a click, then a thud. It was the back door being opened. Walking on his toes, paying attention to his arms to make sure they did not bang into anything, he made his way over to his bedroom door, and listened. There would be at least three of them. He had heard no car. He thought he heard a gasp and a muffled thud. They must be using knives. His mother could be lying in a pool of her blood. He ran to his bed, and in one movement swept his hand underneath, spun around, and faced his bedroom door. In his hand he held a small black throwing knife that he hadn't learned to throw yet.

The house was in utter stillness. Ruggiero stretched towards his bed to reach his pyjama top, but could not get to it without moving, and he found his legs were rooted to the floor. With enormous effort, he forced himself forward, away from his bed, towards the door. His left leg was trembling uncontrollably, he breathed in deeply, and the vibrations abated. He needed to talk to the killers, tell them to leave Roberto, or tell them that if they could murder an infant, it should not be with steel, which served other purposes.

'A knife, a sword, a cutlass: these are called "white" weapons because they are associated with the noble warfare of knights. They demand skill and put the user at risk. A gun is a black thing that does not do this,' his father had told him once. 'But of course there is no honour in using a white weapon on an infant or a woman.'

But another time he had offered a different explanation, saying a knife was white when the light of the sun glanced off the flat of the blade.

Ruggiero's puny black throwing knife reflected nothing. Gathering courage, he quietly slipped out his door across the hallway and into his little brother's room, which smelt of talcum powder and bread. If his mother was alive, she should be here protecting Roberto. And she should be trying to protect him, though he would protect her. He sat down in the dark beside the cot, choked back his tears, and waited.

He heard a footfall on the stairs. The first step was quiet and careful, but the next were louder and more careless as they drew closer, and there were other feet coming up the stairs behind that and more behind that. At least three of them. Five perhaps. He could not count or reason.

Ruggiero touched the side of his brother's sleeping head. The temple was still soft, and the child's brain was pulsing with innocent thoughts beneath. There were voices in the hall outside. He went over and placed himself in front of the door, and pushed his chest out. He realized he had gone completely numb from his feet to the bottom of his neck, and it made no difference in the end if he was bare-chested or not.

They checked his room, and there was a surprised grunt as they found it empty.

Now the door was swinging open, and Ruggiero stood up. He put his arms behind his back and braced himself.

The man who entered the room strode over to Ruggiero, embraced him hard, kissed him on the side of the neck, combed his fingers through the boy's hair, then pushed him back, and looked at him in admiration.

'Were you in here defending your brother?'

'Yes, Papà.'

'No need now, my courageous son. I am here.'

37

Positano

KONRAD HOFFMANN WAS swimming deeper and deeper into the unplumbed depths of a restaurant fish tank and his voice streamed upwards in an angry buzz of bubbles to pop loudly but meaninglessly as they reached the surface, and Blume, observing that this was all far-fetched, especially the bit about the fish tank being bottomless, deep and dark, decided to wake up and grab at his mobile phone. He opened his eyes as he brought it to his ear, shocked to see daylight. If he had been asked to guess, he would have said he had been asleep for an hour at most.

'Maria Itria has called for help. For real this time. She called Magistrate Arconti at around 4:30 this morning, but did not answer a call that he made later. After thinking about it for a bit he called me,' said Caterina on the other end of the line.

It gave him such an unexpected lift to hear her voice first thing after a stupid dream about . . . red fish or something, that he was not sure he had understood the content of her message.

'Caterina? Wait . . . go through that again.'

'Curmaci's wife. She called for help last night.'

'She called you?' Blume shook his head. 'Sorry, dumb question, I was asleep just now.'

'She called Arconti and said if something happened to her husband, she would be willing to turn state witness. Then she said she wanted police protection and an escort the hell out of there. Since then, her phone has been off. Arconti told me and I'm telling you. It's six in the morning, you're usually awake at this time, not that that was a consideration. The woman and her children are in trouble. Your trick has become self-fulfilling, and now she really is willing to reach out to the authorities.'

'She called Arconti on her own initiative, in the early hours of the morning?'

'Yes, he said he definitely got the impression she was either unaware of or indifferent to the fact of his hospitalization.'

'Why didn't Arconti call me?' asked Blume.

'I can't second-guess Arconti, but I can think of several reasons he might not trust you after that stunt you pulled with the false confession.'

He felt a throb in the back of his head. If only it would remain there, but it would not. Within half an hour it would have worked its way to his frontal lobes and would sit pulsing like a toad all day long.

'He's very fucking busy for a man in a hospital bed. Why didn't he call the local police, get them to pick up the Mafia wife and her progeny?'

'Are you really asking that?' said Caterina. 'An order imparted from a magistrate in Rome to the local police would be intercepted pretty quickly, and the police themselves will be under surveillance, especially with the Polsi summit meeting coming up. They can't move without being followed.'

'Fine, but they'd still go and get her. Probably.'

'He didn't make that call.'

'More strange behaviour on his part,' said Blume.

'You write false confessions but he's the one who's acting strange because he does not issue orders from his bed for the police at the far end of the country to go rescue a woman who is now not responding to calls? Apart from the fact he is not assigned to any case, on what grounds could he order a patrol around? For all he knows, it could be a trap or a diversion. She may have called to test his reaction.'

'So what did he say?'

'That he would pass on her message to a different magistrate who would contact her later in the morning. He said she could call the police herself if her need was immediate. At that point she hung up.'

What seemed like a bubble of methane rose from the back of his throat into the back of his head and popped with a thud. He counted six heartbeats, before the next thud arrived.

'Alec?'

'Yes, yes. Still here.' But he wasn't. His mind had darted back to the idea of Curmaci's wife fleeing, Konrad as a fast-moving fish, a fragment from his dream.

'Maria Itria said she would co-operate with the authorities if something happened to her husband, but as far as we know, nothing has,' said Caterina. 'But something is up. Curmaci's acting strangely and his wife and children are in trouble, just like you wanted.'

'What's Curmaci doing that's strange?'

'He was booked under a false name on a flight from Frankfurt to Lamezia Terme, but he never took the flight, and he disappeared yesterday evening,' she said.

'Those geniuses at the BKA lost him?'

'No, we did. The BKA saw him board a flight for Bari instead of Lamezia Terme and alerted us. That is to say, they alerted the Finance Police at Bari airport. The Finance Police registered Curmaci's arrival and reported it to the Carabinieri at the airport, who reported it to the police in the city. Problem is, the police in Bari were in Bari while Curmaci was at the airport, and no one had told the Carabinieri . . . Well, you've seen how it happens. By the time it had been cleared up, and authorization given for the Carabinieri to follow him, he was gone. It appears he rented a car, and they're looking into it.'

'He changed his route at the last minute,' said Blume. 'Three or four hours will take him to Calabria and Locri. Looks to me like he's just trying to shake off anyone who might be following. We can try to pick him up after the Polsi summit, though it's not so easy to find those bastards. They seem to vanish into the Aspromonte wilderness only to turn up a few days later in New York, London, Malaga or Amsterdam.'

'Or he does not want to meet his welcoming committee in Lamezia Terme,' said Caterina.

'You mean because he fears for his life? No. That's not it. If he feared assassination at the hands of his own people, he'd steer clear of Calabria altogether.'

'Typically, Alec, you keep forgetting his family. He has the strongest and most urgent reason in the world to get there. They are vulnerable. Funny how you seem to block that out of your mind since, I presume, that was the original idea behind the forged confession. Or didn't you think about the consequences for the woman and her children?'

Blume paused to think. This was one of those questions Caterina liked to ask in which, whether he replied yes or no, he still came out of it looking like the bad guy. He chose the best response he could come up with: 'I don't know.'

'You don't know,' she echoed, scathing. 'You realize Arconti may be trying to do you a favour by not calling in the local police? A woman from the Ndrangheta, a *sorella d'omertà* confessing to a magistrate, especially one who has become notorious because of the namesake killing, is going to be big news. And if her story is big news, your efforts to force her husband back into Italy via a false confession is going to be just as big, maybe bigger given the poisonous atmosphere in the country against investigators and magistrates.'

'I'm not a magistrate.'

'Arconti is. If the story breaks in the press, every magistrate in Italy will distance themselves as fast and as far as they can from you and all your dubious tactics before Berlusconi's hacks turn this into another weapon to use against the judiciary. They'll throw you to the lions.'

'Those reporters aren't lions. More like trained monkeys.'

'Trained to tear people apart, Alec. You know better than to hope for solidarity . . .'

'All right. Point taken. My thanks to Arconti for allowing me to fix this thing myself.'

'Good. What are you going to do now? What about the German you are with?'

Blume felt a small tingling in his stomach and arms, like a tiny version of the body's aftershock to a near-miss traffic accident. Her question bothered him. 'I think I need to talk with him,' he said. 'Right now, as a matter of fact. I'll call you back.'

'Sure you will,' she said.

Blume ran up to the hotel lobby in his boxer shorts, his mind's eye already anticipating what he would see out the window of the lobby, the silver leaves of the olive trees, the mass of dark green and pale white of jasmine bushes in the background, and, off to the side, nodding in and out of view, a scarlet hibiscus bush he had noticed the day before. His eye immediately latched on to the revolting plant as soon as he arrived in the lobby. Blume stared across the room out at the fat red flowers already opening in the morning sun, their protruding stamens licking at the air. Yesterday, when he had glanced out the window, the plant had been obscured by the rear section of an old orange-and-white camper van. Slowly now, since he knew the answer and because each footfall travelled up his body and thumped on the side of his aching head, he walked out the front door of the hotel and stood there bare-chested, looking at the empty space where the camper van had been.

38

Positano

'You've been very obliging,' said Blume, now fully dressed.
    The manager stood back as he opened Konrad's room and waved a generous arm to usher Blume in. Konrad had left his room not just empty but spotlessly clean. He had even made the bed and folded the towels. The manager then helpfully announced, 'I heard the camper van very early this morning. But it is not my policy to check on the comings and goings of guests, even if they haven't paid.'

'You've got a credit card number for surety,' said Blume. 'I'm sure that helps you sleep through the sound of departing vehicles. What time was it?'

'Around four.'

'Right.' He pushed his arm under the mattress, and swept his hand back and forth. It touched something, a remote control? No, a phone. To lull his controllers into thinking he was still here. Well done, Konrad.

The manager was watching him with interest.

'Oh, listen, I almost forgot,' said Blume, 'I left my weapon in my room. My spare weapon.' He winked as if this had meaning. 'It's in a top drawer . . .' He did not even have to bother making up the rest. The manager had almost squealed in delight as he promised to fetch it for him.

When the manager had gone, Blume pulled out the phone from under the mattress. It was switched on. The *Telefonbuch* contained a short list of contacts, most of them consisting of shortened versions of first names: Max, Rob, Hlmt, Kris, Greg, Bea, Tri, none of which meant anything to him. He pocketed it, and headed to his room, where he told the manager, who was peering under the bed, that he had been mistaken about his weapon. The manager looked up from the floor, his eyes full of disappointment and suspicion as Blume set about stuffing his backpack with his dirty clothes and the copy of the documents he had lifted from Konrad. He then remembered that his suitcase, which should never have left the safety of his home, was in the damned camper van.

He went up to the lobby with the manager, who positioned himself defensively behind the reception desk and glared at Blume. A crackle of gravel outside told Blume, without looking round, that a car had arrived. How many had they sent?

'Those are my colleagues arriving now,' he told the manager. 'Two people, am I right?'

The manager refused to look up.

'Are they armed?' whispered Blume in urgent tones, and the effect was immediate. The manager's eyes lit up and he craned his neck to look behind Blume.

'I can't see. Two of them,' he started retreating towards the back office.

'They are police not assassins,' said Blume. 'I want you to take them down to Konrad's – the German's room. Don't give any indication that I have been confiding privileged information to you. Can you do that?'

The manager winked.

The door opened behind them.

'That means not even mentioning that he's missing,' added Blume quickly.

'I understand,' said the manager, helpless in the face of a confidence and willing to trust Blume one more time.

Blume turned around, and was both relieved and annoyed to see who had been sent. The two men standing there hardly made up his age between them. The one closer to him, a mop of jet-black hair, ankle boots, broad shoulders, momentarily assumed a defensive posture as Blume turned round, then relaxed. His partner, smaller, thin fair hair, wearing a puffed-up Japanese-style windbreaker to give himself some heft, was still twirling the car keys in his fingers.

'Shh,' said Blume, looking at the small one with the keys. He flashed his badge. 'You're not BKA? The person we're looking for is downstairs.'

'BKA?' said the smaller man. 'No, we're . . .'

'You armed?' said Blume. He took out his Beretta, offered it to the same man.

The larger man stepped forward. 'Of course we are armed, but we were detailed just to pick up two colleagues . . . nobody said nothing about a situation developing.'

'OK,' said Blume, holstering his pistol. He pointed to his backpack. 'Let me throw this in the back, then I'll need to explain . . .' He took the car keys from the young man's hand, then turned to the larger one. 'I don't think it'll be a problem. The person you're looking for is unarmed. Do you think you'll be able to handle it, or shall I call in backup?'

'What's his problem? He's supposed to be some sort of colleague, right?'

'We had a falling out. I'll call in some regular police support if you want.'

'He's not armed, you said.'

'No. He's never even worked in the field. Old guy. Older than me, even. Frail. Spent all his life behind a desk.'

The man turned to his nervous colleague. 'Come on, let's go get him.'

Blume nodded to the manager, who was bobbing up and down on the periphery and was overjoyed to be included in the action. 'He'll show you the room.'

Blume watched the three of them descend the stairs out of the lobby, reach the landing, turn and pass out of sight.

'Be right down,' he called after them. He pressed the button on the car key as he reached the front door, walked five paces and hopped into the driver's seat of the car, tossing his backpack on the seat beside him. He put the key in the ignition and reversed out of the hotel courtyard blindly on to the curving coastal road.

Luckily, no one was coming from either direction.

39

On the Road to Calabria

B LUME FOUND THE Class A Mercedes 160 he had stolen a disappoint-
ingly boxy little car, though it ran smoothly, and, half an hour later, he
had to admit it handled quite well as he engaged in the nifty steering
needed to negotiate the alternating one-way lane of the A3 autostrada, in
construction since 1964 and still unfinished.

He was not likely to make up the two-hour headstart Konrad had and
stop him from doing something stupid, but he saw no harm in trying. He
directed the Mercedes into the narrow lane demarcated on one side by
traffic cones and on the other by orange plastic road studs that slapped
against the wheels in a satisfyingly rhythmic way as he drove over them,
then negotiated a hairpin bend formed by concrete blocks.

A faded warning sign with two arrows indicated that the traffic was
now two-way, which, in view of the trucks now bearing down on him,
was self-evident. The effect was so like a video game that he found it
hard to take the threat of an imminent head-on collision entirely seriously. Seeking a soundtrack to his adventure, he turned on the car
stereo, and was horrified as Gigi D'Alessio's wavering little voice started
bleating out a folksy Neapolitan love song. He pushed at random buttons hoping to get the radio, but the stereo flashed some sort of message
and then went quiet. He gave up. It was high time he got his eyes back
on the road.

The stretch of the Salerno–Reggio Calabria autostrada he was now on
had given up any pretence of being a work in progress. The warning signs
were themselves in need of some repair. The temporary concrete dividers
had acquired an air of permanence. They were barriers to the south,
actively discouraging visitors. The smallest act, a dropped piece of

concrete, a broken-down vehicle, a misplaced barrier, effectively cut off road access to all southern Italy.

A truck had stopped next to a cluster of porta-potty cabins, two of them toppled over. A few yards further on, a woman was selling fruit from a stall covered by a tarpaulin, held down by guy lines attached to butane gas canisters, which were sitting in the emergency lane. Blume had allowed a convoy of trucks to go hurtling by, adjusted the trajectory of the car which had been thrown sideways and towards the divider by the heavy slipstream they left in their wake, when he heard a phone ringing, apparently coming from the car stereo. He glanced down at the stereo, which displayed the message 'incoming call'.

A Bluetooth connection between his phone and stereo. Neat. Or it would be if he knew which button to press. There were a few on the steering wheel, and he gave them a try. The ringing stopped.

'*Ma vaffanculo*,' he muttered, banging the steering wheel.

'So you steal a ROS vehicle and then you're the one who starts shouting obscenities at me?' said the stereo speakers.

'You heard that?' said Blume. He found the volume control and dialled down Massimiliani's voice.

'What the fuck, Blume?'

'I am in hot pursuit.'

'Of Hoffmann? The genius recruits they sent have let it be known that Hoffmann's nowhere to be found. So they managed to lose you, Hoffmann and their car. I foresee two short intelligence careers.'

'Not their fault,' said Blume. 'One partner should always be considerably older, and they thought they had been detailed just to act as chauffeurs.'

'Forget about them. Tell me what's going on.'

'I am following Hoffmann.'

'He's in the camper van and you're behind him in a stolen ROS vehicle? So those two also missed an orange motor home pulling out of the hotel as they drove in?'

Blume thought about it. He wanted to talk to Konrad, maybe dissuade him, but he was not sure he wanted to hand Konrad over to Massimiliani just like that. Konrad had a big headstart but in a very slow vehicle, and Blume felt inclined to give him this advantage, at least for now. Also, though he suppressed the thought as best he could, he did not want Massimiliani to know he had been outwitted by Konrad.

'Sure. I have him in my sights.'

'This is unbelievable. Does he know you're following him?'

'No. I had to act quickly, though. No time to explain to the agents you sent.'

'I didn't send those two . . . If Konrad's trying to get away, why didn't he make a run for it during the night, or in the early hours of the morning?'

'I don't know. Ask him. Maybe he just found something out,' said Blume. He rummaged with his free hand in his backpack and pulled out Konrad's phone to make sure it was still on.

'Talk about a loose cannon. Don't let him out of your sight while we arrange a roadblock. We can use the signal from his phone to see where he is. Keep yours on, too.'

'Sure,' said Blume. 'But I need to know where he's going, what he's doing.'

'Not now. I'll call back.' Massimiliani's voice vanished.

Blume was so busy pressing buttons on the car stereo that had turned into a speaker phone to see how it worked that he almost went hurtling into the back of a Y-10 with a number plate from the late '80s dawdling along at around sixty kilometres an hour. His passing swerve took out three traffic cones. Then, unexpectedly, there was a brief section of genuine two-lane divided road, just like a motorway in an ordinary country.

He got the radio working, and turned up the volume the better to hear a woman singing a song, which sounded Disneyesque. He found her voice a bit nasal, too, but was sorry when the song ended, then was inordinately annoyed at the fact they did not identify what it had been. When had they stopped identifying songs on the radio? When he was young, they always told you before the song and then again afterwards. The unidentified song faded into another. But he recognized this as Beyoncé. He remembered sitting in the company of Caterina's son Elia and watching a music video, and actively committing the name to memory. Beyoncé so called because she's bouncy. Maybe it would be a second topic of conversation with Elia besides the perpetually disappointing performance of the Roma football team. Elia was too young for the bouncy woman anyhow. The voice had a nice growl and power and invincibility. *Shoulda put a ring on it, uh-huh-huh.* Good song to encourage reckless driving.

It was possible, if damned unlikely, the extra speed would eventually bring him up behind the camper van. The dangerous driving required his full attention, which kept his thoughts away from the complicated mess he was making of everything. He needed to catch up with Konrad, stop him, talk to him, and then turn him in. He needed to get down to Calabria, find out about this woman, Curmaci's wife. Massimiliani, for all he thought he was subtle, had failed to register any surprise whatsoever that Hoffmann was headed southwards on the A3. Evidently they already knew Konrad's destination.

Blume switched off the stereo that presumed to answer his calls for him, and when his phone rang a quarter of an hour later, he had to hold it against his ear in the normal manner of all the other drivers on the road.

'Can you see him?'

'At this precise moment, no,' said Blume. 'But we are on the A3. There is no other way to go.'

Massimiliani seemed to find Blume's answer believable. 'I'm going to call you back soon.'

He meant what he said. Three minutes later, he was back.

'Look, before I get to asking you about the change in plans, I want you to fall back a little,' said Massimiliani.

'What?'

'You're too close. Your phones started moving away from the hotel at exactly the same time, and have remained locked at the same point ever since. From here it looks like you're tailgating him. Drop back a bit. If he goes off the autostrada, we'll let you know.'

'You'd think Konrad would know better than to leave his phone on,' said Blume. 'He'll probably turn it off any minute now, though I suppose you're tracking the IMEI number, so he'd need to dump or destroy the phone . . .'

'I wouldn't know about that sort of stuff,' said Massimiliani. 'I'm just passing on some advice from a person here who knows more than me, and he says to drop back.'

'OK,' said Blume. He trapped the steering wheel between his knees and pulled Konrad's phone out of his pocket with his other hand and tried to slide the battery cover off with his thumb. It would be suspicious if Konrad vanished from the network just as they were talking about it, but he saw no alternative. Finally, the battery cover popped off.

'Of course, now we know his story, we know his destination,' said Massimiliani.

'We do?' said Blume.

'Sure. He's headed towards Calabria. Where else does that road you're on lead? You're still too close, if you don't mind me saying. Pull back.'

'Konrad speeded up. I need to stay close.'

'Yes, I noticed that. That camper van must have some engine,' said Massimiliani.

Blume fingered the battery in Konrad's phone. 'Suppose you're wrong?'

'About his destination? No. We know it's Calabria, but not for the reasons we thought.'

'What are the reasons?'

'You'll get briefed in good time, but for now . . .'

'Tell me what you know about Konrad. I'll be waiting for your call,' said Blume. He hung up and put both hands on the wheel.

40

Milan

THEY FOUND TERESA Resca's body on Tuesday morning between the railway lines and the quarry lake, half a kilometre from the abandoned buildings they had searched. A team of volunteers, policemen working overtime and, crucially, dog handlers, beginning at first light, had spread out over the area, and there she was, Teresa, a small heap, face down, already sinking into the mud. The great mystery was how she had not been discovered earlier. The other was why whoever had done this to her had not tried to dispose of the body in the lake. Or maybe they had.

By now it was clear there was no organized crime connection. Fossati was not surprised that Bazza had been right. From the start he, too, had doubted that the father's denunciations of the Ndrangheta had had anything to do with the disappearance, thought his articles and opinions, ignored for so long by the mainstream press, were now being reprinted as part of the late-summer horror story.

Be careful what you wish for.

Teresa's mother received the news in hospital, where she had been taken two days before. She was under sedation, suicide watch, and armed guard.

The suspects were Kosovars, already in custody. They had been arrested on charges of loansharking in the past, and now faced life for murder. They started confessing and accusing each other within half an hour of the body being found.

Lost in his political obsessions, Giovanni Resca had failed to notice that his wife, who worked nights in the Policlinico San Donato, the very hospital in which she now lay drugged, though this time legally, was living far beyond her means. The jewellery he had assumed was cheap imitation was real, the clothes he attributed to her innate sense of style were designer, the irascibility, constant running nose, late lie-ins and increased tolerance and liking for liquor were not signs of an unshakeable cold. Nights out had been disguised as night-shift work, requiring her not only to hide the expenditure but to create the impression of earning overtime. She had borrowed €50,000 five years ago, had made regular payments, yet now owed the Kosovars €180,000. Her apartment was rented, her car was a Skoda, and her husband a failure, so when they came looking for collateral, they found nothing but her child.

Whether they had intended to kill the girl was another matter. The woman at the bus stop, who now had a face and a name, Altea Agushi, seemed also to have a conscience, or it might have been an instinct for self-preservation. Whatever it was, her testimony put her partner Dardan, now in San Vittore prison, in a very bad position, even if she continued to insist Dardan had not really meant to harm the girl. They had only wanted to scare the parents. But Dardan was a kick boxer, and hardly knew his own strength.

Fossati believed her, in that he believed the killing made no sense and was unplanned. When the girl started screaming, Dardan probably just lost it for a moment, as his wife said. But the moment was a long one. It had taken more than one blow to silence her, and when the moment was finally over, time had stopped for ever for Teresa.

'I told you it could never end well, this story,' said the magistrate.

The inspector beside him shook his head in disgust at the whole sorry mess, then brightened up a little. 'Amazing that dog. It was like it knew. You'd almost arrest the dog and the handler for the way they went straight to the spot.'

'What can you do with people like Dardan and Altea?' asked Fossati. 'You can't make them care. That would be the best punishment: make them care. But you can't. You can put them away for life, but you can't touch them inside.'

The policeman ignored his musings. 'I hear that the wedding ring we found helped make a breakthrough in that case of the dead Romanians. You know, the one that's connected to the killing of the insurance guy, Arconti, and the judge in Rome?'

'That is no concern of yours or mine,' said Fossati.

'Word spreads,' said the inspector, unrepentant.

'You police talk to each other too much.'

41

On the Road to Calabria

M ASSIMILIANI DID NOT call back for half an hour, so Blume was able to continue his pell-mell driving and listen to young people's music full blast on the stereo. When Massimiliani came back on the phone line, it was with another person.

'Alec, I'm on speakerphone here with Weissmann.'

'*Schiess los*,' said Blume.

Weissmann laughed heartily, '*Aber du sprichst gut Deutsch!*'

'*Ein bisschen*,' said Blume modestly. He removed the battery from Konrad's phone, opened the window, and dropped it out. Bad for the environment, apparently. Couldn't be as bad as the car batteries left on the pavement outside his apartment in Rome.

Massimiliani cut in. 'I already find difficult English, but speak no German. Please use English.'

'*Ja, doch!*' said Weissmann.

'Sorry,' said Blume, raising his voice against the inrush of air from the open window beside him. He flicked Konrad's SIM card out, then crooking his arm and cupping his wrist, tossed the phone itself towards the back wheel of the car. If his wheels didn't crush it, maybe the bastard tailgating him behind would, or someone after that. He rolled up the window.

'OK, now . . . I have some notes,' Weissmann was saying. 'You are aware of course that Italian organized crime in Germany is considered a new phenomenon? I talk of the press, not of us in the BKA. We have been following it for years. But the Duisburg killing on the Feast of the Assumption interested the press, and now they write articles. But of course we are not as expert as you Italians.'

Blume heard Massimiliani say, 'Thank you.' He was not sure if Massimiliani's English stretched to sarcasm, but it might.

'The Ndrangheta was established well before we began to investigate it properly,' said Weissmann. 'I am talking about very recently. The late 1990s, you understand? And resources are still not . . . well, that's not your problem. But the phenomenon is still underestimated, I believe. This is because what we have in Germany are only branches of the main organization, or . . .' Blume heard the rustling of papers. 'Offshoots. That is the word. *Ableger, oder?* They are offshoots of the main tree, which is in Calabria, in a town called San Luca. And so we have hoped that the Italians will someday cut the tree down. But what has happened is these offshoots . . .'

'*'ndrine bastarde,*' said Massimiliani.

'*Wie?* Bastards?' Weissmann sounded delighted.

'That's what the Ndrangheta calls its offshoots,' said Blume, '*'ndrine bastarde*', bastard units. A *locale* is a set of various *'ndrine*. If one of them gets too big, it might split and give birth to an *'ndrina bastarda*. Sometimes a bastard unit grows up to become larger than the whole *locale*. It often happens, in fact, because the new Ndrangheta is more powerful and wealthier than the old. Each generation gets stronger. Maybe *Seitentrieb* in German?'

'No! They must be bastard units,' said Weissmann. 'That is a very good name. And that is what has happened in Germany. Now even without Calabria, the Ndrangheta in Germany has its own base of power.'

'Perhaps,' said Blume. 'But without Calabria as a home base, I think they mightn't be as strong as all that. I thought you were going to talk about Konrad Hoffmann.'

'Commissioner Blume?' It was Massimiliani's voice sounding formal and concerned.

'What?'

'Hoffmann has just disappeared from the network. He must have shut down his phone, taken the battery out and everything. Have you still got him in your sights?'

'I was backing off like you told me to. So he's got a bit far ahead. I can try to catch up.'

'We've decided to intercept you at Atrena Lucana. That's about seventy kilometres ahead of you. You'll need to make sure Hoffmann doesn't turn off before then, but there is no reason he would. He's headed for Locri, San Luca, Africo or Polsi. The Locride zone for sure.'

'I need to know what you have found out about Hoffmann,' said Blume.

There was a pause and Blume could hear someone nearby speaking to Massimiliani. Eventually the DCSA captain said, 'Look, Blume, I only learned about all this just now from the BKA. I'll let Weissmann fill you in, then we need to talk.'

After a few moments' silence, Weissmann's voice came through, clearer than before, as if he had picked up a receiver and was speaking directly into it.

'Commissioner?'

'I'm here,' said Blume, 'and listening.'

'OK, I must tell you this is what we have found out . . . In 1992, a young woman named Dagmar Schiefer was working in the Finanzministerium in the Nordrhein-Westfalen region. She was highly *begabt*, you understand? She was a clever, gifted young woman who had a good eye for data analysis, which was even more important in those days before we started to use good database abstraction layers. Dagmar, who was twenty-five years old and just out of a specialization course at university, became interested in what turned out to be what we call *Karussellgeschäft*, which in English is . . .' He paused, presumably to look at his notes.

'Carousel fraud,' said Blume. 'Almost the same as the German.'

'You are wrong. Here it says the English translation is "missing trader intra-community fraud" . . .'

'Let's just call it fraud. Dagmar discovered fraud,' said Blume. He thought he had glimpsed a familiar orange-and-white slow-moving vehicle disappearing over the crest of a hill. Cones and barriers had turned the autostrada back into a one-lane highway with a surface that ripped at his tyres.

'Dagmar was brilliant,' said Weissmann. 'It is always easy to spot a fraud afterwards, when it has already been exposed, but Dagmar managed to identify profiles and models of behaviour. She created a sort of checklist of suspect actions so that fictitious companies set up to steal VAT from the government could be caught while still in the act. Even now, with all our computer power, it is hard to do this. This is also because everything is legal until one of the companies disappears. Also, we have to operate in different jurisdictions with different police, and that is very difficult,

242

especially with the Dutch and the Spanish. The Dutch can be very unhelpful. *Ein schwieriges Volk*. We have good relations with the Italians in this area.'

'Delighted to hear it,' said Blume.

'Yes. Of course it's not just police but also tax officers, finance ministries, bureaucrats and accountants . . . In 1993, thanks to Dagmar, who also testified as an expert witness, we arrested thirty people, your colleagues in the Carabinieri arrested ten in this country, and there were more arrests in Spain and England. It was a very successful operation, but it was like a raindrop on a hot stone. In Germany, one of those arrested was a man called Domenico Megale.

'More serious charges came later. That is why he stayed in jail from back then until now. Anyhow, we have been observing him for years, because it is clear that he still commands, or it was clear. In the last year of his imprisonment, he had few visits. Agazio Curmaci was one. Then, as you know, Domenico Megale was released a few weeks ago, and remains in Germany. So it seems he will not participate at the general meeting of the bosses in Polsi, but his son will. Also this Curmaci, whose role is hard to understand.'

'It sounds like you are not sure if Megale is still the boss of the Dusseldorf colony, or if he has passed the command on to his son, or if someone else – Curmaci – has stepped in between them,' said Blume.

'This is the sort of information we hope to get by comparing notes with you Italians,' said Weissmann, 'but that is not the subject of this conversation, Commissioner.'

'We were talking about Megale's arrest.'

'*Genau*. It was a very long time ago. His arrest was important, because it was one of the very first, and the authorities finally became interested in the invisible new Italian Mafia. A colleague of mine wrote a special report on the Ndrangheta in Germany. Also, just after my arrival in the BKA, a major inquiry was launched into the Ndrangheta investments in Russia and, in particular, Gazprom, but you know who one of the top managers in Gazprom is?'

'No,' said Blume.

'Gerhard Schroeder, our former Chancellor. So that investigation did not go very far. Then it was discovered the Ndrangheta was funding some politicians. There was a funding scandal with Thomas Schäuble, a regional minister, brother of our current Minister of Finance in Merkel's government. These are complex and delicate matters, and it is very difficult to find out the truth. In fact, most of the accusations are false, but it slows things down and makes it difficult for us to proceed.'

Now it was Weissmann's turn to stray off topic.

'Welcome to the world of Italian organized crime,' said Blume. 'Its three weapons of choice are confusion, intimidation and corruption. But it will always choose confusion first. Nobody really knows who's on whose side. Everything is infiltrated.'

'They cannot infiltrate the BKA,' said Weissmann in definitive tones.

'That is a very comforting thought,' said Blume. 'We were talking about this young woman Dagmar?'

'Yes. Three months after testifying, Dagmar Schiefer, who had just turned twenty-six, disappeared, like the earth had swallowed her. This is 1993. She was still living with her parents in Dusseldorf at the time. One Friday evening, she did not come home. They thought she must have gone to a party or something and did not report her missing until Sunday. But they never saw their girl again. No one saw anything, heard anything. The local police had nothing.'

'*Lupara bianca* is what we call it in Italy. It means "white shotgun". When the Mafia disappears a person for ever, leaving no trace. Usually, they dissolve the body in acid. Sodium hydroxide, I think.'

He managed to pass a line of cars and move up about twenty places, but the van he had spotted had disappeared from sight.

'We think Agazio Curmaci killed Dagmar Schiefer. He was working closely with Domenico Megale at the time of the disappearance. In those days Curmaci was Megale's driver. It is the closest we can get to associating Curmaci with an act of violence in Germany, but there was never enough to prosecute. A few days after Dagmar vanished, he was questioned and released within hours. Megale was in police custody at the time.'

'So, you're saying Curmaci killed this Dagmar back in the early 1990s. Has the investigation been reopened?'

'We do not close cases such as these, but they do eventually lose priority. Last week, a former colleague in the BKA, Sebastian Eich, a man who has since retired, received a call from Dagmar's mother. She called the BKA and asked to speak specifically to him, saying it was of the utmost

244

importance. They put her in contact because she was so insistent. Eich and Dagmar's mother had met many years before, you see. When the BKA finally intervened to explain to Dagmar's parents – and to her fiancé – that their daughter might have been killed by a new Mafia organization, Eich was the person who did it. That was in 1994, more than a year after Dagmar disappeared.'

'I suppose they heard Megale had been released from jail, and all the old pain resurfaced. Is that what this is?'

'Yes, they knew he had been released from jail, and that is connected. Before she disappeared, Dagmar Schiefer had been planning to move out of her family home to live with her fiancé. He was a student, doing a post-graduate degree in archaeology. After Dagmar's disappearance, he quit university, promising her parents that he would find out what happened and bring them proof that she was dead, find out who killed her, discover where she died. But he never did. At least not yet.'

'That boyfriend will have forgotten now. It's a lifetime ago. Unless he's unable to let go . . . Oh, God. Wait –'

'I have no time to wait. This boyfriend has not forgotten. He visited Dagmar's mother the day before she called Eich. He even asked her not to mention his visit to anyone, but she was worried he was about to do something stupid, which is why she called Eich.'

'And federal agents in Germany are at the beck and call of old women with presentiments?'

'*Unterbrechen Sie mich bitte nicht, Kommissar.*'

'Then get to the point, because I think I've already reached it.'

'So you will have realized that Megale received a visit from Dagmar's boyfriend, and that this visit had been observed by us.'

As Weissmann said this, the faded pictures of the young woman in the camper, the sad postcard pictures of journeys past flashed into the front of his mind, the torn Madonna, Konrad's pale blue eyes, his personal quixotic mission.

'Konrad Hoffmann,' said Blume. 'The boyfriend is Konrad Hoffmann. He wants the man who killed his girlfriend, and he has waited until now.'

'Yes,' Weissmann was saying, 'Konrad Hoffmann. He quit his degree, joined the Deutsche Hochschule der Polizei and then the BKA a few years later. At this time, a few people did notice his career choice, also because for a brief period he was under suspicion as a fiancé always will be in these circumstances, but then as the years went by and he carried out his work very well, no one on the force thought about his past, and he never spoke of it.'

Hoffmann distracted everyone with the idea of the Camorra and the Ndrangheta cooperating in toxic dumping, because that is a real phenomenon and part of a real investigation. There was a lot of sides to consider, and that is why no one looked into the deep past. We kept looking at what he does, not at what he used to be.'

Bullshit, thought Blume. The BKA had an agent with a grudge who had decided to set out on a mission against Curmaci; the Italians had the perfect idiot counterweight, him, who had also set out on a personal quest against Curmaci. Two loose cannons, each used to cancel the other out. He could appreciate the elegance of the solution, but felt humiliated at being played in this way. At least Konrad's quest was noble.

'Massimiliani, are you still there?'

'I am, but Weissmann's gone.'

'Why now? Why am I learning this only now? Answer me honestly for once.'

'No one knew. We are all learning this now.'

'OK, why now for Konrad? Why is he acting now, after all these years?'

'Honestly? Your guess is as good as mine,' said Massimiliani. 'But the most likely answer is Konrad needed confirmation from Megale that Curmaci was the killer, and perhaps permission to act. Maybe he just wanted to know where Dagmar's body was. But he can't have approached Megale and demanded any of these things without giving something back. He has something on them. So that is what the BKA want to talk to him about now. Finally, they have a strategy.'

'He built up his own investigative file on Megale,' said Blume. 'He told me. He used it to coax information from the old man.'

'I hope he planned for his investigation to be made available posthumously, if he thinks he can go down to Calabria, single out Curmaci, and revenge himself.'

'Maybe he's looking for information instead of revenge,' said Blume.

'He won't survive. He is completely and voluntarily on his own. Megale sent him down to where he could be killed without the BKA being able to do anything about it, nor even investigate afterwards. Meanwhile, Megale himself stays in Germany with a perfect alibi.'

Blume cleared the crest of a hill. A narrow stripe of road with two-way traffic stretched out below him, visible all the way down to the black oval mouth of a tunnel cut into a hillside of limestone so blindingly white it hurt his eyes to look at it. A red car travelling towards him came shooting out of the tunnel just as a two-tone camper van disappeared into it.

42

On the road in Calabria

BLUME HAD NEVER been able to distinguish between the myths and the realities surrounding the Ndrangheta, the Sacra Corona Unita, Cosa Nostra, the Camorra and the Stidda, but at least he knew he didn't know. Had Konrad, the German who thought he understood Italians and could speak Neapolitan dialect, failed to see the elaborate hoax? The Ndrangheta loved its symbols but kept them internal. A signed piece of paper from Megale would never turn a German federal policeman into a figure the Ndrangheta could trust even for a moment. Surely he knew that?

The road had narrowed further to the width of a country lane. It was going to be like this more or less until the very end. Hundreds of kilometres down to the tip of the boot at an average speed of what, fifty kilometres an hour? Berlusconi had promised a massive bridge at the end of it, connecting Reggio Calabria to Sicily. Presumably the Ndrangheta would build the first span, from the mainland towards Sicily, Cosa Nostra would build the span from Sicily, and they'd never meet in the middle.

He froze his thoughts as a gap opened in the oncoming traffic, and he moved up nine more places. The road now followed a squiggling line and he could not see far ahead. But half an hour later, he thought he saw the camper van, now only half a mile ahead. The phone beside him started buzzing, but he ignored it: he needed two hands on the wheel now. Dipping the right wheels of the car into a ditch on the verge made shallow by the rubble and rubbish that filled it, he managed to create his own emergency lane and pass an entire line of vehicles on the inside. The wheels rumbled and the side panel and fender on the right were taking a hell of a battering, and then he hit an invisibly low divider, but somehow managed to keep going and, after ten minutes, came right up behind the camper van. He swung back into lane behind it, and it was then he saw the yellow-and-black number plate and the 'NL' sticker.

Dutch holidaymakers. Was there any corner of the planet that had not been reached by a Dutch family in a caravan? And now that he was directly behind it, Blume realized the van was twenty years too modern but made to look retro-chic. Finally, he accepted that Konrad had gone.

The land flashing by was soft and lush, the vegetation so fertile that it had invaded the verges. He picked up speed and went racing past a sign indicating Sibari. That was on the opposite coast, the Ionian Sea. If it was signposted here, then he had to be passing one of the narrowest parts of the peninsula. It was possible that Konrad had turned off here. It was not the most efficient way to cross the narrow neck of land to the other side, but it was precisely the sort of mistake Konrad would make. Or maybe he would have been unable to resist the allure of the name. The ancient Greek colonists of the town, the Sybarites, used to be renowned for sex, luxury, wealth and power. Sibari had come down in the world, but they were still there, the ancient Greeks, now Calabrians.

A ping followed by an orange warning light told him he needed petrol soon.

Twenty minutes later, he pulled into an Agip service station, handed the keys to the attendant, and asked for a full tank. A blue-and-white estate car of the highway police, with two uniformed officers in it, pulled up beside him. Blume ignored them. The driver waved at him and, when Blume still failed to respond, got out and walked around.

'Commissioner Blume? We were asked to . . . um, accompany you.'

Blume paid the attendant and reversed out of the forecourt in the direction of the snack bar. He got out, holding the phone Massimiliani had given him in his hand. The police car made a U-turn and followed. Casually, it stopped just close enough to block Blume's exit.

The driver pointed at his warped fender. 'Did you have an accident?'

'No, no, that's . . . collateral damage,' said Blume. 'Accompany me where?'

'Cosenza.'

'Right,' said Blume. 'Are you driving me or . . .?'

'It would be good if you were to get into our car. In the front seat, of course, sir.'

'I can't drive behind you?'

'Well, technically . . .' The policeman bounced the toe of his boot against the tyre of the police car a few times as he avoided Blume's gaze. 'Technically, you're driving a stolen vehicle, sir.'

'And to think I just put 70 euros worth of super unleaded in the car. I've a good mind to suck it out again.'

Blume opened the passenger door, nodded to the policeman seated there who scowled, but got out and sat in the back. For a moment, he imagined himself kicking the policeman out, leaping into the driver's seat, and roaring away.

Just as he was about to get in, his phone rang. He put up a finger warning them to wait, cupped the phone to his ear, and wandered off towards the air pumps.

It was Caterina.

'Can you be quick about this? I've got friends waiting.'

'Still on your top-secret mission, then? Besides getting away from me and avoiding difficult decisions, what else persuaded you to place yourself under the command of a Carabiniere conducting an operation without any apparent judicial oversight? A boyish sense of adventure, was it?'

'Sometimes, magistrates can be called in on a need-to-know basis. They are not always to be trusted,' said Blume.

'You got that right,' said Caterina. 'I can tell from the tone of your voice you still want to play it like you're controlling events. Fine. I just thought you'd be interested to know the magistrate in Milan who's conducting the investigation into the Arconti case is Ezio Bazza. He's also looking into the killing of the assassins, which you forgot to mention to me when you found out, so thanks for that.'

'I wasn't sure . . . sorry.'

'A "sorry": well, it's something,' she said. 'Meanwhile, another magistrate in Milan, investigating the case of a missing girl, came across Arconti's wedding ring.'

'That's good,' said Blume. 'That's really good.'

'It gets better. The ring was found in a sequestered construction site belonging to the Mancuso family.' She let the news sink in.

'So they have found the site where Arconti was killed?'

'Almost certainly. The technicians are still working on it.'

'The property is owned by the Mancuso family?'

'Yes.'

'The Mancusos are allied to Megale,' said Blume. 'Tony Megale married into the Mancuso family. The wife died of cancer. They had a son . . .'

' . . . called Enrico,' finished Caterina. 'He lives with his aunt and uncle in Locri, down the road from where Curmaci's wife and kids live. Panebianco's been helping me with the research.'

'That Mancuso news is definitely interesting,' said Blume. He picked up the air hose and blasted it at a spider on its way from asphalt to a patch of crabgrass. The spider rolled itself into a ball and allowed itself to be blown away, and Blume found he had just covered his hand in filthy oil.

'Is it so interesting that it might cause you to doubt your theory that Curmaci is responsible for ordering the death of the namesake? Because from where I am sitting, it looks like Tony Megale or his father is behind it.'

'I don't follow you,' said Blume. He did, but he wanted to hear someone else voice his own thoughts.

'Were you even listening? The victim was taken to a property owned by the Mancuso family. Tony Megale married into that family. His wife . . .'

' . . . died from cancer, they have a son called Enrico. I know, but why does any of this exonerate Curmaci?' demanded Blume.

'Because, since they used a Mancuso property and got Mancuso help, it suggests Tony Megale carried out the killing, or ordered it.'

'Yeah, but why?' said Blume. 'Tony Megale had no compelling reason to kill Arconti's namesake.'

'Maybe Tony wanted to put Agazio Curmaci in an awkward position just before the Polsi summit. Compromise him, cast doubt on his judgment, and make it too dangerous for anyone to appoint him as head of operations in Germany,' said Caterina. 'Maybe he just hates Curmaci. Maybe, Alec, there are people out there who will do things, like forge confessions, so that the blame falls on others.'

'You are always so moral, Caterina. We're talking about someone killing a guy just to embarrass his rival.'

'You've always told me that people don't need compelling reasons to kill.'

'I have? How wise-sounding of me. How about this: Tony Megale killed the Arconti namesake, just like you say, but he did it because Curmaci told him to.'

251

'Is Curmaci so powerful he can order Megale to do this?'

'You've made enough good points for one call, Caterina, bearing in mind that others may be listening into this conversation,' said Blume, as he turned and headed back towards the forecourt where the highway cops were both eating Cornetto ice cream and making a great show of not watching his movements from behind their sunglasses.

'Is that all you have to say?'

'I realize that I think now I may have been wrong in some of my assumptions and a few of my actions.'

'At last!'

Blume pulled a windscreen squeegee out of a bucket and slipped his oily hand into the filthy water, then, unable to bear the disequilibrium of having one hand dry and the other one wet, transferred the phone into the wet one, which was now dripping black water up his arm, and plunged his clean hand into the bucket. The cops looked on impassively as he reached for the paper towel dispenser and found it empty.

'You didn't ask about the wedding ring,' said Caterina.

'That's right, I didn't,' said Blume, cradling the phone with his shoulder and flicking filth from his fingers.

'He probably took it off himself and dropped it there to leave us a clue.'

'It worked a treat, then,' said Blume. 'Good thinking by the actuary.'

'Or he could have taken it off so they wouldn't rob it from his corpse, or find the name of his wife inscribed inside.'

'Also possibilities,' said Blume.

'Or it could have been a gesture of love and respect,' she said.

'That, too,' agreed Blume, crouching down and drying his hands on his socks.

Caterina gave a sigh of exasperation. 'Listen, that confession from Curmaci's wife . . .'

'What about it? You realize you are speaking on an open line.'

'I know what I am doing, but are you doing what I asked?'

'You mean helping the much put-upon wife? It's hardly my main priority, Caterina. It's not as if a person like that . . .'

But she was gone.

Blume climbed into the front of the police car, crossed his arms and sat back in his seat, resolutely refusing to join in the driver's one or two attempts at light banter as they sped down the autostrada towards Cosenza.

He wished he had a wide-brimmed cowboy hat that he could tilt down over his brow. But by dint of half closing his eyes and squinting trucu- lently at the handbrake, he managed to impose silence in the car. Settling back in his seat and wondering why Massimiliani had stopped phoning, he almost fell asleep. Not until they pulled in under the shadow of the modern grey police headquarters in Cosenza did he bestir himself.

The driver stopped the vehicle and addressed his companion in the back. 'Giuseppe, come round to the front seat. The commissioner gets out here.'

The policeman came round as instructed and pulled open the passenger door. Blume stepped out. The door behind him slammed and the car sped off. In front of him, standing with folded arms beside an outsized blue- and-white Range Rover with cages over its side windows and headlights, stood Captain Massimiliano Massimiliani.

43

Cosenza, Calabria

'YOU HAVE A lot of explaining to do,' said Massimiliani. 'But first of all, where is Konrad Hoffmann?'

'*I* have a lot of explaining to do?' said Blume. 'How did you get here ahead of me?'

'Flew.'

'Cosenza has an airport?'

'No.'

'A helicopter all this way just for me?'

'Shut up, Blume. I took a chartered plane from Ciampino to Lamezia Terme, came up north by car. You've lost our German friend?'

'If I hadn't already, I would have when those two clowns picked me up at the service station.'

'That was not my decision. They couldn't very well leave you with that car. Come on, get in. We can talk as we get out of this horrible town.'

'It's not that bad,' said Blume, looking around for the first time. 'A bit like a seaside town without any sea. But it's quiet and there's plenty of parking. And it's nice and cool because we're actually pretty high up. So there is that.'

Massimiliani looked at him and shook his head. 'I thought I had the measure of you, but I don't know when you are being serious. Please don't tell me you took this whole Konrad Hoffmann thing as some sort of elaborate joke.'

'I didn't take it entirely seriously, not at first. I knew you were testing me . . .'

'Wait,' Massimiliani held up his hand, 'which direction?'

'For what?'

'Konrad. That's still your mission. It's rather embarrassing that we've lost him.'

'You don't seem that embarrassed,' said Blume.

'I learned about Konrad and Dagmar just before you,' said Massimiliani. 'If the BKA doesn't see fit to explain what's happening, then there is no reason *we* should care what happens to their agent. As long as he does not upset any equilibrium here in Italy. Wouldn't you agree?'

'That it serves the Germans right if Konrad gets himself killed? Maybe. But then I would have to believe you when you say you only just found out.'

'I am telling you the truth, but whether you believe me or not is of no consequence to anyone, Blume,' said Massimiliani.

'I'm glad to hear you say that out loud. From the beginning you have had a restrained contempt for me, for the mission, for the Germans. For Arconti, too.'

'Arconti's a friend. He recommended you. Friends make mistakes.'

'Recommended me for what, Massimiliani?'

'For being unattached, dissatisfied with your prospects, pigheaded, occasionally unscrupulous . . .'

'I was not referring to my many qualities. What was the nature of the mission?'

'Where's Hoffmann?'

'Like you said, I lost him. What was the mission?'

'To keep an eye on Konrad. So well done, there.'

They continued in silence for a few minutes until Massimiliani arrived at an intersection. 'So, now what?'

'Go south, back to Lamezia Terme airport,' said Blume. 'Then we can cut across to the east coast.'

'You're sure that's where he's headed? I mean you believe this thing about him looking for Curmaci because of a dead girlfriend from decades ago?'

'Are you still pretending that the Germans so fooled you that you still don't know what story to believe in?'

'The BKA asked me to find someone to keep an eye on an agent whose business in Italy was unclear. I don't know why they didn't share the full story from the beginning,' said Massimiliani.

'Maybe they didn't know either, which is what they are claiming after all. I mean, it must happen occasionally in your world that someone accidentally tells you the truth.'

'Hmm. You could be right. Speaking of which . . . tell me how you managed to lose Konrad on the autostrada.'

'I was never behind him.'

'Thought not. You were carrying his phone.'

'Yes. He left it behind. I picked it up.'

'You were deliberately misleading me?'

'I was,' said Blume. He explained about Konrad's disappearance in the early hours of the morning, the phone, his destruction of it.

Massimiliani smiled. 'I was right about you from the get-go, Blume. You are a devious bastard: the false confession by Maria Itria, the way you walked away from an investigation you knew was going nowhere – or nowhere that would redound to your credit – the way you let Arconti misread you, the way you control what you say on the phone, your air of the innocent abroad in the Tuscolana HQ. What else have you been holding back? Last night you said something about a Madonna.'

'A torn Madonna,' said Blume. 'I was going to tell you, but . . . you seemed uninterested.'

'I am interested now.'

Blume told him about his search of Hoffmann's suitcase and his discovery. He enjoyed seeing that Massimiliani, despite his job, had a lousy poker face. First his expression registered outrage at Blume's reticence, but it was soon replaced by a hungry look as he sought more details.

Massimiliani drove on in silence for some time, then said, 'Well, at least we know something the Germans don't. Even if it's not important . . . And presuming it's true and you're not making it up for some reason I cannot fathom.'

'Now that makes me wonder how good you can really be at your job, Massimiliani. There can be no efficiency without at least a little bit of trust. If you never believe anything anyone tells you, then there's not much point in sending people out to discover things, is there?'

'We had no previous trust between us.'

'And we have less now, I think,' said Blume.

'Not true. I still say we could work well together. Maybe I can give you some more background next time, clarify your position.'

'Next time,' said Blume.

Massimiliani pulled out a Smartphone, tapped it expertly and exchanged a few words with someone, organizing a meeting point and something to do with a car, and hung up.

Blume remembered the Samsung in his pocket. He took it out and set it on the seat. 'Keep that. I've discovered I don't like Smartphones. I suppose you have been listening in to my conversations with Caterina.'

'And Caterina would be . . .?'

Blume laughed.

'Oh, you mean Inspector Caterina Mattiola? No, no.'

'Of course not,' said Blume. It was getting hotter and clammier as they neared the coast, and the tyres rumbled and thudded unpleasantly over the pocked surface of the autostrada. He imagined Konrad in his camper, probably coming down the other side of the mountain range now, the ageing engine finally able to pick up some speed as it rolled down towards the Ionian sea, the land getting harder and rockier and dustier on the descent. That was part of the upside-down world of the Italian south. In the north, where he liked to holiday, the green was below and the land got harder as you went up, not down.

Blume was worried for Konrad, concerned even for the camper van itself and, in particular, his outsized suitcase, which he could picture sliding across the floor as the van began the descent towards the eastern seaboard. Underneath the stratum of old jackets that had grown too tight and trousers that had, unaccountably, become narrow around the waist and short in the legs, were things he really valued. Had Konrad rifled through his possessions as he had through Konrad's? If so, he would have come across some prints, a few signed books his father had collected – including three signed first editions of Pirandello plays. He imagined Konrad holding up the amber necklace his mother used to wear, then frowning at the worthless string of wooden worry beads that Blume had had all his life. He had sucked most of the lead paint off them in his childhood, but the greens, blues and yellows were still faintly visible. His father said it was a rosary of sorts, but his mother denied it. *The Cat in the Hat Dictionary*, which had taught him to read, was in there, too, all the pages loose, the spine cracked by the heat of Rome, the ice of Washington State, and the stress of the movement from one to the other.

Tucked into the corner, lovingly cushioned among his socks and sweaters, were two coffee mugs celebrating the year 1976. One, decorated with a white star formed by the implied space between dark-red and pale-blue lines, celebrated the bicentennial of the USA; the other, which displayed a blue-and-green V-shaped badge with a Viking-style bird's head, celebrated the first year of the Seattle Seahawks football team. Inside the first mug, wrapped in tissue paper, were his parents' wedding rings. Inside the other, also wrapped in tissue paper, was a little leather pouch, and inside that was the diamond engagement ring that his father had given his mother. It wasn't much of a diamond, and it was set off on either side by two blue lapis lazuli gemstones that reminded him of neon lights, and gave the ring a tacky Las Vegas feel. Something that belonged as much to the 1970s as the cup it was hidden in. When he found Konrad, or the camper, or both, the first thing he would do would be to rescue his suitcase.

Massimiliani interrupted his thoughts. 'Did you deliberately allow Hoffmann to escape?'

'No. That was just my being careless.'

'I see. Well, apart from your complete failure to do the few simple things I asked you to, I still think you've got potential. If another case came up, would you be interested?'

'I'd have to think about it,' said Blume.

'You'd be better briefed next time.'

'Good.'

'Almost there,' said Massimiliani.

'Where?'

'The point in the road where you make a decision, Blume. Do you want to continue with what's left of this mission?'

'Someone needs to stop Konrad.'

'We might have picked him up before if you hadn't misdirected us.'

'That was a mistake.'

'I don't really understand why you did that.'

'Partly because even though he had given me the slip I still wanted to give him a headstart on you and the BKA, as a sort of favour to him. Partly because I thought he might sow some confusion among Curmaci and his friends, partly because I was fed up getting only partial information from you and the BKA, and partly because I was embarrassed to admit I had lost him,' said Blume.

'That's good and honest,' said Massimiliani. 'I thought you might want to know Curmaci's disappeared.'

'I know,' said Blume. 'Caterina told me.'

'This ship is leaking in all parts. If she was referring to us losing him in Bari, we found him, then lost him again. Someone else is driving the car he rented. Presumably he took another car and is now in Calabria. Do you still hold him responsible for that killing of the insurance broker or whatever he was?'

'If not, then he is responsible for many other things,' said Blume.

'On the day the murder was committed, Curmaci was in Spain. Malaga, which is almost as big a cocaine port as Gioia Tauro. We got this from the Guardia Civil. Then, just as the charred bodies of the presumed perpetrators were found in the Milan hinterland, Curmaci was in Milan, doing a little tour of certain families, including the Flachi. The Flachi specialize in logistics, by the way. You know the companies that deliver stuff you buy on the internet?'

'I don't buy online,' said Blume.

'How very Italian of you,' said Massimiliani. 'But some advanced Italians do trust their credit cards to the web, especially since they invented those ones you top-up with credit. So, Dutch and German logistics companies have moved in and are opening new warehouses in Milan, and the Flachi are there ready to provide for them. Amazon has just opened business in Italy. It's a growing market.'

'What has this to do with Curmaci?' asked Blume.

'We have no idea. That is why it would be nice to leave him in peace and watch developments. After all, Curmaci's not the person you want. Not really.'

'Are you asking me to leave him alone?'

'I wouldn't advise you to go anywhere near him to begin with. Not without backup. But he's probably not the person you want.'

'No boss is ever at the scene of a hit – or only very rarely. The fact he was in Malaga means nothing,' said Blume. His head was throbbing again, and he realized he had not eaten all day and it was now . . . he pulled out his phone . . . two o'clock. The cold air from the air-conditioning was tunnelling into his eyes like two mini whirlwinds, while the rest of his body roasted.

'From what I hear,' said Massimiliani, 'it makes no sense for Curmaci to have ordered the hit on Arconti's namesake.'

'From what you hear?'

'I am not an intelligence analyst, Blume. I don't think you quite get what I do. Basically I just monitor and report, I don't explore. I have too many subjects to go into the details on them all.'

'Try this,' said Blume. 'Suppose Curmaci orders an execution that breaks several rules of Ndrangheta etiquette and draws a lot of unwelcome attention to himself, he could manipulate the event so that it would look like a deliberate action against him, couldn't he? Think about it. The act insults other 'ndrine in Milan and Rome, angers the command in Calabria, endangers Curmaci's own family, galvanizes investigators, gets the press interested in an organization that is pathologically committed to secrecy. If he asked a friend to carry out that act, the friend – a real friend – would refuse and tell him it was a stupid and self-destructive request. But an enemy posing as a friend might agree to it, seeing it as a way of under-mining him. It is so much to Curmaci's disadvantage that as soon as he claims it was done to harm him, everyone will believe him.'

'Christ, do you always think like that? I mean, I knew you had a devious mind, but maybe you're just obsessing about Curmaci at this point? Could it be you need to justify what you did with that transcript?'

'That's a possibility,' said Blume. 'But maybe his actions are for internal consumption. He wants people to see he has internal enemies, and he wants the internal enemies to declare themselves.'

'If you're right, then he must be mighty pleased with you. That false confession by his wife will help him play the role of plot victim even better. What about Konrad Hoffmann, how does he fit in?'

'Like a gift from God,' said Blume. 'Hoffmann appears on the scene, demanding that Megale tell him about a murder Curmaci committed years ago, and threatens him with the result of some inquiry he has been conducting. Megale calls Curmaci, and Curmaci comes up with the idea. He tells Megale to tear a Madonna in half, sign his name, write a message on one half, and send Konrad to Calabria where he'll meet a man with the other half. That way, they get Konrad not only off their case, but out of the country, into Calabria, exposed and alone. Curmaci pockets the other half of the Madonna.'

'Why bother with the other half?' asked Massimiliani. 'All they need to do is to get Konrad to come down to Calabria, and disappear.'

'If I were Curmaci . . .'

'I'd say you and he must be twins separated at birth. You'd have it that

Curmaci has been feigning persecution in preparation for an attack. He's constructed a casus belli for himself.'

'*Casus foederis*,' corrected Blume.

'What?'

'Sorry, it's Konrad's influence. He liked to boast about his Latin. Curmaci had constructed a false plot against himself and a pretext for action. The enemy posing as a friend, the person responsible for the murder of the Milanese insurance agent, could easily be Tony Megale. Perhaps he thinks his father has succession plans that favour Curmaci.'

'He's not really his father,' said Massimiliani.

'What?'

'Tony Megale is almost certainly not Old Megale's real son.'

'How do you know that?'

'It's all open-source intelligence, Blume. Court reports, newspaper stories, and even a few TV programmes from the 1990s. There was a whole scandal. They say it is one of the reasons Tony went to Germany, though I think he just went for the money and opportunity. I thought you knew about it.'

'No. I didn't think to look into him. Just Curmaci. Tell me the story.'

Massimiliani told him about Tony Megale's alleged abduction and adoption. As he listened, Blume's initial annoyance at having overlooked this aspect of the story gave way to a sense of satisfaction at how well it all fitted. Tony, not quite a bastard son, but not far from it, not the natural heir and successor, feared Curmaci, who had exploited him.

The autostrada curved westwards again, back to the coast. He had never entirely outgrown his childish excitement at catching the wink of blue water when the road he was on came close to the sea. But the sea here could only be glimpsed through the empty floors of the incomplete concrete apartment blocks that framed and monumentalized the failure of the south.

A sign for Lamezia Terme appeared, and Massimiliani slowed down. 'I'm going to pull in just before the entrance road to Via dei due Mari. There should be a car waiting for me.'

'Meaning?'

'Meaning you can take this car, head across to the east coast, see if you can't catch up with Hoffmann. There is an APB out on that camper. No reports of any sightings, though.'

'You're not going to the east coast to help me look for him?'

'Of course not. The operations centre is in Reggio, but maybe I'll see you in a few days in Polsi, just after the Ndrangheta holds its summit meeting.'

'Polsi? The sanctuary itself?'

'Yes, madness, I admit, and not my idea. It's a new policy, a sort of annoy-the-fuckers-till-they-do-something-stupid policy. The authorities are holding a mass and then a celebration in Polsi, claiming back the sacred site for the forces of law and order, as it were. And it's going to be done in front of some BKA observers, whom I'll be looking after, and some German journalists. The police from Reggio Calabria and the Locride area are going to go to the same church used the day before by the Ndrangheta for its summit. All in dress uniform. The idea is to celebrate the Archangel Saint Michael, who's the patron saint of the police and . . .'

'Patron saint of the Ndrangheta. I never liked that coincidence,' said Blume. 'Who's behind the idea?'

'The questore of Reggio Calabria. He comes across as mild-mannered and reasonable but he's a hard-nosed aggressive bastard.'

'Good for him.'

'Maybe,' said Massimiliani doubtfully. 'He went on TV and said the police weren't going to share their patron saint with a bunch of cut-throats and bandits. He said it was time to reclaim the Madonna of Polsi from the criminal overlords. He's got strong Catholic beliefs, the questore. If you ask me, he's a bit too keen on the afterlife.'

'He's a hero,' said Blume.

'I thought you'd be a bit more cynical than that. Are you a big Catholic, too?'

'No, but I like the idea of prodding the Mafia beast.'

'First let's see where that policy gets your German friend.'

He pulled into a layby almost completely obscured by wild oats and reeds. He cut the engine and got out, coming round to Blume's door. Blume shifted into the driver's seat, which was unpleasantly warm and slightly damp. Massimiliani opened the passenger door and leaned in.

'You have made some poor decisions, but you have good instincts, Blume. With a bit of training, and a bit of trust, we'd make a good team.' He pointed down the road. 'Go up the mountain to Gerace, down into Locri, head towards San Luca, Africo, Polsi, wherever you think Hoffmann went.'

'If I take Via dei due Mari, maybe you could send a car over the mountain pass to the south . . .?'

'Send a car over Aspromonte, from where, Reggio? It takes all day to get over that mountain, and our resources are deployed to the full. No, Blume, I am not helping the BKA any more than I have already. As for you, finish on your own what you started on your own, but don't do anything that requires backup.'

A siren suddenly whooped behind them. He looked in the rear-view mirror and saw an unmarked saloon car behind, a magnetic flasher stuck in its roof.

'There's my lift. We'll be in contact soon.'

Massimiliani slammed the door shut, and got into the car behind. Blume drove down the slip road and began to drive east.

44

Locri

'SICILIAN PISTACHIO,' SAID Basile. 'I think it's one of my best. The nuts themselves come from Africa and are processed in China, when Sicily can be seen from the other end of this region, but that's progress for you. I hope you understand my accent?'

Konrad nodded. The ice cream stood untouched in a stainless-steel bowl in front of him, next to the torn image of the Madonna. 'I am not hungry.' He pushed the bowl away from himself and the Madonna. 'You must understand that I am extremely nervous.'

'Everyone here is nervous, Mr Hoffmann. In all my long years, I have never had such a strange request. In fact, it is so unprecedented that I do not know what to make of it. Could it be you came all this way to make fun of us simple southerners?'

'No.' Konrad turned the card over. 'This is Mr Megale's signature.'

'And this is the address Mr Megale gave you?'

'Mr Basile's Café Bar Gelateria, yes.'

Basile shook his head in an elaborate display of amazement and disbelief.

'I thought you would have the other half of the card, and that would be a sign of good faith,' added Konrad.

'Is that what Domenico said?'

'No,' admitted Konrad. 'He never said who would have the other half.'

'I understand you do not want to talk to me. Salvatore tells me you want to talk to Agazio Curmaci, who lives in Germany, where you are from. And he also tells me you are a policeman of some sort. If you wanted to talk to Curmaci, you could have arrested him there on false charges, which is the sort of behaviour we have come to expect from the authorities.'

'I do not want to arrest him. I just want him to answer a few questions.'

'I have to tell you I have no idea where Curmaci is at this moment. His son was in here the other day. Brave kid. But Agazio . . .' Basile took the bowl of ice cream and tossed it into the sink. 'It feels like we are all wasting our time.'

'I am sorry if this is inconveniencing you.'

'*Mah.*' Basile waved a generous hand.

A spluttering noise followed by an engine roar caused Konrad to run to the door of the bar. 'My Hymer. They're stealing it!'

'No one is stealing anything from outside my bar. It must just be the traffic police. You're not allowed to park motor homes in the middle of the town. They'll be taking it to a campsite for you. I'll make sure you're taken there after this.'

'The traffic police don't get in and drive away an illegally parked vehicle,' said Konrad. 'I have the keys here, so how did they start it?'

Basile shook his head in disgust. 'The traffic police are such busybodies, you wouldn't believe it. Are you going out there to stop them?'

Konrad stayed where he was.

'Good. Now sit down, and let's see if Curmaci turns up. I haven't seen him myself in more than a year, and most people seem to be under the impression he is still in Germany, and won't be making it down for the Feast of the Madonna tomorrow. So I will be surprised and delighted if he walks through that door.'

'I'd like to wait here for him, if you don't mind.'

'Mind? Of course I don't mind. This is where I live and work, and it's cool and dry in here. Tell you what, I'll shut up the bar, make sure no customers come in to disturb us!'

Konrad surveyed the empty room. Even the wrinkled bald man who had been serving at the bar when he entered had vanished. It was just him and Basile. People were passing by in the square outside, but it was as if a force field was keeping them from coming in.

Fifteen minutes later, seated across a table on which stood two empty and unused glasses, Basile said, 'And do you mind me asking what you want to talk to Curmaci about?'

'Private affairs.'

'Ah.'

'From long ago,' added Konrad, a hint of apology in his tone.

'Well, I go back a long way, too. Perhaps I can remember something that will help you and him resolve this?'

'I don't think so,' said Konrad. 'It's not a pleasant business.'

Ten minutes later, the door opened and four men came in. The last of them was Curmaci. Basile's face registered no surprise at seeing him, but for the sake of consistency of tone, he professed astonishment. 'Agazio! Your foreign friend here was right!'

He stood up and went behind the bar. The three men and Curmaci himself were looking at the torn Madonna on the zinc counter. Konrad stood up, and walked over, and leaned on the far end of the bar and watched from a safe distance. Everyone ignored him.

'What can I get the gentlemen?' asked Basile.

'*Café corretto* with a drop of Sambuco for me,' said Curmaci, pulling out his wallet. The others all ordered coffee. Curmaci plucked out a 10-euro note and left it on the bar, where it went unheeded by Basile. Curmaci slipped two fingers into an inside fold of his wallet and pulled out a bent piece of thick paper, which he smoothed out on the counter and set beside the torn Madonna. The men looked at it and nodded.

'A perfect match, how about that!' said Basile.

Konrad knew then that he was going to die, and that he had known this from the start of his journey.

Curmaci, finally acknowledging Konrad, motioned him over, and pointed at a seat. The other men disappeared into the kitchen. Basile remained behind the bar, at a discreet distance but not out of earshot from where Curmaci and Konrad were now seated.

'*Wollen Sie lieber Deutsch sprechen?*' began Curmaci.

'As a matter of courtesy in my bar, could you please speak Italian,' said Basile from behind the counter.

'I beg your pardon,' said Curmaci. 'Konrad, your Italian is good, isn't it?'

Konrad nodded.

'You have built up a file that could be very damaging for Megale and our operations in Germany, I believe? This is what Domenico Megale tells me.'

'Yes.'

'And what would you like us to do about it?'

'I want you to talk to me,' said Konrad. 'First we talk about what I want to talk about, then we talk about what you want to talk about. OK?'

'That's a roundabout but valorous way of putting it.'

'Did you kill Dagmar?'

'You don't even give me her last name.'

'I don't need to, you know who I am.'

'But if you put it like that, it sounds too intimate, like we are old friends. You, Dagmar and me. That's not how it is, though.'

'We are not friends, no.'

'Good, that's cleared that up,' said Curmaci, with a quick glance at Basile who was quietly rearranging a stack of cappuccino cups balanced on top of the cream-coloured Gaggia espresso machine. 'Her surname was Schiefer, and I shot her dead in 1993 in execution of a direct order from Domenico Megale, who went to prison as a result of her attempts to impress her superiors. Do you really want to hear this story?'

'Yes.'

'Very well. She had gone to the Edeka supermarket near her house. Her parents' house. She still lived with them. I remember she had chestnuts in her shopping. It's funny the incidental details that come to mind even after so long a time. She had parked her bike in the car park, and we pulled up. Our driver, who didn't even speak any German, started asking directions, she came over. I remember she had a big smile on her face. I got out the back, pushed her in. It was so easy, it almost felt like she climbed in willingly. Are you listening?'

'Yes.'

'We went north out of the city in the direction of the airport, then took a right towards Lintorf. We drove down Lintorfer Waldstrasse, which, as you know, is one of the few bits of countryside left around that area. We pulled in off the road, without even bothering to hide the car very much since it was not going to take long. She walked on her own two legs away from the car. I told her I wanted her to walk into the copse of black poplars beside the road, put her back against a tree trunk, then turn to face me, but I shot her in the back of the head as soon as she had taken her first two steps. It wouldn't have made sense to have to carry the deadweight of the body all the way back from the trees, and doing it that way minimized her suffering and fear. Also there is always the chance of a lucky escape in such circumstances. She might have run.'

Konrad put his head between his knees and retched, bringing up nothing. Basile courteously arrived with a glass of water, set it down before him, then retreated.

'How many shots?'

'Two. I don't remember, to be honest. But it was always two. One to bring the person down, one to make sure.'

'You didn't give her a chance to prepare. She would have faced you.'

'She prepared herself in the car. I could feel it. But even if she didn't, it's not my job to prepare people.'

'Did she mention my name?'

'How would I be expected to remember a thing like that?'

'You remembered the chestnuts. Did she beg for her life?'

'I can't remember. Probably.'

'Did she mention her parents?'

Curmaci shrugged apologetically. 'Again, I can't remember. Parents, mothers in particular, children – if there are any – and God. These are common themes among victims.'

Konrad straightened up. 'And the body? Where is she?'

'I didn't oversee the disposal. Even if I knew, do you really want the details? They will have cut off the four limbs, dissolved her parts in acid, removed the teeth and bone fragments after three days, crushed them, tossed them into several skips. The liquefied body could have gone any-where. There's an industrial park near Neuss we used. It's near the river. That's where it will have been done.'

'Are you telling me the truth?'

'Does it sound like I am holding anything back?'

'So there is no body and no resting place?'

'No. You know how it is . . . *Madonna mia*, show some courage, Hoffmann. What sort of man weeps for news that is a generation old?'

'If I would cry, but I am not, I would not be ashamed. I would be crying for the parents, too.'

Curmaci glanced back at Basile, now straightening the packets of sugar and artificial sweeteners. 'When he gave you that torn Madonna, did you think Old Megale was making a move against me?'

'It is what I hoped, yes,' said Konrad. 'I promised him that if you were killed, I would destroy the evidence I have gathered, eliminate every trace of my investigation, and leave the police force.'

'And you believed he would order that?'

'I am an excellent investigator and I have a good mind. But sometimes hope obfuscates even a fine intellect. It did not occur to me until now that the torn Madonna will have been your idea. Megale is not so subtle. He is just an ignorant pig. I had hopes which were unrealistic.'

'You realize I did not need to tell you anything? I did you a favour.'

'You enjoyed the telling. You knew it would be a torture for me.'

'Speaking of torture,' said Curmaci, 'how can you be persuaded to get rid of that evidence you have built up on money laundering?'

'Not just that,' said Hoffmann defiantly. 'I know about your operations through Rotterdam into Duisburg. Plus several other things. Hotels in Provence, housing projects outside Dresden. I have a lot of stuff.'

'What will it be: money to buy your silence; threats against people you love? You tell me, Hoffmann.'

'I have no one. No family, no parents, no colleagues who are friends.'

'*Frei aber einsam.* What about Dagmar's parents?'

'You can't hurt them any more.'

'Well, that can be tested. But it seems to me the easiest thing to do would be for you to disappear, unless you can give me a better idea.'

'I have sent the evidence to myself multiple times, including by parcel post to the office. If something happens to me, my colleagues will eventually get around to looking at my files. The same files are also attached to an email stored on a site called Time Cave. They'll start arriving in various inboxes in the future unless I go to my account and cancel them from the outbox.'

'You have everything covered.' Curmaci stood up. 'It seems the only choice we have is to let you go and hope for the best. If we do that, can we have your word that you will hold back on these revelations?'

'Yes,' said Konrad.

'But you didn't get the revenge you were seeking, did you?'

'At least I got some information.'

Basile came out from behind the bar, and retrieved Konrad's glass, and placed it out of harm's way. The three men who had come in earlier emerged from the kitchen. Two stood behind him, Basile, Curmaci and the other in front.

'I think your specialization in the Camorra has misled you, Hoffmann,' said Curmaci. 'But I don't think even the feckless Neapolitans would allow you to come down from Germany, sit in the bar of a capo, and threaten the Society. But us? Have you even read anything about our history?'

'I read a lot.'

'You understood nothing, then. We *always* put honour before money. If you don't understand the word "honour", think of it as a willingness to invest in long-term reputation and goodwill at the cost of short-term benefits. That's why the South Americans trust us so much. We will sever our own limbs rather than be seen to give in to threats. There are countless examples of us sacrificing huge business empires built up over years merely for the sake of reputation. You will have noted that fact while studying our Society?'

Konrad nodded, unable to speak. He needed the water Basile had taken from him.

'Your naivety is unbelievable.'

Konrad put up no resistance as they steered him towards the kitchen. The temperature in there was cool and the air was scented with sugar and cleaning alcohol. The ice-cream makers looked like woodchip stoves, and they gleamed. A black rubber hose was attached to the tap above the double sink, and lay coiled on the white tiles that had recently been washed clean and were still slightly slippery. Not quite now, he thought. It would not be in this clean kitchen, the very place the boss himself worked.

But once again, Konrad had misread the situation.

45

Gerace–Locri, Calabria

IT WAS YEARS since Blume had been in this part of the country. After an initial section of squalor in the form of a prefabricated shopping centre and a clutch of apartment buildings cluttered with balconies, which resembled makeshift spectator stands erected to observe the spectacle of cars passing by, the road narrowed and straightened and darkened, as sturdy metal fences and tall olive trees appeared on either side. Sometimes, where a new olive grove with younger trees had been planted in the red earth, the light would intensify and the vista open, but then the tall trees and fences returned to reiterate the relentlessly linear plan. It was like driving up the longest ever avenue to a stately home, an impression intensified by the absence of any traffic coming in the opposite direction. Occasionally, he caught glimpses of parked or discarded small boxy Fiats so old they still had number plates with 'RC', the abbreviation for Reggio Calabria, marked out in pale orange, a system he wished the country had never abandoned, since it was always interesting and sometimes useful to know from which province the fool in the car in front of you hailed. In some of the groves, the bare earth was already overlaid with dark green nets, ready to catch the olives that would be combed off in a few months by African immigrants or shaken off by vibrating mechanical bars attached to tractors.

The olive oil from here was among his favourite things in the world. He preferred the bitter and complex tones of Calabrian oil to the mellow, fruity Tuscan varieties that Japanese tourists came all the way from Tokyo to taste. No Japanese tourists came down here.

After half an hour, the road started turning and climbing. The repetitive but soothing pale grey and silver of the olive groves gave way to a

271

dark composition of greens and yellows. Blume rolled down the window to get the scent of the pine trees, whose cones and needles lay baking on the bumpy asphalt, sometimes causing the wheels to lose grip. Similar to olive trees, but taller and more sober, holm oaks stood behind thickets of juniper and birch, a tree he had always associated with the cool north. Yet here it was, perfectly at home. Hazels, hornbeams and green alder, all heavy, sturdy and oppressive plants linked by chains of ivy, fought for dominance, then fell back as the road continued to climb. Just when he thought he had seen the last of the taller trees, the road dipped downwards and suddenly he found himself driving through a forest of ancient beeches whose rippled leaves fended off the sun so well that the air was damp and mushroom-scented.

As the trees finally began to give way to the increasing altitude and the bushes turned into shrubs, he was able, thanks also to the added height of the car he was driving, to see how insidious the steep banks on the roadside were. Now that he was nearing upper reaches of the range, the vistas he had glimpsed through the side window lay in front of him. Dozens of mountaintops, the shape of upturned egg boxes or cloche hats, lay before him, their slopes sudden, steep and gleaming. His father had once taught him that painters used lighter colours for the background, darker for the foreground, but the hills before him seemed to increase the depth of their green as they stretched northwards, while the one he was driving across was sand-coloured and dominated by yellow flowers and scratching woody plants.

It would be difficult to paint this landscape without seeming to idealize it, he thought, but the solution to that particular problem of representation soon presented itself in the form of a sudden hamlet made up of a scattering of brutal cement houses, most of them missing a top storey but all equipped with satellite dishes. They were fronted by messy gardens containing stubby Indian figs, discarded plastic bottles of motor oil and rotting cars. The larger houses had McMansion gates, and all the smaller houses had yellow and brown aluminium-framed windows and doors.

These people do not deserve their environment, thought Blume. With Naples, one could always hope for Vesuvius, but here . . . three cars came racing around the corner so close together they might have been linked by a chain. Suddenly, as if they had been waiting for a secret command, vehicles appeared behind him and in front of him. The empty road was suddenly busy. He checked the time. Four o'clock. The Ionian sea lay before him; the town of Locri, a modern excrescence of the Norman citadel of Gerace, which he had just driven through without stopping, was visible in the distance.

The escarpments on either side of the road were shallower now, but he still would not want to find himself skidding down one. How had Konrad fared with his big camper van? Two oncoming cars flashed their lights at him. What were they doing? Challenging him to move over, closer to the edge of the road, to hog the middle less? Or were they defying the authority of the state, mocking him in his police car? A policeman alone in a marked vehicle was rare anywhere in the country, down here it may never have been seen. He glanced in his rear mirror and saw the car behind him flash its light. Just friends greeting each other. He was being paranoiac.

He reached a ribbon of breeze-block buildings that, he supposed, represented the outskirts of Locri. A car passed in the opposite direction without flashing its lights, the driver not even looking at him. Blume checked the wing mirror to see if anyone was behind. Nothing. He eased back in his seat, pressed gently on the accelerator when suddenly a shape shot out from the side of the road and hurled itself in front of him. The object had come at lightning speed from the bushes on to the road, but now seemed magnetized and immobile as it stood there, teeth bared, eyes flashing, and Blume was already spinning the wheel. It was only as his foot reached the brake pedal that the word 'dog' formed itself in his conscious mind, but he was already spinning furiously in the opposite direction to avoid a patch of small trees.

He managed to bring the car to a halt, then got out, and looked back down the road. He had not felt any impact, but if he had hit the beast, an ugly thing it had been, then it would be finished off by the traffic behind. But he saw no one swerve or slow down, heard no pitiful yelps or sickening crunch.

The vehicles he was watching slowed down as they passed, as if Blume were an interesting crash. Within three minutes, the oncoming traffic, as well as the cars behind him, had slowed to a crawl, and Blume realized that with his police-marked SUV on the side of the road, he had inadvertently set up a one-man checkpoint. He started waving the traffic past.

Finally, a green Mercedes estate car slowed down and the driver, a woman with piercing blue eyes and long silky hair that looked all the better for being dyed blonde, spoke to him.

'*Ma 'cca sei 'mbarru.*'

'What?'

'You're in the way and you're in the wrong place. Go on for about a kilometre, first left, third right. That's where it is.'

'Where what is?' But she had driven on, waving an elegant hand, made languorous by the weight of golden bracelets.

Blume climbed back into his Range Rover, drove it to the side of the road, and called Caterina.

'Where are you?' she said without so much as a greeting.

'Locri. At last.'

'Have you gone to Maria Itria?'

'No. I haven't even got to the town proper yet.'

'Then you're right next to where she lives. You came in by Highway 111, right?'

'Yes,' said Blume.

'Follow it down to Via Garibaldi, then on to the Provincial Road, first house after a Sidis food mart, number 45. On Google Street View it has a red gate. That may have changed.'

'Give me a bit of time,' said Blume. 'It's still not my priority and I think it might be an ill-advised visit.'

'It almost certainly is, but you shouldn't have started this thing. Just check. You don't have to go in. Check from a distance, bring backup from the town. Has anyone spoken to the local magistrate yet?'

'I don't know . . . Listen, Caterina, I was thinking maybe . . . no never mind.'

'Thinking what, Alec?'

'Nothing. I was thinking nothing. It's nice to hear your voice.'

He hung up before she could reply to that.

He followed the directions of the woman in the Mercedes, replaying her voice in his head. There was something about the accent of Calabria that seemed to imply that the speaker was engaged in two streams of communication, one literal, the other ironic. The Sicilians did it, too, but here it was even more pronounced. No matter how innocuous the subject matter, the Calabrians seemed to be delivering an underlying commentary on the person being spoken to for failing to recognize that the whole idea of speaking Italian was faintly ridiculous. If only the person being spoken to would switch into the local dialect based on Greek, Latin, Albanian, Arabic and Norman French, they seemed to be suggesting, things would be much clearer. Or maybe it was speaking at all that they found ridiculous, when so much about life and the past was better left unsaid.

The feeling of being watched was so strong that he felt if he were to make a wrong turning someone might step out of the bushes and redirect him. But to what?

The road, already so narrow that the Spanish broom was clutching at the wheels, simply vanished ten yards after the turn. A few yards into the field and he could feel the wheels sinking into the sand beneath the scrub, and from where he was, he could already see that the land suddenly dropped away into a narrow gorge. Seeing he could no longer go forwards, he reversed the Range Rover back to the edge of the field and walked. By now he knew what he would see.

The soil beneath his feet was grey and powdery, and the smell that reached his nose was of wet ash and burned rubber, even more pungent than the smell he and Konrad had experienced together near Lake Avernus. As he reached the edge of the shallow gully, he saw the blackened hulk of the burned-out camper van lying at the bottom of the deep ditch. The back section was jutting halfway up the slope, and the driver's cab was buried in a pool of greasy mud at the bottom, like the nose of some sea creature stranded by the tide.

He had a weapon, but it was a handgun, no use against hidden enemies at a distance who had the drop on him. He had a phone, which, when he took it out to call in backup, flashed a little antenna at him to impart the unsurprising news that there was no mobile phone signal in this dimple of wasteland on the outskirts of Locri. The car had a radio, but, he felt sure, there would be people waiting for him at the car, and in any case it was his duty now to clamber down to the ditch and put his head into the black gap where the curtain to the living space in the camper had been and to look inside.

The smell of the charred materials was overpoweringly sour, but, he realized with relief, there was no smell of burned hair and teeth, none of the sweet *porchetta* smell of roasted human. Wherever Konrad was, and he might be lying somewhere in the ditch below, at least he was not in the camper, which, even in the hot air of the late afternoon, was still radiating

275

heat. After hunting around for ten minutes and finding no trace of Konrad, alive or dead, Blume resolved to climb into the camper van. Years of experience had taught him to control his gag reflex, but the evil smells from the burned-out wreck were no less overpowering for that. They entered his nostrils and mouth and seemed to stream into his brain through his eyes and ears. With the inevitability of a digital timer, the migraine went off in his head, obscuring his vision. He clambered through the burned-out door, becoming immediately filthy as he gripped the flaking walls to steady himself against the steep incline. Inside it was as if someone had spent the day burning fat wads of newspaper and scattering the pieces around. A scorched piece of crumpling wood was all that was left of the partition between the living quarters and the cab. There was no trace of the photo of Dagmar.

In the corner, blistered and bulging, as if it had been blown open from the inside, sat his father's suitcase. It had not put up much of a fight against the fire. Blume lifted off what was left of the lid, saddened to find that the shiny shellac-covered case his father had been so fond of had consisted mainly of compressed layers of corrugated cardboard. Nothing inside had survived except for an unwieldy Aran sweater that he had always hated but had kept all these years in memory of his mother who said he would be thankful for it when they moved back to cold Seattle. As he lifted it out, he noticed that some of the threads on the sleeve were still glowing slightly in the dark, like tiny electric filaments. The pictures and sketches from his parents' study, some of them valuable, all of them precious, were gone. The books were all burned halfway in from their sides or else halfway down from the tops. His socks, underpants and polo shirts had melted. As he was rummaging through the mess, the charred sides of the suitcase gave way. For a moment, the incinerated contents retained a rectangular shape, then subsided with a puff of ash, which wafted into his face. He reached his hand down into the heap of clinker that had once held the most valued objects of his life and scooped up the warm shards of an exploded cup. He sieved them through his fingers and then repeated the operation, over and over again. Half an hour later, he emerged from the vehicle, clutching a blackened engagement ring and two misshapen wedding bands in his fist. The air, which had seemed so hot and hostile before, cooled his face. He filled his lungs and expanded his chest and, sob by sob, heaved in oxygen until he was breathing normally.

When he reached the car, he noticed that it seemed lopsided. He soon discovered the cause. Two tyres had been slashed. Not all four, because two was just one more than the available spare, and therefore the more exquisite an act of intimidation. He hardly cared. He opened the door and got a bottle of water that he had seen in the back seat. It was warm and had been half drunk by God knows whom, but took the madness out of his thirst. He wiped his face with his black hands and looked at the results in the mirror. He started the engine and reversed, not bothering to look backwards into the glare of the sun. The Range Rover wobbled and swayed, and the wheels behaved like wooden cubes rather than flat rings. He shoved it into forward gear and headed back towards Via Garibaldi. He found that if he went faster, the car maintained a linear trajectory for longer, and so he pushed down on the accelerator. The sound from underneath the car, echoed and amplified by the walls on the side of the road, was like the rotor blades of a helicopter. He stepped down harder on the gas and the car began sliding unstoppably into the opposite lane where another car, whose driver was either playing chicken with him or texting what might be his last ever message on his phone, continued its head-on approach. Blume pulled at the wheel and aimed at a jagged pothole on his own side. The other car went sailing by and, with a crunch and a pop, his front left tyre disintegrated. The car lurched forwards, showering sparks and making a scraping noise on the asphalt which seemed to electrify every tooth filling in his head and make his balls contract.

Blume gave up. He kicked his way out of the car, even though nothing was wrong with the door, and stepped down into the dingy street, and started walking. Fifty yards ahead of him was a Sidis mini-mart, closed, and after that, on the left, was his inevitable destination, a modest two-storey house with a red gate.

46

Locri

HIS HEADACHE WAS no longer confined to his head nor was it a mere ache. At some point in the past hour the pain had burrowed its way into the centre of his body, and was operating from there. Each heartbeat seemed to squirt a jet of poison up his spine and into the back of his brain, from where it spread slowly, gripping his entire skull before pulsing in his temples as if trying to burst out. Just as the pulsation ended and the pain began to ebb, another heartbeat injected a renewed dose. He imagined the relief of his heart stopping.

The orange shine of the sun flared off the windows of the house behind the red gate and off the metal of a parked car. When the door opened to his knock, he almost stepped straight in, so inviting was the dark dry air from the house. But there was a woman in front of him, younger-looking and smaller than he had been expecting. He thought he could smell lavender and mint, either from her or from deeper inside. He screwed up his eyes against the brightness and tried to penetrate the dark entrance with his gaze. He could make out her shining hair, and when she smiled her teeth glistened.

'Are you all right?'

Blume swayed on the threshold, confused. That was surely the question he was supposed to have asked her. And the voice was wrong, too. She sounded like a girl. He could not fit the voice to the wheedling Mafia-accented matriarch he had created in his mind.

'Do you need to sit down?'

'I have a terrible headache,' said Blume. 'And I think I'm pretty dirty.'

'Have you been standing in the sun?'

'It's not the sun. I often get them.'

Maria Itria stood aside and he walked in. The drop in temperature was immediate and exhilarating, but it made him sneeze and break out in a sweat. He kept his eyes closed, trying to adjust to the shaded hallway.

'Come through to the kitchen,' she said.

He followed obediently.

'Sit.'

He sat at the broad table. Its top was a board of dark oak that was cool against the palm of his hands. He had to resist the temptation to lay his cheek against it.

'My name is Commissioner Alec Blume. Police.'

'Eat this, Alessio.' She handed him a rock-hard piece of bread.

'Alec, not Alessio. I'm not hungry.'

'If you want your headache to go, eat it. Just a bite or two. You need something in your stomach if you have a headache.'

Something wet and alive leaped at his face, and he realized she had thrown him a cloth dipped in water. He wiped his face, turning the cloth dark. Then he stood up and went over to the kitchen sink, which is what he should have done to begin with, and washed his hands and arms and drank glass after glass of water. The woman shied away from him as he did this, but when he sat down again, she resumed her position at the sink.

Back at the table, Blume tried to bite off a small piece of the bread she had given him, but found he had to gnaw his way into it. As he began chewing, it released a fragrance of orange and olive. His teeth cracked a seed, and his mouth filled with the taste of fennel. He realized his lips had numbed slightly and his tongue was tingling.

'There are a few flakes of *peperoncino* mixed in with the grains. It can help a headache sometimes, but I've got something better.'

She walked across to the cupboard. Blume looked at her properly for the first time. She was barefoot, youthful, dressed simply in faded blue jeans and a beige cotton and linen blouse. It looked comfortable, floppy and elegant all at the same time, and he suddenly felt self-conscious about his abject appearance. Nothing about her fitted his image, and nothing in her actions matched his expectations.

She placed a full glass of jet-black liquid on the table before him. He looked down at the glass, then up at her, examining her face. Why had he not pulled up a file on her, prepared himself better for this encounter? This was the woman whose life he had decided to put in danger. The woman he said he had no sympathy for. Her eyes were dark and sloped in a way that would have given her an Asian look had they not been so large. She had a small white scar on her left cheek, a mark from childhood chicken pox or measles. Her childhood, Blume realized, could not have been all that long ago.

'What's in this glass?'

'Your nose must be blocked if you can't smell it.' She stood up again, went over to the drawer, pulled out a large knife, and Blume felt his hand reach automatically inwards towards his sweaty waist and the butt of his gun. The knife flashed as she sliced through two thick-skinned lemons. Cautiously, he brought the glass up to his nose.

'It's a suspension of pure liquorice,' she said, coming over with the lemons, one of which she had halved, the other quartered.

'Liquorice liquor. Then it's alcoholic,' he said. 'I don't drink alcohol.'

She rolled up the dangling sleeve of her shirt, and pushed the lemons towards him. 'If you want to get rid of your headache, drink that cordial.'

Blume drank. It was powerful. He could feel it painting his tongue and the roof of his mouth black, and it burned the back of his throat even though it was extremely sweet. The glass contained at least three measures. He put it down half empty. Already he could feel the fumes going to his head.

'All of it, come on. You're a big man.'

Blume took a second long draught and snapped the empty glass back on the wooden top. It was like drinking a cough medicine.

'Those lemons are sweet enough to peel and eat like oranges, but they will taste sour after the licorice. Nothing is sweeter than licorice. Bite into the quartered lemons,' she instructed.

'I don't think I will. We need to talk.'

'Do it. You can talk at the same time.'

Blume did as she said. She was right about the lemon being sour, but the effect was invigorating and the taste delicious. He finished two quarters with two quick bites, attacked the third, and said, 'You know who I am?'

'For now, you are just an unhappy man with a headache.'

'Commissioner Blume. I am a policeman.'

'You just said that a minute ago.'

'So I did. I apologize. The reason I am here, Mrs Curmaci, is . . .' He stopped. He did not sound credible to himself. He finished the last quarter lemon as he thought of something to say.

'Now take the two half lemons, and press them against your temples.'

'You're kidding, right?'

'No. But if you think you'll look stupid,' and here she smiled sweetly at him, 'and you will, just hold half a lemon in your hand and keep smelling it. Your headache will be gone in ten minutes. In fact, it's already fading.'

She was right. As soon as he thought about it, he felt another pulse, but at least thirty seconds had passed since the last one. And the sensation of the pain trying to break out was diminishing fast.

'You can use lavender, too. Shall I get you some?'

'No. I'm fine. This,' he brought the lemon to his nose and inhaled deeply, 'is working.'

The nausea was fading fast too, and he had finally stopped sweating. He looked gratefully into the face of the young woman across the table and saw her eyes shift sideways and her face become anxious. He followed her gaze to the kitchen door, where staring at them was a youth on the verge of manhood.

Blume raised his hand in greeting, but the teenager continued to regard him in grave silence. Blume looked at the mother for guidance. He had never mastered the etiquette of speaking to children. All he knew was that after they reached a certain age, asking them their names and age sounded as strange to them as it would to an ordinary adult. And yet he could not for the life of him imagine what else to say.

He looked back, and saw the boy was gone. Mostly he felt relieved, but he also found the sudden disappearance and the utter silence that preceded it disturbing.

'That's my son.' She smiled. Her eyetooth was slightly crooked. 'I have another son upstairs, and if he wakes up I'll have to go to him. His name is Roberto. Robertino we call him. The little one. My son here, the one you saw . . .'

Blume ran his mind's eye over files from what seemed like years ago and plucked the name Ruggiero from the air, and said it to her.

'That's right, Ruggiero.' Her voice softened as she pronounced the name, and she expressed no surprise that he should know it.

Blume felt very pleased with his brain and with the lucidity of his thoughts, then realized, almost with a shock, that the pain had simply floated out of his head. Tentatively, he rolled his head backwards to feel the tension in his neck. Nothing. It was gone, and he felt energy returning to his whole body.

'How are you feeling?'

Happy was the right response, but he could not really say that. 'That liquorice seems to have done the trick,' he said. 'Thank you.'

'Don't mention it. Now what am I going to do about having not just a man, but a policeman visiting my house? I hope you're going to make a call and a fleet of cars will drive up and you'll arrest me now. Nothing else would look right.'

'Well . . . I suppose I could . . .'

'And it needs to be made clear that the time we spent together in here was dedicated to discussing what was to be done about the children. I was refusing to leave the house until arrangements had been made for them. In fact, that's true. I am going to make a phone call to the Megales across the road, and send Roberto over with Ruggiero. Can you make the call to your colleagues, make sure there are a lot of flashing lights and squealing of tyres?' She rolled up her shirtsleeve, which had fallen down again, and held out her arms. Blume could see tiny blonde hairs against her smooth brown skin. Her wrists were thin, one encircled by a silver bracelet, and her fingers long, one encircled by a golden ring.

She shook her lovely hands at him. 'Maybe you could put handcuffs on me?'

'I can't just arrest you like that. I need a magistrate to bring charges. And I can't call in the local police. It doesn't work like that.'

She pulled her arms back and folded them across her breast. 'So what are you doing here?'

'I thought you might need help.'

'I don't,' she said. 'In a moment of weakness, I made a telephone call. But you don't look like you came either to arrest me or to help me. You're all alone, aren't you?'

'I'm not here to arrest you.'

'Do you even know what I am talking about?'

'Yes. You made a call to Magistrate Arconti,' said Blume. 'But maybe you had no choice?'

'Of course I had a choice.'

'If you have been under pressure or threat from your neighbours, from people around here, I think I can help you understand why. But first I need to ask you this: has your husband returned?'

She shook her head, not in denial but in refusal to answer.

'I need to ask you this again,' said Blume. 'Has your husband returned?'

This time the shake of her head contained a warning.

'Suppose your husband had returned,' said Blume. 'Do you think he could resolve this problem that has arisen? I am referring to your reputation in this community.'

'I don't follow.'

'Without bloodshed. Because if he could just make sure, without bloodshed, that everyone understood your phone call was made in good faith, then I would be happy with that.'

'Who knows about it?'

'Only a few people,' said Blume. 'It does not have to become known to anyone else.'

Maria Itria bit her lip as she considered this. 'What do you want in return?'

'Nothing. But if you decided to follow up on that phone call and talk to a magistrate, I think it would be a good thing.'

'Betray my husband, my family?'

'Talk openly to someone. Even to me. Not to Arconti, he's leaving the profession. Did you know he has been taken ill?'

'Poor man, it must be the stress of all those lies he tells about honest people.'

There it was. The flash of cynicism he had been waiting for. But still she sat there, beautiful and seemingly vulnerable, a youthful mother with two children in the house.

'Did you hear about the murder of Matteo Arconti?'

'I thought you said he had been taken ill.'

'Not him. His namesake.' Blume told her the story, watching her face as he did so. She seemed keen to hear the details, and her eyes shone with interest when he spoke about how they had tracked down the van to the abandoned Falck steelworks in Sesto San Giovanni. She grimaced sympathetically as he described the bullet wounds in Arconti's body, shook her head sadly as he remembered how Magistrate Arconti had been overcome by apoplexy on the floor of his office.

'And you think my husband planned all this?'

'I certainly think he is capable of it.'

'That is an evasive answer, Commissioner. My husband has so many enemies. Some of them very close. I am still trying to see how my phone call last night to Arconti is supposed to be connected to all this that went before – and to your presence here in my kitchen.'

'Months ago, Arconti phoned you, and you refused to answer his questions. Do you remember that?'

She nodded.

'Someone altered the transcript of that call to make it sound like you had made a willing confession. The idea was to force your husband to intervene, to get him into the open, and maybe even to force him to break with the Society.'

'What Society? Are you implying organized crime? And what sort of evil person would risk the life of a mother and her two children on the strength of a mere suspicion, a misplaced one at that?' she said, looking straight at him.

Blume returned the gaze. 'What sort of sick community do you live in where the life of a mother and her children would be at risk because she had spoken to a magistrate of the Republic? What sort of evil peasant culture have you chosen? And don't deny that you chose it.'

'My call yesterday was a moment of weakness. That can be suppressed and forgiven. It can be made to have never happened. What I want to know is what sort of person altered my conversation with the magistrate . . . Hush!'

Blume listened, and heard nothing. He was about to speak when she held up a warning finger and he heard the sound of an infant making a few practice sounds like little coughs, a clearing of the air passages in preparation for the bawling phase, which began almost immediately.

'He wakes up hungry,' she said and slipped quickly out of the kitchen, leaving the door ajar, her footsteps thudding quickly up the short flight of stairs.

The speed with which the infant's cries filled with desperation was remarkable, as was the immediacy with which his lament turned into contented burbles as he was picked up. Blume could hear the mother softly talking and comforting the child as she made her way downstairs again. She stood outside the door for a moment, muttering something to the baby. He heard another voice, presumably the elder boy.

She opened the kitchen door slowly, still leaving it open. Framed in the doorway, cradling the baby, she was a lovely sight, and her expression still seemed tender and comforting as she looked up from the child's face and across the kitchen at him, but there was an expression of alarm there, too.

'I see you haven't moved, Commissioner,' she said. Then, instead of taking a step forward, towards him and the table, she stepped aside, and pulled the baby up to her shoulder protectively cupping the back of its head, while she pressed it against herself and squeezed her eyes shut. Blume was still smiling at her when a dark shape he had begun to pick up in the corner of his eye came through the door at speed, seeming to grow in size as it moved. The figure moved across the narrow space that separated them, holding a black pistol at the end of an outstretched arm as if it were a smoking pan he intended to dispose of.

Agazio Curmaci merely clicked his tongue twice in rapid warning as Blume's hand reached across his stomach towards his side holster, then he hit Blume's forehead hard with the barrel of the pistol and even then continued advancing, forcing Blume's head back and finally toppling him off the chair. Another person appeared, a hefty ageing man in heavy trousers, a filthy shirt and an incongruous red silk handkerchief knitted around his throat. He, too, was holding a weapon, a massive old shotgun, probably legally owned since its ends were not sawn off and he was clearly some sort of peasant hunter. It was characteristic of the Ndrangheta to use buckshot and to aim for the face. Blume was so intent on looking up the barrels of the shotgun and waiting for the flash, the pain and the eternal darkness afterwards that he hardly noticed as Curmaci squatted down and disarmed him. Curmaci patted his hands up and down his body looking for other weapons. He found and confiscated Blume's mobile phone.

'OK, you can stand. We're leaving here,' said Curmaci. He was different in the flesh from the photos Blume had seen in Arconti's office. For a start, he had aged and gained in girth. In the photos, he had been scowling or tight-lipped, but from up close, despite the circumstances, he seemed to have an open face and a ready smile. He came across as likeable, solid, frank, dependable.

Blume got to his feet. The shotgun man, who stank of game and meat, grabbed the back of Blume's filthy jacket, bunching it up, and marched him past the doorway where Maria Itria stood, one child still in her arms, the older wordless child standing beside her, his arm around her waist either seeking or giving comfort.

'Was your husband here all the time?' said Blume as he passed her. It was the only question that came to mind, or the only question he could ask without feeling completely foolish in the eyes of this woman. He was concerned not to cut too bad a figure in front of her, even though he might be dead within minutes.

'No, I was out on business, Commissioner,' replied Curmaci, answering on his wife's behalf. 'I got a call.'

'Who called? No one knew I was . . .' Blume saw the bright blue eyes of the boy looking unblinkingly at him.

'Here, Ruggiero,' said Curmaci, tossing Blume's mobile phone into the boy's hand. 'Get rid of this, and destroy it completely. Not here. It can't go offline at this address. Can I trust you to do this?'

'Yes, Dad. You can always trust me.'

'I know I can, son.'

The look on the boy's face as Blume filed past was of ecstatic pride.

47

Ardore, Locride area

THE STINKING MAN with the shotgun tied Blume's wrists behind his back, but did not show much interest or skill in the task, simply wrapping the cord casually like he was trussing a chicken. Blume felt the knot loosen almost immediately.

They bundled him into a car, a small Fiat Ritmo from the 1980s that seemed to be made of tin. The stinking giant drove. Blume sat in the back, Curmaci beside him looking pensively out the window, like he was a train passenger keen not to enter into conversation. Blume could almost sympathize given the state of his clothes and skin, and the sour stench of soot he could smell coming from himself. Curmaci was casually but immaculately dressed in a Zenga polo shirt with stripes so narrow they could only be seen close up, an elegant pair of lemon-yellow slacks, slip-on moccasins, a pair of designer sunglasses tucked between the buttons on his shirt. His hair seemed to have been cut an hour ago, so precise was the razor and scissor line above his ear. Where it swept elegantly down towards the back of his head, Blume could see individual strands of white. He wondered if Curmaci was aware of them, and if they bothered him. Blume had been rather pleased with his first white hairs, but disliked the emergent salt-and-pepper look he now had.

They were headed inland and upwards again, though not on the same road Blume had come from. Either the car had only one gear or the moron driving did not know what the clutch was for, but after half an hour, the constant screaming of the engine being forced to do everything in second was beginning to weigh more heavily upon Blume's mind than the thought of his own imminent death. And now the driver seemed to forget how to steer. Instead of following the curve of the narrow road, he drove straight at a shiny green bush of buckthorn and myrtle. Blume braced for impact, but they were already through what had been no more than a curtain and, in fact, were still on a road hardly any worse than the one they had left. As they came to a downward slope, the driver finally stopped gunning the overworked engine and allowed the car to free-wheel. Blume tried to grip the seat with the back of his tied hands, but was quickly jolted sideways, banging his ear against the window. As the car hit a ditch and bounced out again, he experienced a moment of zero gravity that ended when his forehead hit the back of the driver's skull. He was almost knocked unconscious, but the driver growled and swatted blindly at the back of his head and neck as if he had been attacked by a mosquito. For the next fifteen minutes, they continued like that, up and down fields, and Blume concentrated on bracing his legs and not biting his tongue. Finally, they stopped at the bottom of a valley next to a clump of oaks.

Curmaci got out first and politely held the door open as Blume, exaggerating the difficulty of movement, extricated himself. Curmaci brushed himself down, looked at the clothes he was wearing, and sighed theatrically.

'I am not dressed for the part. Zio Pietro here is right never to wear anything but his hunting clothes.'

He started walking ahead, his expensive shoes crunching on the broken acorn shells as he went into what turned out to be a far deeper woodland than had first appeared, leaving Pietro to prod at Blume with the shotgun. Pietro took delight in telling Blume to hurry, then kicking the back of his legs to trip him up. When Blume stumbled, Pietro would jab at him and order him to move faster. By now, the strands of cord binding Blume's hands were dangling loose, but Pietro did not seem to notice, and Blume decided it was more expedient to keep them clasped behind his back. At one point, Pietro delivered such a hard blow to his kidneys that Blume thought he had finally been shot. It was only as he hit the earth he realized that there had been no corresponding sound and that he was still thinking and feeling.

Blume struggled to his feet, and looked around. Curmaci was just disappearing into the thickets ahead. Pietro raised the two barrels and crooked his finger on the triggers.

'You're Pietro Megale?'

He got no reply, but the weapon dipped slightly. No matter what the circumstances, people liked to be recognized and hear about themselves.

'You're Tony's older brother,' added Blume.

The barrels rose again, this time to eye level. 'I am Domenico Megale's first-born son,' he said.

'And Tony is the interloper,' said Blume, but the dirt-caked face in front of him showed no flicker of comprehension. 'A usurper,' said Blume. Still nothing. 'Your brother's a bastard.' He braced himself for a blow, which did not come. Instead, Pietro smiled broadly, displaying missing eyeteeth.

'He's not my real brother.'

'Curmaci told you that?'

'What would I need to tell him that for?' said Curmaci's voice from behind him. Blume turned around to see Curmaci standing there, a friendly smile on his face. 'Pietro clearly remembers the day his father brought the screaming infant Tony into their family home, don't you, Pietro? And he remembers the anxiety it caused his mother, God rest her soul. Just as he remembers the day that his father left for Germany, leaving him in charge of protecting Tony as his brother, which Pietro did with steadfastness and courage.'

Blume watched in amazement as the dirty thug in front of him blushed modestly and crossed one foot over the other in embarrassment.

'I know you don't like to be praised, Pietro,' said Curmaci, 'but sometimes praise is so evidently merited that to refuse to listen to it is like asking for it twice.' Curmaci waved a hand as if presenting Pietro onstage. 'This man protected Tony until he was seventeen. He lived through scandals brought into the family through his brother. When Domenico Megale invited Tony to Germany instead of Pietro, they said it was because Tony had brought too much attention and trouble to the family. When Tony married, Pietro was his best man. When Tony's wife died leaving an infant behind in whom Tony showed no interest, it was Pietro and his wife Rosa who stepped in and raised the child. I tell you all this, Commissioner Alec Blume, because you seem to have an unnatural interest in the private affairs of our families. I have been keeping an eye on you ever since Arconti recruited you.'

'He's a magistrate with jurisdiction over my ward. He does not need to "recruit" police, all he has to do is order.'

'Oh, he recruited you, all right. He brought you round to his way of seeing things, kept you on the case well after it left your scope of competence, got you looking into me and my affairs. Then he passed you on to other people, and here you are. Pietro, try not to let Commissioner Blume fall down again or we'll never get there.'

After twenty minutes' walking, with the light finally dimming and the air growing colder, they came to a lake, bright blue in the middle but scummy green along its edges where the water was teeming and plopping with thousands of frogs. Newts and salamanders slipped into rather than out of view as they approached, little reptile spectators interested in the show. Where the green scum stopped and the water cleared, fat black fish swam lazily, ignoring the millions of water-skating insects above them. Blume had never seen so much life concentrated in so small an area. They followed the edge of the lake, Blume trying to anticipate where his captor behind him wanted to go, since he had once again lost sight of Curmaci.

He had now also lost sight of the water, which was hidden behind and below banks of reeds, sedge grass and cattails with insects feeding off their sausage-like heads that nodded in the slight wind. He imagined parting the reeds, and peering down into the water, the colour of a dark beer.

It was hard to credit his own feelings, but Blume was still enjoying the absence of his headache, and the idea of a bullet tearing through his skull seemed such a waste. Finally, they caught up with Curmaci, who was standing in a field of asphodels meticulously picking pollen and burrs off his clothes. As they arrived, he started pulling at a translucent piece of corrugated green plastic like a conscientious hiker trying to clean up the mess left by others. He flipped the plastic neatly over to reveal an opening in the ground out of which the two uprights of a wooden ladder barely protruded. Pietro pushed Blume forward towards the pit that looked like a waterless well. The ladder descending into it had a dozen or so rungs. The important thing for Blume at that moment was that the cavity was too deep, too narrow and too carefully constructed to be a grave.

Curmaci nodded amicably at Blume. 'There are dozens of these in this area alone, thousands in the region, I would say. Some have lighting and running water, sewage, dehumidifiers, all sorts of amenities. This one has none of those things, but it does have a certain history.'

'Did some teenage kidnapping victim from the north spend his last days starving to death in here back in the '80s?' asked Blume.

'For a kidnap victim, you'd want to go farther back, to the '70s,' said Curmaci, displaying no sign of anger at Blume's provocation. 'But this dates from the '20s, no less. It was a refuge for bandits. It's an entrance to an underground cave, see?' He pointed, and Blume looked again into the pit at the bottom of which he now saw the narrow opening of a tunnel high enough for a child to walk into.

'As I say, it's got no amenities,' said Curmaci. 'The access corridor at the bottom is long and dark, and it gets lower in the middle, where you have to get down on your knees and crawl. There's been some subsidence in there, too. You get to be a police mole.'

'Very funny.'

'It opens up again almost immediately afterward. I'll be in front, Pietro behind. Pietro, unbind his hands.'

Pietro gave a careless pull at the loose strings behind Blume's back, which fell away. Curmaci plucked at the knee of his expensive slacks. 'I am definitely not dressed for this. That should tell you how unplanned this is, right, Pietro?'

'What is all unplanned?' asked Blume, but Curmaci had stepped onto the ladder and was out of sight. Two shotgun barrels prodded him in the back and Blume, even though he realized he was more afraid of being buried alive than being shot dead, nonetheless found himself clambering down the rungs, feeling his legs shake with adrenalin, or just from exhaustion. The air was immediately damp and earthy, and the rocks crumbled at his touch. The floor of the pit was only about three metres below ground, but the walls were too smooth to climb. He looked up at the sky and tilted back his head to allow the sunlight to flood his whole face for a moment before the shadow of Pietro cut it off. He ducked his head and went beneath the ground. The bottom of the pit, which had looked soft and earthy from above, turned out to be formed of a flat rock with only a thin layer of soil, like a dirty flagstone. The floor sloped gently towards the mouth of the tunnel into which Curmaci, dressed in his city clothes, had already gone, and with him the feeble light of the mobile phone, which was all he was using to light his way. Blume considered resisting, but the giant with the shotgun literally had the drop on him and blocked out all light and thoughts of escape as he filled the gap and, to make matters worse, closed the green trapdoor. Blume had no choice but to stoop and enter the tunnel, where it was immediately completely black.

Breathing through his nose to keep calm, resisting the temptation to open his mouth and gulp down extra oxygen because he knew panic would set in if that failed to work, he allowed the sloping roof to push him closer and closer to the floor. There was no light, no sign of anyone before him or behind him, and the only sound was his own breathing and grunts. The rocky roof now came so low that he was forced on to his hands and knees. To calm himself, he started counting backwards, randomly choosing seventeen as the starting point, and subtracting one number for every two shuffles forward of his knees. If he reached zero and the tunnel had not widened – he did not want to think about it. Maybe he should have started at thirty. His forehead hit a wall of stone.

'Oh Christ.' Being killed in the open air with the sound of the gunshot racing across the open waters of the lake was what he had wanted, not this. He was at a dead end. Although impossible to do so, he must somehow have taken a wrong turn. He pushed himself backwards, and his knees became wedged against each other, and the walls of the tunnel pushed slowly in, he could feel them moving.

Stuck! Like a rat in a sealed pipe. He could not go backwards!

Without his mind having anything to do with it, his mouth opened in a moan. Then something pushed at him from behind. It was the animal with the shotgun, which meant that he had not taken a wrong turning, but this was worse, for now he would be pushed and crushed against the rock face by the oversized brute to his rear. Blume's mouth opened again, and this time he tasted the slight movement of air from in front of him. Where had Curmaci gone? He understood his forehead had hit a ledge, not a full wall, and that the air and now also a sheen were coming from directly in front of him, where Curmaci was using his telephone to light his way. He ducked his head below the ledge, and plunged in, resolving to bludgeon himself to death against the sides if he became stuck. He squeezed deeper in, and found he could no longer lift his legs high enough to give his feet purchase. Using his stomach muscles, he wriggled forwards, stretched out his arms, and dug his fingers into the hard ground. Finding a little bit of lateral space, he started using his arms and shoulders in a sort of swimming stroke, and effected an agonizing front crawl.

He'd dragged himself a body's length along the ground when his hand touched something hard, metallic, and familiar. It was his Beretta. He knew it at once, like a neglected old friend. The nicks and imperfections on the grip, the tiny chip out of the hammer, the stickiness of the release catch, now on. It must have dropped out of Curmaci's pocket. Almost without thinking, he scooped it into his hand, even though it impeded his movements. Curmaci would no doubt have noticed and would be waiting at the end of the tunnel, but even so it felt like a providential gift. Even better, the collapsed section of the tunnel was over. The cavern opened upwards and outwards, suddenly becoming a spacious chamber in which he could stand up. In front of him was a metal door with a sliding bolt like the one to the communal roof of his apartment in Rome, and behind that a larger room where white LED-bulb lanterns were hanging. He saw all this with absolute clarity after the darkness of the tunnel.

He walked into the cavernous space, tucking his Beretta into the back of his waistband under his shirt.

Curmaci was waiting for him, but at a distance, and half hidden behind a rock. Already he could hear Curmaci's henchman wheezing and cursing as he emerged from the tunnel. It must have been even tighter for him.

'It's a limestone cave, ten or twelve metres high at the centre, shaped like a big tent. Most of the tunnel into it was already there,' said Curmaci, switching on another lamp and lifting it up to reveal the last corner of the room with a camp bed and neatly folded blankets. The room contained piles of old newspapers, what seemed like a complete collection of Dylan Dog comics, chipped mugs, plates, a few food cans with faded labels. A bench-chair was fashioned from fruit crates, and was placed in front of a truncated section of a single log of heavy wood that served as a table.

'The door and that log are far too big. How did they get down the tunnel?'

Curmaci shrugged. 'Why do you care, Commissioner?'

'Everything needs a logical explanation.'

'I don't agree,' said Curmaci.

'But the metal door . . .'

'Shh!' said Curmaci. 'Listen, this place has running water. You can hear it.'

A creaking sound of reluctant water came from the back of the cavern.

'It takes a while to fill a cup, but you just leave one there. Basile stayed here for eight months once, during the Second Mafia War, venturing out only at night. But maybe you don't even know who Basile is?'

Blume shook his head. How had Curmaci failed to noticed the missing pistol? Behind him, smelling even worse than before, stood Pietro, shotgun pointed straight at him. All that bulk and a shotgun through the narrow tunnel. It was an unwelcome marvel to see him here.

Curmaci inclined his head in the direction of the corner of the cavern, and Pietro waved the gun in Blume's face and, finally, verbalized the death sentence. 'Over there, into the corner.'

'This also doesn't make sense,' Blume said over his shoulder to Curmaci, pleased to hear that the cavern deepened and echoed his voice, removing the tremor of fear he could feel in his chest. 'All the way down here just to shoot me.'

'That's what Pietro said, too, but it does make sense. You'll see in a minute, won't he, Pietro?'

'If you say so,' said Pietro.

'I do say so, and that should be good enough for both of you.'

'What happened to Konrad Hoffmann?' said Blume.

'My idea for Hoffmann,' said Curmaci, 'though I need to check the logistics of this, is to ship what's left of him back to Germany, throw the pieces into the same sewage pipes into which they poured his girlfriend all those years ago. What do you think, Blume? Will I make all that effort and run the risk of detection just so as to lay the grounds for an ironic story that I could tell to myself and two, three other people at most?'

'I think you might.'

'Is that how you see me? OK, Pietro, do your stuff.'

Blume moved back into the depths of the cavern in the direction of the water, drawn there by thirst as much as anything. Pietro came up behind him. Just as it was becoming too dark to see, Blume stopped dead, causing Pietro to lumber into him. Pietro stood back and aimed a vicious kick at the small of his back.

The kick was hard and sent him lurching forwards, but he exaggerated his fall. The floor was irregular and jagged, and he took his full weight on his left hand as he went down, but in his right he had the Beretta, and as the shotgun appeared over him, Blume fired directly into the space where Pietro's stupid face should be, realizing as he did so that this was the first time he had ever killed a man, and surprised at how quick it was, and how easy. His would-be assassin did manage to utter a half-shout half a second after the gunshot. The acoustics of the cave seemed to combine the two sounds into a single angry roar that ricocheted off the walls, and returned with renewed vigour just as Pietro's body hit the floor. Even his going down worked out nicely. He fell neither forwards nor backwards but crumpled in on himself, like a smokestack being demolished by expert engineers. After the gunshot and shout, the flop of his body on the stone was like a whisper.

Blume stood up, Beretta in hand, but Curmaci was there, a pistol inches away from Blume's forehead.

Ah well, thought Blume.

Curmaci stepped back, and beckoned with the pistol. 'Come over here and sit down.'

'I think I'd prefer to be shot standing up,' said Blume.

'Who's talking about shooting? Come over here, away from that shotgun. Go over there and sit down.'

Blume stayed where he was, his own pistol still in his hand.

'Please?' said Curmaci.

Blume started walking towards the makeshift seat, and Curmaci picked up the shotgun by its barrel and tucked it under his left arm.

Blume was shivering, because it was damp and ghastly in the cave and because he had just killed a man. He recognized the plastic LED lanterns now: from the home and garden section of IKEA. They were one of the last objects displayed for impulse buys before the warehouse section. Caterina had wanted one, even though neither she nor he had so much as a balcony, let alone a garden. There were four of them in the cavern. They shone pure white unto themselves, but bathed everything around them in shades of yellow and grey and did not nearly penetrate the darkness behind.

He was sitting underground with Curmaci. He was still holding his weapon, and Curmaci did not seem to mind. Their voices boomed and echoed as they spoke. He was pretty sure it was not a dream, but it didn't feel very real either.

Curmaci popped the shells out of the shotgun. He pocketed them and tossed the weapon carelessly in the direction of the incongruous door at the entrance. He propped a foot on the log table, and contemplated Blume.

'Was that your first time to kill a man?'

Blume nodded.

'It's not as hard as you'd think, is it? The first thing to do is to persuade yourself it is not a man, which will have been easy with that stinking goat Pietro. Easy for you, I mean. For me, it would have been a bit harder. He and his wife virtually brought up my boy along with their fat spoiled nephew, Enrico. Pietro, for all his faults, was like a father to his nephew Enrico, and like an uncle to my son. And you have just shot him dead. A single shot, that's all you had, and that's all it took. You didn't pull the trigger again, which is not just a sign of your self-confidence, but also of your humanity.'

'Obviously you left me just one round in the pistol.'

'Yes. I took out the others. Then left it for you to find. You were hardly going to use it on me while Pietro was behind you, and you could not use it on him while you were in the tunnel.'

'What if I had not found the gun or missed my shot?'

'Then you would be dead and I would have had the sad task of killing Pietro myself,' said Curmaci. 'Now he has a bullet from a police-issue weapon in his head, which is good for me, and possibly good for you, since it gives us a bit of wriggle room. For example, you could take the blame for killing Megale's only son, as indeed you should, and I would make sure the revenge attack on you never happens, especially since the Megales are about to lose all power.'

'Why was he working for you and not his brother?'

'Because his father told him to. Domenico ordered Pietro to side with me against Tony. Pietro, without quite knowing it, had been waiting for years for this moment to come, the moment his father would finally change his mind about the viper he brought into the bosom of his family. Tony was plotting to take over from the old man. Everyone knew that for years except Old Megale himself. Tony felt he had been overlooked too long, and wanted me in particular out of the way. But Megale had time to think in prison, and he noticed the frequency and enthusiasm of the visits he received. Tony should have worked out that if Old Megale could adopt an outsider once, he could do it again. Finally Old Megale listened to me. I told him Tony was going to kill him, me, and Pietro, his one real child. I persuaded him that I had no ambitions to take his place but he needed to do something about Tony.'

'And he believed you.'

'Of course. I spoke the truth. I cannot be a boss like Megale. It's not how I fit in.'

'Then why kill Pietro?'

'Sooner or later, he would have been taunted into revenging the man who killed his half-brother. He'd have killed me as a question of pride and appearances.'

'So have you killed Tony?'

'Not yet.'

'You might have let Konrad Hoffmann live.'

'Again, a question of appearances,' said Curmaci. 'He came out of the blue. What was I supposed to do, let him threaten us?'

'I understand,' said Blume. He raised his Beretta quickly, almost touching the bridge of Curmaci's long Greek nose with the barrel, and pulled the trigger.

The click was obvious, embarrassing even as it echoed in the cavern. The ensuing silence was very deep, only the dripping water breaking it. Curmaci seemed to stir as if he had been asleep, and lifted his eyelids, heavy and reproachful, and stared at Blume in the half light.

'That sort of hurt my feelings,' he said.

'Sorry about that,' said Blume. He put his useless Beretta down on the table between them. 'But supposing you had miscounted, or there had been one in the chamber? You can hardly blame me for trying.'

Curmaci was staring upwards at the roof. 'The first time I killed a man, a boy it was – but I was no more than a boy myself – I was in agony for months. It was the worst thing in my life, and my father made me do it. I didn't speak to him for almost a year, and he patiently accepted that. I thought of becoming a monk, of going to the police, of killing myself, of killing my father and the person who ordered him to induct me into the blood ritual of the clan. I thought of approaching the brothers of the boy I had killed and letting them deal with me. And yet you, Blume, who say you have never killed a man, lift up a steady hand, put a gun right in my face, and pull the trigger on the off-chance. Have you acquired a taste for blood?'

'A taste for life,' said Blume.

'You want to stay alive at all costs. Good. Your bullet is in the head of an Ndranghetista. The repercussions of this depend on you and me. I'd like to come to an agreement with you. I think you would make a very good contact for me. The rewards don't stop with my allowing you to live now. Money and probable career advancement would flow from any understanding between us.'

'What sort of understanding?'

'Not on anything specific for now. I'd like to come to an open-ended arrangement with you.'

'I see,' said Blume.

'But I can't offer anything concrete right now. I am not even sure a deal will be possible. I need to seek opinions. Old bosses like to have their outmoded opinions sought after.'

'And first you have to win your internal feud,' said Blume.

'It's not a feud, just a minor coup. Tomorrow I will attend the Polsi summit meeting. Among other things, I will tell them I have a police commissioner captive – I'll mention your name but no one really knows who you are. Then we'll discuss three choices. You die and are never found, which would be seen as a muted declaration of war on the police, but not the sort that would get the attention of the public like Cosa Nostra did when they started killing magistrates and bombing monuments. The second option is you die and your body is put somewhere symbolic. Maybe in front of the sanctuary of Polsi when the police are about to celebrate the Archangel Saint Michael. I know that option is going to look very tempting to some bosses who are enraged at this proposed violation of the sanctity of the sanctuary of the Madonna by the forces of the State. Having a captive police commissioner will definitely work to my advantage when explaining my position. I'll try to talk them out of using you as a scapegoat though.'

'Gee, thanks.'

'Not for your sake. Clamorous declarations of war on the state are not good for business. Still, if they do decide to send out a signal of defiance, you'll become posthumously famous, have streets named after you, Via Falcone, Via Borsellino, Via Blume. What sort of name is that, anyhow?'

'Magistrates, not policemen, have streets named after them,' said Blume.

'Let's hope it doesn't come to that. But if you live, it will be on borrowed time and I am the lender you have to pay back. You will need me and soon enough you will want me on your side. For example, your career prospects will have to be advanced through certain channels rather than others. Because no matter what you say or do, certain anti-Mafia fundamentalists in the force will always remember that at a certain critical point, you and I had a common enemy, and you took him out for me. They will recall that you and I must have sat and talked as we are doing now. So you will need to align yourself with those of your colleagues who see the world in shades of grey, and understand the value of cooperation. I think you can live with that. Especially after I saw you put a gun in my face and pull the trigger.'

'It was empty. We both knew it.'

'Then why pull the trigger? You did not even flinch.'

'Nor you,' said Blume.

'I knew absolutely it was empty.'

'What about killing Dagmar, was that easy?'

'Don't take on such a moralizing tone. You never even knew her.'

'I am just curious,' said Blume.

'As a matter of fact, it was not easy for me at the time. I think you'd find it easier than me, Blume.'

'I would never kill an innocent young woman.'

'Sure you would. You'd be even easier to persuade than I was. I can tell. You're the type, only you don't know it yet. Right now, take a measure of your regret for Pietro over there. Go on. How sorry do you feel? It's not even registering, is it? You feel so completely justified and right. Not everyone is like that.'

'I'd have let Konrad live.'

'No, you wouldn't. He was about to cause no end of upsets and upheavals, and in this business that means bloodshed. Killing him saved lives.'

'Who had the other half of the Madonna picture, you?'

'Yes, I did. Basile, he's the local boss, says he wants to frame the two halves of the Madonna in his bar. Basile, by the way, is completely on my side, which is good news for you. And one of the reasons he is on my side is that he believes firmly that Tony set up an elaborate plot against me. The namesake killing, the arrivals of Konrad and you, the rumours of a confession by Maria Itria. So you helped my case too, by setting my wife up as a snitch. See the way you're prepared to sacrifice a young woman for your own convenience?'

'Not for my own convenience. I am protecting society.'

'You have some political ideas in your mind that aren't even yours to begin with. You love yourself so much you think certain ideas are sacred just because they happen to live in your head. My actions will probably save lives, but you don't count them. Mafiosi killing Mafiosi is more than OK, it's something you welcome. You get to decide whose lives are worth more. Does my wife deserve to die more than your girlfriend, what's her name . . . that female inspector? Caterina, that's her.'

'Don't.'

'I'll try not to, Commissioner, but maybe you could have thought of her beforehand. Now I go back to my family that you put in danger, I instruct them to stay put, to fight. I forgive my wife because in the end your lie became a reality and she called Arconti for help, and I tell her that anyone who knows this is in danger, and anyone who reveals it is dead, and I tell Basile and others I have a policeman in captivity, though I won't say where, awaiting our decision.'

'How do you know it was my lie? How do you know I was behind the altered transcript?'

'Word gets around. If all this works out for the best, join me and you'll find yourself meeting the most surprising people in the most unexpected places.'

'Massimiliani informed on me?'

'No, Commissioner. It's simpler than that. I knew it wasn't Arconti, because I know his style. It had to be you. All I had to do was listen and find out a few details, like where they found the transcripts – your office and in Arconti's office after you had been in there. Logic works better than spies.'

'You ordered the murder of an innocent man simply to intimidate an honest magistrate.'

'Wrong again. The murder of that unfortunate Milanese man was a declaration of war against me.'

'So you didn't order it?'

'I can't *order* Tony Megale to do anything. What I can do, and what I did, was give him enough space to make a serious mistake. Ever since he murdered his mother – did you know he did that? Ever since then people have been waiting for someone to wipe the slate clean. There is another branch of the Megale family in Africo that is keen to see the surname purified, and will support me.'

Curmaci picked up his pistol from the table, then the shotgun and backed away towards the edge of the cave. 'The meeting's tomorrow. You had better hope for the best. The batteries on those lamps last for ages, but you might want to save them.'

He made broad sweeps with the shotgun pointing around the cave. 'Some cans. An old opener. Camp stove, hope there's still gas. Water on the right; catch it in a cup. Oh, you had better shit away from the water. That's important.'

'You're leaving me here?'

'You want me to shoot you? I'd prefer to give you the chance to think about my offer. If I come back for you in two or three days, and next week you find yourself walking on the right side of the earth and enjoying the sun, then maybe you'll have learned to trust me a bit. I've got some walking to do myself now. All the way back to Ardore.'

Curmaci went towards the steel door, keeping him covered with the pistol and fading into the darkness. Blume did not see him open the door, but now he heard him close it and slide a bolt on the other side.

Curmaci's voice came muffled through the steel. 'Just wait for me. Trust, Commissioner, and if you can't trust . . .'

But his next words were lost as he moved down the passage.

Blume stayed motionless for ten minutes examining his options. Then he stood up and went around the cavern, unhooking the four lanterns from steel nails hammered into the rock. He brought them over to the table, and turned them off one by one. After the last had gone out, he sat there, waiting for his eyes to get used to the dark. When he had been sitting there for what seemed like half an hour, he accepted that the darkness was total. He lit one lantern, and went over to the door and gave it a few kicks, each harder than the last, exorcizing the deathly silence, pleased to be able to declare his presence through noise, but managing to unnerve himself too. Hammering on doors was what the incarcerated insane did.

Over the next few hours, how many he could not tell, he twice went over with a lamp to where the body lay and looked at the white face staring as if at something on the roof behind him. Twice he raised the lantern to see what Pietro was gazing at, knowing that his action made no sense. Blume had seen many dead bodies in his time, but never one whose death he had been responsible for. He gave it a kick, then whispered,

'Fuck you,' and waited to see if he felt any sense of angry triumph, but he didn't. Then he cleared his throat and said, more solemnly, 'Sorry.'

But he didn't feel sorry either.

He returned to the entrance, gave the door a few more kicks. It did not budge, and even if it opened, there would be no ladder at the end of the nightmare corridor outside. But he could not think of any better plan. He went back towards the table where he had seen some pieces of cutlery, a fork. He was but four steps from the table when, without any preliminary flickering, the first lamp died with the suddenness of someone switching it off. He walked till he felt himself hitting the wood.

Wednesday, 2 September

48

Locri

WITH JUST THREE hours to go before the Polsi celebrations began, Enrico Megale phoned Ruggiero Curmaci and said, 'Are you coming today?' His voice was full of excitement, perhaps because of the day ahead, perhaps because his father was there.

'Sure,' said Ruggiero.

'You need a lift?'

'No, I don't think so,' said Ruggiero.

'No? How are you getting there?'

'By car, I suppose,' said Ruggiero.

A few beats passed before Enrico said, 'OK. I'll see you there. Call us if you need a lift, OK?'

'Sure,' said Ruggiero. 'Are you going with your father?'

'Yes! Great, isn't it? Look, I'm sorry your dad couldn't make it back. I hear there are problems. Maybe he'll arrive at the procession at the last moment, huh? Did he say anything?'

'We've not heard from him.'

'So, your mother's going to drive?' asked Enrico.

'I guess,' said Ruggiero.

'We won't be leaving for another hour and a half, so . . . you know.'

'Thanks, Enrico. You're a good friend.'

'Yeah, oh listen you haven't seen my uncle anywhere, have you? Zia Rosa is out of her mind with worry. Pietro got a call yesterday afternoon, went out, and hasn't come back since and has turned off his phone.'

'I've been here all the time, Enrico, so I never saw him. Who called him?'

'He didn't say. He didn't even say someone had called. My aunt heard his phone ringing, then it stopped and he left without saying a word. He took the car. Did I tell you about the car?'

'No,' said Ruggiero. 'You mean the old Fiat Ritmo?'

'Yeah. The other night it slipped out of gear, went rolling out of the drive on to the road, and got stuck in a ditch. Wild! Imagine if it had hit someone. It would have been like getting hit by a car driven by a ghost. Yesterday morning, Uncle Pietro looks out the window and says, "They've stolen the fucking Ritmo!" And then my aunt says maybe it slipped out of gear and rolled away, and he says, "No, they've stolen it, the bastards." Then my aunt, she puts some cheese on his bread, waits till it's all in his mouth, and says, "How much do you think they'll get for it?" And my uncle almost died from laughing, choking on his bread, and had to spit it out, the two of them like kids, howling at the idea of someone trying to sell the Ritmo. It turns out it was her fault. She was the last one to drive it, and she remembers not bothering to put it into gear when she parked under the kitchen window. My uncle says women drivers are so bad they even have crashes after they've parked, which was a good one.'

'That's a hell of a story about the car.'

'Yeah. It's gone, too. Zio must have taken it. It's a pity your father's not here for you.'

'Maybe he went straight to Polsi, to avoid certain people,' said Ruggiero. 'You never know.'

'Yeah, could be. Our dads were booked on the same flight, but yours pulled out at the last moment.'

'He'll have had his reasons.'

Enrico lowered his voice. 'My dad is fucking raging at Uncle Pietro for disappearing like this. Says Pietro never acted responsibly. Says that's why no one ever tells Pietro anything.' He raised his voice again. 'Let's hope we meet there, then. Let me know, huh? Also if you see Pietro . . .'

'No problem,' said Ruggiero, hanging up, and tossing his phone onto his bed.

Ardore

Lacking a watch and deprived of his phone, he measured his time in cups of water and in the inches of progress he was making in scraping away the sharp limestone and daubs of cement around the bottom hinge of the door. He was using a rusted fork and a flat butter knife for the purpose. In his pocket was an old lever-type opener with which he had stabbed open a can of soup and drained the unheated contents into his mouth. He might make better progress on the cement if he used the opener, but if it broke, he would not be able to open any of the remaining cans, though some of them had swollen so much that they looked like they might explode if he merely tapped them.

Sometimes he turned off the lamp and worked for as long as he could in the darkness. Occasionally he thought he heard buzzing and saw a glow from where the body lay in the corner of the cave, but he knew it was just his mind playing tricks. Rigor mortis, livor mortis and algor mortis. The rigor had come and perhaps was gone already. The body temperature should be coming down to that of the cave, which, to Blume, seemed increasingly cold.

It was a fork, not a knife, that first penetrated through to the other side. Blume tried to peer through the tiny hole he had made, but could see nothing. His hands were puffed and watery with burst and swelling blisters, but it would surely take only five or six more hours increasing the size of the hole, weakening the hinge, though he could hardly remember why he wanted to.

A shiver ran down his back and shot forward suddenly into his stomach making him gasp. His bowels seemed to loosen. With great effort, he controlled himself, clutching his stomach and sweating. He needed to find a place. But after he had gone a few paces, the sensation passed. It would return, and he needed to choose a place to serve as his latrine. Not near the water. Next to the body was too disrespectful. He picked up his lantern and walked over to where the corpse lay, whiter than ever, the mouth a black hole, the eyes devoid of all colour, the pupils not even visible. He passed by it hurriedly, and found a small declivity that could be used.

When he was finishing up, he gathered up the lantern again, then roared and instinctively flung the lamp beside him at the corpse. The head that had been staring up at the roof of the cavern had turned and was watching him as he squatted. The mouth was grinning, and making a sound.

The lantern bounced, cracked and went out and the dark arrived at the speed of light. The totality of the darkness caught him unprepared again. He struggled upright, brought his fingers up to his face, and touched his eyelids a few times, checking that his eyes were in fact open. By rubbing them, he could produce deep purple blots that floated in the air and comforted him a little. Pietro's face had been so white it must surely still be visible, yet it, too, had been completely swallowed by the darkness. He closed his eyes, opened them: no difference. But the tiny buzzing sound persisted.

If rigor mortis had just worn off, it was perfectly possible for the head to move, the jaws to slacken. The faint buzz he had heard had not necessarily come from the mouth, and it was still going on. Faraway flies made that sound. He thought he could smell the beginning of the decay, or maybe it was just the smell that Pietro had carried with him in life. How much time had passed?

Extending his hands in front of him, he took a careful step forward and immediately almost tripped on the irregular surface. He needed to take baby steps. He could not afford to fall and injure himself. In his mind's eye, he tried to replay where he had hurled the lamp, how it had illuminated the corpse, then dashed itself against the rock behind. It made better sense for him to get back to the table, which still had two more lamps. But the table was so far away and he was not sure of the right direction.

He reckoned he was a third of the way back when his foot stepped on something soft and yielding. He poked at it for a moment, then kicked in frustration and heard something like an exhalation followed by a sloshing sound. He had hardly made any progress and was only now drawing level with the corpse. He edged his way past, tapping at it with his feet, finally finding the skull, and then took a larger step into the darkness.

His foot tried to find purchase in empty space and he found himself falling, banging his knees and elbow. To save his face he put out his hands. He heard his skin rip, and felt pain, but it was poorly localized. He could not tell which hand he had damaged until he felt the blood tickling his left arm. He lay there for some time, promising himself that he would not panic. All he had to do was cover twenty paces. The length from his desk in his office to Caterina's desk in the next room. How he missed that now. He wanted back all that he thought he hated about Rome: the extravagant noise, the idiots outside bars broadcasting their opinions. He thought of the vile cologne-scented politicians striding by in silver suits and fluffed-up ties who passed through Piazza Collegio Romano, bawling obscenities into their phones, mainly for the benefit of the people they knew were watching. He even missed that. He missed people.

At a certain point – he had no idea how long it had been since he started his interminable journey across the floor of the cave – he sat down and gave up. It had been long enough for the blood to stop flowing so freely down his arm and turn sticky and hard. The costive trickle of water was no longer functioning as a point of reference. It seemed to be coming from everywhere. The sensible thing was to catch some sleep and rest his mind.

His hand found a smooth slab. The rocks behind were jagged, but the slab was comfortable, if cold. Lying down might be dangerous: he was exhausted, he had lost blood, he had not slept properly and all he had eaten was a can of cold soup. He could taste its saltiness now, and he dearly wished he had had another. He decided just to sit for a while, without sleeping, and let his thoughts collect themselves. He had read somewhere that it took only a few days after the onset of blindness before the brain started remapping some of the mind's spatial functions to the ears. Or maybe a few months. Whatever: he'd be dead before he was Batman.

He wondered how Caterina was getting on. She was probably in bed now, deep asleep and warm. He could have taken the suitcase stuffed with his parents' memories round to her place a few days earlier. Sort of like inviting the dead parents round. What had made him throw it into a camper van travelling south? Those were among the last things he had belonging to them. Except . . . he put his bloody hand into his pocket and felt the three rings.

There was the buzzing again, so faint it was no more than a whine, but it interfered with the sound of the water. Two sounds plus his own breathing, and sometimes, he had noticed, he talked out loud to himself. He sniffed at the darkness, but could not smell. Was the whole cavern impregnated with the stench of death and he no longer noticed? Not noticing could be a sign that he, too, was dead. He opened his mouth and swallowed the air, as black as the inside of Pietro's mouth. No, I am still alive. *Cogito ergo sum*.

It was evident that he would never get to sleep and evident that he would never be found. What sort of death would he have chosen instead of this?

'A painful death?' he said out loud, hearing his voice at once echoed and muffled. 'Stabbing?' He held up his injured hand, stared at it, put it to his nose, and tried to smell its shape and colour.

'Dying in a bed surrounded by weeping children, wives?'

Wives. That's very funny. Five wives. Seven! Let's see, there would be, in order of good sex, Kristin, Emilia, Daria, Caterina of course. It's a pity Caterina wasn't higher up the sex list. Top place for everything else, of course. He could call them up, all his exes one by one, out of the blue.

'Who shall I call first?'

'Why me, of course,' said Caterina. 'You never call.'

'I will from now on,' said Blume. 'Promise.'

'You don't even answer when I call.'

'That's because I have it on silent.'

'But it buzzes, doesn't it?'

'I met a beautiful woman who cured me with licorice. She had a handsome son with blue eyes and a white smile. But then her husband put me in a cave.'

'If this is a bedtime story for Elia, he's too old for that.'

'Old enough to betray. To call his father, who comes along to put me in a cave.'

'Elia's father is dead. He can't be called.'

'I'm not so sure,' said Blume.

The buzzing grew louder. The air seemed to press in on itself. He felt it had become so thick it would block his lungs, so he held his breath. Now the only sounds were his heartbeat, the dripping water and a footfall. Three heartbeats, one footfall. Coming in his direction.

'Caterina? You're here?'

The footsteps stopped. The thick air smelled of sewage, gutted hare, boar.

The voice that spoke to him was hoarse with rage. 'Answer and you'll find out who's calling you.'

'I don't want to know.'

'Coward.'

'They confiscated my phone. I can't answer.'

'Open your eyes, *infame*,' ordered the voice.

'My eyes are open.'

'Then you can see me.'

Pietro was standing several paces off, taller than Blume remembered him. His blackened tongue poked out between his teeth. The darkness hid his lips. Walking sure-footed and soundlessly over the rock, he approached Blume and held out his arm, which was blue marbled on top, livid below. He grinned showing his missing eyeteeth, opened his stinking mouth, and said, 'They're calling you.'

Blume stared into Pietro's misted eyes, the blasted forehead, through which a whirl of black air was passing.

'There is nothing in your hand, Pietro.' Blume checked his own hand, but it was invisible in the dark, which had a significance he couldn't quite work out.

'*Infame di merda*. Where did you get that gun? I took it off you. I destroyed your phone, gave your pistol to Curmaci. How did that happen? This place stinks of treachery. Do you think Agazio is coming back for you?'

'He promised he would.'

'Answer the phone.'

'I am under tons of rock. There's no signal down here. It cannot be ringing. This is some diabolic trick.'

'Such a logical line of thought. Logical to the very end. But look who you're talking to, where's the logic in that?'

'No one is calling me.'

'Where is the buzzing coming from then? You'll have to frisk me to find the phone. Watch out for the mushy bits. Those flies, tiny creatures now, but just you wait. They'll like your fresh blood better than mine. Lick it off your arm. Before the flies eat you.'

'I won't touch you. The dead are unclean.'

'Dereliction of duty. Dead people are what pay your salary.'

'The Calabrian dead mean nothing to me.'

'As a people we have noticed that. A lot of the trouble stems from just that.'

Pietro glided back, illuminating the cavern as he went. When he had returned to the place where he had fallen, he lay down, getting right back into his previous position with absolute precision. He turned his head once to grin at Blume, before becoming perfectly immobile and then dimmed the light around him until he had returned to invisibility.

Polsi, Calabria

The bishop bent down with some difficulty and picked up the silver crown, which he held up so it flashed in the light of the sun. He kissed it, then placed it on the head of the Christ Child. A vigorous cheer went up. He repeated the gesture, kissing the far larger crown of the Madonna three times, straining as he reached up to put it on her head, turning it to screw it into place. A cheer, wilder now, greeted the action, and the bishop smiled and patted his stomach, pleased with the acclamation.

The Madonna was lifted onto the processional throne supported by long oak beams carried on the shoulders of the faithful. Basile would be there towards the end, at the steepest part of the hill, his hands pushing the Virgin and Child skywards as they were carried back to their place of sanctuary. The slaughter and butchering of kids, lambs and calves began. Already Curmaci could smell the spices in the copper pots ready to receive the fresh meat. Children ran around. Some women wept. Some men, too. The musicians were here, the tambourines jangling. They would dance the tarantella. No matter how fat, old or powerful, everyone always had a go at the tarantella. No youth was allowed to feel the dance was below his dignity or that he was above tradition. The dance was for everyone.

He could see his son Ruggiero standing there, at ease, laughing, joking, suddenly solemn as the Mother and Child were borne aloft, now joking and pushing and messing around again. Everyone clapped as the procession passed, after which they followed behind.

A hand on his shoulder. Tony Megale.

'I am overjoyed to see you here. I thought we had lost you in Germany.'

'No, I'm here. I'll tell you all about it afterwards.'

'My brother's missing.'

'Pietro? Do you think he's on a binge?'

'I'm worried. God help anyone who's harmed him.'

'Don't let your imagination run away with you, Tony. Maybe he's in the crowd somewhere with too much wine and veal stew in his stomach.'

'Agazio, will everything be all right?'

Curmaci clasped the back of Tony's neck, pushed his friend's head forwards into a bow, and kissed him on the brow. 'Everything will be fine. Whatever changes are to come, we'll both be part of it, won't we?'

Milan

'You should have ordered the fish. It's very good.'

'It's very childish of me, Giudice,' said Caterina. 'But I can't eat fish. I never learned to like it. I think it's the fact that you see the entire dead animal on the plate. The eyes, the little teeth jutting out . . .'

Bazza put down his fork and held up a hand. 'Please.'

'Oh, I am sorry. I didn't mean to put you off.'

The magistrate did not speak to her again until he had quite finished. Caterina pushed away her own plate and waited for him, registering in the back of her mind that she had already forgotten what she had just eaten.

'How well do you know Massimiliano Massimiliani?' asked Bazza eventually.

'Not very well. Not at all. Commissioner Blume had a new mobile phone number, which I called. Massimiliani answered, and I told him I was worried about Blume who wasn't answering his proper phone either. He told me not to worry. That's the extent of our conversations so far. Massimiliani gave me another number to contact him on and told me the number I had just called would be deactivated.'

The word was so full of ill omen that she wanted to say something about Massimiliani but failed to think of a way that didn't make her sound superstitious and foolish.

'I don't know much about Massimiliani, either,' said Bazza. 'What I do know, I don't like. Nor do I much like what I know of Commissioner Blume. But I like you.'

Whether as a woman or an investigator was left ambiguous. She remained silent and held her head firm, neither nodding in stupid acquiescence nor shaking it in embarrassed modesty until Bazza himself became uncomfortable.

'As an investigator, of course.'

Caterina allowed her neck muscles to loosen a little.

'I called you up to Milan, not because I need you to do any more investigative work but, on the contrary, because I don't want you to persist with your inquiries.'

'And to apologize.'

'Apologize?' Bazza smiled generously. 'Not at all. Your investigative work, the way you tracked down the van used to transport Arconti's corpse, was exemplary. We could do with people like you in Milan. There is nothing to apologize about.'

'Not me to you. You need to apologize to me.'

Bazza opened his mouth in a way that reminded her of the fish he had just consumed.

'For holding back on the discovery of the bodies in Sesto San Giovanni. For allowing me and my team to spend a weekend away from our families working our asses off to track down people who you knew were dead. All it would have taken was a call.'

'Don't be insolent!' Bazza raised his voice loud enough to cause the only other occupied table in the dreary velvet-curtained trattoria to glance over at them. 'That was confidential information. Phone up a bunch of policemen in Rome and tell them where our investigation is going? I don't think so.'

'Fine.'

'In fact, I demand to know who told you that we had found the bodies of the van driver and his accomplice.'

'Nobody. I just phoned up the Chief Prosecutor, gave him my name, explained I was working with you, and asked him to have you call me once you had the autopsy report on the victims in the van. He didn't ask me what van. So I knew. Then, on Monday, you called and let me know the investigation was out of our hands. I've been following progress ever since, making a few calls here and there. Another magistrate, a former colleague of yours, found Arconti's ring. I won't say I have all the details, but I do know enough to say that your story about a gang of East European kidnappers is risible and transparent.'

'How much do you know?'

'I'm beginning to think maybe more than you.'

'Have Blume and Massimiliani been giving you details? If so, I need to know.'

'Is that why you called me here, Magistrate?'

'No, it's not,' said Bazza. He wiped his brow with his napkin. 'Look, we got off on the wrong foot. I called you because I need your help. I need you to sign off on a simplified story about an East European kidnap gang. I know you know better, but I need you to help persuade other people that it's true.'

'What other people?'

'Your colleagues in Rome, the press, and, above all, the victim's family. We have already told them it was an East European gang that was trying to intimidate Magistrate Arconti.'

'What difference does it make for the family? An East European gang murdering their husband and father because he happens to share a name with a magistrate, or an Italian criminal organization doing exactly the same? How could one version possibly be better than the other?'

'We need to let Curmaci go. We want to give him rope to hang himself. In any case, he is untouchable for the Arconti killing, and possibly unconnected. It is hard to tell. Now that we are watching him very closely and know a bit more about him, we wish him success in a way, because it is good to know the enemy. So we let him walk away from this. For now. You understand that this is part of what we have to do.'

'I understand,' said Caterina.

'You know, you're wrong about the story making no difference for the family, because as far as they know, the people who dreamed up and carried out this atrocity are dead. They think they have had their revenge, and so they have closure. If they were to find out it was the Ndrangheta . . .'

'What would happen if they found out?'

'Then,' said Ezio Bazza, Deputy Director of the Milan section of the Anti-Mafia Prosecution Bureau, 'they would know Arconti was the victim of an organization that Italy can never defeat.'

Polsi

Towards the end of the day, Basile raised a glass of wine, and said, 'I am a man of peace. A man of peace must know how to turn the other cheek. I know that many of you are outraged at the desecration that the authorities, accompanied by a horde of Germans and journalists, intend to visit upon this holy site tomorrow, but we shall not rise to the bait. It is not in our interest. Let them provoke us all they like, for now. We shall have other occasions to show them the error of their ways.'

The sixteen men seated below had feasted, negotiated, drunk and danced all day, and now sat in the soft orange light of the evening sun, and yet his words caused a murmur of discontent to run down the table before they finally raised their glasses and joined in his toast.

They drank and smoked, and exchanged some bawdy jokes. The women came in with liquors and aniseed biscuits, and some of the younger children broke through and started running around the table, receiving caresses, pretend punches and hugs from the men. When sufficient time had passed for it to be clear that no contradiction of Basile's toast was intended, a man named Macrì addressed himself to Basile.

'Capo, I have heard a rumour that the police intend to return at the end of the month and perform their own procession in honour of the Archangel St Michael. Twice in one month, they intend to come here.'

'Yes. It will be an empty gesture. And they will not do it next year. That is a promise.'

This time, the murmur sounded more satisfied.

Later, when the noise level had gone up again, Agazio Curmaci came up and sat down on an empty chair near Basile.

'We have already spoken, Agazio.'

'I know. But if you'll forgive me, I want everyone here to see you speaking with me.'

'If I wanted to be seen speaking to you in front of these men, I would have called you over. What you are doing is disrespectful and arrogant.'

'I am sorry. I also wanted to say something that I hope may be of use. We have a bargaining chip with the police.'

'We have more than one. Are you referring to the commissioner who was seen entering but not leaving Locri?'

'If they found his body, mutilated and strategically placed . . .'

Basile held up his hand. 'Did I not just say I was a man of peace? We will not respond to the provocation of the authorities. You have this commissioner alive in a safe place?'

'Immured where he cannot be found.'

'They do not seem to be looking for him yet.'

'No, but they will. And they will also start looking for the German.'

'Agazio, the next few days promise to be troublesome on several fronts. Let's not add to the confusion. Two vanished policemen is more than enough.'

'I understand.'

'Stability and continuity are what we want. Return to Germany at the first opportunity. With my blessing.'

'Thank you.'

'No more initiatives. I shall see to the rest.'

'Thank you. What about the policeman?'

'For the sake of peace, let him rot.'

Thursday, 3 September

49

Ardore

B LUME OPENED HIS eyes to the dark. Smell was the most primal sense. Eyes, ears, touch could all be fooled, but it was hard to fool the nose. What you saw was not always there, what you heard could be an echo, but a smell was a smell. He stood up and inhaled with mouth and nose like he was on a mountaintop. It had seemed that Pietro had walked in his own light, then stretched himself out directly opposite, but his memory was not real, so there was no point in using it to find the body. Instead, he stooped down and, sniffing like a dog, moved towards the corpse. His nose did not lead him astray and, within minutes, he was on his knees, arms outstretched over the dead body. One hand touched hair, the other something wet and cold. He almost wept at first contact, but he was not going to give up. Using the tips of his fingers, he established the position of the head, the neck, and then he touched the greasy denim fabric, and began to search systematically, feeling for pockets, buttons, his sense of urgency and hope driving away his revulsion.

Milan

Magistrate Bazza had been quite put out when Caterina announced her intention to stay in Milan and visit Arconti's widow, Letizia, and children. She had planned the visit before he called her up one day ahead of her schedule.

'It would be better if you did not visit the widow. It's asking for trouble.'

'It's planned. Besides, you want me to lie to her about the case, don't you?'

'I want you to comfort her with a half truth. Why tomorrow?'

'The family has been staying with Letizia's parents in Tuscany. They come back this evening, and I'll see them in the morning. My visit will coincide with their first day back in Milan.'

'Do you expect me to authorize your hotel bill?'

'No. I wouldn't get the reimbursement for a year anyhow. Just sign a piece of paper saying you needed me here for two days to conclude the investigations. That way I don't have to use my holiday time.'

'But you were prepared to pay a hotel bill and lose a day of holiday because the widow of a murder victim asked you to?'

'Yes.'

Bazza shook his head in disgust. 'That's not how it's done.' But as they left, he said he would look into a way of reimbursing her.

She slept badly in the hotel room, thinking about Blume and, sometimes, wondering whether to break her promise to Bazza and tell Letizia Arconti the truth. It was supposed to set people free.

The next morning, sitting in a bar eating a second pastry with a bad conscience, Caterina watched the trams and was quite impressed by their regularity. The one that would take her to the Indro Montanelli Gardens came every five minutes, but being nervous, early and full of carbohydrates to which she should never have succumbed, she decided to walk instead. Heaving her overnight bag on to her shoulder, she pushed in a pair of earphones, double-checked that incoming calls would interrupt the music, scrolled down, and selected a playlist dominated by Einaudi. A tram went clanging by and ruined the lush opening of 'Out of the Night'. She restarted the track and set off at a brisk walk down Via Conservatorio. Now all she had to do was walk to the end, go left, then right and wait for the gardens to appear. In the middle of the busy street, she paused like the worst sort of lost tourist, and called Blume's number yet again, which went to voice mail yet again.

The road opened into a piazzetta. To her right was a church with an ugly façade. Rome did this sort of thing better, she thought with pride. She checked her map. Basilica Santa Maria della Passione. Her appointment was simply for the morning, not at any fixed time, and she did not want to arrive too early. She crossed the cobblestones and entered the church that turned out to be far larger, brighter and more beautiful inside than the façade had led her to expect.

Caterina dipped her finger in the holy water font and touched her forehead, allowing a drop to run down the bridge of her nose. She centred herself in the aisle, genuflected briefly, politely, professionally, she hoped, and walked down towards the transept and the high altar. Blume would have been able to tell her stuff about the frescos. When it came to art, he always said he knew nothing. His parents had been experts, not him. He was just a policeman. After he had gone through this tiresome rigmarole, based more on anger and hurt than false modesty, he might relent, and if the artist was one he knew a lot about, his enthusiasm would soon displace his reticence and unhappiness. In fact, once he got going, it was hard to shut him up.

She stared for a while at a Last Supper. The red-haired Christ, seated at the end of a foreshortened table, gazed back at her. Applying Blume's advice, she suspended her automatic reverence and looked for what was intentionally or, better, unintentionally funny in the painting. According to Blume, irreverence was the key to understanding whether a work was any good. If it made you laugh, maybe it contained subtle humour or maybe it was simply laughable. Never trust to reputation. This Christ, she reflected, looked a bit feminine and He definitely had a stoned expression in his eyes. A tripping Christ with hair the colour of copper. The apostles around Him seemed to be more professional, the efficient staff of a boss whose best days were behind Him and whose immediate future was looking pretty bleak.

But try as she might, she could not keep her reverence for the Son of God and the ancient artist at bay, and the painting ended up making her feel smaller. She went in search of a more intimate side chapel that Blume would have censured as kitsch. She sat and stared at a Virgin holding a child. Blume would thrown his head back and scoffed; Caterina bent her head forward and prayed.

Twenty minutes later, she was on her way through the Indro Montanelli Gardens, the trees and open space a relief after the unfamiliar streets. She did not trust Milanese drivers; you could never tell what they might do next. In Rome, you needed to make sure the driver had seen you, and then you were OK. Here she was not so sure.

She was still in good time. She was increasingly nervous about her meeting with Letizia and the children, if the children were there. All she had to tell them was a lie.

It was hot on the exposed white pebble path, but she soon entered an avenue of handsome straight-trunked trees with rich foliage through which the sunlight reached her fragmented and fruit-scented. She wondered what type they were.

Ardore

Blume's search netted him a lighter, which he held triumphantly in the air as he lit it. In the flickering flame the dead man's face took on various expressions, most of them malignant, some of them amused, some of them horror-filled. Blume ignored them all, his mind being fixed on practical considerations. The next prize given up by the corpse was a shotgun shell stuck into the bottom of his jeans pocket, where the fabric touched the groin. Clicking the lighter on and off to stop it from burning his fingers, he pushed his hands into the back pockets of the trousers, and finally, there it was, the real treasure that had had to be revealed to him in a dream, since his waking mind was not working right. Reverently, Blume pulled it out, slid the cover up, and was bathed in the white light of a functioning Nokia mobile phone. He checked it. No signal, of course, and just one bar left on the battery.

Using the lighter, he made his way back to the log table, picked up a lamp, turned it on, and enjoyed the light. He retrieved the cup from the corner of the cavern and drank. He picked up a can from the ground and hacked into it with the opener. Peeled San Marzano tomatoes. He tipped the contents into his mouth. Lovely. Now he had to leave before the battery on the phone died.

50

Locri

B ASILE STOOD NEXT to the repaired ice-cream machine that buzzed softly as it cooled down the mixture. Tony Megale was there and had brought his own firepower, Peppino and Giacomo. Basile smiled to see Giacomo looking so grown-up and self-important now, big '70s-style sunglasses, a flame tattoo poking up from beneath his silk shirt.

'Are you the same little Giacomino who went missing, you had half the town out looking for you, then it turns out you were at home, playing a trick on your brother, but got so scared by all the fuss you stayed hiding for hours?'

With a curt nod, Giacomo acknowledged that this might be so.

'You were eight at the time. What age are you now?'

'Twenty.'

'Twelve years.' Basile shook his head in amazement and sadness. 'Would you like an ice cream, Giacomo?'

Giacomo gave the old man a cool stare and declined the offer with a contemptuous click of his tongue.

Basile smiled indulgently and turned his attention to the other. 'And you are Nando's son. Beppe was your grandfather?'

The youth nodded, pleased to be recognized.

'Your grandfather and I were friends. Did he ever mention that to you?'

'He died when I was very young, but my father always said there was no one could beat you . . .'

Tony Megale interrupted. 'We'll have all the time we want to talk about this later. Where is he?'

'Who?' asked Basile.

'Agazio Curmaci, of course. Who else?'

'I thought you might mean your older brother, Pietro.'

'I fear for him. He is a simple man who is easily led astray. I even fear he may have chosen the wrong side, but if that's the case, I will forgive him as he is my brother.'

'Is everyone sure they don't want any ice cream . . .?' Basile looked at the three of them. 'All right. Your loss.' He sighed. 'This is a bad business. Curmaci is a repository of some of our deepest traditions and has ensured that they are replicated, honoured and enforced in Germany. The loss of such a subtle and fluid man could set us back, unless, of course, there was someone equally qualified and skilled, ready to take his place . . .'

Tony Megale put his shoulders back and expanded his chest, creating a tiny regal space for himself between the two kids he had brought along.

'Even then,' continued Basile, 'it would be a self-inflicted wound, and forgiveness and compromise are still options.'

'The Honoured Society,' said Tony, 'is the Tree of Knowledge. The Capo Bastone is the trunk. If a branch is diseased and grows crooked, it shall be lopped off. One who collaborates with the authorities of the Italian State, with the Federal Police of Germany is no longer a man. My father, *Megale u Vecchiu*, spent years in prison because of an act of betrayal by Curmaci, and the decades of incarceration have destroyed his wisdom and discrimination and rendered him less than half the man he used to be. Curmaci is the *infame* who alerted the woman in the Finance Ministry about our carousel VAT system. That's why he was so keen to make her disappear afterwards.'

'That is a serious charge against him, Tony. So serious that I wonder why you are reporting it only now.'

'I only found out now. The crazy German called me a few days ago. He says he has papers to prove it.'

'So now we must believe the crazy German, who came down full of wild accusations, with a Madonna ripped in half claiming to represent your father's will?'

'My father no longer speaks with reason.'

'The German said nothing about this to me,' said Basile.

'He was finally thinking about his own life,' said Tony, 'instead of trying to ruin ours.'

'And these papers that prove this betrayal?'

'The *scagnozzi* you engaged gutted the camper without searching it properly.'

326

'Young people have no foresight,' said Basile. 'Tony, you have a mature mind. Are you sure of the decision you have made? I see from your face that you are. It is terrible that this should come so soon after the joyous festivities in celebration of Our Lady. The sanctuary is now crawling with policemen, our common enemy, and yet we find ourselves fighting each other again. Will you reconsider?'

'I will not.'

'You will meet Men of Honour from Reggio and Crotone. They will be waiting for you at the end of Via Garibaldi. Before you take any action, they must be persuaded that this is not a mere personal vendetta and that it will not lead to a debilitating feud. If one of them objects to your course of action, you shall do nothing. Is that understood?'

Tony Megale nodded impatiently.

'Please listen to them carefully, *Antonino mio*. They are courteous men versed in diplomacy and negotiation. An objection might be expressed as a question, the voicing of a misgiving or regret. I expect you to be sensitive to the nuances of their conversation. I think subtlety will serve you well in your future.'

'I understand,' said Tony. 'If Curmaci is with his wife and children?'

'He is a man of honour. He will walk out of the house in your company. I am sure of it. Go now, all three of you, and God's blessing be on you all.'

'Come in here, Ruggiero. I'm in the kitchen.'

It was strange to hear his father's voice echoing through the house. His mother had come into his bedroom early that morning to give him a kiss and tell him she was going with Robertino to visit family in Cosenza that she had not seen in years. It would be an opportunity to try out the brand-new Nissan Pathfinder sitting outside the front gate. Pepè's father, Mimmo the mechanic, had driven it over personally the day before, and Ruggiero and Agazio had ridden in fine style to San Luca and Polsi. When they returned that night, the old car with the mysterious engine trouble was gone.

Ruggiero walked into the kitchen. His father was seated at the far end of the table. Set in front of him, diagonally across the table, was the old Carcano carbine, the *Modello 1891*, which his father liked to take down and clean whenever he came home. Next to his hand was a small glass with what appeared to be water in it, and beside that, one of Ruggiero's throwing knives.

'Someday we must find out if this old Carcano can still be fired,' he said. 'I doubt it. You know, no one seems to know if the Carabinieri are named after the carbines they used, or whether the carbines are named after them. You would think such a simple question of history would be easy to resolve. I have always had some respect for the Carabinieri. The police . . . not so much.'

His father picked up Ruggiero's throwing knife, frowned at it, then launched it at the cupboard above the sink. With a dull thud, the blade embedded itself in the wood.

'That cupboard is worth nothing. Layers of woodchip and glue. If I had thrown it into this table, it might have bounced off it, but maybe that's also because I've never used a throwing knife. Have you been practising?'

'A bit,' said Ruggiero.

'I'm not sure that knife is good quality. It doesn't even seem to have bitten deep into that cheap wood. You can imagine how pleased your mother would be if she thought we were throwing knives in the kitchen.'

Ruggiero retrieved his knife. When he turned round, his father had placed on the table a dagger with a four-sided blade that tapered to a point so thin as to be almost invisible.

'This is called a *quadrello*. The metal of the blade remains four-sided all the way to the top. A *stiletto* has a triangular tip. I would have liked a Norman dagger, but you can only get worthless replicas. Sit down, Ruggiero.'

He reached over to the wooden fruit bowl, tapped a lemon off the top of the pile, and allowed it to roll towards him. Then he sliced the lemon in two with the dagger. 'Nowhere in the world has lemons that smell like the lemons of Calabria. The rind itself is sweet enough for a dessert.' He pressed his finger into the grain of the oaken wood, and then lifted it.

Ruggiero saw what seemed like one of his mother's sewing needles was stuck to his father's finger. His father rolled the needle between finger and thumb, and pressed it back on to the table, where it became almost invisible.

'Hard to see against the wood, isn't it?' said his father. 'That's because it's gold.' He picked it up again and quickly pricked his forefinger, index finger and thumb, and squeezed them till pearls of blood bobbed to the surface. 'A carbine, a golden needle, a dagger, a lemon and a glass of water with poison in it. These are the symbols that were laid out before me upon my induction as a *santista* for the Honoured Society. It is both wrong and right for me to be telling you this.'

Somewhere in the distance, something made a hollow pop, followed immediately by two more, then a pause. Suddenly there was such a volley of pops and cracks that they became innumerable, and then there was silence, like the end of a fireworks show.

'Papà?'

His father held up his hand. 'Wait.' Three more popping sounds reached them. Then they heard the sound of tyres screeching on hot asphalt.

'Papà?' said Ruggiero again.

'It's all right, son. We are safe now.'

A car roared by the front of the house. Someone beeped timidly at it as it took the corner and started heading out of town, up the mountain.

His father let out a long breath. 'When you are sworn in as a *santista*, only another *santista* may take your life. If a *santista* should commit an error, he is expected to punish himself, because no one else may touch him. That is what the glass of poison represents.' So saying, he picked it up and drank it.

'No!' cried Ruggiero, leaping up and running over to him.

His father grabbed him and almost squeezed the life out of him, and laughed. Ruggiero could smell alcohol on his breath.

'Don't worry. That was Aquavit I just drank. Maybe you'd like one? But no, your mother would not approve.'

He squeezed some drops of lemon onto the beads of blood and winced a little, then licked his fingers. 'There are thirty-three *santisti*. When you receive the title, you leave the Honoured Society. You no longer swear in the name of the angels and saints, but take an oath instead to the secular heroes of the Italian Risorgimento: Giuseppe Mazzini, Giuseppe Garibaldi and Giuseppe La Marmora. These are men of the state, men of law enforcement. Like other *santisti*, I pledged allegiance to them. By this act, I left the Society, yet continue to work exclusively in its interests and for its benefit. We members of the *Santa* collaborate with the authorities. We have friends in uniform, lunch with Senators, negotiate with the political parties of the Republic, and have even helped design new laws. Our peers are not men with guns, but bankers, lawyers, developers and investors. All that we do, we do to advance the fortunes of the Society and enrich its members. When a man joins the *Santa*, he is condemned to a life of loneliness, exile and betrayal. The first thing he must do is undertake to keep his status secret from the group to which he belongs, from his closest companions, from the *'ndrina* that brought him up, and even from the boss that commands him. In the case of a conflict of interests, the *santista* shall always prevail. To do so, he calls on the help of other *santisti*. Usually, but not always, he will call on the three fellows who were present at his induction. They will act personally or through the agency of *sgarristi*, *camorristi*, or even mere *contrasti d'onore*.

'Eventually, circumstances will conspire to make the real status of a *santista* become known even to his former companions. If they are wise and farseeing, and if they are not greedy for power, they may recognize that their brother has become a *santista* and withdraw their claims. If they are not, they will accuse him of calumny, collaboration, theft and betrayal.

'A *santista* can also become a *vangelista*. This is a great honour, and there are but twenty-five such persons. But the life of the *vangelista* is even lonelier. A *vangelista* writes the rules of the Society. He determines the rites, and enforces them, maintaining unity of purpose, discipline and clarity within the Society as it expands. A *vangelista* should be a man who is steeped in history and tradition, but one who also knows how to maintain those traditions in this violent and rapidly changing world. A *vangelista*, for instance, might live his whole life in Germany, or Australia, or Canada, making sure the traditions and lines of command are obeyed, preventing infiltration from the authorities while ensuring the Society has representatives within the authorities. It would be hard, say, for anyone to challenge a *vangelista* on the protocol of revealing some of the secrets of his work to his own son, since the *vangelista* is endowed with *magisterium*. Like a Doctor of the Holy Apostolic Church, a *vangelista* is the ultimate arbiter of moral codes and the scriptures. It would take another *vangelista* to challenge him.'

'What's higher than a *vangelista*?'

'A *trequartista*. So called because he has access to and command over three-quarters of the entire Society. A *trequartista* must be an old man, as I hope to be some day.'

'Is Mamma coming home?'

'Of course! She cannot be touched. Neither can you. But I don't think you want to have the reputation of one whose valour derives from his untouchability, do you?'

Ruggiero shook his head. 'No.'

'Although I have seen proof of your courage on many occasions, none so striking as the other evening when I found you standing guard, with a throwing knife that would barely scratch a cat, you have not had any opportunity for a public display of this strength of character and determination.'

Ruggiero heard the low wail of sirens as Carabinieri cars shot out of the fortified compound in the centre of the town and came racing up the hill towards the place where the popping noises had come.

His father picked up the golden needle and dropped it into a tiny cylinder pouch and tucked it into his pocket. He grasped the antique carbine, and said, 'I'm going to hang this back on the wall in our bedroom. I suppose you are dying to get out of the house and see what has happened. The men you will see out there thought they were coming for us. If their wounds shock you, consider that that is what they intended for me, your mother, you and the baby. I will almost certainly be gone by the time you get back.'

51

Ardore

WITH ALMOST THE last of his strength, Blume rolled the heavy log table across the floor, trying to get up some speed without losing aim. It hit the door full on, but without much force, and the weakened hinge stayed firmly in place. He heaved the log away, realizing that he would never manage to gather the strength to try again.

He lifted the lantern and examined his handiwork. Around the hole he had chipped away, the pozzolana cementing the metal frame of the door to the wall of the cave had cracked and begun to crumble. He was able to pull away quite large slabs of it, though some of it stayed hard and unyielding. He went back to the table and took the final lantern as backup. He was pleased at his foresight when the third one died. For a while, he worked in the dark, pulling and punching, breaking his nails and bruising his knuckles. A hot trickle down his arm told him he had reopened the gash in his hand, but he continued working in the dark, putting off the moment of truth.

Finally, he switched on the last lamp to see what he had achieved. Between the frame of the door and the wall was a gap large enough for him to insert his arm and shoulder. He sat down, placed the lamp beside him, leaned his back against the overturned log, and rhythmically, but without violence which would lead to injury and desperation, started kicking at the edges of the gap he had opened. Pozzolana dust and shards of limestone fell on his leg. The frame showed no signs of giving way, but its position relative to the wall seemed to have moved very slightly. He kept at it, alternating from left foot to right every thirty kicks, until the misalignment between the bottom part of the steel frame and the cavern wall was a question of inconvertible fact and not blind hope. A lump of cement, biscuity and welcome, fell on his leg. He rested, slept, had no visitations, woke, and continued.

Eventually there was space for his head. What was the rule? If a cat could fit its head through a crack, then the rest of its body could follow? Or was that a rat? At any rate, he didn't think it applied to large policemen. And yet, he was going to try. He stretched out his arms and clasped his hands religiously together, then pushed them through the gap and followed with his head before he could stop himself. Immediately he was stuck, but he had been expecting this. Using his elbows and pushing with his foot against the log on the other side, he half turned, and his right shoulder slipped through the breach, wedging his body very firmly against the sharp upper part of the gap, but the sensation of one shoulder going through had given him courage. If the only barrier was pain and not the laws of physics, he would get through. He pushed and heaved and thrashed, and then something came loose in his shoulder and he screamed and cried, and found to his chagrin that he was calling for his mother. But the dislocation of his shoulder saved him. His upper body was out, the rest followed. Weeping with pain, he started edging forwards, realizing that he had left the lamp burning in the darkness behind him out of reach.

He got to the partially collapsed section of tunnel, and was so overcome with anguish at the idea of pushing his head into the jaws of the rock, that he thought he might prefer to die where he was. He remembered the hope he had felt when his hand, emerging from the narrow space, had touched the warm polymer of his pistol.

He pulled Pietro's lighter from his pocket and used it to illuminate the space around him. Right in front of him, touching his feet, though he had not felt it, lay Pietro's shotgun, cracked open and discarded by Curmaci before entering the narrow space. He pulled the shotgun to him and poked and pushed it into the black hole in front of him. It came up against an obstruction that had not been there before. He probed at the blockage, which yielded. Curmaci, deliberately or not, had caused a small avalanche of rubble to fall. As he bent down, an unmistakable taste of fresh air streamed into his dry mouth, and it was this that drove him on. Squirming like a worm, floundering like a fish on dry land, and scrabbling like a rodent, he managed to make his way through the narrow section and emerged in the first section of tunnel that had seemed so dark before, but now seemed bathed in soft light. The tunnel roof rose in height, and he walked the final part stooped but on two legs.

The light that came down from above was green, filtered through the corrugated plastic cover that hid the entrance from police helicopters and anyone else who might be interested. The ladder had been drawn up. This did not surprise him, yet it brought tears to his eyes, and he felt ashamed. The glistening rocks and silt that formed the walls of his new prison were appalling in their smoothness. Even with both arms functioning, he could never have scaled them.

He took the phone out of his pocket again and slid the cover back. The small antenna symbol flashed at him, and the reception bars were still absent. He walked around the walls, holding the phone above his head. Nothing.

Blume retreated to just inside the tunnel entrance, and banged the shotgun barrel against the dry rock shaking out as much dirt as he could. He cleared out the left bore and, holding it up to the green light from above, peered into it. The barrel was filthy, but it was a shotgun. With no rifling in the bore, even quite a lot of dirt would not be a problem. The only thing that needed to be precise was his aim, because he had one shot only. He put the left barrel of the shotgun into his mouth, and blew down it. That was as clean as it would get.

He could not suppress the thirst that was taking over his whole being, but in between thoughts of water, he patiently gazed at the green plastic above, watching the play of the sun and shadows on its surface, looking for the hinges and for signs of any objects weighing it down. The best point to hit it would be where the border of the plastic rested on the rim of the hole. He fixed the spot in his mind, stared at it, and imagined how, when he had blasted a hole through it, the sunlight would come in as an angled beam hitting the walls of his deep prison halfway down like a searchlight.

He fished the cartridge out of his pocket, inserted it into the left chamber of the shotgun. The only way this was going to work was if he was lying down. He pressed the recoil pad against his right shoulder and slowly, pausing now and again to let the pain subside, brought his left arm over to steady the barrel. No. He was shaking with pain, and would bury the shot in the sides of the pit. He set the recoil pad on the ground below his armpit and, crooking his arm, pressed the stock into the side of his body. He focused on the pain in his left arm. It was all in the shoulder, not in the finger that was going to pull the trigger. The finger that was going to pull the trigger was steady, and firm. Steady and firm. He looked upwards and fired.

The roar deafened his ear, the shotgun leaped away from him like a pogo stick and a pile of dry dirt and stones tumbled down onto his face, and for a desperate moment he thought he had hit the walls. Instead, he had blasted a patch of blue sky into the green trapdoor and a sunbeam was shining down, not at an angle but straight down upon his face.

He tried to shout for joy, but his voice came out as a dying croak.

He slid open the phone, worked out its menus. There was one bar left on the battery. He found the option for redial, and set it to maximum, which was just five. The phone would dial the same number five times, then give up. And there was no point in calling emergency services, since none of the operators would give a second thought to hanging up on a mute call from a mobile phone.

Blume tested the phone by lobbing it up half a yard and allowing it to fall. As the phone hit the ground, its front panel snapped closed and the call was shut down. Even the slightest bump snapped it closed. He scraped at the earthy parts of the walls till he had come up with some twigs and pieces of root. He shoved them under the sliding panel of the phone, pushed in small pebbles and dirt, and let it fall. The panel stayed open. He stripped his shoelaces from his shoes, and using his teeth and his good hand, bound them tightly around the battery cover.

Blume only had one phone number in his memory. He dialled it with reverential care and lobbed the phone upwards towards the hole he had blown in the corrugated plastic. He missed twice. The first time he caught the phone one-handed before it hit the ground. The second time, it clattered at his feet, but the battery cover stayed on and the panel stayed wedged open. He brushed it down, pressed disconnect, kissed and blessed the phone, then dialled the same number again. He could already see the message flashing no signal as he lobbed it skywards again. This time, it sailed through the shining gap above.

52

Milan

SHE NEED NOT have worried about her reception in the bereaved household. Letizia Arconti did not expect Caterina to answer angry questions. She was just thankful, immensely thankful, that Caterina had taken all the trouble to come up here and talk to her. She had heard that the East Europeans who had done this to Matteo were dead and that it had all been part of some warning to a judge in Rome. What she really wanted Caterina to tell her was how he had looked when they found him.

'You came down to identify him in the morgue in Rome. You saw what he looked like,' said Caterina.

'But they had cleaned him up then, closed his eyes, his mouth. My father died at home, and I remember how my sister and I smoothed away the rictus of pain on his face before we let my mother see him again. What did Matteo look like when you found him? Were his eyes open? Could you see fear?'

They taught you that it was better to withhold as many details as possible from the family of a murder victim. It did no one any good.

'No, no. I could not see fear,' said Caterina.

'That's because it was a stupid question. Of course, you can't see fear. The dead are dead. I'm sorry. I'm doing the hysterical widow act.'

'That's all right,' said Caterina. 'And it wasn't a stupid question. I've seen fear on the faces of the dead. Immigrants who suffocated in the back of a semi. I promise you he didn't have that sort of fear in him.'

'Are you trying to be kind?'

'Yes, but I'm a widow, too. I lost my husband in a road accident.'

'I'm so sorry.'

'He was on a motorbike, got hit by a car. His body was broken all over, his face pulped, and so there was no recognizable expression on it, but I can guess it would have been shock and anger. He would have been so angry to die at that age. I knew him, knew what he was like. I see the same look of stunned anger on my son's face, sometimes. You knew your husband. How you imagine he faced his death is probably how he died. They didn't torture him, you know.'

'The hours before they killed him would have been torture.'

'As long as people are alive they don't really believe they're going to die. If the realization came to him, it will have been in the last moment, maybe with a sense of resignation.'

'Thank you, Caterina.' Letizia clasped her hand. 'You've restored my faith in the system of justice in this country. You people can never get paid too much for what you do.'

Caterina freed her hand as gently as she could.

'Sorry,' said Letizia. 'I have no right to throw myself at you like this. Where are you going now, back to Rome?'

'Yes,' said Caterina. 'There's a train . . . The Eurostar.'

'Matteo used to fly. I always told him he should take the train, but he preferred flying. Come into the kitchen, the children are there.'

'No, really . . .'

'Please? It'll only take a moment.'

She led Caterina down the hallway. It was a beautiful apartment. The hallway was broad enough to be a room in its own right. Arconti must have been doing well for himself.

'Children, this is Inspector Mattiola. Caterina. She has a train to catch, so she's just saying hello.'

An adolescent girl and a boy who probably thought he was an adolescent but was only a baby, sat at the table, a jar of Nutella between them. Caterina lifted her hand in awkward greeting. The boy slowly scanned her face and sought out her eyes; the girl examined her face and then her body.

'I am a policewoman. I was assigned to investigate your father's murder.'

'The killers got killed, didn't they?' said the girl.

'Yes.'

'So it's all over?'

'Yes,' she said without any hesitation in her voice.

The boy put down the knife with Nutella on it, came over to her, put his arms around her waist, and hugged her. Instinctively she found herself caressing his hair, while his mother stood at the kitchen door.

A phone rang.

'Wait!' said Caterina, pushing the boy from her, then, seeing his face, pulling him back and kissing him quickly on the forehead before running into the living room. 'That's my phone. I absolutely need to get that. I've been waiting for news from a friend.'

She fumbled around in her bag hunting for the phone, mentally imploring the caller not to hang up. The phone was still going. Twelve or so was the maximum number of rings before an automatic disconnect. She looked at the number, and frowned. In a voice that startled even herself, she shouted at Letizia to get a pen and a piece of paper, 'Now!' The phone would record the number, but she wanted physical backup.

'Hello?' She listened. Letizia handed her a piece of paper and she scribbled down the number. 'Hello?'

Silence, or almost. The connection was live, and she could hear rustling and a crackle. She had her notebook out now, and with her phone pressed to her ear had gone across the room and picked up Letizia's house phone without even glancing at her for permission.

She dialled Massimiliano Massimiliani's personal number. Come on, come on. The sounds from the mysterious mobile phone sounded like the background to one of those new-age relaxation pieces, all rushing air, faraway birdsong. Blume hated that music. Said it was bad enough when Pink Floyd started doing it forty years or so ago.

'Alec? Is that you? Maybe you can't speak, but can you hear me? Alec? Answer.'

The mobile phone said nothing, but Massimiliani answered on the other line.

'At last, Blume's calling me. You need to track the number, now.'

'Inspector Mattiola?'

She collected herself, also because she was being watched by the startled widow she had come to comfort. 'Yes, Inspector Mattiola. Commissioner Blume is calling me at this moment from this number.' She read out the digits on the piece of paper, and then gave him her own mobile number.

'Where did you say he's calling from?'

'Shit! The line just went down. He's not calling now.'

'I'm taking it he said nothing and you need a location?'

'Yes,' she said, thankful Massimiliani was quick on the uptake. 'But what I gave you wasn't his number.'

'Right. I'll get back to you.' He hung up, without asking any pointless questions.

'Are you all right?' asked Letizia.

'Yes. Can I have a glass of water?'

'Sofia! Bring a glass of water in here.'

Sofia arrived followed by Lorenzo. Caterina accepted the glass, and gulped it down gratefully.

'Thank you, Sofia.' The girl blushed self-consciously. Laden with hurt and fear, yet still able to suffer social embarrassment as if it counted.

Lorenzo stepped forward and relieved her of the glass, and offered to get her another.

'No thanks, *tesoro.*'

She turned to Letizia. 'As you may have gathered that was something of an emergency. What's a good taxi number for me to call? I need to get to Linate airport.'

Letizia picked up the phone and dialled a number. 'I thought you were going by train.'

'Change of plan. I need to get a flight to Calabria. Are there many flights from Linate, do you know?'

Cinquefrondi, Calabria

It seemed the traffic policeman wanted to expend as little energy as possible on waving the oncoming traffic to a stop, no doubt trusting that the presence of a small aluminium sign with 'Deviazione' written on it and the two cars marked 'Polizia Municipale' sitting on the central reservation with their flashers on would make his intentions plain.

Curmaci rolled down his window.

'What's going on?'

The cop's face was glistening in the heat. He wiped his brow with the back of the dark blue sleeve of his jacket. 'The viaduct is out. A subsidence of the central section this morning.'

'I need to get to the A3,' said Curmaci.

'No problem. You just go straight through the town and rejoin the highway on the other side. It'll add an extra five minutes to the journey. Take the ramp there, where my colleagues are.'

To Curmaci's left stood two more traffic cops, one of them beckoning with a red lollipop-shaped wand, the other making sweeping gestures at the side road, as if directing a thick flow of vehicles.

A car came up behind, and the driver rolled down his window as Curmaci had done. The traffic cop let out an exaggerated sigh of exasperation, then winked at Curmaci and went to deal with his next customer. As Curmaci turned his steering wheel, he could hear the same exchange starting up with the driver behind.

Lousy job, he thought to himself as he drove down the ramp onto a pock-marked country lane below the highway. Imagine standing there in the middle of the road waiting to get knocked down by a speeding car, explaining the same thing over and over, sweltering in those jackets.

Except – the thought hit him like a sucker punch – *the policemen should not have been wearing jackets*. The standard issue in summer is pale blue short-sleeved shirts. Was it possible . . .?

He looked into the rear-view mirror.

The car that had come up behind was following him down the narrow lane, which would have been all right, except he now also saw the two Municipal Police cars behind it, occupying the full breadth of the road as they drove side-by-side in slow pursuit.

The road curved rightwards leading to a square-mouthed cement underpass that went below the highway he had so foolishly left. He slowed down as he entered it and stopped even before he had properly made out the two cars positioned nose-to-nose forming a V in the centre, cutting off his escape. Leaving the engine running, he stepped out, pistol in hand.

'Agazio! You've grown fatter and slower since I last saw you.'

He could not see the speaker yet, but knew the voice. As his eyes adjusted to the gloom, he could make out three or four other figures in front of him. The cars behind stopped at the mouth of the tunnel, but he did not even bother turning around to look.

'And stupider. You should have said stupider. Is that you, Daniele?'

A short man, unarmed, wearing a pink Lacoste T-shirt and perfectly clean tennis shoes, stepped forward. Curmaci kept his gun dangling by his side.

'I'm afraid it is.'

340

'Why?'

'Too much confusion, a loss of trust. A new beginning. It appears a German policeman was gathering evidence for years, and no one stopped him.'

'But he's gone.'

'The information itself remains, and with it so many doubts. Far too many doubts.'

'My wife? My sons?'

'They will be fine. I give you my word.'

Curmaci tried to crack a smile. 'I am glad I can trust you. You'll let me phone them now and say a few words?'

The man in pink shook his head. 'That would just make it harder on everyone concerned. Harder for them when they hear your voice, harder for you when you hear theirs, and harder for us to decide whether you passed on some sort of message. Don't call.'

Curmaci nodded. He walked back to his car, got back into the driver's seat, closed the door, and switched off the engine. At a signal from his old friend, the man who had instructed him in the ways of the *Santa*, the cars in the tunnel made three-point turns, then left. The vehicles from behind then filed past him in slow procession. As the last one drew level, the fake policeman, now out of his heavy jacket and wearing a yellow T-shirt, glanced at him and winked.

He waited till they were all gone. Then he waited some more until the rumble of a truck passing overhead had died away. When he was sure the silence was as good as it was ever going to get, he put the gun in his mouth and, before the unexpected sob swelling from his chest had time to reach his throat, he pulled the trigger.

53

Milan

Massimiliani did not call her back until she had already bought her ticket in Linate airport. The next flight from Milan to Calabria was in forty-five minutes. The first time her phone rang, it was Panebianco back in Rome asking something stupid about a file she was supposed to have regarding the murder of a shepherd. A shepherd in Rome. He lived in a camper on the Via Portuense, had a flock of sheep that fed on municipal grass and a criminal record going back to the 1960s. A shepherd who rented out firearms, according to Panebianco.

She told him she might skip the next day at work.

Panebianco did not seem to mind. 'How's Blume getting on, any word?'

'I'll let you know when I know.'

She was at the boarding gate when Massimiliani phoned.

'That was a very interesting number you gave us. As it happens, we had a trace on it already. Are you sure it was Blume calling?'

'Yes,' she said.

'What did he say?'

'He didn't say anything.'

'So you don't know it was him.'

'Look, I know it was him. Are you on your way to where the call was made?'

Massimiliani hesitated. 'Yes . . . it's a large area. There are a number of problems. First, the signal has died in the meantime.'

'I know,' said Caterina. She had only called it twenty times.

'Second, it's an old phone, no GPS positioning, so we're using multi-lateration, and third, it's in a rural area with quite a large area covered by the masts. Also, it'll be dark in a few hours, so if we're searching outside . . .'

'Where was the call made from?'

Massimiliani remained silent.

'Tell me where the call was made from or I'll kick up such a fuss about Curmaci, Bazza, Arconti – all of them – your phone-tapping activities, SISDE wrongdoings, everything, that you won't know what hit you.'

'You're bluffing.'

'I'm not. And you're surprised I know so much. Where?'

'In the Locride district. Ardore is the nearest village.' He hung up, which meant even if she had wanted to, she couldn't tell him she was on her way down.

Twenty minutes later, the flight assistant reminded all passengers not to use their mobile phones.

Locri

Enrico Megale sat in the bar, a large bowl of yellow ice cream completely melted in front of him. The seats around him were empty, and the exclusion zone extended to the next table. Even Pepè was treading carefully, treating Enrico with as much respect as suspicion. All the glances in his direction were furtive, but they could have looked straight at him, because Enrico was staring into space, unaware of his surroundings.

'Enrico? It's me, Ruggiero.'

Enrico ignored him.

'Enrico, you're needed at home now. Your aunt wants you. Zia Rosa needs you.'

'I'm the only one left.'

'Your uncle could still turn up.'

'I don't understand what just happened,' said Enrico. His button eyes stared out unblinking and uncomprehendingly at Ruggiero. Suddenly he lurched across the table in what seemed to have been an attempt to punch Ruggiero.

'Take it easy, Enrico,' he said, parrying the blow with ease. 'We'll find out what happened.'

'The way I heard it . . . It was supposed to be your father. That's what I was hearing.'

'Vicious rumours, Enrico. Some people have no souls.'

'My father has gone. I hardly got to see him.' Enrico started sobbing.

Ruggiero put an arm around him. 'This is the sort of thing they do when they want to take over. Divide and conquer, turn friends into enemies.'

'I didn't know my father!' Enrico blurted out. 'He never fucking visited. Never told me anything, never . . . I may as well not be his son.'

'Well, maybe that will make it easier to accept in the long run.'

'He was a bastard! My father was a foundling bastard. Everyone knows it. I am not a Megale. I am no one.' Enrico stared defiantly around the bar and everyone averted their gaze.

'You are a Megale,' said Ruggiero softly. 'You will be treated as a Megale deserves to be treated. And you are your father's son, now more than ever.'

'I miss my uncle! Zio Pietro was more of a father than he was.'

'And your aunt misses you and him. A family needs to be together at a time like this. I'm sure she's been calling you ever since you saw what you should never have seen in the car park.'

'Giacomo and Peppino,' said Ruggiero. He clicked his fingers in the air. 'Pepè,' he said, 'we're borrowing your bike.'

Pepè came over and handed Ruggiero the keys.

Enrico's grief was momentarily trumped by astonishment. 'How did you do that? Since when has Pepè snapped to attention when you click your fingers?'

'That's not it, Enrico. I knew he would want to show you an act of kindness. In times of trouble and sorrow, we stick together. Come on. On a *motorino* we'll be there in no time.'

Basile started cleaning the coffee machine and making a lot of noise with the foaming arm as Ruggiero escorted Enrico out.

Ardore

The sunlight was no longer shining on the walls of his prison, and his thoughts were no longer able to resist the idea of water. But if he tried to crawl all the way back into the darkness, he would never come out again. This knowledge, along with the piercing pains in his shoulder and a physical weariness such as he had never experienced, kept him where he was. It was embarrassing, too, to die because he was unable to climb out of a three-metre-deep hole, like drowning in two inches of water. Drowning in cold water would be good.

He lay down. The phone he had thrown to the gods above had shown the date to be 3 September, but he didn't believe it. Surely, he had been in there for far longer than that? If it was just one day after the Polsi summit, then there was still time for Curmaci to keep his word and come for him. Curmaci had seemed a decent enough type. Most people were pretty much the same. It just depended on the system they found themselves in. Or maybe Curmaci was evil, but Blume was too tired to try to hate him. There was nothing particularly awful about Curmaci, even if he was a demon.

The sky was darkening nicely now, and there were no clouds visible through his blasted gap. He decided he would prefer no moon, so he could see the millions of stars and lie back and think his way into them.

Ardore (village)

Two hundred euros to cross to the east coast, fifty up front, and the taxi wasn't even legal and the driver was completely unimpressed by her police badge, but she was lucky she had found him. Not all taxi drivers at the airport, legal or not, would have been willing to have a policewoman from Rome as their fare, no matter what the price.

'How much longer?'

'Fifty minutes.' The taxi driver, like Blume, measured out his journey in units of time rather than distance. At least he did not ask her who she was or what she was doing, or why she wanted a taxi to drive her at nightfall into a wilderness on the lower slopes of the mountains. There were a lot of questions the taxi driver was making a point of not asking.

On calling Massimiliani from the airport as soon as the plane landed, she was furious to learn that she was only an hour and a half behind him. Surely he should have been there hours before? Her anger swept away Massimiliani's half-hearted objections to her arrival.

Twenty minutes into the taxi journey, Massimiliani called with news that was good when she looked at it one way, ominous when she looked at it another.

'We found a vehicle belonging to Pietro Megale. The call you got came from his phone. I am assuming there is no connection between you and him beyond this call?'

'You assume right. Blume has his phone. That means he is dead.'

'Blume's dead?'

'No!' shouted Caterina. 'Pietro is dead. If he's missing and Blume has his phone, he's either dead or incapacitated. Blume is strong. But now he needs our help.'

Caterina realized the taxi driver had heard every single word; she didn't care. She looked at her watch. Seven o'clock. It would be dark when she got there, wherever 'there' was.

The taxi driver's sense of timing was spot on. The sun was dipping below the mountains, a perfect orange disc and soft on the eyes as they climbed the curving road to Ardore. Massimiliani had asked her to call as she arrived, and she did. He told her to have the taxi leave her in the main square, where a squad car would be waiting for her. It wouldn't do to have a taxi drive all the way to the scene.

The taxi driver looked at her askance when she produced a Bancomat card.

'What, you don't have one of those swipe machines?' she asked.

'Sure I do.' He pulled one out of the glove compartment, switched it on. 'It takes time to boot up, find a phone signal, especially out here. Are you sure you don't have cash? It would be much faster.'

'I'm sure,' said Caterina.

'That police car is waiting for you?'

'Yes.'

'Always with the flashing lights. Maybe if you police turned off the flashing lights, you'd catch someone unawares someday, but no, the lights have to be flashing. Sirens, too, blaring away in the night when the only things that'll be listening are children trying to sleep and the only things on the roads have four legs . . . there we go, we're online now. How much shall I put in for the tip?'

The police car swept down the hill, siren blaring, then took a series of bumpy roads and tracks. The driver did not turn off the siren until they left the road for a field. He remained grimly silent and concentrated even as the vehicle dipped and shuddered across a rough field, tossing them up and down uncontrollably in their seats like two children in a bouncy castle.

Parked by a thicket of myrtle bushes were three other police vehicles, one of which was a van, all of them with their lights flashing.

'Is that all?' said Caterina.

The policeman shrugged.

They parked and Caterina had to hurry the policeman who was supposed to be accompanying her to wherever they were going. She saw no sign of generators or arc lights. The writing on the side of the van said *Squadra Cinofilo*. The dog handlers were here.

Locri

When Ruggiero came downstairs, showered and in fresh clothes, Zia Rosa was in the kitchen. The familiar folds and lines in her face seemed to have been drawn taut as if the white skull beneath was straining to get out. He had had no idea she would be here. She and his mother had not been talking, so he had not heard their voices. Nor had anyone been crying. Only now did he remember hearing whispering and murmurs too tense and disjointed for it to be his mother talking to Roberto. He had walked into the kitchen without thinking, and when he saw his aunt there, sitting in the same chair where his father had been a few hours earlier, he recognized this meeting was inevitable and he had been childish not to anticipate it.

His mother looked startled to see him there, as if a stranger had just walked into the room.

'Zia Rosa,' said Ruggiero, his voice full of pleasant surprise. He went over to the kitchen sink, and filled a glass of water and drank it down, making an appreciative and slightly jocular 'ah' as he drained the glass, then filled up another, annoyed to see his hand was trembling. He let the water run, rinsing out the glass several times before turning off the tap, and taking another drink of water, more slowly this time. He reached out and touched his mother's elbow, and held it for a while.

'Any news from Zio Pietro?'

No one answered.

'We are all shocked at what happened to your brother-in-law. I'm sorry for your loss. Tony was a good man. We did not see enough of him in these parts. I am sure whoever did this . . .'

'Where is Enrico?' said Zia Rosa, her voice husky and harsh, almost a growl.

'Enrico? You mean he hasn't called? He must be . . . I don't know, have you tried Basile's bar? I was there today and they were saying that Enrico had been in. I thought he would be home by now. But I've been in for a while, you know, on PlayStation. So, I don't know. He's not really my responsibility. If he wants to disappear, have some time to himself after all that's happened . . .'

'Maria! Get out of the way. I want to see your son standing there.'

His mother pulled her elbow away, and seemed to shudder as she did so.

'Look at me, Ruggiero,' ordered Zia Rosa. 'Look into this face from which you have received thousands of kisses. Look at me.'

Ruggiero raised his eyes, and looked at Zia Rosa, and allowed his feelings to drain out of him. He could feel the light go from his eyes as he stared at what was in effect nothing more than an ugly old woman, her skin like an uncooked chicken, her eyes full of despair turning to hate. If he concentrated on that alone, he could suspend all sympathy.

'I have not seen Enrico,' he repeated, using his standing position to try to stare her down. 'I have not seen him. You cannot ask me if I have seen him.'

The moaning sound that came from the old woman at the table seemed to fill the entire room. With a sudden scream, she leaped up and went for his face, clawing at him with her hands, slicing his lips and bloodying his gums with her nails, spitting, biting, pulling his hair and hurling maledictions into his face. She screamed curses against his health, his reason, his prick, balls, gut, the follicles in his head, the shit in his intestines, the ice in his blood; she invoked deformities and pain on his children and his children's children, and called down every human and animal disease upon the whole Curmaci family. She begged God to blast him, men to rape him, burn him, scatter his parts, and she called upon the wind to sweep him away as if he had never been.

He accepted all this, and even willed her to strike him harder, but she was too feeble. Across the table, his mother was weeping.

Ardore

Massimiliani was standing in a field of white flowers, three policemen wearing reflective jackets by his side.

'We're near, but there's no sign of anyone,' said Massimiliani. He looked at her again. 'You're different in person. I saw your file.'

'What about a helicopter? Searchlights, a full team?' she demanded.

Massimiliani puffed out his cheeks. 'We're not looking for a missing child. And I'm not even in charge here. I am about to call in extra help, though.'

Something nuzzled her knee, and she glanced down to see a white Labrador. The handler, dressed in blue fatigues, was grinning at her.

'How many dogs are out here?'

'Two,' said the handler.

'And this is one of them?' she pointed to the Labrador, which was lolling in the grass and licking her shoes. 'Why isn't he helping?'

'It's a she,' said the handler. 'She's not much use at this sort of thing.'

Caterina pointed at an unleashed black dog walking slowly away from her across the field. 'And that one?'

'That's a cadaver dog,' said the handler, following her gaze. 'It sniffs out, well, it's self-explanatory.'

'And the Labrador?'

'She's great with scent articles. You know, a piece of clothing or something worn by the victim.'

'By the missing person,' corrected Caterina.

'Yeah, whatever. But there is nothing belonging to the victim for her to use . . . so.' He shrugged.

'Wait . . .' Caterina pulled open her bag, and started fumbling around in it. 'Did no one here think to bring a fucking torch?'

'Use your mobile phone,' said the handler helpfully.

'This is a night-time search and no one . . . Hold on.' She dropped to her knees and the Labrador raised its face and looked at her expectantly, then, out of sheer friendliness, gave her mouth a lick. Caterina cupped her hands and the dog stuck its nose into them.

The handler caught the dog by the collar and dragged it away. 'Hey! What do you think you're doing? What are you giving her?'

'It's his watch. He only wore it for a short time, but – it might work, mightn't it?'

'A watch? That's not ideal. What you really want is a piece of cloth. And if he only wore it . . .'

'But he kept it in his pocket for months, used it like it was a pocket watch.'

The handler dropped to his knees and ushered Caterina away. 'OK, but I'll do this. She's still young and a bit stupid, but she's good.'

'It's a full moon,' said Massimiliani. She jumped, having forgotten about him, being completely focused on the handler and his stupid Labrador, who were now running back and forth through the flower stalks for all the world like they were playing a game.

'Anyway,' said Massimiliani, 'here's the torch you were looking for, though we hardly need it.'

Caterina looked up at the moon. That was why she could see the Labrador and the handler so well.

The Labrador barked and the handler cried out, 'She's got something.'

Hadn't he asked for a new moon, a dark night and stars? But the moon would do just fine. He couldn't see it yet, but it was lighting the patch of sky he was watching. Soon he would have moonbeams for company. In the morning, he would think about ways of getting water out of the soil. Or he might crawl back into the hole.

A shadow blocked out the view through the hole he had made, and Blume felt immeasurable sadness at the loss of sky. The shadow vanished, then suddenly popped back and poked a face in. An animal. A goat? It must be a goat.

The goat barked. The sound was very loud as it echoed down the walls of his prison. It barked and barked and barked. The clamour was tremendous, overpowering. If he had any voice, he would have shouted back, and they would have created a feast of noise.

The lid came off and a bright light shone straight down into his face. He gazed up at it, too lazy to blink. If it was Curmaci, or some other demon, the odds were not good.

'Alec? Alec!'

His throat and tongue were too swollen and dry for him to speak. There was the ladder, coming down from the sky. A second person was holding the light now. Ah, someone on the ladder now. He would have liked to stand up for the occasion, if only to check that it was real. The pain in his shoulder, the cramp in his legs were reassuring in this respect. Dreams tended to gloss over the body's pains.

A woman in blue was descending towards him, and Blume stared up at her beautiful smiling face, illuminated from above.

'Let's go home, Alec,' she said.

Glossary

AISI   *Agenzia Informazioni e Sicurezza Interna* is the 'Internal
                 Intelligence and Security Agency' of Italy. The British
                 equivalent is MI5, but it is more difficult to draw a
                 parallel with a US agency, the closest being the FBI
                 and Department of Homeland Security. AISI is a
                 relatively new name for what used to be known as
                 SISDE, the covert role of which in modern Italian
                 history is ambiguous, to say the least.

BKA   *Das Bundeskriminalamt*, the Federal Criminal Police
                 Department. The German FBI, effectively.

Camorra   The Mafia of Naples and Campania. Its reach extends
                 to southern Latium (Lazio, *q.v.*) and Rome.

Camorrista   Either a member of the Camorra of Naples or,
                 confusingly, a rank in the 'ndrangheta. There are several
                 different levels of *camorrista*, much as a legitimate
                 military might have several different levels and types of
                 lieutenant.

Campania   The region south of Lazio, the beginning of the
                 'Mezzogiorno' (southern Italy), capital Naples.

Carabiniere The Carabinieri Corps (*Arma dei Carabinieri*) is the
(pl Carabinieri) national gendarmerie of Italy. Although the Carabinieri
                 Corps carries out police and investigative work, it also
                 operates in its military capacity in theatres of war and
                 – an important distinction – reports to the Ministry of
                 Defence rather than to the Ministry of the Interior.
                 Most of the 112,000 members of the Corps operate

as 'policemen' rather than soldiers. It also functions as the Military Police for the Army, Navy and Air Force. It specialises in investigations into terrorism, forgery, art theft, food adulteration and provides protection to Italian missions and embassies.

Commissario   Police Commissioner. Blume's rank, translated literally. Its US equivalent, however, is not 'Police Commissioner', which is far too high and corresponds more closely to the *Questore* in the Italian system; rather, it is roughly equivalent to Captain or Major. The British and Canadian equivalent would be (Detective) Superintendent or Chief Superintendent. In Australia it would be the Commander.

Cosa Nostra   The Sicilian Mafia. It literally means 'Our Thing'.

Crimine   The word means 'crime' or 'felony' in standard Italian. In the context of the 'ndrangheta, the *crimine* is a person in charge of coordinating criminal actions and assassinations – the head of a death squad.

DCSA   *Direzione Centrale per i Servizi Antidroga* – The Central Anti-Drug Directorate. The DCSA has a broader remit than its name implies, because drug running is a crime that covers so many other areas, from homicide to high finance. Like the DIA (*q.v.*), it is an elite inter-force organisation bringing together members of the *Polizia* (Police, Blume's force), the *Carabinieri* (*q.v.*) and the *Guardia di Finanza* (the Finance Police).

DDA   The *Direzione Distrettuale Antimafia* is the judicial arm of the anti-Mafia apparatus of Italy. Its members are magistrates, often with a pronounced level of expertise and commitment. It imparts executive to an interforce agency called the DIA (*q.v.*). Strictly speaking, a DDA is a regional branch of a national body called the *Direzione Nazionale Antimafia* (DNA).

DIA   The *Direzione Investigativa Antimafia* was formed in 1991. It is an anti-Mafia force whose members are drawn from the three main police forces of the country (the *Carabinieri*, the Police and the Finance Police).

Magistrate Giovanni Falcone, murdered by the Mafia in 1993, had long campaigned for the institution of the DIA, which he explicitly compared to the FBI.

Giovane d'onore A young man of honour, a new adept in the 'ndrangheta. A private soldier, so to speak.

Giudice Judge. The word may also used as an honorific when addressing a magistrate.

Lazio Also known by its Latin name Latium, a central region of Italy whose capital is Rome.

Lira, lire The old Italian currency was worth around 2,000 to the euro, so that a million lire was, very roughly speaking, 500 euros or 600 dollars.

Locale In the parlance of the 'ndrangheta, a 'locale' (*locali* in the Calabrian dialect) is the collective name for a series smaller criminal units called *'ndrine* (*q.v.*) operating in cooperation with each other in a given (local) area. The most important of these, is the Locale of San Luca, next to the Sanctuary of the Madonna di Polsi. Each district, in Italy and abroad, will have its own locale.

Mafia Italian uses the word Mafia in much the same way as English. It may refer to any organised group of criminals, and can even be used in a loose and facetious sense. Thus the 'ndrangheta can be called the Calabrian Mafia. In the absence of any qualifying adjectives or gloss, Mafia will refer to the Sicilian criminal organisation, which is also known as *Cosa Nostra*. The main Mafia groups in Italy are: *Cosa Nostra/La Mafia* (Sicily); the *Stidda* (Sicily); the *Camorra* (Naples); the *'ndrangheta* (Calabria) and the *Sacra Corona Unita* (Apulia).

Mastro di Giornata In Calabrian dialect, this would be *mastru i jurnata*. Effectively the person in charge of the internal communications of the 'ndrangheta. He keeps members up to date and keeps tabs on where any member is at a given time.

Ndrangheta ('ndrangheta) The proper orthography is 'ndrangheta, with an apostrophe and lower-case 'n', but an editorial decision was made to spell it as Ndrangheta to make it clear that it is a proper name. It is pronounced with the stress on the first 'a' and with a hard 'g' (*en-DRAN-gehta*) It refers to the Mafia of the Region of Calabria (the 'toe' on the boot of Italy). The source of the name is uncertain, but it seems to come from the Greek *andragathía* meaning 'Valour, gallantry, courage'. The *andr-* stem of the word means 'manly', or characteristic of a man. Other names for the 'ndrangheta are: The Montalbano Family, the Honoured Society (*Società Onorata*), the *Santa*, and la *Picciotteria*. In the past it has also been called the *Maffia* and the *Camorra*, the latter of which is now used exclusively for the criminal gangs of Naples.

Ndrina (properly 'ndrina, pl. 'ndrine) Etymology uncertain, but possibly from *malandrino*, which means 'ruffian', 'bandit' or 'scoundrel'. It is the smallest collective unit in the 'ndrangheta and consists of criminal members of blood-related family with a smaller number of external associates. An *'ndrina* controls a small district, and several *'ndrine* together form a *locale* (*q.v.*). Sometimes, however, an *'ndrina*, especially if it has sent members abroad, can become more powerful than the entire locale. The *'ndrina* will be known by the surname of the controlling family.

Picciotto A rank in the 'ndrangheta, below that of *camorrista*. If we use the analogy of the army, we might compare a *picciotto* to a corporal.

Puglia Also known by its Latin name Apulia, a southern region corresponding to the 'heel' of Italy.

Sgarrista A rank in the 'ndrangheta, above that of *camorrista* (*q.v.*). If we consider a *camorrista* as analogous to an army lieutenant, then a *sgarrista* is a captain.

SISDE Now called AISI (*q.v.*).

Sorella d'omertà A 'sister sworn to the code of silence'. A female member of the 'ndrangheta. It is the highest rank a woman can have in the organisation, and seems to fall somewhere between *sgarrista* and *santista*.

Squadra mobile 'Flying squad'. The term, referring to a group of police officers who investigate serious crimes, comes from the idea that they are mobile so that they can get quickly to the scene of a crime. Blume is part of Section III (Crimes against the Person) of the *Squadra Mobile* of Rome.

A Note on the Author

Conor Fitzgerald has lived in Ireland, the UK, the United States, and Italy. He has worked as an arts editor, produced a current affairs journal for foreign embassies and founded a successful translation company. He is married with two children and lives in Rome. He is the author of *The Dogs of Rome* and *The Fatal Touch*. *The Namesake* is his third book.

A Note on the Type

The text of this book is set in Bembo. This type was first used in 1495 by the Venetian printer Aldus Manutius for Cardinal Bembo's *De Aetna*, and was cut for Manutius by Francesco Griffo. It was one of the types used by Claude Garamond (1480–1561) as a model for his Romain de l'Université, and so it was the forerunner of what became standard European type for the following two centuries. Its modern form follows the original types and was designed for Monotype in 1929.